The House that Jack Built

Diana Mayo

Barefoot Books
Celebrating Art and Story

This is the house that Jack built.

This is the malt
That lay in the house
that Jack built.

This is the rat

That ate the malt

That lay in the house that Jack built.

This is the cat that chased the rat,

That ate the malt

That lay in the house that Jack built.

This is the dog

That worried the cat,

That chased the rat,

That ate the malt

That lay in the house that Jack built.

This is the cow with the crumpled horn,

That tossed the dog,

That worried the cat,

That chased the rat,

That ate the malt

That lay in the house that Jack built.

This is the maiden all forlorn,

That milked the
cow with the
crumpled horn,

That tossed the dog,

That worried the cat,

That chased the rat,

That ate the malt

That lay in the house that Jack built.

This is the man all tattered and torn,

That kissed the maiden all forlorn,

That milked the cow with the crumpled horn,

That tossed the dog,

That worried the cat,

That chased the rat,

That ate the malt

That lay in the house that Jack built.

This is the priest all shaven and shorn,

That married the man all tattered and torn,

That kissed the maiden all forlorn,

That milked the cow with the crumpled horn,

That tossed the dog,

That worried the cat,

That chased the rat,

That ate the malt

That lay in the house that Jack built.

This is the cock that crowed in the morn,

That waked the priest all
shaven and shorn,

That married the man
all tattered and torn,

That kissed the maiden all forlorn,

That milked the cow with the
crumpled horn,

That tossed the dog,

That worried the cat,

That chased the rat,

That ate the malt

That lay in the house that Jack built.

This is the farmer sowing his corn,

That kept the cock that crowed in the morn,

That waked the priest
all shaven and shorn,

That married the man all tattered and torn,

That kissed the maiden all forlorn,

That milked the cow
with the crumpled horn,

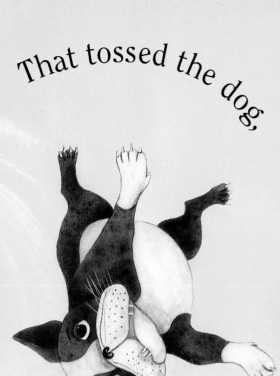

That tossed the dog,

That worried the cat,

That chased the rat,

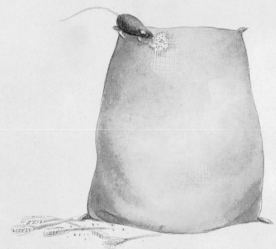

That ate the malt

That lay in the house that Jack built.

DEAD LETTERS

DEAD LETTERS

GERALD HAMMOND

First published in Great Britain in 2004 by
Allison & Busby Limited
Bon Marché Centre
241-251 Ferndale Road
London SW9 8BJ

http://www.allisonandbusby.com

Copyright © 2004 by GERALD HAMMOND

A catalogue record for this book is available from
the British Library.

10 9 8 7 6 5 4 3 2 1

ISBN 0 7490 8327 1

Printed and bound in Wales by
Creative Print and Design, Ebbw Vale

GERALD HAMMOND is a retired architect and the creator of the mystery series featuring John Cunningham, a dog breeder in Scotland, and Keith Calder, a gunsmith. He also writes under the pseudonyms Arthur Douglas and Dalby Holden.

Book One

HONEYPOT

THE COLLECTED EMAILS OF HONORIA POTTERTON-PHIPPS.

Foreword

The emails collected in this volume required substantial editing. Some were irrelevant, others (most but not all to her fiancé) contained matter of a nature too erotic for publication even in this day and age. Between them, they provide a comprehensive picture of her part, and that of Pippa, in the investigation into the death of Fred Fraser.

(I need hardly add that the events and characters are all fictitious. The only real character portrayed is Pippa who, as I write, is lying with her head weighing heavily on my right foot, wondering when we are going out for another lovely, smelly walk. And Suzy was my dog-of-a-lifetime, now long gone but not forgotten. This book is a tribute to her memory.)

G.H.

11 June

Poppy – lovely to hear from you after all this time. So you've come back from sunny California. At least the present fine weather should give you a chance to re-acclimatise yourself to dear old rainswept Britain! Sorry to hear that you've parted from Andrew, but if he's that much of a bastard you're better off without him.

Of course I'd have loved to meet up with you again, but for the moment it's impossible. Your message only caught up with me because I've kept the same email address for yonks. You gave me your news and asked for mine, so I'll update you and explain.

Soon after we made our escape from Bath Ladies' College, I was sent for a final brush and polish in Switzerland and you were preparing to plunge so early and disastrously into holy bedlock. That was when Daddy dropped his bombshell. I had had enough and more than enough of a cloistered existence and what I had in mind was to stay in the Cadogan Street flat, taking it easy until my number came up in the matrimony stakes, in the meantime enjoying all the ineligible bachelors in town, with occasional visits to Daddy's place in Perthshire for a little rest and recreation. But that wasn't good enough. He would continue my (admittedly very generous) allowance and even increase it, but only on condition that I went to university and took a degree. What he had in mind, I think, was a science or business degree, preferably both, a place in one of his research labs and eventually a seat on one board or another.

Boring! And, worse, it would see me confined to some dull university town until my tits sagged. So I looked through the prospectuses of London University and Imperial College and other metropolitan seats of learning; and the one course that looked like being not too much of a yawn was Criminology.

I had all the necessary passes – you remember from our schooldays how facts stick in my mind – Miss Ardlington used to say that I had total recall, but that was overstating it. However, I do have a very retentive, photographic memory, I love finding things out and I respond well to examination conditions. I had no difficulty getting a place.

The course was interesting, which is more than you could ever say about my fellow students. I stayed in Cadogan Street and kept open house for some of the old friends of my youth, studying by day and partying at night, sometimes all night. Ah, life was good, I kept telling myself! Tiring but good.

When I emerged at last, blinking, into the daylight with a parchment in my sweaty paw, I expected the Age of Leisure to dawn at last, but Daddy dropped another bombshell. He would keep my allowance going, and even increase it again, but only if I got a proper job and kept it. The sound of my jaw dropping could have been heard in Bootle, wherever that is. Instead of the Age of Leisure we were into the Age of Negotiation. I settled, in the end, for an even more increased allowance plus the handing over of Daddy's second best, top-of-the-range Range Rover, complete with all mod cons from air-conditioning to DVD player. I think he was going to change the car anyway. The ashtrays were full or something.

Actually, he was putty in my hands, because he was still thinking of a ladylike job in an office somewhere, or lecturing. He nearly had a stroke when I started lingerie modelling and it was a great relief to him when I finally joined the Met. I had been wondering how to do something useful with my Criminology degree and I had a picture in my mind of looking very smart in the new uniform and pacing slowly along Park Lane beside a hunky PC, pausing only to have it off in a police box now and again. And again.

Of course, life is never quite how you imagine it. I don't think they have hunky PCs any more, and if they still have police boxes I never saw one. Not that it mattered. I did my eighteen weeks basic training at Hendon and then went on the beat. I found myself in some of the toughest neighbourhoods. I'd always been rather insulated from *hoi polloi* and I was nervous at first, but I liked the people and when I put on my best Scots accent (deepest Perthshire with overtones of Glasgow borrowed from McClaggan the gardener) they accepted me. It was an exciting life. I was attacked once by a large and hopped-up non-white, but you don't grow up with four brothers without learning a thing or two and I did his matrimonial prospects a lot of no good. He tried to sue me, but my mates (yes, I actually had mates!) took him aside and promised to fit him up on every charge in the book if he didn't drop it. (You can always have mates in the Force if you can stand your hand and have a reliable source of racing tips. You remember George Haverton? He runs his father's racing stable now and does some training on the side.)

About then, somebody took another look at my file and noticed the degree in Criminology for the first time. I was promoted sideways into CID, which I'd wanted all along. I did another training stint at Peel Centre, Hendon. Then another somebody, or possibly the same one, realised that there was a use for a young lady who could pass among the nobs without standing out – at least not in the wrong sort of way. I was sent on an advanced firearms course with a view to bodyguarding duties.

That's how I came to meet Sandy – Detective Inspector Alexander Laird to you. He was on the same course. I think he wrote me off as a piece of superintendent's totty at first, but I noticed that he got muddled identifying the Browning Hi-Power from the Colt Combat Elite. A DS of my acquaintance had been swotting for the same course and he had a chart of all the different pistols blue-tacked to the ceiling over his bed and I had it imprinted on that photographic memory of mine. I saw it often enough before he two-timed me with a civilian computer operator and I had to dump him or look a complete prat.

When I corrected him, Sandy was most impressed and soon we became rather more than good friends. When he went back to Edinburgh I became quite celibate. We stayed in touch and even managed weekends together. I had only been using the Potterton part of my name (just try being hyphenated in the lower ranks of the Met!) and when I finally let him know who Daddy was (and is) he went into shock. But in the end he took it on the chin and I even managed to take him for a break to the place in Perthshire, where he fitted in rather well. I think Daddy liked him because Sandy isn't quite as good a shot as he is and can't cast a salmon line quite as far.

This was all very well, but with me in the Met and Sandy in Lothian & Borders, life was complicated. When we managed to co-ordinate our weekends the travelling was hellish and you know by now how the cost of fares has shot up while you were away. Sandy would have got on his high horse if I'd offered to help with his fares. You'll realise how difficult life was getting when I tell you that he finally proposed...by email! I emailed back accepting, and on his next visit to the Smoke I took him to see the ring I'd chosen. Actually, I'd deposited one grand with the jeweller beforehand, to bring the price within Sandy's grasp. (Result: the ring's dangerously underinsured so I have to be careful with it.)

Our situation was not a whole lot better. I was now an engaged person and I had said farewell to my male friends. I hope that Sandy had done likewise. But I like my nooky and I like it best of all with Sandy who, to be frank, is a bit of a stud. Anyway, nothing would have dragged him to London whereas I'm half-Scottish and, to tell the truth, the urban life was beginning to pall. When I fretted in school or in the wilds of Perthshire, I had thought how marvellous it would be to be loose in the Smoke; but I had discovered for myself that streets are hard and smelly and lacking in privacy, clubbing is overrated and the pleasure of live theatre (as opposed to TV) is outweighed by the nuisance and the rigid timetable. Also, I was tired of being looked on, when out of uniform, as a bit of a glamour pants and a brainless Sloane. I found that I was thinking of myself more as I had been, in green wellies and a Barbour, up to my bum in heather.

The solution was obvious. I applied for a switch to Lothian & Borders, who were delighted to get a Scots-born DS away from the Met. (I was a detective sergeant by then, believe it or not. I can write a good report, thanks to Miss Jenkins, and I can touch-type. These things count.)

I had expected to get Edinburgh, which is where the HQ is and where Sandy hangs up his hat. But Lothian & Borders covers a huge area. I was posted to Newton Lauder, which isn't as bad as you'd think. A small, old town, rather beautiful, very inward-looking but prepared to accept a stranger and it's little over an

hour's driving to the south of Edinburgh if you go like the ham-
mers of hell. So any time you find yourself in the rural
Caledonian wilds, look me up. Leave it for a few weeks though or
you won't meet Sandy – he's been sent on an exchange to LAPD,
to see if there's anything they do better than we do it. Keep me
posted when you settle and I'll pay you a call if I find an excuse
to come south. It would be good to get together again, talk over
old scandals and do a little backbiting.

All the best,

H.P-P

15 June

Jeremy – your bitch arrived as expected. Very beautiful, intelligent and well meaning but – oh my God! – she scratches, she farts and she eats anything. Anything at all. Coprophagic, like a high proportion of dogs (although many owners prefer to turn a blind eye and swear that Bonzo never eats anything but doggy chunks). But to be fair, she doesn't steal food unless you drop it; then she'll catch it before it hits the floor.

The Guide Dogs named her Pippa, rather commonplace but you could change it. Better to keep to something similar, though. Kipper, Flipper or Dipper. Yipper suits her at times. Or Ripper. To be fair again, she never chews anything indoors but she's ripping her blanket in the car to shreds. After my childhood and youth, spent in a house that was usually as full of Labradors as a blanket is with fleas (plus the occasional spaniel or GSP), I thought I'd met every fault to which Labs are prone, but not all in the same dog! And I don't think that I've plumbed her depths yet.

Shall I tell the Guide Dogs to take her away and lose her? To be fair yet again, she's a handsome dog, intelligent, eager to please and quick to learn, it's just that she's slow to unlearn the bad habits. I can persevere, but do you really think you'll be able to cope at the end of the day with a strong willed and impetuous dog? Instructions please.

Honey

11 June

Daddy darling – I'm so glad you liked Sandy. Yes, he is well thought of and his prospects are good.

Well, here I am, getting settled in Newton Lauder. There was no police accommodation empty for me, thank God, so I checked into the hotel, very stuffy, quite expensive but very comfortable and the cuisine is surprisingly good. There was some eyebrow-raising among my new colleagues at the extravagance because I never let on that there's any lolly in the family – I explained the plushy car by saying that I'd had a win on the lottery and blown most of it on wheels. They quite understood, it's what they'd have done themselves. Most of them wouldn't know a Givenchy original from an M&S copy, but I think my immediate boss has his suspicions. So do several of the women (I caught them eyeing up my ring) but they have more sense than to say so and divert the attention of the men from themselves.

Anyway, I only stayed one night in the hotel because I was in the local gun and fishing tackle shop, just across the so-called Square (it's really triangular) and discovered that the chap who served me had just moved, for the sake of a heart condition, into a bungalow and out of the flat upstairs and it was to let. So I took it on straight away. It's very small but cheerful, two bedrooms, living-dining and all the usuals with a nice outlook over the Square, past the Police HQ, between trees to the hills beyond. Mr James left the curtains and carpets but I found quite a good furniture shop just round the corner and bought a bed, some chairs and a few necessities like crockery, cutlery and utensils. I hope you don't mind the bill being sent to you because, after all, you were the one who insisted that I get a job.

I'd better explain what I was doing in the gun shop in the first place. I came bombing up the M6. (An exaggeration, I was never over 70 – perish the thought! But your Range Rover is a sweet mover.) More than one road cuts up diagonally after Moffat, but I was aiming south of Edinburgh so I took a far from major road across the wilds of the Scottish Borders. Getting peckish, I realised that I was passing Tinnisbeck Castle. You'll remember

Jeremy and Hazel Carpenter; you invited them up for the grouse one year. He'd contacted you about some obscure point in an ancient family scandal and you rather liked him. She's something in antiques and she pointed out a Rembrandt or something hanging in a dark corner. Their castle's at least as old as the hills, mostly in a single large keep, but they've made it very comfortable inside, hot and cold running everything.

Anyway, I called in on spec and found them in a tizzy. Jeremy's a historian and he had a sudden invite to meet up with an archaeologist and a scientist to test his theory that the enormous explosion of Santorini, as well as wiping out the Minoan civilisation, coincided with the exodus from Egypt. You know how the water sucks out just before a wave arrives? Jeremy's theory is that just before the tsunami reached the Suez isthmus the Med receded, letting the Israelites cross the creeks and mudflats in the dry. The pursuing Gyppos were not so lucky, which, he says, explains the Bible story without any need for miraculous intervention.

So they were desperate to get away but they had arranged to adopt a Labrador that had failed its Guide Dog tests – for wanting to follow a scent instead of leading the blind around, Jeremy was told, and since he wants the dog for his shooting that seemed ideal. The snag was that they had agreed to receive the dog the next day. The re-homing officer, who was making other visits, would already be on the way with it, the local kennels had closed, the next nearest is a slum and they didn't know anybody willing to take it who wasn't going away and didn't have a savage mutt of their own complete with ticks and fleas.

I offered to turn round and vamoose if the time was bad, but their little eyes lit up. They remembered me working Brutus on the moor and I expect that I had pontificated just a little bit, as I'm inclined to do, so you tell me. They hailed me in, gave me a cup of tea and a large gin and in about ten minutes they were on the phone arranging for the Lab, a spayed and microchipped bitch, to be delivered to me. My visit to the gun and fishing tackle shop was in search of leads and a whistle etc.

The bitch duly arrived. Lovely dog, lovely nature. We developed an instant rapport. But I never thought to see all the vices that Labs are prone to in the one dog. (Life in Newton Lauder looked like being a bit bland, especially with Sandy abroad, so I was in need of a challenge – but this is definitely over the top!) So, if they're not all in use, could you have one of the keepers send me down a dummy launcher with dummies and blanks, a Halti headcollar (because she pulls like a train) and an electronic collar. Yes, I know we agreed that they're a rotten idea because they can camouflage a heritable fault in breeding stock, but I reckon they're the only way to eradicate an existing fault in a spayed worker, especially one who goes deaf to the whistle if it scents a juicy morsel fifty yards away.

One more thing (if I don't think of something else). She's a scratcher. I've tried a shampoo with Head and Shoulders (which worked with that spaniel of Barney's, if you remember) but no dice. The vet says there are no mites or fleas. What was the name of that feed that worked so well on Brutus?

The clothes I bought for London aren't quite the thing in the Scottish countryside. Please get Mrs Wallis to pack and send me down my blue-grey tweed suit, the three or four dresses at the left end of my wardrobe, my good grey coat, my Barbour, a pair of wellies and some good country shoes.

Thanks.

Love

Honoria

25 June

Sandy darling – yes, of course I miss you at least as much as you miss me and probably much more. I'm glad you're enjoying LA; but don't enjoy it too much. I want you back here in full fettle, snorting and pawing the ground.

There may not be a lot of time for writing. Believe it or not, we have a murder here. I don't suppose it will be reported in LA, where they have enough murders of their own to think about, so I'll put you in the picture. I'm making a start to this email on my laptop in the car while we wait for the brass to arrive from Edinburgh and for the police surgeon, the photographer, the pathologist and Uncle Tom Cobleigh to do their stuff. Then I suppose we'll be plunged into all the usual house-to-house visits, fingertip searches and arguments with suspects' solicitors. So I'll write what I can while I can and send it off when I get home tonight. Always, supposing, of course, that we don't turn up a confession or an obvious suspect straight away, but that seems unlikely this time around.

I'm writing this in the car during one of the long waits that seem to be part of a detective's life. Pippa is putting me off by snuffling in my ear as I write and, as I think I told you, she's coprophagic, so her breath smells foul. (Her teeth are all right, I had the local vet check.) If this is a bit disjointed, blame her. I must get a dog guard so that I can confine her to the distant back.

I allowed myself a few days break to get settled in. I must say that I like Newton Lauder. Do you know it? A handsome, cosy old town, almost unspoiled, with trees carefully preserved. Flowers in beds and tubs and hanging baskets, which sound a bit twee on paper but in fact lifts the town above its neighbours. The locals have stopped noticing it except to despise everywhere else.

When I reported for duty my boss, DI Fellowes, knew that I'd been on the advanced firearms course so he appointed me Firearms Officer to help out the uniformed branch. Have you met Ian Fellowes? I think we're going to get along. He isn't one of those seniors who keep their subordinates in place by finding fault; he seems absolutely fair. I'm told that he can be firm with anyone who lets him down but that he's always ready with thanks and praise for a job well done. He and I and two DCs represent CID in this neck of the woods and it seems mostly to be minor offences – vandalism, petty theft, sheep stealing and some poaching – so I could be spared. This suited me quite well, because I could be out and about, inspecting firearms certificates, checking gun numbers and security, inspecting territory where applicants want to use rifles and generally getting the lie of the land. I've been called a busybody once or twice, but when they've found that I'm a reasonable person with a Labrador they get quite friendly and I've had some useful chats over a cup of tea and now know more of the facts and scandal about the area. I've even had an invitation for both of us to shoot, next season.

I walk Pippa morning and evening, and usually take her with me in the Range Rover during working hours so that she can get an extra walk and a little training whenever we get the chance. I was walking her this morning before starting work (rather late, by agreement) when I got a text from my boss, DI Fellowes, and when I called him he told me to meet him near Moorfoot Loch Reservoir, at the bridge below the dam.

As it happened, that was exactly where I was parked, because I usually walk Pippa there. Around Newton Lauder, you're expected to pick up any turds your dog drops and, though I always carry a supply of bags, I prefer not to have to use them. Well, you know me. If you had to describe me in one (repeatable) word, what would it be? My guess is...fastidious. I like things to be nice (in the best sense of the word) and, though dogs are my favourite people, intimate contact with their by-products makes me squirm. Newton Lauder is very much dog-owning territory and just around the outskirts of the town the area is usually deep in dog crap, which I might have tolerated if Pippa had not been a shit-eater, which is what coprophagic means if you didn't know the word. A little further out we have sheep and cattle and crops. The moors abound with sheep ticks (and more sheep). But the territory around Moorfoot Loch Reservoir is as clean as you have any right to expect.

In case you don't know the area, I'll explain. (If you do, you can skip this bit). The reservoir is, of course, in a valley, what else? The hills on either side climb fairly steeply, the grass and whins soon giving way to heather. The dam is at the southern end. The west side of the reservoir is developed, with a very upmarket clay pigeon club at the dam end, an equally upmarket hotel and timeshare complex with stables and squash courts etc. near the other and a championship standard golf course in between. There are also sailing dinghies and almost every other toy you could think of.

The other side is quite different. I gather that a rather run-down village was drowned when the reservoir was impounded, but the local gentry occupied half a dozen villas higher up the slope and almost opposite where the timeshare now stands. These narrowly escaped the flood. You might think that a group of Victorian villas miles from anywhere would have been left to rot, but in fact I'm told that they're highly desirable to the retired, to those who can work from home and (being almost within commuting distance of Edinburgh) to others who don't have to commute too often, because the residents can, without the expense of hotels or timeshares, pay their fees and get the use of the golf course, trout fishing etc. The houses even have frontage to the reservoir and one or two have their own boats so that they can cross the water without resorting to nasty, smelly motor cars.

The new B-road runs up the west side of the reservoir, where dogs might not be welcomed either round the clay pigeon club or the golf course. But an older road crosses a bridge below the dam, becomes single-track with passing places and arrives eventually at the houses. Beyond them it stops at a smallholding. The maps show it resuming further on but there are only traces on the ground. I usually park at the dam and walk up the east side, not going quite as far as the houses because there are dogs there and I'm trying to keep Pippa away from other dogs' poo. Honest to God, Sandy, she's so habituated that if she meets another dog doing its business she'll catch the plonk before it hits the ground. No wonder the Guide Dogs gave her up – you couldn't have a blind man led on a circuit of the dog turds and never mind the traffic. But I bet they didn't mention that little foible to Jeremy. I expect that they just told him that she liked to use her nose, which might attract a shooting man; and he wouldn't be able to say that he wasn't told.

I think DI Fellowes was impressed by my quick response when he found me waiting at the bridge. He beckoned me and I followed his Vauxhall along the single-track road. We stopped less than half a mile short of the houses at a place where the ground is level enough to get cars off the road. A little further on I could see a small group of people. DI Fellowes and one of our constables set off, the DI beckoning to me again. I had no idea that there had been a murder; I thought that it was probably a stolen car dumped in the water or something. When I tried to leave Pippa in the car she made it quite clear that she resented my taking a walk in her territory and leaving her shut in a car to starve, so I put her on the lead and took her along, trying to look as though she was a fully-trained and officially recognised police dog.

As we got closer, I saw that the object of interest was a rowing boat moored to a stump. Sitting on the middle thwart was a man. He was obviously an angler because a trout rod was sticking up over the side. It was equally obvious that he was dead. There was that total immobility about him that you only see on a corpse (and I saw a few of those in the Met). I thought that rigor might have begun, but he had been supported by the oars and was sitting up in a remarkably lifelike position except that his head was down on his chest. I could see a number of puncture wounds and he hadn't been killed by the first or even the second because there was some blood to be seen. They could have been stab-wounds but I rather thought that he had been shot, because one or two looked like exit wounds. Anyway, it's not easy to see how somebody could be stabbed half a dozen times while sitting in a boat and not even let go of the oars. There was an outboard motor lying on the floorboards, with clamps for attaching it to the transom. The boat was a neat, clinker, varnished dinghy.

The man was dark haired and blue chinned, which was about all that I could make out at the time. From the traces of grey in his hair, he was no chicken. He had on a fishing waistcoat with bulging pockets but no lifejacket or self-inflating collar.

The DI pulled the boat in and had a good look at the corpse. Then he looked round the bystanders, a group of three women and a man, and asked who found the body. A rather formidable lady with a huge bust (you'd have been thunderstruck!) put up her hand and admitted it. She is Mrs Dawson, of the second house along. She was walking the dog, she said, when she saw the dinghy drifting near the bank and could see that something was far wrong. She hurried home and sent her neighbour's husband to secure the dinghy while she phoned us. Then, of course, she couldn't resist spreading the tidings before returning to the scene. The other onlookers were from among her neighbours.

The DI thanked her very sweetly for her very sensible actions. Mrs Dawson said that the dead man was a Mr Fraser from the third house along, next door to herself in fact. The man from among the onlookers said that Fraser was in the habit of angling in the reservoir, usually without going to the trouble of buying a ticket, and that he had been seen going out very early in his dinghy. He spoiled the value of his evidence by saying 'Or was that yesterday?' I noticed that he was wearing an angler's waistcoat like that on the corpse.

At that point, DI Fellowes rather put his foot in it by assuming that the man was Mr Dawson. For a reason not clear at that time, Mrs Dawson seemed shocked at the suggestion and hurried to explain that her neighbour's husband had had to leave to attend to his business in Newton Lauder. 'Mr Berenson – my neighbour – said that those were bullet wounds,' Mrs Dawson said. 'They look very small.'

'Nobody's mentioned hearing the sound of shots,' said the third woman.

'Jim Berenson has a rifle,' Mrs Dawson said. 'He should know. This is quite a long way from the houses, so the sound might not have carried. Anyway, the dinghy could have been blown from further along.'

There would have been no way, short of mass arrests, to prevent them discussing this exciting interruption to their daily routine, but we did not have to listen to it until the time came for gathering hard facts. The DI suggested that they return to their houses, without disturbing what might or might not be a murder scene, and promised that they would be interviewed later. He worded it as a suggestion but what came across was 'Get the hell out of here'. He's the nicest man you could meet, he even looks a little like you, the brawny fair-haired type of southern Scot, but when his voice snaps people jump. The constable (DC Bright – nobody was ever so misnamed) took the names of those present and identified the two witnesses. They turned reluctantly home-ward, the man hurrying ahead but the ladies talking as they went, no doubt to exchange pleasurable murmuring over the coffee-cups.

'That's all we can do for the moment,' the DI said to me. 'Superintendent Blackhouse is on his way from Edinburgh.' (From the way that he said the name I could tell that he had no affection for the Super. That attitude turned out to be almost uni-versal.) 'We won't get any thanks for disturbing the scene. That woman was right about one thing. The boat could have drifted from anywhere, but he could have been shot here so we'll have to go through the proper motions. McFadden –' that's our other constable '– will be bringing out the gear and we'll tape off and search a path to the body. You may as well go and sit in your car.'

So that's how it stands at the moment. Lots of love and you-know-what. Further details when I have time and energy to write again. Watch this space.

Honeypot

26 June

Jeremy – you ask for an update on Pippa. I'll keep it brief because we are in the throes just now. The Guide Dogs, of course, had tried to teach her all the wrong things, like walking in front and chasing a ball, instead of the things she has a talent for.

First the good news. She is walking reliably to heel (except when tempted away by anything that was ever edible) and is pulling much less on the lead. The sit-stay-come exercise (which is fundamental) is now performed reliably at up to 50 yards provided there are no distractions such as people, other dogs, rabbits, birds overhead, butterflies or bits of paper blowing in the wind. To be fair, we must expect some puppyishness at sixteen months. The average Lab matures at around two years, but that's only an average. Some of them never grow up at all. We can only hope.

The new diet is a success. She has almost stopped scratching and the diet, combined with a lot of raw parsley added to her meals and a lot of charcoal biscuits, seems also to have almost cured the farting. (I swear I would have been afraid to strike a match.) Her coat now shines like patent leather.

She looks like being a brilliant retriever. I give her some retrieves with the dummy launcher whenever I can find time and although she is enthusiastic to the point of morbid passion I've brought her to the point of sitting and waiting to be sent instead of chasing after it. She took hand-signals from the first and we haven't lost a dummy yet.

I've been making much use of the electronic collar. She now returns reliably. The bad news is that it has little effect on the coprophagia – the attraction of a between-meals snack is greater than the fear of an electric jolt. You saw how many Labs there were at the Perthshire place, between Dad, my brothers and the keepers, so you won't be surprised when I say that the problem is not exactly a novelty to me. The vets all say that it's very unlikely to be harmful between dogs (although sometimes the dung of wildlife can carry nasties.) So it does little harm except to the sensibilities of squeamish owners. But, of course, it would be a damning defect in a guide dog. (As far as I know, nobody's tried the electronic collar to desensitise an over fastidious owner, but it's worth considering.)

They say that coprophagia starts when puppies see their dam cleaning up after them. I have a different theory. You have to put yourself in the place of a creature with four legs, no hands, no real language and not a lot of brain. It has to subsist, somehow or other. Nowadays, dogs are dependant on humans but their ancestors had to be hunters and opportunist scavengers. So modern dogs don't eat for taste, they eat more for the comfort of a full stomach; but the clean-up instinct may have survived because it makes it more difficult for a larger predator to follow the pack.

Whatever the motivation, you won't want Pippa shaming you on a formal occasion. I tried a muzzle designed to deter but she was so determined to scrape it off that she was rubbing a sore onto her beautiful black nose.

Another downside is that the breath isn't too sweet. I clean her teeth every evening, which solves the problem for the moment but it isn't easy, she absolutely loves the taste of the toothpaste so I'm trying to get at the teeth around a huge tongue that is lashing around, trying to lick the brush.

The experts say that there's no cure for coprophagia. They also say that some dogs grow out of it but they don't say it with any great conviction. We shall see. I haven't given up yet.

Regards to Hazel. Pippa sends love. All the best.

Honey

26 June

Sandy darling – sorry to hear you've got lost in the smog. Why don't you try for a shift to San Francisco? Much pleasanter if you turn a blind eye to the eccentrics. Tell your bosses you've learned all you can in LA and that we do everything much better here.

I had to break off yesterday because Superintendent Blackhouse showed up, in a rather tatty Jag and a bad temper. I already knew that you must have had the pleasure of his acquaintance. Reading between the lines of your email (at which I'm becoming adept) you have no great affection for him. This I can understand. As you must know, he's one of those people, the opposite of DI Fellowes, who don't believe in letting the lower orders have any delusions of adequacy. I'm told that he has favourites but that if he takes against you, nothing that you do will ever be right. He arrived just after we'd taped off the area – a fat pig of a man with terrible posture. He took in the scene in one glance, gathered that the dinghy when found had been loose and was moored by one of the finders and he said that Fraser had almost certainly been killed elsewhere, which we had all worked out for ourselves. All the same, he wanted the tapes shifted, more area enclosed and a different entry path. He had his own DS with him, a thin man by name of Tomlinson, who looked totally fed up as well he might.

We all got off on the wrong foot with him, none more so than your beloved.

The police surgeon had already arrived, certified death and confirmed bullet-wounds as the probable cause. A photographer had done his thing. A SOCO (from Edinburgh) and the entire strength of Newton Lauder CID were standing by. If we had already done anything at all, he'd have damned us for messing up the scene. Instead, he damned us for standing idly by. DC Bright started to say that the holes seemed very small even for .22 bullets but a glare from the DS stopped him in his tracks and I took Bright aside to explain that skin is elastic and bullet entry holes always do look smaller than the calibre.

It was another sunny day but there was a brisk and gusty

breeze. At the moment it was from the west, bringing with it a faint popping sound from the gun club. 'Somebody's shooting,' the DS said in awful tones.

'Probably my wife giving somebody a little coaching at the clay pigeons,' DI Fellowes said. His wife has been European Skeet Champion and acts as shotgun coach at the club.

That set the DS off on the subject of the iniquity of allowing any kind of firearm to be held in civilian hands. I knew that I was taking my life in my hands but I couldn't contain myself in the face of so much ignorance and prejudice. 'Sir,' I said, 'according to the statistics, more people are killed by accidents in the gymnasium than by firearms. You have more chance of choking to death on food than of being killed by a gunshot.'

DI Fellowes looked grateful to me for diverting the wrath of God. Mr Blackhouse looked at me as though I had farted or confessed to eating babies. He then glared down at poor Pippa. (Pippa was still wearing the electronic collar with its little aerial, which gave her a suitably official appearance, resembling all the personal radios clipped to the lapels around us.) The DS had only grunted when I was introduced to him. He grunted again, goggled at me for a few more seconds and decided to say nothing. He is one of those men who hate to be seen to be wrong and he probably thought that if he argued with me I might produce those very statistics out of my shoulder bag (which at the time actually held only the dummy launcher, some treats and my mobile phone). But from then on whatever I did was wrong, wrong, wrong. I may not look like your stereotypical police officer and I'm quite used to being looked on with suspicion until superiors realise that I'm a hard worker and not exactly dim; but with Mr Blackhouse I could have walked on the water or healed the sick without him ever looking on me as anything other than a know-all and a presumptuous Barbie doll. I would have thought that only a fevered imagination could suspect a Barbie doll of being a know-all, but he seemed to have no difficulty with the concept.

Moments later the DS looked into the wind and said that Fraser had probably drifted from the direction of the timeshare. I was spared having to point out that among the hills the wind can blow from all points of the compass in succession because DI Fellowes said it first. He was told not to quibble.

Mr Blackhouse decided that, if we didn't turn up a suspect bloody quick (his words), we'd need more men from Edinburgh and an incident room.

'We could get on with gathering all the two-two rifles held legally around here for testing,' DI Fellowes suggested, showing keen.

The DS looked as though he had been about to suggest the same thing. It would, after all, be routine. 'Too early for that,' he snapped. 'We won't know for sure what calibre we're looking for until the pathologist's dug out the bullets. Somewhere around this reservoir there must be some spent cases lying around which may tell us rather more.'

The reservoir is two or three miles around, so there was no eager rush to start a fingertip search. I pointed out that there were other dinghies locally, so the cases could well be on the bottom or in the bilge of another boat. 'If he didn't take them home with him like a sensible killer,' DS Tomlinson said gloomily.

Mr Blackhouse would have none of this defeatist talk. 'Find them and we'll find our man,' he said. 'The firing pin marks will identify the rifle.' Just how we would know which spent cartridges had been left by the killer, as opposed to any left behind by somebody local shooting rabbits, was left vague.

Just then DC Bright, who had been back to the cars for something, returned. 'Is this of any interest, Sir?' he asked. He held out his hand on which was a cartridge case resembling a .22 Long Rifle case. You know what they look like, just over half an inch long and less than a quarter inch diameter, quite tiny. The Super's eyes lit up but he cursed Bright for handling it without gloves. 'It could have held fingerprints,' he said.

'If it did,' I said, 'they were probably mine.' Then I had to explain, quickly before he had me arrested on suspicion of something or other, that it had been a blank cartridge for the dummy launcher. Before he'd believe me, I had to point out the originally crimped end with its red colouring, show him a matching but unfired blank from my pocket, fit a dummy and the launcher together and give a lengthy explanation of gundog training and its purpose. When that had sunk in, he conveyed his total contempt by one huge sniff.

Given a little time to shake off his prejudices and think, the DS was capable of logical reasoning. Until the pathologist and Forensics had done their stuff, he said, we could make little progress except for getting the lie of the land and taking the most preliminary of statements. That gave us time to get organised. He sent his Sergeant Tomlinson off to the timeshare to get a list of people who might have been around during the previous twelve or fourteen hours, what boats had been out and to ask whether anybody had seen or heard anything relevant. Bright and McFadden were left behind, one to seek similar information at the houses and enquire about next of kin; the other was to attend, help and spy on the specialists and to stand guard over the boat when they had finished.

He, DI Fellowes and (for lack of any contrary instructions) your beloved would go in to Newton Lauder and organise an incident room. The fact that it was by now nearing lunchtime may have had some bearing on the plan. The only car not otherwise committed was mine but, as we walked towards it, I caught DI Fellowes's eye. We agreed, almost telepathically, that the DS would not appreciate being driven by a female sergeant who he considered to be a flibbertigibbet and that it might be better not to emphasise that the Range Rover, which distinctly outclassed his own transport, was mine. Already knowing that he was a careful driver, I slipped the DI the key surreptitiously. Mr Blackhouse, of course, took the front passenger seat as of right. After stowing Pippa in the back, I had to re-arrange two coats, a muzzle, a whole lot of dummies both canvas and rubber, a bag of biscuits (for bribes), a walking stick, a thumbstick with integral whistle, the extending lead and several rubber toys, all on the rear seat, before I could get in.

We travelled in silence towards Newton Lauder, each busy with his (or her) own thoughts. Pippa was breathing foul smells into my ear. Mr Blackhouse was managing to radiate equally foul disapproval of the world in general and me in particular. We had been in a dead area for radio among the hills and as we came out onto the main road the car's radio suddenly picked up Classic FM. Mr Blackhouse seemed mollified. 'That's nice,' he said. 'I've heard it before. What is it?'

DI Fellowes said that he wasn't sure.

'*Meditation*,' I said, before I had time to think.

'Oh. From?'

The wiser course would have been to pretend ignorance. '*Thais* by Massenet,' I said.

He switched off the radio and we travelled in thunderous silence to Newton Lauder. Mr Fellowes parked behind the Police HQ.

As we dismounted there was a sudden flurry of activity. Pippa came over the back of the rear seat to join me on the tarmac. Her bowels are very regular. She is also very clean about the house and car. Our morning walk had been cut short and she had since been confined to the car or kept on a very short lead on tarmac. The prospect of being left in the car again proved to be too much to bear. She thumped down onto the ground and deposited a huge dollop beside Mr Blackhouse's brightly polished black shoe. DI Fellowes, I could see, was busting a gut not to break down laughing.

'What,' Mr Blackhouse cried in awful tones, 'is this?'

By that time, I was not exactly enamoured of DS Blackhouse. I decided that disciplinary proceedings would not be called for if I gave him a precise and literal one-word answer to what had, after all, been a rather silly question. Before I could utter it, thankfully, I realised that he was not referring to the turd itself but to something half-embedded in it. Peeping out of the still steaming brown and winking in the sunshine was a very small brass cartridge case.

It's been a hard day, as you can imagine. That little episode would have made sure of it even if nothing else had done so. And now it's nearly midnight. I'll continue the saga tomorrow. For the moment, you can cliff-hang and allow your imagination to run riot.

More than love,

Honeypot

27 June

Sandy, my angel, if this saga seems disjointed it's because I'm writing when I get a minute's peace (which, as you know, becomes a rare commodity after a murder) and then sending it off as soon as I get the chance. That way, I can use the hard-drive memory as little as possible and if my laptop gets pinched out of the car it will be that much more difficult for the thief to recover deleted material that is certainly confidential and might be used for evil purposes. The floppy disk remains with my person.

Yes of course I miss you, desperately. Just keep your hands etc. off those starlets who are no doubt making you offers you can hardly refuse. Or, if you succumb to temptation, don't tell me openly. Just slip a codeword into one of your emails (off the top of the head, I suggest that *slinking* would be appropriate). Then we'll never mention it again but I'll know that you're suitably contrite and that I can take a lover to fill the gap (if you'll pardon the expression) until your return. (Only joking).

I left you cliff-hanging at the point where a spent .22 cartridge case had just been deposited beside DS Blackhouse's shoe. Apropos nothing in particular, I was surprised to see it shining so brightly. I remember swallowing a chromium-plated key when I was three or four years old and it came out jet black. It was the key to an important box, which is why they took so much trouble to recover it, and so it was around for years and it stayed black. But brass, of course, is chemically quite different.

Fortunately, I had a supply of small nylon evidence bags in my pocket (I had been running out of polythene bags and Pippa has been known to do her business in the streets of the town). So I gathered up the cartridge and, before turning the bag inside out, confirmed that it was indeed a case that had fired a .22 bullet and not a launcher dummy.

I then had to explain, still standing in the police car park with more and more grinning woodentops gathering around, about coprophagia and Pippa's unfortunate habit. Closely questioned (mostly about the speed of a dog's digestive system), I said that it had almost certainly been ingested that morning, but whether that was so or it had been the previous night's bedtime snack, she had only had the chance to collect it somewhere along the southern half of the eastern side of the reservoir. To my surprise, Mr Blackhouse said nothing at the time. If I had known him better, I would have realised that he was saving it up for the most devastating opportunity to drop me deep into the same mess as was still clinging to the cartridge. I had to clean up the plonk in a second bag and hurry to wash my hands and catch up.

There is a former gymnasium and recreation room in the old part of the HQ, made redundant when the building was massively extended and now called into service for functions and for use as an incident room. Basic furniture was quickly available. Up to that point, I had wondered how Mr Blackhouse had ever made it to superintendent. I could see him going from sergeant to inspector, but after that his manner would have been against him. But now I saw what an organiser he was. He soon had people producing all the resources and equipment he really needed, including one computer and a switchboard, and as his team assembled he was parcelling out jobs and dictating questionnaires, apparently without pausing to draw breath. Lunchtime had passed by almost unnoticed but tea and sandwiches made a miraculous appearance.

When the whole team was assembled, he gave a briefing. Some of us had been on our feet for most of the day, but he had a chair so that was all right. He had taken off his jacket to reveal the gaudiest braces I ever saw. (I thought at first that he was being fashionable and then realised that he was just being a slob.) By that time, the pathologist had extracted the first small and badly damaged piece of lead, which he stated had once been a .22 bullet, and two others with identifiable rifling marks. The pathologist had also given a preliminary opinion that the man had been dead for 24 hours or more, which caused a bit of a stir. Thus it seemed that he could have been drifting around on the reservoir for a day and a night. This depressed me. I had been assuming that there had not been time for the spent shell to pass through two or more successive digestive systems.

The local team (Mr Fellowes, me and the two DCs) would take

the east side of the reservoir while the visitors (an inspector, his sergeant and four DCs) would cover the hotel, timeshare, golf course and gun club. There would be a meeting of sergeants and above every morning at 8 a.m. sharp.

Accommodation was dealt with in about fifteen seconds and then he looked at me. For a moment he was almost smiling as he told the whole company how my dog (he called Pippa a cur) had deposited a potential clue in the car park. I had not credited him with a sense of humour so I was surprised when he made a funny story out of it – at least, it had the others rolling about. I had to point out that the nature of coprophagia meant that the deposit could easily have been second or even third hand (if hand can be the proper word).

As you know, I don't embarrass easily. Anyone who has ever modelled lingerie has had to learn the hard way to conquer embarrassment. But I was embarrassed then, with them all looking at me and grinning like apes. Fortunately I had had time to tidy my hair when I washed after Pippa's episode and I was confident that my pale dress and the cream flannel blazer had not picked up any marks. The whistle and the transmitter for the radio dog collar hanging round my neck may have spoiled the effect a little, but I kept my cool. I considered bursting into tears, to enlist the sympathy of the hangers-on, but decided not to give him the satisfaction. Instead, I took heart from the fact that the men, other than Mr Blackhouse himself, were looking at me in a way that was not exactly disapproving. When the DS asked me what I meant by excretion I looked him in the eye and said 'Shit!' and I meant it to sound as if I was referring to him. I think some of them got the point, including the DS. There was some sniggering.

He really did smile then, the smile of a crocodile gripping an antelope, as he explained that it would be my special task to poke through every dog-turd on the eastern side of the reservoir. Somewhere, possibly beneath the water but more probably not, there was a deposit of spent .22 cases and he wanted them found. And every .22 rifle was to be collected for examination.

There was still some of the working day left but, sandwiches or

no, I was ravenously hungry. And so, apparently, was DI
Fellowes. DC Bright had not brought his car back so he joined
me in mine and directed me to his house where he persuaded his
wife to microwave a quick snack for us both, which I thought was
handsome of them both. She's very attractive, dark and rather
plump, and I had seen her going in and out of the gunshop –
apparently she's the daughter of the joint proprietor. As well as
being shotgun instructor at the club, she's a time-served engraver
and a general gunsmith and she still helps her father out. They
have a school-age son who came in while I was there.

Back in the Range Rover, he reminded me that I could claim
mileage expenses for use of the car on police business, which had
never even occurred to me, but he apologised that the appropriate rate for a sergeant was not calculated on the fuel consumption
of Dad's thirsty beast. I said that I forgave him.

He then asked, again rather apologetically, how I proposed to
carry out the DS's orders. I don't know whether he expected me
to rebel or what else he expected me to say but, whatever my personal attitude to dog shit, I do not shirk duty. When I told him
that my first step would be to seek out any dog-owners in the
houses, find out which were known to be coprophagic and
arrange for the dog owners to show me where their dogs had,
first, gathered up their little morsels and, secondly, deposited
them again, he agreed. He decided to kill two birds with one
stone and come with me. Maybe he wanted to keep tabs on the
new kid on the block.

When we got back to the reservoir, the specialists had done
their several things and departed and the dinghy was being carried up the slope to the road and lifted onto a trailer by two uniformed PCs. It was my first chance to take a good look. As I said
earlier, it was a neat clinker dinghy, brightly varnished. I thought
that a forensic scientist could tell a lot from what his colleagues
had left behind – fingerprint powder, reagent for showing up
bloodstains and so on. We took a good look. The blood spatter
only told us what we already knew, that the shots had come from
the man's right. One bullet had gone low and passed clean
through the dinghy from side to side, passing below and behind

the man's bottom by my calculation. It had made a larger hole on exiting – above the waterline, or the dinghy would eventually have sunk.

There was a small fishing box on the boards. The boffins had had their go at it so I opened it up. It only held the usual jumble of flies and leaders, a few spinners, a priest, two reels of thin nylon or polycarbonate for leaders and one of those combined pliers and scissors that don't do either job very well. If he caught a fish, one of the forensic lads had taken it home for his tea.

On the water, there were several sailing dinghies making what they could of a fluky breeze. There was also at least one sail-less dinghy with a hopeful angler waiting in unrewarded patience, so I supposed that a dinghy with a dead angler sitting in an attitude suggesting a somnolent wait for a bite might easily have passed unnoticed. Beyond, the hotel and timeshare half a mile away stood out clearly. We could see golfers on the links and two riders heading for the stables. The heather has yet to bloom, so the hills above were only relieved by the moving shadows of clouds. A peaceful scene, full of harmless recreation, but such impressions can be illusory. Of the fifty or so people in sight, two or three might well be harbouring thoughts of hatred or violence. That, in my experience, would be about par for the course.

By now, DC Bright was overdue for rest and refreshment. He went off to Newton Lauder while DI Fellowes and I drove on towards the houses. This would once have been a back lane, used by delivery vehicles and dust carts. The houses would originally have fronted on a better, lower road that had been drowned, so the fronts of the houses had gardens running down to the water. I noticed one or two boathouses. At the back, the slope of the hill had been partly dug away to allow for parking and turning, but most of the houses had had garages built in the former back garden.

A small traffic car was parked with two wheels up on the grass just short of the houses. The uniformed PC had been borrowed by the DS to keep reporters and nosy rubbernecks at bay. He had not been overworked.

The day clouded over, bringing a breeze for the sailing dinghy to use. The first house was dark and proved unoccupied, but the second, the lair of our informant Mrs Dawson, showed lights. It also showed, as we opened the wooden gates, Mrs Dawson at what was evidently the kitchen window. The garage was obviously much newer than the house, which was Victorian, two storey, with a slated roof. The walls were probably stone but were almost covered by a mixture of ivy and Virginia creeper through which neat rectangular holes had been maintained for the sash-and-case windows to peer through like animals from their lairs. A Japanese motorcycle with L-plates stood beside it.

Mrs Dawson opened the back door as we reached it. (I have explained that the houses are now back-to-front.) The house was pulsing with the sort of music that used to set me gyrating on the disco floor but I was surprised to find that my taste had moved on and the cacophony had become only a nuisance. Mrs Dawson shooed us into the front room while she clattered upstairs and had words with somebody called Julian. The volume of the music dropped a little though it was soon turned up again. Tacitly, we agreed to ignore it and raised our voices to be heard.

The room was fussy, filled with ill-assorted ornaments, unmatching furniture, badly chosen wallpaper and the ugliest curtains I ever saw; yet somehow it was comfortable and seemed homely. The unnecessary fire in the Adam fireplace may have helped. (I am telling you all this because you said you wanted to know all the details. Also, it helps me to remember. I am writing this on my laptop while making out my own report on my desktop computer, all this while Schumann is on the Hi-fi. Why limit yourself?) There was a Labrador/golden retriever cross paying us no attention from the white hearthrug – name of Hannibal, we were informed when Mrs Dawson returned. Julian is their only son, a final year student at Dalkeith.

Mrs D is large and busty but sharp-featured, with reddish hair permed into improbable waves. I guessed that she had prepared herself in expectation of our visit, because she had changed her dress (moss green, totally unsuited to her hair colour) and was now wearing rings and earrings that looked like real diamonds but from the lack of colour in the sparkle were mostly zircons.

The interview took some time because the lady, as well as being naturally garrulous, was full of the excitement of something actually happening in a life usually filled with lots of nothing. The interview was rather a waste of time. She couldn't add much to what she had told us that morning. She hadn't seen the dinghy drifting on the open water and had not heard any shots. I had the impression that what happened on the water was of no interest to her and if dear Julian was in the habit of playing music at that volume I doubt that she would have heard the last trump.

At that point, DI Fellowes had to go and supervise the removal and labelling of the refuse bags from every house but I stayed with Mrs Dawson. She had no more relevant information (or none that I managed to dig out of her) but she did, however, provide me with some useful background about the other denizens of the Moorfoot Road Houses, information that I'll give you as we go along. She also promised to bring her dog out on a turd-hunt next morning though she swore blind that her Hannibal would never eat anything so revolting.

For the moment, I'm exhausted and I need to get to bed if I'm to be at Mr Blackhouse's meeting tomorrow at 8 a.m.. So to cut it short I'll just explain that the houses have names that nobody uses and if they ever had numbers they've been forgotten. The postman simply knows the names of the inhabitants. So for our purposes I'll number the houses from the point of arrival, making Mrs Dawson No. 2.

I already knew that the only .22 rifles on certificates were at houses No. 1 (Berenson) and No. 4 (Andrews). I collected Mr Andrews's rifle, but Berenson was out and remained out – at a meeting, his wife said when she cast up, but more probably the golf club and spreading the story of his part in the gruesome find. She was on the point of opening his gun cabinet for me but I headed her off. If she had admitted that she knew where he hid the keys, I'd have had to do something about it, probably prosecute. (You remember the man who was prosecuted because his old mother, who had no firearms certificate, knew where he kept the keys?) Mrs Berenson promised to walk with me next day, with the family Labrador.

That was not the end of my day but this most definitely is the end of this one. I'll finish now before I fall asleep on the keyboard. Goodnight, lover. I'll catch up with today tomorrow.

Yours,

Honeypot

My very dear Sandy – your emails are a great comfort to me and, yes, I do still love you, but don't let that sense of humour run away with you. We both know that I was joking when I suggested *slinking* as a code word for confessing infidelity, but there was no need for you to work in every word that can be mistaken for that one out of the corner of the eye. All the same, I have to admire the ingenuity with which you worked *stinking, drinking* and *blinking* all into the same sentence.

When I wrote to you yesterday, I only recounted my saga up to the evening of the 25th, the day after the unfortunate Mr Fraser is believed to have died and the day on which he was found, still seated at the oars. So I have to bring you up to speed by filling in the succeeding couple of days, including today. I could sum them up by saying that they've been... I nearly wrote *bloody murder*, but the words would be a little too apt.

For a start, the reporters have been around. Praise be, I've been in plain clothes and I don't look anything like a journalist's mental picture of a detective sergeant, while my colleagues were only too glad to hog the limelight. Otherwise my scavenging would have been subjected to the scrutiny of TV cameras and no doubt reporters would have carried off every dog dropping in the hope of beating the police to a valuable clue. Come to think of it, that might have been a blessing. But most of the police activity has been over on the other side of the reservoir so, although the residents have been pestered with the daftest questions that anyone could possibly dream up, we've largely been ignored.

The morning briefings, while a necessary way of keeping everybody pulling in the same direction, have been depressing. Mr Blackhouse has his knife firmly into me and has enlivened the meetings and amused my colleagues by dragging me through a description of my researches. I have tried to maintain a dignified cool and to respond with the air of an adult amusing the children, which hasn't endeared me a lot.

The completed post-mortem showed that Fraser died not long after drinking coffee. There was no coffee flask in the dinghy, so that suggests that he was shot soon after setting off. It was pre-dictably vague about the time of death. It produced several bullets though others had gone through soft tissue and presumably have vanished into the depths. One had hit bone and was too distorted to be of use, but two were said to be in good enough condition to be matched to a firearm if we could find it.

So far, the two rifles from the Moorfoot Road Houses, the several belonging to visitors at the hotel and timeshare and the six at the gun club have all been proved innocent by comparison with the bullets removed from the body. Nothing else of any interest turned up in the post-mortem examination. No drugs or poisons, no significant bruises, no marks of strangulation. Forensic study of the body, its clothing and the boat produced a huge amount of material that may or may not prove to be significant if we ever have a suspect and if the killing turns out to be anything other than a shooting from long range, but at the moment seems to consist of the sort of traces that any of us might be carrying around.

Several witnesses remember seeing the dinghy and the presumably deceased Mr Fraser on the 24th, drifting here and there on the reservoir, but because he was in a fairly natural attitude had assumed that he was a somnolent angler waiting for the rise. Any shots heard had been presumed to come from the gun club although an experienced ear could surely tell the difference between the sound of a shotgun and that of a small-bore rifle. Small-bore rifle ranges sometimes use low velocity cartridges which are very quiet but the opinion of the pathologist was that the damage to bullets and bone would not have resulted from an LV cartridge.

Spent .22 cartridge cases by the score have been examined – mostly from the gun club and none from our side of the reservoir except for my launcher blanks. So far, each has been linked (by way of the impression of the firing pin) to a rifle already proved innocent; except for some which came from the gun club and may have been fired by visitors long departed. The tracing of such visitors goes on, together with checking for firearm certificates and local connections.

But to return to my chronological account; when we returned to resume our enquiries at the Moorfoot Road Houses, we were in for a shock. DC Bright had been led to believe that Fraser was a widower, but on our arrival we found DC McFadden confronted by a ladylike female person (I can't express it more clearly than that) who announced herself to be Fraser's widow. (When I tackled Bright about this piece of inaccuracy, he was adamant that Mrs Dawson had said that there was no Mrs Fraser. Mrs Dawson later explained that she had thought that the Frasers had been divorced.)

We now learned that Mrs Fraser was not only alive but resident in the staff accommodation at the hotel. Fraser, it seemed, had got her a job as bar staff, and when she decided to leave him she kept on the job and moved into the building. Mr Blackhouse was informed by radio and he arrived post haste to collect the widow, but not before she had made it clear that she believed the house and everything in it were now hers and had made a spirited attempt to take possession.

DI Fellowes and I, with our two DCs, did a thorough search of Fraser's house. Since we did not know what, if anything, might be significant it is hardly surprising that we didn't find anything much. So it was necessary to list and photograph everything. He had lived at No. 3 for about ten years, since he took early retirement from one of the police forces in the south of England. His wife left him about two years after they moved in. He had originated somewhere around here and by the time of the rift he was too comfortably established to move again. If there had ever been any children, none of the neighbours had seen or heard of them. Mr Blackhouse removed Mrs Fraser before we got around to asking her.

Mrs Fraser had told us little about her estranged and now deceased husband, and none of it good. Mrs Dawson was a little more informative. She said that Fraser had a female cousin to live with him for a while after his wife's departure but it was not a success and she moved away again. He loved his trout fishing and devoted most of his time to it in summer.

Still according to Mrs Dawson, he was a cantankerous old cuss, which probably explained his wife's departure, but he kept himself much to himself and so far we haven't turned up any quarrels more significant than the usual niggles between neighbours about noise, garden rubbish and thoughtless parking. He objected regularly to Julian Dawson's taste and volume of music, threatening to make a complaint about noise pollution, but who wouldn't? Julian's parents tried to make the youth keep the volume down, so perhaps the ear-bending noise when we visited was in celebration of new-found freedom from a complainant. Fraser had an old but sound Ford estate car that he used for shopping and to fetch a lady from Newton Lauder who cleaned and did his laundry every week. She says that he was harmless but uncommunicative and always paid on the dot, which seems to be her criterion of excellence. The car was just as uninformative.

Fraser's house was clearly too large for a single man. Another neighbour said that while his wife was with him they had had frequent visitors. Some of the rooms were shut up and obviously disused. The furniture had been good, well chosen by a person of taste – a woman, I could tell by the pastel colours. DI Fellowes came to the same conclusion because, he said, the furniture had been chosen for looks rather than comfort. The fabrics and decoration were showing signs of wear and tear so the choice was probably that of Mrs Fraser. No pets. The sitting room was as you might expect – a huge television facing the most worn of the easy chairs with a video recorder, books and a drinks cabinet all within reach. The books showed a catholic taste in reading but tended towards what you might call the romantic adventure. The videos in their own rack were similar. Girly magazines were confined to his bedroom, which was otherwise unremarkable. The kitchen was a surprise. Instead of the usual male slum it was sparkling clean and well supplied with equipment and materials. Evidently, even on his own, he went in for *haute cuisine*. The wines in the rack were good value for money – well chosen for a mediocre budget and in boxes to allow for modest drinking. There was a room in use as a study although half of it had been turned over to fly-tying – all trout flies, I noticed. I got a look at the fly that was on his line when he died and it was definitely his own tying, I could tell.

We found his will, which left a small legacy to the widow and the rest, including the house and contents, to his female cousin. I'm not at all sure how this will be regarded in Scots law – the will was made on a form and witnessed, apparently without the advice of the local solicitor who was named as executor, so I can foresee all sorts of complications. We bundled up his financial papers for study by Mr Blackhouse and transmission to the solicitor, an elderly fusspot named Enterkin.

One item of possible interest was a large desk diary. He had few appointments and those were all things like doctors and dentists plus reminders about his cleaning lady; but there were notes about when the music from next door was excessive and what complaint he had made about it, all sounding like the groundwork for a complaint of noise pollution. It also contained some Xs, averaging five or six a month, starting last April, but without explanation except that the first was labelled *bastard!* Are these the records of happenings past or reminders of appointments to come?

The garden is short and, like the house, showed some signs of neglect. There were several untidy vegetable beds, somewhat nibbled by rabbits, and the grass seemed to have been mown fairly regularly. I would guess that some handsome floribunda roses had been properly pruned and the flowerbeds forked over now and again. Beyond that point, the shrubs and plants were left to look after themselves. The garden, like the others, reaches down to the waterside where some duckboarding had been laid, presumably to give him a dry footing for his trout fishing, and there was a small stage for his dinghy.

My trawling for dog poo with the ladies (by tradition wives are the dog-walkers, but don't count on it) proved as unsatisfactory as you can get. I had to take Pippa along, because dogs don't usually bother with their own droppings. Pippa has not had much experience of socialising with strange dogs and wants to romp, so we all ended up with arms and leads stretched. Pippa, of course, had to remain on the lead in case she devoured the evidence again (in which event we would have had to wait for it to re-emerge);

but this had the side-effect that, in letting her sniff out each target and then pulling her away with a command and a reward, the idea that the eating of other dogs' by-products is unacceptable seems to be getting through to her at last.

God knows, in view of the time that had elapsed it was asking a lot of busy ladies to remember exactly where their dog had crapped on 24th June, but at least they could take me on their usual walks and point out the most common stopping-places. I had armed myself with many small evidence bags and the local chemist had managed to provide me with a stock of the sort of gloves that come with hair-dye kits. The large suede shoulder bag that you gave me for my birthday is proving very useful!

I need hardly say that all the effort produced precisely no cartridges but, between the dog-walks, visiting about guns and taking statements with DI Fellowes, at least I've encountered all the residents. I'll give you a summary. If you know any dirt about any of them, let me have it.

One preliminary point. I'm usually very good on voices, but these are educated people and Scots from good schools tend to have neutral accents.

Mr Berenson, at No. 1, is tall and fair-haired with a bushy moustache. He is one of those men whose long bones went on growing, so he is gangling and with a pronounced jaw. The name sounds Scandinavian but his family has been in Scotland for generations so the name is probably a relic of the Vikings. (Or did the Viking leave names?) He has an office in Newton Lauder dealing in agricultural supplies. He uses his Anschutz .22 rifle on rabbits and also at the range at the gun club. He has a multichoke over-under shotgun that he uses for clay pigeons and on a local shoot.

They have two daughters at school in the town; they travel in with him in the morning and wait for him at a friend's house after school. Their house and garden are untidy in a comfortable sort of way.

Mrs Berenson is plump and fluffy, very much the Earth Mother type and very friendly. She brought along the family Labrador (Garfield), who is very dignified and didn't really want to know. Mrs Berenson thought the whole expedition was super fun and joined me in poking through the dog plonks with great enthusiasm, undimmed by the revolting nature of the job and our total lack of discoveries. She had no recollection of her walk on the 24th but she always goes along the waterside, heading south towards my walking territory, which makes Garfield a definite suspect although I did not see him indulging in any snacks during our walkies.

Neither Berenson admits to having seen anything on the 24th. He was at work. She spent some time in the garden but without looking over the water. The first she knew of anything untoward was when Mrs Dawson pointed out the dinghy and the corpse.

Mrs Dawson at No. 2 you have already met. (Similarly the late Mr Fraser at No. 3.) I put her at 50 dressed for 35. Mr Dawson, when I came to meet him, turned out to be considerably older than his wife. He retired some time ago (from the civil service) and seems to have let his mind go to pot. He spends a lot of time watching the news and gets the wrong end of the stick almost every time. His short-term memory comes and goes, and when I first met him it had definitely gone.

At No. 4 we have Mr and Mrs Andrews, one rifle, one daughter and two dogs. They are comparative newcomers, arriving only about four years ago but in the meantime Mr Andrews seems to have built up a small shop into a thriving wholesale business. There is one son, now left home. Mr Andrews is mild and gently spoken, slim and spectacled. He uses the rifle with subsonic ammunition, this being much quieter than a shotgun and so not disturbing the neighbours, on rabbits. (These have reached plague proportions around the reservoir and although the gardens are walled the rabbits get around the reservoir end, swimming if necessary, or else they get under the gates.) Mrs Andrews is busty, forceful and has a strong jaw and tightly crimped grey hair. Her voice is loud and metallic. I gather that she and Mrs Dawson are friends on the surface but in a state of rivalry.

Our jaunts with their two spaniels produced precisely nothing. She swore that they would never eat anything disgusting. They all say that, but she seemed to be correct. Her walks took us up the hill where I saw traces of sheep, foxes and rabbits but none of dogs. On the other hand, we mustn't forget that Mr Fraser could have been shot from quite high on the hill. Conversely, the hole in the dinghy suggests, to me, a flatter trajectory – unless the dinghy was heeled at the time. (Fraser could, for instance, have leaned over at the critical moment to look into the water.)

Their house is furnished in the best of contemporary taste, straight out of *Home and Garden*. The garden and the house are both inhumanly tidy.

At No. 5 we have a Mr Glashan, Herbert by name. He was the man among the female bystanders when I first saw the body. He is thin, dark and intense looking, with a moustache that suits him, giving him a deceptively masculine look. His house looks much like the others, but inside it shows great imagination and flair. Colours, dividers, indoor plants and fabrics have all been used to define the functions of the different spaces. (If it all sounds a bit precious, I can only say that when we get around to setting up house I would like him or his twin brother, if he has one, to do the décor.) His garden features a lot of bright paving and coloured gravels among the flowering shrubs, thus keeping the work of maintenance at the irreducible minimum for quite an attractive garden.

Several of the residents dropped their voices when his name came up. Only Mrs Andrews was forthright enough to say that her neighbour was gay. (She actually said *homosexual* and, linguistically, I agree with her even if I have less sympathy for the horror with which she mouthed it.) He's on his own at the moment but I gather that the house is sometimes the scene of parties that may last for several days, quite discreet and exclusive, apparently, to gays of both sexes. You may know him by his *nom de plume* of Roderick Gardner, under which he writes, very successfully, the kind of romantic adventure that Mr Fraser enjoyed. I noticed one of his books on Fraser's shelf, but unsigned.

Glashan was quite frank about his shooting. I had in fact heard of him in that connection although I hadn't realised that he was the writer. He was, and probably is, a very successful pistol shot, having won medals at the Commonwealth Games and been European runner-up. I gather that he was reserved for the Olympic team but never called on. The Firearms (Amendment) Act 1997, banning private ownership of handguns (which most serving police officers knew to be a political gesture of no benefit to the public) hit him hard. (You'll know as well as I do that in a six-year period encompassing the ban, the figure for homicides by pistol doubled.)

Glashan now keeps his target weapons with a friend in France and goes over to practice as often as he can afford it. His diaries for several years back refer entirely to his shooting and a comparison with his recent novels suggested that he places the plots of his books wherever the next major competition is to be held so that his trip there becomes a research trip and therefore tax deductible. When I suggested this to him he smiled and made no comment. I know better than to let my personal likes and dislikes intrude, but between ourselves I'll admit that I liked him. He shoots small-bore rifle at the gun club range, using one of the club's rifles.

He is also a keen angler. A large sycamore in the Andrews's garden had been lopped on his side, to give him easier casting, but a long branch had been left over the water. Mr Fellowes was shocked to see (and smell) the corpse of a rabbit hanging from it. I explained that it would be there so that maggots would drop into the water and act as ground bait. The dead bunny, I discovered, had been supplied by Mr Berenson, the only male local resident to admit to being on good speaking terms with Glashan.

His house and No. 6 were originally one larger house, now divided into a pair of semis. The work was sensibly done and the soundproofing seems good but there is only a fence between the two gardens. This has proved a source of friction because the family next door is in a state of disorganisation and, from the state of their garden, has been for some time. Also their terrier, mostly what's loosely and inaccurately known as Jack Russell but with signs of other ancestry, comes and craps in Glashan's garden. (He showed me some of the evidence of this but no cartridges showed up.)

The family in No. 6 is named Fenwick. Mr F is tall and angry looking with every feature prominent, giving him the look of a caricature. He has high colour and pop eyes. He is the catering chief at the hotel and timeshare complex. In good weather he crosses the reservoir in his motorboat. His estranged wife is bar staff, so they never usually meet. When it's windy, the speedboat stays in a neat boathouse and he drives the much longer way round. His wife's name is Betty but he calls her everything under the sun. She is stocky and equally angry looking, but this may be because the pair of them are permanently angry, mostly with each other. He has a very loud voice and it is rumoured that he once emerged from the hotel to shout at his wife across the width of the reservoir, but this I do not believe. I understand that he is very meticulous in his work and incredibly untidy at home. He has a shotgun, which he uses only on clays at the gun club.

Mrs Fenwick stated that she never walks the dog but she admitted that their gate is sometimes left open and she had no idea of the days when that had happened.

They should divorce and they keep talking about it, but claim that they stay together for the sake of three children. I gather that the real reason is that the house still belongs to her father, who is definitely senile and occupies most of the attic floor. Neither has anywhere else to go.

Mr Fenwick states that he crossed to his work by motorboat around 9 a.m. on the 24th. He had quarrelled with Fraser, as with almost everybody else, so he admits that he drove past Fraser's dinghy fast and close. At this morning's meeting, Mr Blackhouse argued that Fraser must still have been alive at that time or his body would have fallen over when the boat was rocked, but I'm not so sure. It was a hot day. We all know how much hotter it can be on the water where the sun reflects off the surface; and rigor can develop very quickly in heat and especially so after exercise such as rowing.

No. 7 is the smallholding, rented from the Water Authority by a family called McPhee. They have no dog or firearm so I have not had much contact with them, but the smallholding is down to vegetables with a pair of pigs in a sty at the far corner. It all looks well kept. In contrast to the tidiness of the plots, the family is as untidy as the Fenwicks next door, which may explain why the two families get on well to the exclusion of most of their neighbours. The McPhees give the impression of having a hundred children but it's probably only three or four. They treat the Fenwicks' house as their own and seem welcome. They all deny ever seeing Fraser on the water, which I find unlikely. Children are usually very observant.

So those are the occupants in the Moorfoot Road Houses. If you know anything about any of them that might not be on record, please let me have it. I'm going to copy the salient parts of this to Dad, because a big commercial organisation probably knows more about people's dirty linen than the Police National Computer does.

My attendance at these enquiries was interrupted by an urgent summons from Mr Blackhouse. I hurried round to the hotel and timeshare and met him in the lobby of the hotel. Mrs Fraser, it seemed, had declined at first to open up to him or any of his officers. (One suspects that he had used his finely honed interrogation technique to put her back most thoroughly up.) Eventually she had agreed that she might open up – but only to a female officer and definitely not a local one. Apart from yours truly, the only two females on the team had been born locally, so the die was cast.

I saw her in the hotel manager's office. She is a presentable and quite smart woman, more dignified than cultured, in her forties, and no beauty. She refused to speak into a tape recorder and only allowed me to make notes on the very clear understanding that anything not relevant to the enquiry would stay confidential. I soon discovered the cause of her concern. She already had an idea as to when her husband died which turned out to be fairly accurate (rumour and tittle-tattle travel fast in these rural communities) and she had spent the whole period in the hotel. Her alibi seemed to be shatterproof. When not on duty, she spent her afternoons in what passes for a staff common room, working on a tapestry and under the eyes of several other women. Her nights were spent in the company, and the bed, of the bar manager. She places a high value on her reputation in the neighbourhood and was deeply afraid that her nightly romps would become the talk of Newton Lauder. I gathered from one of my colleagues that Newton Lauder was already well aware of them but not particularly interested.

She still did not have a good word to say for her late husband who, she said, was an irritable and mannerless bastard (her words, not mine) who didn't deserve a decent woman. She had seen little of him for several years, but unless he had changed his tune, his habits, his morals and his socks she could well understand somebody wanting to shoot him. I pointed out to her, as gently as I could, that her lover would have to be checked out. She actually laughed aloud at the idea that her lover – McNaulty by name – would have wanted Fraser dead so that he could marry the widow but she finally accepted that both their alibis would have to be confirmed, insofar as one can confirm that sort of statement. Mr Blackhouse accepted my report without comment but I could see that he was both interested and amused.

So far, our efforts seem to have been, as the French say, beating the water with a stick. But cases often seem to look like that until one gets a sudden break. I will report further.

All my love and everything else,

Honeypot

29 June

Jeremy – you ask for another update on Pippa. You also ask what is the electronic collar. The two questions go hand in hand.

For the electronic collar you get a battery charger with two leads. One is used to charge a small transmitter that hangs round your neck and is adjustable. The other charges the dog's collar, which has a small box of tricks on it with a short aerial and, on the other side, two blunt prongs. You can vary the strength of signal and also have a choice of a high strength and a low strength button; and so you can give anything from a tickle to a jolt. This facility gets you over the problem of a dog that thinks it can do what it likes if it's beyond your reach (and, of course, it's much too late to punish a dog for not coming when it comes at last!). Pippa must have spent much of her life on the harness and the rest running free. In theory, of course, if the dog refuses to come you run after it and catch it for a good shaking. Unfortunately Pippa can run faster than I can; but a good electric jolt at a distance soon had her coming reliably and when she found that this brought praise and a reward she started answering the whistle immediately.

The diet is reducing the scratching; her coat shines and with the addition of a lot of chopped raw parsley to her meal the farting has almost stopped. Or else you can't smell it any more, I'm not sure which. But the diet is rich and she tended to put on weight, so I cut her meals down slightly. She thinks that she's hungry all the time, which makes it doubly difficult to cure the coprophagia; but it's amazing what you can teach a dog with perseverance, tenderness and preventing wrong behaviour.

She delights in rolling in things and she had developed a talent for sniffing out the most disgusting, long dead carrion, especially fish, from miles away. I got fed up showering her in the flat. I walk her twice on most days at the reservoir, so now I give her a dummy retrieve from the water, then rub her with shampoo and give her another retrieve. What this does to the water supply of the towns round about I hate to think, but nobody has told me to stop. Sometimes I think I can taste her in the tap-water, but that's just imagination, probably. Patience and the electronic collar seem to be modifying this behaviour.

In short, she's a loveable dog, eager to please, but no brighter than the average Lab. (Face it, animals are not as intelligent as humans, with occasional human exceptions. Dogs come fairly low in the scale of animal intelligence and Labradors are near the bottom of the canine intelligence scale. Where Pippa comes in the scale of Labrador IQ I'll leave you to find out for yourselves, but by the time of your return I think you'll have a dog you don't have to be too ashamed of.)

I told the lady in the vegetable shop that all the parsley was for a farting Labrador. She said that she'd have to try it on her husband.

Love to Hazel. All the best,

Honey

29 June

Sandy, my dearest – you won't believe what a day I've had. Yesterday evening, late, I was called in for a sudden conference. Mr Blackhouse explained that we still had no idea where the shooting occurred. The alibis of Mrs Fraser and her lover appeared to stand up – unless they were acting in concert – but if either of them had the opportunity to get their hands on a .22 rifle he would certainly root it out. The possibilities remained open that Fraser had been shot from the vicinity of his own house, from the hotel-timeshare complex, from a boat on the water or, indeed, from anywhere along the banks. Today would be the last chance to trigger the memories of witnesses before the occupancy of the timeshares changed. Somebody would therefore spend today in Fraser's dinghy, drifting around on the reservoir, while every available person buttonholed potential witnesses to pin down where the dinghy had been seen and at what times.

DI Fellowes pointed out that a dummy would do as well as a person, to which the DS retorted, correctly for once, that a person would be needed to return the dinghy to the middle of the reservoir whenever it nudged the bank. Then he looked at me and said that, while he hated to spoil my fun by taking me away from a task to which I was admirably suited, he was going to remove me from my turd-hunt for the day. I was to be the person in the dinghy. I would be provided with a shirt and hat similar to those that Fraser had been wearing. And Fraser had had a trout rod sticking over the side of the boat, so arrangements had been made with the shop below my flat for the loan of fishing gear and would I please try to look as though I knew something about fishing.

It sounded like a boring sort of day, but at least I would get away from confronting peevish strangers or poking through dog plonks. I was up early this morning, made some sandwiches, took soft drinks out of the fridge and put some meal for Pippa into a freezer bag. I was on the doorstep of the shop when it opened. Mr James was there again and he lent me his personal trout rod. He seemed a bit surprised when I wanted the rest of the gear but he gave me his bag and a net.

The dinghy was waiting for me near where it had been found, which happens to be about the nearest point of shore to the geometrical centre of the reservoir. The oars were there but not the outboard motor – Mr Blackhouse probably thought that I was too ladylike to row and would have to admit it. Pippa seemed surprised to be put in the dinghy. It was a new experience for her, but she's a confident and trusting bitch. She settled quite happily in the bottom and I rowed out into the middle.

The day was warm and dry but dull with insects all over the water, perfect for fishing. Mr James's fly-box held some brilliant imitations of the insect life, even including the damsel flies, but there was no sign of surface feeding and anyway I decided that Mr Blackhouse might well have objected if his supposed corpse had spent the day casting dry fly. I rummaged in Mr James's bag and fitted up the rod with a floating line, a goofus bug as float and bite indicator and then a long polycarbonate leader to two Montana nymphs. There was just enough breeze to keep the dinghy moving gently (although obviously it could not be expected to retrace the path of its previous voyage), so all I had to do was give the line an occasional twitch to give the nymphs some life and shorten it whenever we drifted into shallower water.

When there is a general breeze it tends to blow along a valley, but on a calm day the breeze tends to be catabatic – cold air rolling downhill from the high ground. Today, as on the 24th, the breeze was light, so it came from any point of the compass.

As you can imagine, I had plenty of time to look around and to think. The air was very clear. I could see every boulder on the hills, every sheep and probably every rabbit. I saw deer on the skyline. Lower down, I could see the golfers and riders although from my low viewpoint the course itself was mostly hidden. I could also see my colleagues pointing me out and taking statements, accompanied by a lot of head shaking and more pointing. I had a much better view of the waterfowl than ever before. I counted four species of duck, three of geese and the usual waders.

As usual among the hills, the wind came in puffs from varying directions. My drift took me several times past the construction in the middle of the reservoir where new stock is released weekly and fed daily. The larger fish evidently hang around there and feed deep on the leftovers. By the time the trailer returned, with DS Blackhouse come to enjoy my misery, I had five rainbows of up to three pounds and I'd returned several tiddlers of only a pound or so. Mr Blackhouse graciously accepted one of the trout although I suspect that he dumped it in a ditch as soon as he was out of my sight.

People are not very good at pinpointing a position on open water, so you may well feel, as I did, that the whole exercise was unlikely to produce any results. The reported sightings were plotted on a single map as they came in and, to everybody's surprise, after making allowance for errors in positioning, it seemed clear that Fraser had started from the vicinity of the Moorfoot Road Houses and described an attenuated and wobbly M or W (depending on which way round you look at it), drifting homeward during the night to fetch up only half a mile from where he started. Unfortunately, each witness could only speak to seeing a seated figure and had no idea whether it was alive or dead. What course he followed during the night is anybody's guess but probably irrelevant. The likelihood is that he was shot close to home in the early morning but, although nobody saw him rowing or motoring across, it remains perfectly possible that he let himself drift to somewhere around the timeshare and was shot there. I find it hard to envisage Mrs Fraser as the kind of woman that men would kill for, but there is no accounting for passions. Would you kill to get possession of me, Sandy? No, better not answer that in case some day I'm found with my toes turned up and not from natural causes. After all, you may well be the guilty party.

As soon as I had gutted and bagged my fish I popped them into the freezer and descended to return his fishing gear to Wallace James. By then, the shop was manned (womanned?) by DI Fellowes's wife, the coach at the gun club and who had kindly provided us with lunch. We got on like the proverbial house fire. Her husband had already obtained a photocopy of their sales of .22 cartridges for some months back, but she promised to run me off another copy for my own interest. We then closed the shop and adjourned up to my flat, talking scandal and relaxing over microwaved prawn balls and Chianti, after which she was so relaxed that she had to phone for her husband to come and fetch her. I rather suspect that he had to cook for himself or eat out.

I, of course, was sober enough to sit down and write to you but I think I'll feed Pippa and go to bed now.

Your ever loving,

Honeypot

Sandy, my angel – it hadn't dawned on me that you'd have to go armed in LA. If confronted, do remember everything we were taught on that course. Wait until you can swear, on your heart or whatever part of your body you hold most sacred, that you had no alternative and not an instant longer. Then shoot fast and straight. I want you back, complete, in one piece. And preferably soon, but I'd rather that you had to wait over there for a board of enquiry than that you got yourself punctured. I know that you have quick reactions; just don't let that compassionate heart slow you down.

The Incident Room must have been waiting for my line to clear when last night's email was going out to you, because as soon as I signed off my phone went again. DS Blackhouse had already decided that enquiries and searches on the west side of the reservoir had been exhausted without result. That and the result of yesterday's experiment combined to suggest that Fraser had been shot near his home in the early morning (which is what we'd all thought in the first place). While the full team remained assembled, there would be a search of the hillsides behind the houses.

At the morning meeting, to which everybody was bidden, he elaborated. Fraser might have been shot from one of the houses. (Enquiries revealed that a helicopter had flown over early, which would have covered the sound of small-bore shots.) In that case, a small team pursuing local enquiries should produce the answer. Meantime, there was still the possibility of spent cartridge cases or other evidence lying on the hillside and the search was going to be thorough. (He had earlier mentioned the possible use of magnets but I left it to DC Bright to point out that brass cartridge cases would not respond.)

Though I held my tongue (I had learned my lesson at last) I had serious doubts about the benefits of a search. I knew how tiny objects could vanish down among the roots. I had already looked in all the places from which a marksman could take a shot without being obvious to the casual viewer. If such a hillside

sniper existed, he had surely had the sense to take his spent cases
home with him and chuck them in the reservoir. And it had been
occurring to me to wonder how the cartridge that Pippa had produced so inopportunely had ever got into the food chain at all. I
could imagine it being passed from one coprophagic dog to
another, but why would the first dog have picked up and swallowed a small, brass object. There was, I suppose, the faint chance
that a cartridge case had been left in the open and a dog had come
along and deposited a tasty morsel on top of it, but that figured
very low in my list of possibilities (Sherlock Holmes's dictum
about *whatever remains* notwithstanding). However, Jove thun-
dered and we all jumped to it. Knowing the quality of refresh-
ments usually provided on such works outings, I had provided
myself with a packet of pâté sandwiches with lettuce, tomato and
a little mustard, with a bottle of tonic water not uncontaminated
by gin, and also a bag of meal for Pippa. I carried a good thumbstick. When the time came to line out up the hill my earlier
researches came in useful. I knew that the lower slopes were thick
with very prickly gorse. Higher up, the slope became steeper and
the heather long. I slotted myself into the line where I reckoned
the walking would be easiest and I noticed that our two local
DCs, Bright and McFadden, had also learned a lesson and were
on either side of me.

It was a leisurely progress. There was no hurrying what should
have been almost a fingertip search and, of course, we had to
linger to wait for those who were struggling, especially those who
had been too lazy to climb higher up the hill and found themselves deep in gorse. My early training on hockey fields and
grouse moors proved itself – some of those whose main exercise
had been strolling a beat or cheering on a football team were
floundering. As I expected, nothing of obvious value was found
although there was plenty of rubbish, most of it paper which had
probably arrived on the wind from miles away. So at least the hillside is now tidier than it was. Pippa, determined to be helpful,
brought me several empty plastic bags and a beer can. We disturbed a few grouse, one or two hares and more rabbits than you
could shake a stick at.

The effort was abandoned at last, when exhaustion set in. We had more or less covered a stretch about half a mile long by three hundred yards wide, which I reckon might be about a tenth of the area required to embrace all the possible places from which a competent shot could have shot an oarsman on the water but near the bank between the houses and where Fraser turned up. Everybody hurried home for a proper meal. I was met by Mrs Fellowes, who had been watching for me from the shop while in theory helping her father and Mr James with stocktaking. She brought me my photocopy of the cartridge sales. I think she was glad of the excuse to get out of the shop, because she was willing to join me for a drink again. (I don't know what my boss will think about my leading his wife into temptation.) It was easy to detain her for a chat. I had hoped for some revelations about the gun club (where, you will recall, she is the resident coach as well as being a life member) but they seem to be a dull bunch there with no usefully guilty secrets – except for the secretary/steward. He, it seems, looks after the rifle range while Mrs Fellowes sees to most of the clay pigeon shooting.

Deborah – Mrs Fellowes – praised this Ewan Henderson with only the faintest of damns. He was, it seemed, efficient, careful, polite and – her highest accolade – a damn good shot. Then she added that he could be trusted never, ever to make a pass at the female members or members' wives. 'Ho ho!' I said to myself, because experience leads me to believe that, though many men may refrain from making passes there isn't one born with normal orientation who can be trusted to do so, always excepting your usually good self I hope.

Deborah, I noticed, had turned slightly pink and was avoiding my eye, which confirmed my suspicions. 'But you can't trust him not to make passes at the men?' I suggested.

'He doesn't do that either,' she said. 'He has more sense. But, yes, he's what they call gay. Not the obvious, effeminate kind or he wouldn't be tolerated. He doesn't flaunt it but he isn't secretive either. He had a man friend visiting at one time and the two were touching hands and whispering in the clubhouse like an engaged, heterosexual couple. They acted as though it was the most natural thing in the world, so the members accepted it the same way. If they had been either surreptitious or blatant, I expect that all hell would have broken out.'

I said that Mr Glashan, from the Moorfoot Road Houses, sometimes shot at the club and he was gay too. She didn't know Mr Glashan by name until I described him. She hadn't connected him with the distinguished pistol shot and she said that he was only moderately competent with a rifle and would never make an adequate performer with a shotgun in a million years. She had occasionally seen Glashan and Henderson talking together but there never seemed to be any special relationship between them. I asked whether she had told her husband about Mr Henderson's orientation and she said, 'No, should I?' I told her not to bother him, because I wanted to produce this faintly promising lead myself.

After she left, I put a frozen chicken supreme into the oven and settled down to the computer; and – *mirabile dictu!* – up came your email with another possible lead. So Mr Fenwick has had trouble with the law in the past, quite a long time ago. If you were gifted with my kind of recall you would remember what, when and where, but I dare say we can dig it out.

I caught a news item on the car radio to the effect that there has been a series of killings in Edinburgh, presumed to signal the outbreak of gang war between drug overlords. I would not be flabbergasted if Mr Blackhouse grabbed at the excuse to step back from an investigation that seems to be bogging down and leave it to the locals who can then be blamed if it fizzles out. We have here a case with a body, no obvious motive, some bullets, one possibly relevant cartridge case, no crime scene, no suspect, no weapon, no fingerprints, no DNA, no contact traces, nothing. It has all the making of a long-term unsolved murder or a long wait for a lucky break. There is some talk of soliciting help from the entire public by way of *Crimewatch*.

Sandy, my angel...(*The remaining page of this email is of an amorous, not to say erotic, nature. It is neither relevant to the enquiry nor proper for publication.*)

Jeremy – so you've moved on to Suez. I hope the desert bears fruit for you and that the samples you've sent to the lab contain the four-thousand-year-old deepwater diatoms you're looking for, but don't hold your breath – it's been a long time and even in the desert a lot of rain must have percolated through the sand. The stone tablet you found could be Commandments Eleven through Fourteen, had you thought of that?

Pippa continues to progress well. I had to visit the gun club today and my boss's wife was coaching a duffer on the springing teal stand. The duffer kept lifting his head and I could see that she was on the verge of losing her temper. I could hardly get Pippa past there because she sat down at the sound of every shot. So the work with dummy launcher and blank cartridge pistol is paying off. I'm sure you'd rather start the season with a sticky dog than a chronic runner-in. She's naturally exuberant, so you'll have difficulty keeping her subdued rather than in getting her going.

She gets bored easily. I got her a Kong. This is a hard rubber ball with a hole each end, one large and one small. You put food inside. I'm using two bits of carrot, which can be jammed in hard with scraps of apple. She then spends time figuring out how to extract them, but I'm afraid she's getting very clever at dropping the Kong on the wide end to shake them loose. She has also learned to shake apple trees to bring down the fruit. She says to tell you that she sends her love and looks forward to working for you.

The parsley is doing its job. I still don't know whether it stops the farting or you don't smell it, but things are better. The parsley keeps well frozen and crumbles easily onto the meal. The lady in the vegetable shop says it worked on her husband too but she is having difficulty finding recipes to which parsley can be added. He was surprised to be served a green pizza.

Regards to Hazel. All the best,

Honey

1 July

Sandy, my loveboat – I am not usually one to say 'I told you so,' but I did. I told you! At this morning's meeting, the DS announced that he was needed back in Edinburgh. And the next stages of the investigation would be plodding local enquiries that could safely be left to the local idiots – subject to his personal supervision from long range, of course. So the Edinburgh contingent could return to civilisation and those borrowed from uniformed branch (I must get out of the habit of referring to them as 'woodentops' – an expression acceptable in the Met but resented here) could go back to harassing drunks and motorists, especially when those are one and the same.

When DI Fellowes emerged, looking fed up, from a private briefing with the DS, I took him aside for a conference of those lumbered. (By which I mean that, as I need hardly point out, a successful outcome will reflect well on Mr Blackhouse but a failure will be down to us.) He brightened up a little when I told him about Fenwick having had trouble with the law and a little more when I mentioned the sexual preference of Ewan Henderson, the gun club secretary.

Mr Blackhouse had already shaken off the dust of Newton Lauder in his hurry to get back to Auld Reekie and all the comforts of home and, presumably, Mrs Blackhouse. To be honest, I think we drew out our discussion to give him time to go. Then Mr Fellowes got on the phone to Edinburgh. But here we hit a bit of an impasse because some of the matters dated from before the records were put onto computer; they remained on microfilm and were not as accessible as the experts would have had us believe. Such staff as was capable of getting sense out of the system was on leave.

'One of us had better go in to Edinburgh and ask some questions,' he said, 'while the other has a word with Mr Henderson. And you're the firearms officer, so you'd better go to the gun club.' I don't think he fancied questioning a homosexual too closely. No more did I although I usually get on well with the male ones.

As you know, days off seem to get forgotten during a murder enquiry. I had rather hoped for a day in Edinburgh – my shopping is seriously out of date – I'm getting withdrawal symptoms – and I desperately need the attention of a big city hairdresser. (You can tell at a glance which of the two local salons a lady prefers because they only have one style apiece.) Though locally I'm coming to be regarded as the very arbiter of London fashion, some of my London friends would fall about laughing if they saw me now. However, what the boss says goes. I left word for DC Bright to join me at the gun club.

Moorfoot gun club had been high on my list of visits to make – as Firearms Officer – and I would have made it before now if a little matter of murder had not intruded. From force of habit, I nearly turned right over the bridge before the dam. Instead, I climbed a steep incline in a new-looking road between the top-heavy hills. The reservoir came into view and a little further on I came to a perimeter fence of chain-link. The gates stood open. Beyond the cool green landscaping of the golf course, the hotel and timeshare complex looked welcoming but expensive. Across the reservoir, I could make out the small gathering of Moorfoot Road Houses.

It was another hot day, close and airless. The clubhouse was too low to offer much in the way of shade and what little shade it threw fell on a bed of mixed shrubs. However, a chestnut tree had been preserved and threw a shadow that overlapped the parking area. I was able to squeeze the Range Rover into the shade, where it stood a good chance of being habitable when we came back to it without the necessity of having to wait for the air-conditioning to do its thing.

I was pleased to see that the clubhouse was well protected with security locks. I knew that an alarm system was connected to Police HQ. The clubhouse was locked but a bell push was accompanied by an invitation to ring for attention. I guessed that it would be connected to bells or buzzers among the shooting disciplines.

Deborah Fellowes had told me that she would be coaching a novice game-shooter and I could hear shots. Because of Mr

Blackhouse's meeting, Pippa had not had much of an outing, so I was glad of the excuse for a walk. I descended one of several flights of steps to what had probably once been a flood plain. There had been some considerable earth shifting, probably when the reservoir was constructed, and noise attenuation banking had been added around the whole area. I could see Deborah with her novice on one of the clay pigeon layouts. She gave me a wave, but I was more interested in exploration. I followed what seemed to be the main path past the layouts. It led me to another flight of steps up the further banking where a prickly hedge made certain that there was only one approach to the small-bore rifle range beyond. This was in the open except for a shelter over the principle firing position where two ladies lay prone, bums sticking up like the Cuillins of Skye, competing with each other in their attempts to make small groups with single shot small-bore rifles. From the sound of the shots, they were using high velocity ammunition. They were brooded over by gentlemen who I assumed to be their husbands and the group was supervised by a man who came to meet me as soon as I appeared.

My guess that this was Ewan Henderson, the gun club secretary, was confirmed when we introduced ourselves. He was a thin and nervous-looking man with a bandit moustache and very dark eyes. He was roughly dressed but I did not hold that against him – a gun club is no place for an official in a business suit. If I had not already known that he was homosexual I would have guessed it from the way he looked at me as a person rather than a sex object, ignoring my figure. (I can't help the way I look. I dress to be smart and neat, not to look sexy, but I can detect the covert lust in the eye of any heterosexual male between puberty and senility – not excluding yourself, I'm pleased to say. Conversely, I can usually tell a lesbian on sight.)

Quite sensibly, he asked to see and then checked my identification. 'I can't come away just yet,' he said. His accent came from further north, Dundee I thought. He lowered his voice. 'The men are Italian; and Eyeties can get careless.'

I sympathised with that view. I have done a lot of picking-up, as you know, and if there are Italians in the party I shelter behind a tree. 'No hurry,' I said. 'I want to look at your security and check gun numbers. But first I have a few questions.'

He nodded. 'There's a seat up on the banking.' It was a very suitable place. We would not be overheard. He would be able to watch the target shooters and I could keep an eye on Pippa. I unclipped the lead and sent her out into the rough ground towards the reservoir.

'If it's about the man who was shot a week back,' he said wearily, 'I'm not sure I can help you. In fact, I'm damn sure I can't. I've answered every question I could think of, and a whole lot more.'

'I've seen your statement,' I told him. 'But this kind of enquiry depends on asking the right people the right questions and you never know what the right question is until you've heard the answer.'

'I never thought of it that way,' he said.

'So let's run over it again. You were here all day but you didn't look out at the reservoir?'

'Correct.'

I decided to check his frankness, his veracity and his reliability as a witness. 'Were there many sailing dinghies out?'

He smiled faintly, perhaps with a trace of superior amusement, not fooled for a moment. 'I've already said that I didn't look at the water.'

'None of the club's rifles left the premises?'

'Definitely not. That's never allowed. Members sometimes ask to borrow a rifle in order to deal with a vermin problem. We tell them that we'd insist on the production of a Firearms Certificate with the particular rifle specified on it. They usually find it quicker, cheaper and easier to buy an air rifle or get a friend to come in and deal with the problem.'

'And no shots were fired except down the range, at your standard targets and against the earth banking?'

He was positive. As a matter of fact, so was I. Evidence from the previous day suggested that Mr Fraser had never drifted so far south. However, a few simple questions might continue to settle him down and get him used to being precise. 'You could swear to that?' I asked him.

He looked defiant. 'I thought I already did.'

'Not on oath. Could you swear to it on oath and stick to it under cross-examination?'

He began to hedge. 'There were several groups came to use the range. Yon inspector from Edinburgh got all the names. I couldn't be down here every minute. As soon as I had each group settled and a mannie in charge as I could see knew the rules of safety, I attended to other club business – taking money, serving drinks or food, selling shotgun cartridges, loading the clay pigeon traps and the like.' He paused and looked through me. 'If anybody had taken shots from the top of the banking, he'd have been seen. And I'd have noticed the difference in the sound of the shots.'

That was unlikely but probably irrelevant. I headed in the direction in which I wanted to go. 'Did anybody take away any live rounds?'

He began to sweat. That may have been the heat of the day, but allowing live rounds to be removed would clearly be a breach of the Firearms Act and could be serious for the club. 'I'm sure they didn't,' he said.

'Did you count the shots?'

'Well, no.'

Having established that I was not going to be palmed off with any answers he couldn't substantiate, I moved on. I could always come back to the subject if I needed a stick to beat the dog with. 'Tell me about the people from the Moorfoot Road Houses,' I said.

There was a long pause. The two women handed over the rifles to the men, who began a more serious competition of their own. The two women, standing nearby, chatted in Italian and laughed. It was a musical sound but it must have been very distracting. One of the men objected and they moved further away.

'People come,' Mr Henderson said at last. 'They shoot, they pay their money, maybe they eat in the clubhouse and they go. I don't mingle with them socially.'

'So you said in your statement,' I told him. I gave him what I like to think of as my most penetrating look. 'The officer who took that statement may not have been around gun clubs much, but I have. You're not just a shop assistant. The secretary and the steward know all that's going on, and if you combine those functions you'll have had some kind of business dealings and a good long chat with any one of them who comes here. In fact, I bet you could tell me their hat sizes.'

He shook his head but he smiled faintly, sighed and said 'Try me.'

'Start with the members. And please don't try to tell me that you don't know who comes from those houses. What can you tell me about Mr Fenwick?'

He shrugged. 'Doesn't come here very often but he competes now and again. Mostly skeet and never on the small-bore rifle range. He has a Spanish over-under twelve-bore and he's quite good with it if he keeps his temper. Once he starts missing, he loses his temper and his confidence and never hits a damn thing. His wife came with him once but she tried to tell him how to shoot and he blew his top. She never came again.'

'Who else has he blown his top at?'

'I remember him niggling and narking at other members sometimes, but nothing that you'd call a quarrel.'

'And Mr Andrews?'

He looked blank. 'I don't think we have a member of that name.' I described Mr Andrews and he shrugged again, which was fair enough. The mild Mr Andrews had said that he only used his rifle on rabbits. 'Doesn't ring any bells.'

'Mr Berenson?'

'Tall man with a moustache a bird could nest in?' He saw me hiding a smile. 'Yes, like mine or even more so. He's here quite often. He shoots with his own target rifle but he's better with a shotgun. He's well co-ordinated and his reactions are quick. His wife's a chatterbox but I like her. She stays in the clubhouse and drinks gin while he's shooting and she tells me how well the girls are doing at school.'

It was time to put the boot in. 'Now tell me all about Mr Glashan.'

I felt his twitch through the slats of the seat. 'He's a member.

How would I know all about him?'

'We both know how.'

'Say it aloud.' He wanted to be sure that I knew before he blurted out any confidences.

'You are both gay,' I said, quite kindly. 'That isn't illegal any more. He comes here. You would certainly have recognised each other.'

'Aye, we did,' he said. He held my eye for the first time. 'But that doesn't mean a thing. He wasn't my cup of tea any more than I was his. You're a woman. If you can meet a man without starting an affair...'

'I do quite accept that,' I assured him. 'I wasn't suggesting that there was any kind of liaison. Just that you would recognise each other. Now tell me about him.'

I was watching his body language. He was very nervous, but that could have been concern for a fellow gay or any one of a dozen other reasons. His nervousness made it very difficult to detect any signs of lying. 'He comes here now and again, shoots small-bore with one of the club's rifles. He joins in the competitions we run at weekends. He's good with a rifle but his heart isn't in it. You know?'

'That he was a champion pistol shot? Yes.'

'Still is, but he has to go abroad all the damn time.' Mr Henderson became heated for the first time. 'That ban in 1997 was the stupidest piece of legislation even our daft buggers of politicians have ever managed to foist on us. The one discipline we used to walk off with most of the gold medals for and it's gone down the drain. And for what? There was no effect on the crime figures at all.'

I could have gone further and pointed out that the total of homicides by pistol in 1997 had been 39. Four years later it was 59. As you know, Sandy, nothing can lie like statistics but it's hard to argue with that one. And statistics through the civilised world show that allowing the responsible citizen to have and to carry arms is a remarkable deterrent to the criminal. Mugging the victim seems a lot less fun if he may be better armed than you are. But it would not be appropriate for a serving police officer to say so aloud. Retired officers can speak more freely and some of them are saying so quite loudly.

'What do you think of him as a person?' I asked.

'I like his books. And he can write about a man and a woman as if he knew what it was about, which is unusual for one of us.' Henderson paused while he thought about it and then shook his head. 'Beats me. I couldn't do it. He's reserved. And I think he's sensitive about being gay. Me, I didn't ask to be this way and I don't have this orientation on purpose, but this is what I am. I don't broadcast it but I'm not secretive about it. Most people have habits or beliefs that seem a damn sight less justifiable to me but I don't get on to them about it and I don't expect them to lecture me.' He flushed for a moment.

'Who lectured you?'

'Just some damn woman who came as a guest.'

I asked him to describe her and it seemed that her appearance had been burned onto his memory. 'Big woman with a bust you could drown in if it wasn't held in by a miracle of engineering. Grey hair tightly curled. One of those rosebud mouths with a mole near it. Nose like a Roman emperor. And a voice like a foghorn.'

That sounded more than a little like Mrs Andrews. 'Whose guest was she?' I asked.

'No idea.'

He either wouldn't or couldn't say any more about the lady. 'Did Mr Fraser ever come here?' I asked him.

He shook his head emphatically. 'His photo was all over the papers and the telly. I'd never set eye on him.'

We were interrupted as the party on the range finished their shooting. He left me while he recovered any unfired cartridges and took their money. I saw a good tip change hands. He returned but did not sit down. 'Are we finished?'

'You've told me about the members,' I said. 'What about casual visitors from the Moorfoot Road Houses?'

'If any of them come as casual visitors, I wouldn't know them. Take a look at the visitor's book, if you like. You might recognise the names.'

'How about Mrs Fraser and the bar manager from the hotel, Mr McNaulty?'

He shook his head. 'I know them both from visiting the hotel. I've never seen either of them here. There's only one other I can think of. A girl called Sandra. I think her name's Andrews. Is she from the houses?'

I said that she was.

'She's been here several times with a boy, Julian something, on the back of his motorbike. They meet up with some other young people for a small-bore competition of their own. They're all of legal age, I checked. I keep a careful eye on them anyway, but they're always careful. I'll tell you this much. She's older than she looks. And I've seen her at the hotel with one of the timeshare owners, a single man who comes regularly all summer. I've watched her.' His nostrils flared slightly. 'That young woman, let me tell you, is just one large clitoris with minor appendages for walking and talking and eating.'

I might have pursued that interesting topic a little further, but Pippa chose that moment to return. I could have sworn that I'd been watching her closely, but she had somehow managed to find and roll all over in the foulest, smelliest, most revolting something indescribable on earth. At a different season I would have supposed that it had been a spent salmon that had died and been brought ashore by a mink, several weeks earlier, but it was probably trout. The fishing is cheap on the reservoir but they make a substantial charge for any fish you keep, so there is a temptation for an angler to dump any surplus. She presented herself to me with a look that said 'Aren't I clever and don't I smell lovely?'

Mr Henderson, I must say, was very good. He hid his amusement and lent me the hose at the clubhouse to wash her down. It took three lots of shampoo to get the reek out of her coat. I left her out in the sun to dry off and he let me buy quite an adequate lunch inside.

I inspected the security, the club's guns and the stock of ammunition. Nothing seemed out of order and I was just getting ready to leave for an afternoon of catching up with the paperwork in Newton Lauder when Bright turned up at last, spouting feeble excuses. I told him that he was certainly not the young fellow called Bright in the limerick. When he looked at me blankly I recited the rhyme about the young fellow called Bright who travelled much faster than light. He set off one day in this relative way, returning the previous night.

He gave me another of his vacant stares and said that he couldn't possibly have travelled that fast. I asked why. 'Because,' he said, 'at the speed of light the mass of matter is infinite, which is impossible.'

People can always surprise you, can't they?

Love and sloppy kisses,

Honeypot

2 July

Jeremy – just another update about Pippa. We have made one amazing stride forward. She is progressing well, but I wanted her to behave less frantically when food is within sight. (Some time, I'll tell you how to offer her a biscuit without getting your fingers bitten.)

So I started by making her wait for her dinner until told to take it. We went on to putting down her late night biscuit and telling her to leave it. Last night I forgot to give her the go-ahead and, believe it or not, when I came through in the morning she was still looking at the biscuit and the floor was covered with drool.

That shows at least that she is capable of learning as well as of forgetting. She is, however, still puppyish and impetuous. Many of these lessons go by the board when the novice encounters the real thing. You won't be back in time for the opening of the grouse. When you arrange your first shoot, if you like, I'll come and work her at picking-up for you, just to get the message across.

No, you don't owe me any money. I've had too much fun from having her. I needed a challenge and something to get me out into the open.

I was only joking about the Commandments.

There was a Mr Symes, a 'keeper working near where you live, who was trying to contact you. He knew about Pippa so he tried the Guide Dogs who referred him to me. I gave him your email address. I hope that's all right.

Regards to Hazel. All the best,

Honey

Sandy, my dream of delight – I wrote yesterday's email in office time and spent the rest of the afternoon digesting and tabulating the statements that had gone before and the comparisons that the now departed collator had made between them. I needn't bother you with all the irrelevancies; I'll give you a potted digest later, with reminders about the characters, who have probably begun to merge together in your mind.

When I made it home, your email was waiting. Apart from all the sweet nothings, which lifted my sagging morale, you asked whether nothing useful had come out of the garbage bags from the Moorfoot Road Houses. This morning, I checked and found them tucked away in a dark corner, unopened but stinking to high heaven. The snag to a bullying insistence on everything being done exactly as you decree is that whatever you don't decree doesn't get done. DS Blackhouse had never specifically told anybody to search through them, so nobody had done anything about them. Well done, Sandy, and black mark Mr B!

My week of poking through dog turds has not exactly cured my squeamishness although I'm now better at hiding it. I felt that I had done at least my share of the less agreeable tasks. I still had to confer with DI Fellowes, which gave me the perfect excuse to delegate the garbage-hunt to our two DCs, with instructions to refer anything of even faintly possible relevance to Forensics.

Ian Fellowes – he asked me to call him Ian whenever we're alone – had had an interesting day. Sandy, you were brilliant to point out that the garbage bags had been overlooked, but I do think that you might have had the sense to mention that, when Mr Fenwick had his earlier run-in with the law, he had had it in a different police area. After some chasing around, Ian discovered that Mr F, on whose temper, especially when in his cups, several people have remarked, had been involved in a punch-up in Fife while he lived in Dunfermline. It had drawn the shortness of his fuse to the attention of the police, who had jerked his firearm and shotgun certificates. When he removed to Stirling, Central had granted him a renewal of his shotgun certificate but either he had been refused a firearms certificate or he had never applied for a renewal. On his removal into Lothian and Borders territory, this history had been left behind except for a residue in the memory of a smart and handsome police officer who had once served in Fife.

BUT, and it's a very big but, Ian Fellowes had dug up a very interesting titbit, aided by a knowledgeable sergeant in Dunfermline. It seems that Mr Fenwick, in addition to a two-two rifle, had owned an adapter tube enabling him to fire two-two Long Rifle rimfire cartridges from his twelve-bore shotgun. This, of course, had been on his firearms certificate. When he forfeited that certificate and had to dispose of his shotgun and firearms, he could not produce the adapter. He had reported it as either lost or stolen only a few days earlier. His story, that it had simply vanished from the boot of his car, was regarded with suspicion; but there was no proof to the contrary. His car boot had shown signs of having been forced and in any case the appropriate penalty – revocation of his firearms certificate – had already been applied.

This was very interesting. Of course, Mr Fenwick's story might be perfectly true. And even if, as some suspicious minds would have it, he had invented the loss and made a false report in order to retain an unusual and expensive piece of equipment, it did not follow that he had made use of it or even that he still had it. As you know, one of the worst but commonest mistakes in crime investigation is to pin your hopes to one suspect and neglect all others. We would see Mr Fenwick. There was no justification for disturbing him at his work and getting him in bad odour with his employers. He had no reason to believe that he was any more suspect that he had been yesterday. Over the phone, his wife confirmed that he was expected home in the late afternoon. We could wait that long.

What with the beauty of the day, a possible break in the case and the fact that Mr Blackhouse was now a long way away, there was a definite feeling of school being out. Neither of us felt like being cooped up in the 'factory', so Mr Fellowes and I climbed the hill behind the houses and settled down in the heather, looking over the whole scene while we reviewed the earlier statements on record plus whatever I had found out that morning. Ian sat down in the heather but I preferred to stand. There are no sheep this side of the hill, but there may have been sheep in the past and sheep ticks can live on rabbits.

Heights seem to be exaggerated, looking down. The reservoir was laid out before us almost like a map, with the houses below us and the timeshare and hotel across the water, the golf course spreading to the left and the gun club beyond. This unlimited view over the whole area freed our deliberations wonderfully. And a fat lot of good it did us!

We started from the premise that Mr Fraser had probably, but not necessarily, been shot close to his home, early in the morning of 24 June. Nobody admits to having heard the sound of shots. The helicopter, on its way to do a survey of overhead electricity lines, passed over at 7.15 a.m. This would probably have covered the sound of any shots. A clattering noise made by a moving helicopter over houses tends to be perceived as a series of loud and soft echoes.

I'll summarise house by house in the same order as before. This is a mixture of our own interviews and what appeared in the formal statements already given.

At No. 1, the Berensons. He owns a rifle and a shotgun, but the rifle did not fire the fatal bullets, nor did the firing pin match the impression in the cartridge case deposited by Pippa. Mr B is adamant that his gun safe is never left unlocked and that nobody but himself knows where the keys are hidden. (This is hardly ever the truth, if for no other reason than that wives usually keep their jewellery in the gun safe.) Their Labrador, Garfield, may have been the first to pick up that cartridge case, but he isn't talking. The Berensons were woken by the sound of the helicopter and rose shortly afterwards. Mr Berenson and the girls left the house around 8.15 without, they insist, noticing anybody or anything.

Mrs Berenson took the dog for a walk around 10.00. At first, she was sure that she had seen nothing. She says that the wind at that time was from the east ('coming down the hill behind the houses') which is in line with other statements, and that there was a dinghy, without sails, drifting in the middle of the reservoir with a figure, presumably Mr Fraser, seated in it. While this seems not unlikely, it may well be the product of her imagination or a recollection from a different day. The rest of her morning was spent in the garden, not looking up.

On closer acquaintance, the Berensons come across as one of those normal, close-knit and well-intentioned families beloved by TV commercials and early films. Nobody had an ill word to say about them and, while not inclined to gossip, they claimed to love all their neighbours. They seem to have been the only family on comfortable terms with the late Mr Fraser. In a whodunnit, this would make them prime suspects.

At No. 2, Mr and Mrs Dawson know nothing about guns. Mrs Dawson claims that they are anti-bloodsports. She admits disliking Fraser but, when asked why, she retreated into an unintelligible mumble. Her husband is older, retired and so vague that he is already unsure who Fraser was. He knows that somebody is dead but keeps coming back to believing in a heart attack. Nobody wants to say the word Alzheimer's aloud. They saw and heard nothing until Mrs Dawson, returning from her dog walk, spotted the body.

According to Ewan Henderson, the gun club secretary, the son, Julian, visits the club with the Andrews girl to shoot small-bore with the club's rifles, so no doubt either of them could purloin ammunition. (If he carries her on his pillion while he is still a learner, that's an offence and they had better not let me see them thus mounted.) His parents seemed quite unaware of these visits or of any contact between their son and Sandra Andrews. The boy is definitely the tearaway type and, though I have never seen him in a baseball cap, he would certainly wear it with the peak over his pimply neck. Although it was so half-hearted that I didn't recognise it until later, would you believe that he made a pass at me?

At least he was frank about the neighbours. Nothing against the Berensons but, according to dear Julian, Fraser was a vicious old bugger who hated everybody and didn't mind them knowing it, Mrs Andrews is a domineering old bitch with a voice like the last trump, Glashan is a perverted poof, the Fenwicks are just plain nuts and the McPhees are peasants and beneath his notice. Those are, in fact, pretty much the views expressed less vigorously (or even implicitly) by the others, except of course the person or persons concerned in each libel.

Julian Dawson produced one other gem. Apparently Glashan had a visitor on June 23rd who Julian thought stayed overnight. One or two witnesses mentioned being somnolently half-aware of a vehicle driving off just before dawn, but this can be assumed to be before Fraser was killed. It could, one supposed, have dropped an assassin who lurked in the heather (which has enough dips and depressions to hide a regiment of hitmen). This might not be as unlikely as it sounds. Fraser had been in the police in southern England and guarded enquiries were met by equally guarded hints that he had been encouraged to retire by colleagues who could no longer work with him. This can only mean that there had been threats to expose some misdeed, but nobody speaks of this. A .22 rimfire, however, is not the professional's weapon of choice. Too many people have been perforated once or twice by the tiny bullets and survived. This surely makes significant the fact that Fraser was hit by eight bullets and may have been missed by one or two more. Somebody meant to kill and knew enough about firearms to make sure. This may prove a significant argument if a case ever comes to trial.

Not dwelling on the late Mr Fraser, we come to Mr and Mrs Andrews at No. 4. Mr Andrews uses his rifle to knock off the rabbits, which get into his garden; though being in the middle of the row he is less vulnerable to their arrival from the waterside than the others. The rabbits are then cooked and fed to the two spaniels. (I have warned him to have a care, because rabbits can carry tapeworm.) He is certain that his rifle has never been left out of his gunsafe and that nobody knows where the key to his gun cupboard is hidden. His wife (who, you will recall, lectured the unfortunate Ewan Henderson at the gun club about his sexuality), was as outspoken about Glashan, which can't have made for good, neighbourly relations. Mr A left early for the office on the 24th, his wife followed him into Newton Lauder in her car to do the shopping and neither of them admits to seeing or hearing

anything. Mr Andrews has nothing against any of their neighbours, but Mrs A considers Mr Dawson an old fool, the Fenwicks
and the McPhees a rabble, and what she said about Glashan I
leave you to imagine. She seems to be generally feared and disliked, but this means that nobody confides in her, so as a fount of
gossip she was a dead loss.

Ewan Henderson referred to the Andrews girl as a walking clitoris. She struck me as being very feminine – not aggressively
sexual but in the soft, passive way that is so often more alluring
to men. She is nineteen going on twenty, but living at home and
under considerable restraint from which she escapes whenever
possible. Her parents flatly refused to discuss her. From hints
and fragments of information dropped by others, I have the
impression that she left home to work elsewhere but was hurriedly fetched home to where her parents could at least pretend
to keep her under supervision. I suspect that an abortion figures
somewhere in the equation but, medical confidentiality being
what it is, it would be difficult to confirm this. Just what threats
or treats are used to keep her at home we do not know, but if I
ever have a daughter like that, I'll make sure that she has a thorough understanding of the less savoury facts of life. I'll also mix
the Pill with her breakfast cereal. She seemed barely aware of any
neighbours except Julian Dawson. We have only Henderson's
word for it that she has a lover who frequents one of the timeshares.

Glashan, living alone at No. 5, seemed isolated in a little pod
or cocoon of his own. Apart from Mr Andrews, his neighbours
seemed reluctant to discuss him. I had the feeling of a general
inability to decide on what attitude to take without seeming
homophobic and therefore politically incorrect – or appearing to
be the opposite and thus casting doubts on their own sexuality.

Glashan admitted that he had had a visitor who had left before
dawn on the day of Fraser's death. He pointed out that, because
his visitor had left when Fraser could safely be presumed to be
alive, he had seen no need to mention the visit earlier. He flatly
refused to name the visitor nor to comment on what had taken
place between them, which suggests that the visitor may have

been someone who would be seriously embarrassed by any word of gay goings-on. Glashan did agree to contact his friend and ask whether he had encountered any other vehicles or noticed anything in the least out of the ordinary when he made his departure. For the moment, we have let it go at that.

At the smallholding, the McPhees are also shunned, not because they are offensive in any way but because, with the exception of the Fenwicks, they simply have nothing in common with the others. Those others would go to the stake denying it, but it is a snob thing. The McPhees are down-to-earth peasant types, toil-worn and stooped but eternally cheerful. The other households buy provisions from the smallholding and there it stops, at a customer-to-tradesman relationship. The McPhees are quite happy to have it that way. Ian had spent some time with them and he said that the McPhee children mingle freely with the Fenwick brats and their parents take the sensible attitude of exchanging the time of day with any of the others who care to speak to them but accepting the drawing of an invisible line. Ian had the impression, however, that they noticed far more than they admitted to.

Mrs Fraser and her lover, McNaulty, make tempting suspects. I went along to the hotel yesterday, ostensibly for a bar supper, and spoke to them both. She was coy at first but she came far enough out of her shell to deny absolutely that they had any intention of marrying, a statement that he repeated with even more vehemence. She is slightly better off with a widow's pension than with the allowance that Fraser made her, but otherwise they seem to have neither means, motive nor opportunity.

While we were still discussing the happy couple, a small motorboat approached across the water. I whistled Pippa and we went down to confront Mr Fenwick.

The front door was answered by Mrs Fenwick, a small, stout woman with uncontrollable hair. (If she were a more likeable person I would put her on to a good stylist.) She looked, as usual, furious with the world in general and her husband in particular, but on this occasion we gathered that it was the aged father in the attic who was getting up her nose. She told us (but not quite so politely) that she was much too busy to waste her time on the likes of us and if we wanted to speak to her louse of a husband – though why anybody in their right mind should want to do so was quite beyond her – we could walk down the garden and help ourselves, and the best of British luck to us. The door then slammed with a violence that rattled every window in the house.

We still had to wait for several minutes, like fairies, at the bottom of the garden, because the motorboat, from steering an almost straight course towards us, came to a halt in the middle distance while its occupant took several drams from a silver measure that he refilled each time from a large flask. I sympathised. I would want a good drink inside me before facing that harpy. Whether there is anything in Scots law about being drunk in charge of a motorboat I have yet to find out, but he was not endangering himself or anybody else. The matter, I suppose, would be covered, if at all, by a by-law.

To be fair to Mr Fenwick, he did bring the motorboat quite neatly alongside a very small landing stage beside his boathouse and moored it against a row of old tyres, snug and secure.

When he straightened up (to his considerable height) he goggled at us. He had all the high colour, broken veins and unsteadiness of the steady drinker. In a voice that seemed ready to trip over his tongue, he enquired just why the hell we had come to bother him again. He did not quite say 'bother'.

Ian explained later that he decided Fenwick might be drunk enough to blurt out the truth, so he asked him outright what had really happened to that adapter.

Either Fenwick had been telling the truth or *in vino veritas* did not apply. He invited us to go forth and multiply, or words to that effect. This, of course, put Ian in a quandary because, if we did indeed go forth, Mr Fenwick would be free to toss his adapter or anything else into the reservoir. So Ian told him quite politely that, in order to demonstrate the truth of what he had told us, we would like his permission to search his house.

We did not receive it. Instead, we got a tirade of abuse. It seemed that we would have to go through the tiresome business of setting a guard on the house while a warrant to search was obtained. Fenwick, however, played into our hands. When Ian invited him to come to the station and make a statement, he first declined, then swore loudly and then took a poke at Ian. Thus we were able to arrest him on a comparatively minor charge. Ian managed to hold onto him while I produced the cuffs (your shoulder-bag still proving its worth) and we bundled him into my car, struggling all the while and uttering such curses that I may have to have the Range Rover exorcised.

It was left to me to go and inform Mrs Fenwick of the arrest. To say that she took the news well would be a gross understatement. She cackled like a hen and said that we could keep him. She offered to pack a suitcase.

And there the matter rests for the moment. Fenwick is cooling his heels in a cell and Ian will ask the sheriff for a search warrant in the morning.

The hour is late and my lonely bed is calling. Hurry back and share it.

Love,

Honeypot

3 July

Jeremy – in answer to your first question, Pippa is coming on great. She's a lovely and loveable dog. She may not be the crispest biscuit in the bag, but even her follies are somehow charming. She has a very good nose. A large part of a dog's brain is given over to interpreting what it smells and much of the rest to what it sees or feels. That doesn't leave a lot for thinking. All the same, I'm sure you'll be proud of her.

Your second question makes the mind boggle. What the hell is going on? You want to know if I can be foster-mother to ANOTHER Labrador bitch until your return and to give you an assessment. Are you starting your own kennels or something? I would like to point out that I am not a professional trainer and I don't have a kennels. It's not a question of money, so don't bother sending any more money orders; I am a serving police officer with responsibilities and calls on my time.

However, I would hate to let down any friend of my father's and I do understand that your Mr Symes has to take up his new job in the metropolis almost immediately. If it had been more than one and anything but a Labrador, I'd have drawn the line but, all right, tell him to drop her off to me, WITH all her accoutrements, papers and inoculation certificates. And this is on the understanding that your return is not too long delayed. I refuse to wonder what I'm going to do if she doesn't get along with Pippa.

If the above sounds a little peevish, put it down to the fact that I've had a hard day and I'm expecting a worse one tomorrow. Also, my fiancé has been in the States for several weeks and I don't know when I'll get him back. I have every respect for the demands of scholarship and I sympathise with anyone who can't resist a dog, but I have a life of my own to live, if you can call it living.

Your dog-tired friend,

Honey

Sandy, my demonic lover – the world is going mad and I'm getting mad with it. Would you believe that the Carpenters, owners
of Pippa, have decided to lumber me with another Labrador bitch
until their return? They must be the sort of people who can't
resist a bargain, and having decided to become dog-owners they
don't know where to stop. If you have to give way to a mania for
compulsive acquisition, I must admit that dog ownership is
understandable and comparatively harmless, but still... At least
they're sticking to Labradors. It could have been an Irish water
spaniel.

You've been attached to the Vice Squad now, you tell me?
Please bear in mind that you're supposed to be against it. You will
be rubbing up (figuratively speaking, I hope) against a number of
ladies who will be only too willing to indulge your carnal appetite
in exchange for a little looking-the-other-way. Just remember
that there are some nasty infections going around over there. I
have some outrageous boudoir attire that you have never seen
yet, but if I think that you have misbehaved I will reserve that and
every other delight for a more faithful lover. (The word *boudoir*
is French for *to sulk* and, believe me, I could sulk for Scotland in
the Olympics.)

While French is the tongue, *Revenons a nos moutons.* The murder of Mr Fraser. On Ian's orders, I left him to charge Mr
Fenwick with raising lumps on a police officer. First thing this
morning, he sent me out (with Pippa and our two constables) to
keep an eye on *chez* Fenwick just in case there was any attempt to
dispose of any fiendish devices. As a result, I gathered up the
story piecemeal, then and later.

It seems that Mrs Fenwick, though despising her hubby, was
not totally disloyal. She phoned his solicitor, who turned out to
be the same Mr Enterkin who is Fraser's executor. (I see a possible conflict of interest arising later, but sufficient unto the day
etc.). I have since met this legal eagle and can report that he is fat,
elderly and very much on the ball. He has a reputation for sloth
but he was round at the nick in three jumps and, after a quick

word with his client, tried to bail him out. This, for obvious reasons, was refused.

Fenwick was brought before the sheriff this morning and Enterkin was on his feet immediately, wishing to object to the granting of a search warrant. Ian, however, had already had a word with the sheriff and obtained his warrant and Enterkin was told that this was not within his purlieu. He then offered to plead his client guilty with grovelling apologies to the officer concerned if the case could be dealt with there and then. The sheriff, however, having seen Ian's black eye, decided that assault on a police officer was too serious to be dealt with summarily and he bailed Fenwick to appear again on a date to be specified.

The pace of court proceedings being what it is, this had all taken some time and I, meanwhile, had taken Pippa for a walk, ostensibly to keep observation and to familiarise myself with the layout but in fact to stretch my legs and give Pippa the exercise she had so far missed. I had gone a little way up the hillside and worked round behind the smallholding. I intended to take a seat in the heather (while remaining wary of ticks) but, before I could pick a spot from which I could watch for the arrival of Ian, a voice spoke to me. 'Aye, there,' it said. Or it may have been 'Hi'.

A boy of twelve or thirteen was sprawled in a dip. To judge from the cigarette ends and the reek of tobacco, this was a favourite place and he had been having a secret smoke. I recognised him as the oldest boy of McPhee, the smallholder. The family had arrived from somewhere further north and east, coming from a family farm which, I gathered, was not large enough to employ a son as well as several other relatives. They were a broad spoken lot, but I don't have to talk 'pan loaf' if I don't want to. I dropped into the accent that had impressed and amused the Londoners. 'Hello there,' I said. 'Which of the McPhees are you?'

'I'm Duggie,' he said. 'And you're the police wifie speering about old man Fraser.'

I said that I was. I knew from a note attached to his father's statement that Duggie had been interviewed only briefly and in the presence of his parents, but I could see that he was bursting with something. Whether this was curiosity or information was anybody's guess, but I decided to play him gently. 'Did you see his corp?' I asked in subdued tones.

He shook his head regretfully. 'I was in school that day,' he said.

I made a guess from the age and number of the cigarette stubs. 'You dinna gang tae the school an awfu' lot,' I suggested.

He looked at me cautiously but decided that I wouldn't clype to the truant officer. 'Nah,' he said. 'I'll come intil my Granddad's farm some day, so whit do I need with history and geography and the like of that?'

He had a point there. We chatted for a while about what subjects might or might not prove useful to a Kincardineshire farmer and I managed to convince him that a sound grasp of arithmetic might prove more than useful.

By that time he had accepted me as a pal and almost a contemporary and I had recognised him as a Heaven-sent potential source of information. A teenager can prove both garrulous and observant on the right occasion but may turn sullen and reticent if approached by authority in a heavy-handed manner – which I gathered had been the case when Mr Blackhouse's detectives had visited the smallholding. He referred to them as *glaikit* and *massie* (which latter, as you probably know, is Doric for pompous).

I mentioned, as if revealing a great secret, the police theory that Mr Fraser had been killed the day before he was found. If that news had reached the parents it had been kept from the younger McPhees and he brightened up immediately. He had been at home that day – with a bad knee – but before helping his dad on the smallholding he had come up to his favourite place for a quick puff or two and a little peace and quiet while his siblings were readied for school and conveyed there in his father's Subaru pickup. He had watched Fraser casting his fly under the bank below the houses. His peace and quiet must have extended throughout his father's school-run into the town, because he had seen Fraser drifting further out on the water. This, he was quite sure, was after the passing of the helicopter. Fraser, he rather thought, was dozing at the oars by then because he had stopped casting and was just drifting with his line in the water. You don't catch trout that way, he said, just the coarse bottom-feeders.

'That's all you know, Laddie,' I told him, and I described my catch of a few days earlier. We talked fishing for a few minutes. Mr Glashan he respected as a competent angler. His mother, he told me, cleaned for Mr Glashan. She thought very highly of him but told Duggie never to go near him. Duggie wondered why. So young, so innocent!

Dragging the subject back to Fraser, I asked Duggie, casually, whether he had seen Mr Fenwick set off in his motorboat. After another few minutes on the subject of motorboats, he said yes. He was quite sure which day. He said quite definitely that the motorboat passed close to Fraser's dinghy without stopping and Fraser never even turned his head. I said that I thought that Mr Fenwick had stopped for a word with Fraser, but no. He insisted that the motorboat passed the dinghy once and once only 'at a good lick' and went straight on.

I need hardly point out the significance of this. It rocked me, but before I could pursue it any further I saw Ian Fellowes's car pulling in at the houses, bearing also Mr Fenwick. I hurried down to join them. Fenwick was in no better mood than yesterday but he was restraining himself better. Sobriety may have had something to do with this. His wife offered him a late breakfast but he said that he could get a better breakfast at his work. He set off hurriedly in the motorboat.

The rest of the day was, well, interesting. Ian was hell-bent to get on with directing the search in the hope of having a result to show before Mr Blackhouse got down to reading his report and came galumphing through to grab the credit for anything that turned up, but I managed to get him aside to drop the bombshell into his lap, to mix my metaphors. Ian was shaken but not stirred. He said, rightly, that we only had the word of one boy to say that the motorboat had not paused long enough for a sequence of bullets to be fired; and the boy, he added, might be buddy-buddies with Fenwick or bribed or coerced. He added, without much conviction, that it might not be impossible to steer the boat while firing the whole series of shots through the adapter. Before I had time to point out that the adapter would be very slow to reload and that Duggie McPhee would certainly have noticed any such carrying-on, he changed tacks and pointed out that it would be almost as useful to exonerate Fenwick as to incriminate him.

Betty Fenwick, now that I was meeting her properly for the first time, gave me the impression of a wise but grumpy owl, but for this her round face and horn-rimmed glasses were mostly to blame. My next impression, based on her attitudes, was that she was retarded. In the end, I concluded that she was one of those people who are born with a certain native intelligence but given no education to bring it out. In short, nobody had ever taught her to think. The result was a creature very much like a badly trained Labrador, potentially affectionate but inclined to snap. She was given to unreasoned beliefs which became set in concrete. She had learned to snarl and bark at her husband in response to his snarls and barks at her, but when speaking of him in his absence she spoke with the sort of amused tolerance that a mother might show towards a wayward child.

The house, at least on its lower two floors, was in a state of disarray. This was understandable. The Fenwicks were blessed or cursed with three young children, which suggested that their relationship was not always one of enmity. For minutes at a time the house was a haven of peace. Then the Fenwick children and Duggie McPhee's younger siblings would crash in, whooping and firing pretend guns, accompanied by the Fenwick's terrier in full voice, only to vanish again into one garden or another. Glashan's garden on the other side, separated from Fenwick's only by a flimsy fence, was not inviolate, but I gathered that the writer protected himself from their noise and that of telephones or doorbells or vacuum cleaners by the simple expedient of wearing a pair of his shooting ear protectors while at his writing.

Ian had served the search warrant but a proper search was impossible while the children were tearing through the house, moving things around and asking questions. Mrs Fenwick offered to take them all for a long walk. The offer was probably well meant, but Ian suggested that we would prefer to have a witness present during the search. In point of fact, I suspect that he wanted the chance to question her informally while she was in such a complaisant mood.

If so, however, this proved to be a disappointment. The lady was happy enough to talk – it was difficult to stop her talking – but she said little to the point. She remembered the trouble over her husband's firearms certificate ('Served the old fool right', she said) but she was quite sure that the theft of his adapter was genuine. An alternative theory, of course, was that he had kept the adapter and that one of his neighbours had borrowed or stolen it. We could hardly make such a suggestion to Mrs Fenwick but, when I led the conversation in the direction of the social life of the little enclave, she agreed that neighbours did occasionally visit but insisted that these were invariably the wives rather than the husbands. She was also positive that the gunsafe was never left unlocked and that her husband always had the keys on his person. (They always say this and it is seldom true, but I had taken Mr Fenwick's keys off him before he left and there was a set of gunsafe keys on the ring. We never did see the spare set. At the last minute, I remembered to open the safe and check that the adapter wasn't fitted in his shotgun, but no such luck.)

Mrs Fenwick was very attentive with tea or coffee. She wanted to cook lunch for us but the most that we dared accept was an open sandwich apiece and a mug of very good soup.

She was as attentive to her father, who occupies the attic. He has his own bathroom up there and seldom ventures downstairs. She warned me that the old man was very vague, 'usually away in the clouds' although, she said, he had his lucid days. According to the officers who had made earlier visits, the old chap was several peas short of a pod. This was one of his better days, because I visited his two rooms (well decorated and furnished, properly heated) to find him finishing a good lunch and delighted to have a visitor. He is a well preserved seventy-eight, tall, skinny, wrinkled and with only a silver fringe around his scalp, but his eyes were bright. His name, he told me, was Trowbridge.

I felt bound to chat with him before beginning another (abortive) search. I asked him how he was keeping and he said, 'My body's wearing well but my mind's going. I can't remember names or what I was doing five minutes ago.' I assured him that he was not alone.

A minute or two later I asked him how he kept occupied. 'Waiting for death,' he said simply. Sandy, if I ever get to that state, shoot me and damn the consequences. I'll do the same for you, I promise. His eyes, he said, weren't good enough to read with for more than a few minutes at a time but his hearing was still good, so he listened to a lot of the radio. His mind and memory were working that day. He knew that Mr Fraser had died of gunshot wounds and on which day and he understood that I was an investigating officer. When he complained that he always woke early, I asked him whether he had heard shots. His memory clicked into gear and he shook his head. 'That was the morning the helicopter went over early, wasn't it?' he said. 'I was awake from then on and there was nothing that I could have taken for gunshots, even if it was only a two-two.'

One mildly interesting titbit that he did manage to produce concerned Mr Glashan next door. (The homosexual, in case you've forgotten.) Apparently the sound insulation between the two houses is good but it doesn't go all the way up into the roof-space and he can hear most of what happens in Glashan's house. He confirmed Duggie McPhee's statement that Glashan had a visitor that night. He could hear them talking and laughing into the small hours and then a car which, he could swear, was not one of the cars belonging to the residents, driving off just before the helicopter came over. He knew all the cars belonging to the neighbours and he even knew, from the sound, that I had a Range Rover. He chuckled at my surprise and said that he'd been in the motor trade all his life. He could tell most models by the sound of the engine and exhaust, and this had been a small, sporty car and not a cheap one, perhaps a Lotus Elise.

Searching for the adapter was not as quick as looking for a stolen car nor as slow as searching for a diamond ring; but we were keeping an eye open for anything else of possible significance, so that the search of the house and garage took four of us most of the day. At the end, it proved fruitless. The adapter could have been buried. It could have been dropped into the middle of the reservoir. But if it was in the buildings it was hidden with monstrous ingenuity.

We gathered around my car while I let Pippa out for a quick pee. 'That doesn't prove Fenwick's innocence,' Ian said, 'but taken together with an apparent lack of motive he seems a less likely suspect. Who else do we have?'

We looked at each other in baffled frustration.

'Did nothing interesting come out of the garbage bags?' I asked Bright.

He avoided my eye. 'We haven't exactly finished there,' he said, which probably meant that they'd hardly started. 'Well, you keep giving us other jobs like today.' I had a feeling that the unpleasantness of the task led them to seek any excuse to get away from it.

Ian had the same feeling. He skewered Bright with a gimlet glare. 'Usual meeting at eight-thirty,' Ian said. 'Unless we come up with something, you can finish those bags by midday tomorrow without fail, you hear me? Go and get on with it.' He waited until the two DCs had made a disconsolate departure. 'For now, you and I will have an evening off and rest our brains.'

I could have appreciated a rest of my brain and everything else, but chores had been piling up – I still haven't found a cleaning lady – and I'm writing to you, physically exhausted, at nearly midnight. A restful period checking firearm certificates is overdue but I shan't be so lucky until this case is either solved or shelved. If you have any inspirations, for God's sake let me have them.

This goes to you with love, kisses and promises of silken dalliance as soon as you can tear yourself away from the starlets.

Honeypot

3 July

Dad – very many thanks for the information. Well what do you know? My thunder has never been so struck nor my flabber so ghasted. He's the last man you'd suspect of such going-on. Still, I suppose that outward respectability has to be the hallmark of the fraudster.

On the other topic, many thanks for the offer which looks like saving my sanity if not my bacon. I knew that June and her mum came from the Borders but not that she was local to here. I don't know what my colleagues will think if I'm seen to have a resident maid, but they can think what they like if I can only have somebody to do the dysoning and the laundry and generally look after me like a mother. Being of local origin, she would also lend me a little extra credibility with the neighbours. If Mrs Spence could spare her at least until I get better organised, she would be a godsend. I do have a spare bedroom. I'll need another bed etc., but I'll pay for that myself. And I'll pay her wages and stamps and things. It's the least I can do. How much does she get?

In all other respects I am settling in well, thank you for asking. I love the place and like the people and, apart from the small matter of an unsolved murder, the job seems to be going well. And now you have solved the problem of trying to do a full-time job and keep house. When Sandy comes back from the States, my cup will be running over.

Love and blessings on you, my noble benefactor.

Honoria.

4 July

My very dear Sandy – so you'll be coming home in three weeks! That's the best news I've had since I grew breasts. Flying to meet you halfway would not be exactly practical. Unfortunately, I have not been here long enough to be due any worthwhile leave and, living as I do almost opposite the factory, I can hardly pretend a recurrence of leprosy. You, on the other hand, should be due leave, but even if that is not forthcoming perhaps you could commute from here for a period of illicit honeymoon? It is possible that my spare bedroom may not be available but I made sure that the main bedroom was superbly furnished. Take a hint, why don't you?

When I logged on to send your email last night the device told me, in its disinterested way, that I had email waiting. I thought that you must have written to say that you were only joking and that you weren't coming back after all. However, it was from Dad.

A little research by some minion in one of his companies had revealed that the mild and gentle Mr Jim Andrews is also a certain Charles James Andrews who is regarded with suspicion by many businesses and most insurance companies. He has never been prosecuted because the ill luck to have your business wiped out by a remarkable succession of very expensive fires is not of itself a crime. By strange coincidence, the contents of the building on each occasion were both valuable (at least on paper) and so flammable that it was quite impossible to tell from the residue whether the goods had been as stated in the claim. How, for instance, do you prove whether all the expensive periodicals in a burned-out warehouse had been next week's issues or the unsold accumulation of several years past? In addition, he was now finding it difficult to raise loans or overdrafts because he is notoriously slow at settling accounts and each fire has been followed by an expensive liquidation. Threatened with lawsuits, the insurers had usually reached a settlement.

These events had occurred in various parts of England and Wales and it was suggested that Mr Andrews had migrated to

Scotland several years ago to where different banks and insurance companies might never have heard of his successive misfortunes. The minion had also noted that Mr Andrews's present business was in the wholesaling of paints and the flammable chemicals that go with them.

As you may imagine, I went to bed in a thoughtful mood last night. Pippa had to make do with a hasty amble beside the reservoir this morning, as I wanted to be at work in good time. I checked with the Police National Computer, which had plenty of entries under Andrews but none resembling our man. The only Andrews appearing in any of the categories of arson or insurance fraud was a Glaswegian specialising in expensive motor vehicles.

I arrived for Ian Fellowes's eight-thirty conference a few minutes early. I did not have a chance to produce my fresh lead with a suitable flourish because, firstly, Ian had been informed that Mr Blackhouse was on his way to join us and, secondly, now that our team was running down, our incident room was required for a larger team being set up to deal with a number of incidents in which schoolgirls had complained of being 'interfered with'.

DCs Bright and McFadden, still in paper overalls and smelling to high heaven, had joined us for the conference. They were sent away to remove the offending overalls while other help was sought from the uniformed branch and we were in the middle of the removal of all our files and equipment into DI Fellowes's own room when Mr Blackhouse made his appearance.

At that point, confusion began to rein. Mr B had come through to be briefed on the latest development and he was not going to be denied. The visiting chief inspector, sent through with his own team (some of them the same faces that had been on our team the week before) to mastermind the other enquiry, had been promised the larger incident room and by God he was going to have it. He invoked the support of everyone up to and probably including the Archangel Gabriel and got it. The outcome was that Ian Fellowes took Mr Blackhouse into one of the interview rooms and broke the news that nothing had been found in Fenwick's house and that a possibly reliable witness was prepared to swear that his motorboat had swept past Fraser's dinghy without a pause.

Meanwhile I bossed around my own team of our two DCs and two PCs borrowed from Traffic while we moved our papers, exhibits, disks and computer into Ian's room. The DCs seemed surprised when I was prepared to dirty my hands but, believe me, compared to searching dog turds on a steep hillside under a hot sun, this was a doddle.

Ian's discussion with Mr Blackhouse went on for some time because the Detective Super had come with the intention of winding up the murder case and returning in triumph to Auld Reekie. He did not give up his adherence to Fenwick as prime suspect without a struggle. In the end, he accepted that we would have to continue studying the field and took himself off.

Ian was pleased to approve the disposition that we had made of our chattels in his room. The two PCs from Traffic were sent back to harassing motorists, our two tried slinking off on unspecified duties but were sent back, complaining bitterly, to finish searching the binbags and I was able to settle down with Ian to tell him about Mr Andrews. I concealed the identity of my informant in the guise of protecting an important source but in fact because I was uncertain whether tapping one's own family for information was quite in accordance with established procedures.

He listened in silence, thought it over for a minute and then said, 'Of course, finding a probable former criminal among a group which – also only probably – includes a murderer would not be stretching coincidence too far. It's difficult to see how the two could be connected – unless, of course, Fraser happened also to be a blackmailer. That could make sense. He was a police officer with – am I right? – Somerset and Avon. Did any of Mr Andrews's suspected frauds occur in their territory?'

I said that one of them had been in Bath. We were slightly euphoric after Mr Blackhouse's departure and I nearly added a joke about many a sin being committed in the bath, but decided that it would not be a good moment.

Ian thought for another few seconds and then asked, 'Did we ever get Fraser's financial paper's back?'

'There's a note on the file,' I told him. 'The executor uplifted them to copy, so that he could take control of his finances, if any. He promised to return them to Mr Blackhouse but I don't think that he'd done so before the DS ran out of patience and decamped. I'll get them off him, or copies from the bank, whichever's quicker.'

He nodded. 'We'd better get a move on,' he said. 'Andrews may be planning another quick coup and then to disappear abroad. At least that would be evidence of guilt.'

'Somebody might get burned. We could suggest a visit from the FPO,' I said.

He nodded again. A visit from the fire prevention officer should see anything rectified that could later have been blamed for a fire.

We had hardly begun to discuss who would do what when DCs Bright and McFadden returned, back in overalls and bringing with them a definite smell of long rotten garbage. This was forgiven, however, because, wearing on their faces the proud and delighted expressions of Labradors returning with a difficult runner, they also brought with them a small nylon evidence bag containing nearly a dozen spent .22 cartridge cases.

'Whose binbag were they in?' I asked.

'Andrews.'

Gasps, of course.

'These should go straight to Forensics,' Ian said wistfully.

'There's no rule that says we can't look at them,' I said. 'If we had the cases that were fired from the two shotguns, we could at least see whether the firing pin imprints look similar. That would tell us whether or not we're looking for Fenwick's adapter.'

'The woman tempted me,' Ian said. 'In point of fact, I had Forensics put an extra cartridge through each shotgun and rifle, in case I wanted to make a quick comparison. They should be in the box-file with my notebooks and gloves. Where did you put it, in your maddeningly tidy way?'

'It's where it should be, on the shelf behind you,' I said. 'I suppose cartridges fired from a shotgun through an adapter are always hit by the shotgun's firing pin?'

Ian took down his box-file. 'They were, in the only one that I've ever seen. A shotgun's firing pin would soon be ruined if it was always hitting a steel pin in the adapter.' He took out his magnifying glass and looked at both sets of cartridges while we waited – with bated breath, whatever that may be. He compared the firing pin indents in the new cartridges with those in the shotgun cartridges fired from Fenwick's shotgun, the rifle cartridges from the Andrews rifle and cartridges from Berenson's rifle and shotgun. 'I'll leave it to Forensics to make comparisons with all the rifles from the gun club and the visitors,' he said at last, 'and a fat lot of good may it do them. It's their job to make a final pronouncement, but I don't think that there's any resemblance at all. Which means that we're looking for an entirely different weapon or the Fenwick adapter and another shotgun.'

'What are those red smears on them,' I asked before he could put them away.

Ian looked through his lens again. 'They don't look like blood. Too red. Blood would have turned black by now. I think they're tomato juice. My guess would be ketchup.' Using tweezers, he returned the tiny cartridges to the evidence bag. 'These go to Forensics straight away.'

'I could run them in to Edinburgh tomorrow morning,' I suggested. My hair was long overdue for some TLC.

He looked at me sharply and said, 'Go now.'

That didn't suit me. Estelle was very unlikely to have an appointment free at such short notice. But my plea that I wanted to check out certain facts at the reservoir fell on deaf ears. 'You can do that on the way back,' he said.

So I bowed to *force majeure* and set off, blessing Dad for installing a hands-free mobile phone kit in the Range Rover. As I feared, Estelle was booked up but she promised to squeeze me in somehow. I shot in to Edinburgh, pausing only to give Pippa a run on top of the Lammermuirs, and delivered the cartridges to a bored science technician who promised to make the comparison as soon as reasonably possible, to confirm the nature of the red smears and to phone us the result. He then went back, I presume, to filling out his Lottery coupon.

My shampoo was delegated to a Work Experience child with an IQ less than her cup size, but Estelle found time to do my cut and shape. I had her trim me shorter than usual, in case I did not manage another visit before your return. I will not have you see me looking like a chrysanthemum. When she realised that I was now based in Newton Lauder, she wanted to talk about the murder. Estelle is a great gossip – like every hairdresser, I think they're taught it in coiffeuring school – and she knew that I would be avid for any scandal about the residents of the Moorfoot Road Houses. Apparently Mrs Andrews is in the habit of visiting the shop (no surprise, as Estelle, though expensive, is quite the best). She is often accompanied by one or other of the ladies from those houses and had been in only two days earlier with Mrs Dawson.

The two ladies had tried to be discreet but had tried to converse over the sound of the hair-dryers, unaware that their raised voices reverberated through the shop. If they said anything to the point, Estelle failed to remember or repeat it but she whispered that Mrs Andrews's credit card had been rejected a fortnight previously, to her great embarrassment. Happily her Switch card had proved to be still valid. When the two ladies were about to leave after the later visit, the Mastercard went through without a hiccup. This was interesting. If Mr Andrews had been cancelling credit cards, or more probably spending to the limit on them, it might be a straw blowing in the wind. There could be a reason for a sudden reversal.

It was late by the time I got away and a whole lot later before I cleared Edinburgh. My God, Sandy, I don't know how you stand it! Rush hour seems to last for four hours at a time. Of course, the City Council can be seen to be doing everything possible to embarrass the motorist in the hope of driving him or her onto a public transport system which is adequate if you are following a main route but impossible for some journeys. I mean, what business man (or a mother with shopping and push-chair for that matter) is going to put up with changing buses twice in the rain and walking half a mile at each end?

All the same, there was still daylight when I neared home. I had an unexplained call from the nick to ask when I would get home but I gave them an evasive answer and turned off the main road to satisfy my curiosity at the Moorfoot Road Houses. I could tell that Pippa was becoming anxious about her dinner but, as I pointed out to her, she was not alone in being hungry.

At the houses, I checked. The layout was pretty much as I recalled it. Outside each back gate there was a binbag in a wire mesh protector. As I feared and thought I remembered, the Andrews refuse bag was the only one that was out of the view of every window, which made it the logical one for the disposal of incriminating material. The fact that the cartridges had been put there suggested either that Mr Andrews (or not impossibly Mrs Andrews) was remarkably careless or else that somebody had a reason to prefer that method of disposal to scattering them in the water. Which, in turn, meant that any other evidence against the Andrews couple had to be regarded with at least a pinch and a half of salt.

Home, then, to find a visitor waiting on the doorstep. Three quick meals, some hasty organising of sleeping arrangements and a quick session at the computer to keep you abreast of developments. No time for more now. To bed, exhausted and alone.

Love,

Honeypot.

5 July

Dear, sweet Dad – your email was sent in good time but I didn't open it until I got home from Edinburgh last night, by which time poor June had been in Newton Lauder for some hours. Like a sensible girl, she found the flat and first enquired at the shop downstairs. Just as sensibly, Mr Calder was not going to give the spare key to any girl who walked in off the street. She went to the police station, which explains a guarded phone-call that reached me as I set off for home. She was on the doorstep when I did arrive but quite happy, having managed to make quick visits to childhood friends between returns here to see if I was home yet.

She seems pleased with her little room and I am positively basking in the delight of having somebody to do the shopping, cooking, Dysoning and bedmaking for me. She knows where to go for the freshest vegetables and the choicest cuts of meat. She loves dog-walking and Pippa thinks that she came down from heaven in a gilded dog-basket.

Rather than confuse my colleagues by letting them know that I have live-in domestic help, I have told them that one of my father's by-blows is staying with me.

Love,

Honoria

5 July

Sandy – my God! Did I really use the code word? It was totally and absolutely accidental I do assure you. All the same, your sudden outburst of jealousy is very gratifying. Unfortunately, you have nobody to assault or to challenge to a duel – it seems ages since I had two grown men fighting over me.

Hurry home. I desperately miss having a man's hairy legs in my bed and a stubbly chin ruining my complexion, but only your hairy legs and your stubbly chin, Sandy, only yours. I am remaining celibate and hating it. The visitor I referred to is female and relieving me of domestic chores. June is the daughter of Dad's housekeeper. She was surplus to requirements at home so she has come to me on semi-permanent loan. If you get along with her adequately but not too damn well, we might think about keeping her on after we're married.

Ian had reported to Mr Blackhouse about the cartridge cases but Mr B said that he would defer action on his own part until Forensics had reported. I suggested to Ian that we put off relaying any such report for as long as possible and Ian asked me if I really thought he hadn't thought of that for himself. What it is to be loved! In preparation for my own elevation to exalted rank, I am filing away a mental list of behaviour to be avoided so that the rank and file will not make similar efforts to keep me in the dark.

(Do my emails seem excessively flippant? I have to present such a serious face to the world in my guise as a responsible detective sergeant that my emails are the only outlet for what one of my teachers called my excess of unnatural exuberance.)

I wised Ian up about my researches and he told me about his afternoon yesterday. He tipped off the FPO as I suggested and then went to see the executor. Mr Enterkin huffed and puffed but eventually handed over Fraser's bank statements, going back years. Ian spent the rest of the afternoon studying them. There were no untoward deposits, only the expected pension payments and some dividends from modest investments, mostly PEPs and TESSAs. On the other hand his withdrawals were very interesting. Until about four years ago (which is about the time that

Andrews moved in) he made regular withdrawals of cash – nothing extravagant but about what one would expect for household and personal expenses. His regular outgoings such as fuel and council tax and his allowance to his estranged wife were covered by bank mandates and those continued. The only large items were cheques for such items as the replacement of his car when the old one failed its MOT. But around four years ago there was a change to his cash withdrawals, which diminished suddenly to a spasmodic trickle.

'This is all very interesting,' Ian said, 'but we mustn't do anything hasty. I told the FPO to be thorough but not to suggest that his visit was other than routine. If we let Andrews know that we suspect him, he could get rid of anything incriminating. When we've got the forensic report I can ask for a search warrant.'

'Hoping for sight of his bank statements?' I suggested.

'Yes. It could be very interesting if Andrews's withdrawals increased just when Fraser's were reduced. And we might be very lucky and find some sign of a weapon. He wouldn't keep it on hand, but even a smear of gun-oil might be enough to start him talking.'

I said that there was still something I wanted to check up on out at the houses and what did he want me to do after that? He looked at me a bit oddly and pointed out that I'd been working a ten or twelve hour day including the weekend and didn't I want a little time off? He was quite right but, thinking back, I'd been so caught up in the case that I hadn't really noticed any lack of quality time. Now that I have June, there shouldn't be any chores to be caught up on. Since arriving in Newton Lauder, my time had been taken up with settling in and then the murder case. I seemed to have lost the impetus to get on with any leisure activities. Perhaps I should take up tapestry or indoor bowling or something.

Meantime, the prospect of an afternoon in the sunshine, feet up and novel in hand, certainly attracted. But first, I felt in need of a good leg-stretch. I had left it to June to walk Pippa but the car was back in the Square. Pippa seemed relieved to be installed in her usual place by her usual walker. Dogs hate a change of routine. I headed out to the reservoir and parked behind the houses. I think that we were both pleased to be back on familiar territory.

We set off up the hill. I knew from experience of brothers, nephews and nieces that children and teenagers are often much more observant than people give them credit for; and many parents would cringe with embarrassment if they knew how much their children and the children's friends knew about their goings on. I also had my suspicions about Duggie McPhee. Sure enough, he was settled in his nest in the heather, surrounded by discarded cigarette stubs. I was intrigued to note how well chosen was the place. Due to a slight ridge and a strip of dead ground invisible from below, one could, with a little care, arrive there without being seen from the houses.

I settled on a flat rock beside him and assumed a conspiratorial air. 'You never go to school,' I said. 'Do you?' He looked at me uncertainly and then decided that I was to be trusted. He shook his head. 'You're still putting in sick lines?' I asked.

'Nah. I gied 'em a letter from my dad to say we were moving away.'

'But your dad thinks you're at school?' I had stopped bothering to use dialect and he seemed to accept the other me. He nodded. 'Your folks will expect to see your end-of-term report.'

'They never have yet.'

'Well, you're a complete card,' I said, pretending admiration. 'And your lunch money goes to buy cigarettes off the van. Don't they wonder why you come home starving?'

He patted his pockets. 'I bring an apple and a piece of cheese, or something like that. I'm no' daft.'

'No, you're certainly not that.' We had spent enough precious time on courtesies. It was time to get down to the nitty-gritty. 'And you've nothing much to do but keep watch. Tell me something. I see binbags in the council's wire mesh holders outside the gates but I've also seen the bags beside the back doors. Is there a system?'

'Aye, of a sort.' He explained that most households produced more rubbish than one black bag would hold and any bag put outside the gate but not within the protection of the holder got ripped up by cats, foxes or even dogs. Most housewives kept the bag in use by the back door, putting the first one out to the holder when it was full. Any later bag filled was put out just before the refuse lorry arrived.

'Duggie, you still remember that morning, when you saw Mr Fraser drifting?' He nodded. 'Up to about that time, who did you see walking along behind the houses?'

He pursed his lips in thought until I was afraid that his memory no longer differentiated between the days. I should have had more faith in the short-term memory of the young. 'A'most a'body,' he said at last.

'Forget about anybody who went straight out to a car and drove off,' I told him. 'And forget the dog-walkers unless they went near the bins. I just want to know about anybody who went close enough to the bins to have put something in.'

After another pause for thought he said that Mrs Berenson had walked along beside the bins. I asked why he thought she should walk towards the smallholding. 'She's fat,' he said. (I would have described her as no more than plump.) 'She likes the bins to lean on while her dog has a shite among the whins. Mrs Dawson went to Mrs Andrews's house, but that was later. They aye go to each other's houses for coffee. And I mind Mr Glashan walked along behind the houses. He stopped and lit a fag and dropped the match into a bin.'

'Which bin?'

'Don't know.'

Thinking back, there had been ashtrays in Glashan's house but no sign of cigarettes. The smell of air freshener would have covered any smell of tobacco. 'I didn't know that Mr Glashan smoked,' I said.

'He doesn't,' Duggie said. 'Not ciggies. This was a funny one. Wacky baccy. A reefer. You can smell them on him sometimes.' Duggie suddenly remembered who he was talking to. 'You'll not tell him I told you?'

'I'm not after anyone for smoking pot,' I told him. If I started a pursuit of this red herring I might find myself back on scavenging duty, picking up every dog-end in the region. 'We're still very much concerned with who shot Mr Fraser.' It occurred to me that he might have been among the many who disliked Fraser and would therefore be reluctant to point towards a public benefactor who could turn out to be one of his favourite people. 'You see,' I said, 'anybody who's killed once finds it easier the next time and sometimes they kill somebody who they think might be dangerous to them. So the sooner he's locked up, the safer for everybody.' Duggie remained silent but from his expression I thought that he took the point. The idea of people killing people had not horrified him – TV and the films had inured him to the concept – but that death should be visited on somebody close to him, or even on himself, well, that was different.

'The problem we have,' I went on, 'is that the grown-ups are all neighbours and don't want to tell the police anything bad about each other in case it starts everybody telling tales. There must be plenty of disagreements and scandals but nobody's going to tell us.'

'They're not going to tell me either,' he said, but I could see that he was getting my drift.

'And you're up here most of the day, where you see everything but hear very little, right?' (He nodded seriously.) 'But your brothers and sisters mix with the Fenwicks and the young Fenwicks are in and out of more houses. Talk to them and see what they can tell you. I want to know the sort of things people won't tell the police, about who dislikes who and what did they quarrel over and anything that seems strange.' While I spoke, I fumbled a few pound coins out of my purse. When I offered them, they vanished instantly. 'For some real good clavers, there'll be more.'

I felt a bit mean, Sandy, involving the children like that, but as long as the adults stuck to the bald facts and were hesitant about criticising each other (except for Mr Glashan and his orientation) we were unlikely to be given the sort of lead that solves cases.

Anyway, I knocked off at that point and headed for home. This was as well, because I was just finishing typing the above when I had a phone-call about another visitor and the tattered remnants of my long overdue period of leisure were blown to the winds. I'll tell you all about it next time.

I'm still counting the days, Sandy.

Yours,

Honeypot

5 August

Jeremy – please bear in mind that I am not a dumping ground for inconvenient dogs. The line is now drawn. *Finis*. That's the lot!

That said, Suzy arrived this afternoon, complete with bedding and toys. Mr Symes was very helpful, producing her pedigree (which looks excellent), inoculation certificates etc. He also produced pedigree information and signed a set of forms for all the pups. Yes, pups! Did you know that she is in an advanced stage of pregnancy? I asked when she was due to whelp and Mr Symes became vague (which is a polite way of saying evasive), so I suspect that it is not far off. There are signs of milk. For God's sake hurry back.

I have put her on a diet suited to an expectant mum.

Apart from an understandable plumpness she seems to be in excellent condition, almost as glossy black as Pippa. She is slightly smaller than Pippa and seems to be the shy and anxious type. Many people get on well with these – they can turn into brilliant and devoted workers. But I admit that I prefer the stubborn, confident ones – when they learn a lesson it is there for keeps. (The problems I still have with Pippa are all concerned with getting her to unlearn what the Guide Dogs taught her.) The two have settled together with only a little jostling to settle the pecking order. Any desire to romp together is inhibited by Suzy's delicate condition.

I repeat, please hurry back. Depositing one black Lab with me was acceptable. A second was pushing it. But eight or nine! I boggle!

Your disgruntled friend,

Honey

6 August

Darling Sandy – yes, I do only have two bedrooms and, yes, June is in one of them, but, no, the new visitor is not a bloke. The Carpenters (Dad's friends, not the singing group) have dumped another black Labrador bitch on me, would you believe? And a pregnant one to boot. A keeper, local to them, is taking up a city job with some rural quango and had to give up a trained dog that the Carpenters already knew and fancied. They're still abroad but due back soon – before P-Day, I hope. (That's Pup-Day, in case you hadn't figured it out.)

I take it that your LAPD bosses are not making full use of the Limey visitor who has been forced on them, or you wouldn't have had idle time to put my Mr Andrews through the computer. Of the four names cast up, Charles Andrews could be the one. According to the brief history produced by Dad's staff, there was a period among his English activities which is at present a void. This coincides with the fire in Santa Monica, with loss of life, for which you tell me Charles Andrews is still wanted. Hold off for a few days until we've investigated him more thoroughly from this end and we may be able to help you to make your departure from LA trailing clouds of glory.

During yesterday afternoon when, but for the arrival of Suzy, I would have been having a little leisure time, Ian had received the report from Forensics. Photomicrographs have confirmed that the firing pin imprints in the new batch of cartridge cases did not match anything so far turned up in the case except for the single-ton deposited by Pippa, the one that unfortunately missed Mr Blackhouse's foot. After some serious thought, Ian decided to go ahead anyway. He already had blanket approval from Edinburgh to request any search warrants that might be justified, so he caught the sheriff in chambers at close of play and asked for a warrant to search the Andrews house and business premises. The sheriff pointed out that the evidence against Andrews was mainly inference and that a neighbour could easily have deposited the spent cartridge cases. He granted the search warrant but left Ian in no doubt that, if we were going to search any more houses of respectable residents, he would want to see something a little stronger in the way of evidence.

Today's task, therefore, began with a search of *chez* Andrews – interview or arrest to follow depending on whatever turned up. We caught Mr Andrews before he left for the office and served the warrant. He was surprisingly eager to go to the office and leave us to get on with a search of his house, which suggested that he was either perfectly innocent or very confident in his hiding place. However, it might also have meant that he had something hidden at his place of work or even that he intended to torch the place straight away. Mr Andrews was invited, in no uncertain terms, to remain where we could see him, on the pretext that he would be able to see us and satisfy himself that we were neither purloining nor planting anything.

The FPO had been grateful for the tip-off. He had found loose papers scattered around; open containers of paint and thinners; and in the heart of the worst corner some electrical wiring which showed signs of damage, possibly by tampering. His recommendations were sweeping and urgent, and once carried through will make an innocent-looking blaze very, very difficult to arrange.

The Andrews, residence was somehow soulless. I put that down to the fact that the furniture was newish and cheapish but well chosen without being co-ordinated. The place was much tidier than the Fenwick's, which made searching easier. I suspect that Mrs Andrews is the sort of lady who tidies out all her cupboards just to keep occupied, looking for things to throw out whether her husband has finished with them or not. (I shall not be like that, Sandy. If you want to hoard, go ahead and hoard.) This unusual tidiness may account for the formidable lady's placid acceptance of the search. Conversely, she was most insistent that everything was replaced exactly as it had been and, although she had no legal right to such consideration, it was easier to comply than to face the Police Complaints Committee.

The only one in the household to raise an objection was the daughter, Sandra. She was pacified when it was agreed that I, and I alone, would search her room; and she managed to persuade her mother not to accompany us. If I should ever be blessed (or cursed) with a daughter and she gave off the same signals, I would be intensely suspicious. Mrs Andrews gave in with no more than token argument. It may be that she preferred not to see the state of the room which was far and away the untidiest in the house, looking rather like the aftermath of an explosion in a laundry. But I rather think that she also preferred not to know about the various contraceptive methods and the extremely provocative underwear that were the only items of any interest or significance that I found.

The same unnatural tidiness as in the house pertained through garage and car. They were not only devoid of guilty secrets – they were conspicuously blameless. The tidiness and house-pride of Mrs Andrews might account for the lack of any informative debris in the house, but it is a rare garage that is not filled with those of a man's precious possessions that have been refused house-room. Your average family car usually contains a clutter of objects that may be wanted some day or were required on some now forgotten journey; but not this one. Apart from fair wear and tear, it was as it came out of the showroom. The garage contained a few basic tools, a can of engine oil and some bottles of things like screenwash and distilled water. (Yes, we did check that the container of oil contained only oil.)

By now, we were into mid-afternoon and we had no grounds on which we could lock Mr Andrews, or even the whole family, up for the night. I could possibly have suggested holding him for extradition to LA. Not that that would have washed for long without a direct request from your present overlords. The information we needed might be in his office, so we adjourned there immediately. Mr Andrews followed in his own car. He remained quiet and polite.

His business was in a recently formed factory unit, but this had been created in some old farm buildings with plenty of timber to sustain a good blaze. The office was as tidy as the house had been and the warehouse area was well on the way to being the same. Evidently his two men had taken the FPO's visit to heart and had been busy. Paper and shavings had been cleared away and his stock properly racked. Andrews, showing real or feigned delight, thanked the men and told them that they could knock off early. An electrician from a local firm was already at work on the wiring. Fire extinguishers and sand-buckets had been installed. While we were there, a man from the fire protection company called to leave a quotation for sprinklers and hose-reels. Mr Andrews was innocent, or else he was making sure that his insurers had no grounds for rejecting a claim.

The business had one female employee who seemed to double as secretary, bookkeeper, filing clerkess and receptionist. I recognised her as one of those invaluable people who are the unrecognised mainstays of their employers, miracles of quiet efficiency and devotion. She was ready to explode with curiosity yet hid it very well and, at her boss's request, produced his insurance policies before she gathered up her things and set off for home on her bicycle.

At that point, Mr Andrews announced his intention of going home and leaving us to lock up when we had finished, but Ian was having none of it. The search of the scrupulously tidy office took only minutes and the warehouse only a little longer. There was nothing under the pallets. The larger drums of paint might have been emptied and, though none of them would have held a rifle, a pistol might have been hidden inside. I took Ian aside and mentioned the possibility, but he was sure that the two men would have had to know. Even so, he said that he would interview them in the morning, during the period when blue collars are at work and white collars are still breakfasting. Then, while McFadden and Bright crawled through the dusty old roof above the modern ceiling, we sat down with Mr Andrews in his office.

From his papers it seemed that Mr Andrews was considerably over-insured, but when I tackled him about that he explained that it was a busy time of year. Contractors were busy on exterior painting while the dry weather lasted and a whole lot of stock had been going out, to be replaced during the coming week. (Vacancies on the shelving supported this; on the other hand it made it a good time for arson.)

Ian decided that it was time to take the gloves off. I went through Mr Andrews's papers, paying attention to his personal accounts, and found that his personal withdrawals had increased during much the same period as Fraser's had diminished. I put a note to that effect in front of Ian and resumed work. Ian only nodded. Neither the current account nor the only deposit account to be seen contained balances sufficient to raise the eyebrows. And while I was busy with the other papers, I was also listening to Ian giving Mr Andrews a thorough going-over.

Mr Andrews began to take his situation more seriously when Ian put two small tape-recorders on the desk. 'I want a record of this conversation,' Ian said, 'and you may wish to keep a copy. Of course, if you wish, we can talk at the station in a room with video camera and all the gubbins, but I'd rather keep this informal and I expect you would too?'

Mr Andrews agreed, but he was beginning to sweat.

Ian began, quite gently, by gaining confirmation that this was Charles Andrews and getting, on the pretext of confirming which Charles Andrews we had with us, an account of Mr Andrews's stays in various parts of England. Andrews did, however, stretch two of the periods to hide his time in the States encompassing the fire about which you so timeously advised me. Ian pulled him up about the dates (making no mention of fires or loss of life) and, when he realised that we knew far more about him than he had realised, Mr Andrews began to sweat bigger drops. He pleaded a lapse of memory. Ian then asked him whether his memory had also lapsed about the fires that had terminated each of his periods of residence in various parts of Britain. After a long pause, Andrews said that he had been unlucky.

'You could easily have been unlucky again, couldn't you?' Ian said. No reply. Ian then asked him whether he had any other insurance policies than the one that we had been shown. Andrews denied it, but by this time he was looking like a man who has found half a worm in his apple. He was very white and he clasped his hands together to prevent them shaking.

Ian suggested that any future fire damage in Mr Andrews's premises would be examined with great care and that Mr Andrews would be well advised to be satisfied with having a sound little business. Mr Andrews, for the first time, showed signs of indignation; but they were unconvincing signs. They looked even less convincing when Ian moved onwards, to the question of blackmail. Andrews was loudly insistent that he had never encountered Fraser except as a neighbour and that any apparent relationship between transactions in their bank accounts was another distressing coincidence. They fenced around the subject for some time. When it became clear that that real subject under discussion was the murder of Fraser, Andrews suddenly said that he would answer no more questions except in the presence of his solicitor, the ubiquitous Mr Enterkin.

'That will be all then, for the moment,' Ian said, 'unless you'd care to explain the cartridges that were found in your binbag.'

At that, Fraser looked astonished and his surprise looked genuine. He had already shown himself to be a less than adequate actor. He was almost certainly a successful serial insurance fraudster, but I guessed that he had negotiated his claims through lawyers on each occasion. He had the telltale habits of the bad liar. Whenever he departed from the truth his normal little movements ceased and he looked from one to the other of us making unusually firm eye contact. And so I found myself inclined to believe him when he absolutely denied any knowledge of the spent cartridges and swore that he had never seen any adapter or even known that such a thing existed.

Nothing else of significance had turned up in the papers and our two PCs came down from the roof-space, dusty and demoralised, with nothing to report. We uplifted the firm's computer and every floppy disk. Ian gave Mr Andrews a receipt and warned him not to contemplate leaving the district without consulting him and we made our departure.

'You didn't warn him,' I said.

'I'd have warned him damn quick if he'd made any admissions,' Ian said. 'Eight-thirty tomorrow, then.'

'You were going to come back and see the men,' I reminded him.

'True. Make it nine.'

Unless Mr Andrews is rash enough to attempt another fire or we turn up something incriminating in his computer, it seems unlikely that we will have enough to proceed against him. I'll keep you posted. You will get your chance to recommend a request for extradition, but life will get complicated if you put us in the position of delaying because we may or may not have a case against him here.

I headed for home, tired and hungry, but there was still a light on in the shop downstairs. The door was locked but I tapped and Mr Calder opened it for me. He is a man in his fifties, at a guess, grey haired but very fit looking and still retaining good looks. By reputation he used to be, and maybe still is, a lady's man, but he never tried it on with me – which must say something about either me or him, preferably him. I asked him about silencers and he said that he knew of half a dozen. (So do I, from the certificates.) He added that any fool could improvise a fairly effective silencer from a plastic bottle.

Then it was home, to a disappointing welcome from the two dogs, who had been perfectly happy with June all day and hadn't missed me at all.

This is a hell of a case, Sandy. Nothing to get your teeth into at all. We have a man shot in an uncertain location and from an unknown distance. We have cartridge cases found where they might have been planted, with firing-pin impressions not matching any local firearm and not a witness around, not even to the sound of shots. If we had the weapon or the locus or one single damn fingerprint or strand of DNA, a contact trace or a flake of the murderer's dandruff, we could get moving, but all the obvious places have been searched and the obvious questions asked with little result and where we go from here God knows. The information is waiting somewhere, if only we asked the right person the right question, but who and what? I'll have to hope that my juvenile informants come up with something.

What have we missed, Sandy?

June is proving a huge blessing. What a difference, coming home to a tidy house, a hot meal and dogs that have already been fed and walked!

Love and all the usual fringe benefits,

Honeypot

7 August

Jeremy – Suzy has settled down and with only a little skirmishing the two dogs continue to get on well together. I gave Pippa a workout with the dummy launcher yesterday evening but only worked Suzy over short distances with thrown canvas dummies – the signs, to my eye, are that whelping is a lot nearer than Mr Symes would have had me believe, so violent exercise is out. (She has shown signs of nest-building so I have given her a corner of the kitchen all to herself, where the dishwasher will go when I get around to buying one, and a lot of old newspapers to tear up.)

All in all, I was most impressed. There has been no attempt to steal each other's retrieves, each was absolutely steady and Suzy shows all the signs of having been very well trained. She is biddable and responds well to whistle, voice and hand signals. She never even farts (or if she does, Pippa gets the blame). Of course, there is no such animal as an ugly black Labrador, but they make a handsome pair. You will be proud of them.

I love them both but, please, no more.

Love to Hazel.

Yours,

Honey

Darling Sandy – bless you for your suggestions, and Ian says to convey his thanks as well, but I think we've...covered all the bases is the vernacular where you're lurking at the moment. The previous collator already charted, up down and sideways, where everybody was during the critical period, and I've been analysing where they say they were and where each says everybody else was, with no discrepancies that can't be put down to lapses of memory. How many witnesses, after all, can be precise about where they were and what they saw three weeks earlier and at what time? When such a paragon makes such specific statements, you can be sure that somebody's trying to set up a false defence of alibi.

One valuable witness has turned up, however. McFadden noticed a man fishing for sea-trout below the dam – a soldier on long leave after foreign service, it turned out, who spends most of his leave at the water. Sea trout, as you probably know, move and feed mainly in darkness and he had fished through the night of the 24th. He can be sure of the date because that was the day after his leave began. He is prepared to swear that no car crossed the bridge until the departure of Glashan's friend just before the helicopter arrived. His testimony makes the possibility of an assassin from outside visiting the small group of houses even more improbable.

Mr Andrews remains our most hopeful suspect if motive counts for anything (it usually doesn't) but any other kind of evidence against him is thin on the ground. If we can't hang anything on him and if he keeps his hands off the matches, we'll let you know and you can reveal all to your present colleagues with a view to extradition. Ian got nowhere with the warehouse men, by the way. They told him that Mr Andrews seldom comes out of his office except to greet new clients and they would certainly have noticed if he had been messing around with the paint-cans.

While Ian was out gathering that negative bouquet, I set about opening up the computer from the Andrews business. The security codes were easily cracked and so, after a rather despondent

morning conference, I set McFadden, who is comparatively computer literate, to plough through the files and floppies in the hope
that something significant might emerge and be copied onto our
own disks. I might then be able to give Mr Andrews his computer
back later today before he sets Mr Enterkin on us. Ian and Bright
then went off to attend to a break-in at a country filling station
and I put both dogs into the Range Rover and headed up to the
Moorfoot Road Houses, parking where I had parked the day we
found the body.

Please delete the next section, Sandy, and do not include it on
disk, because I did not behave strictly by the book.

Suzy, with P-day looming ever closer, looked even less fit for
an energetic walk, so after a short stroll I put her back in the car
and set off with Pippa, thinking that I would not be at all surprised to find a puppy or two squeaking away when we came
back. We climbed the hill and approached Duggie's secret hollow
by way of the dead ground. Pippa was following a scent higher up
the hill and I had come off heather onto grass, so I was moving
quietly when I came across a scene that could have been regarded
as depraved, titillating or tender according to the point of view.
Actually, the expression 'point of view' is rather apt. By chance
their heads were towards me or I might have been looking
straight up at least one bottom and possibly two. The boy was
unmistakably Duggie McPhee but it took me some seconds to
identify the girl as Sandra Andrews.

Just what I should have done at that point still baffles me. She
is undoubtedly of age and he is just as definitely not. Sex with a
minor is a crime. But had the crime already been committed or
was it still in process? What should I have done? Poured a bucket
of water over them? Leaped at them shouting 'Boo!' or 'You're
under arrest!'? I'm not at all sure.

You know me, Sandy, in every sense and you know that I'm not
exactly anti-sex. In my view it may be disappointing or squalid or
fun or, when it's a demonstration of great affection as between
ourselves, inexpressibly beautiful. From the boy's gasps and gig-
gles, I guessed that this was his first introduction to the mating
game and it was proving to be a mind-blowing experience.

Drawing on certain whispered confidences, I have concluded that a boy's first experience should be early and good, rather than the present system which aims, usually unsuccessfully, to keep him celibate for his sexually most active years, thus allowing him time to develop every known inhibition and fetish. As importantly (from my reading of psychiatrists' reports in certain rape cases), any taint of guilt around that first experience may be just as disastrous.

Rightly or wrongly, I took two paces backwards until my head was no longer within their view except possibly through the stems of heather, and waited for the final paroxysms to subside and the breathing to slow. This took some time and I was wondering for how long I would have to contain my impatience when Pippa settled the matter by appearing from the opposite direction and, being the affectionate dog that she is, set about licking Duggie's ear. To judge from his lack of reaction, he may have thought that the tongue belonged to Sandra. If so, it says little for that young lady's breath. The attention failed to rouse him again and it was left to the girl to protest and push Pippa away.

The two sat up and began to tidy themselves, so I stepped forward and picked up the girl's pants (white cotton, nothing fancy) which had been spread tidily in the heather and put them in my already crowded shoulder-bag. The boy was looking definitely pleased with himself. Careful not to include him in my look of reproof, I said, 'You do realise that having sex with a minor is a serious offence?'

She looked me in the eye and said, 'He told me that he was eighteen.'

I said that that wouldn't stand up for a minute. She then said that it was my word against hers and I pointed out that if I whisked her down to the nick it would be her word against mine and the word of several forensic scientists and a doctor.

At that point, she began to get worried. She was too stubborn to plead but she argued, pointing out how upset her parents would be and was I really going to make such a fuss about a little harmless fun?

I took a seat on the heather, first spreading a piece of plastic that I carry in my bulging bag for that very purpose. As far as I was concerned, those two young fornicators were welcome to emerge with sheep ticks all over them but I had no wish to contract Lyme's Disease. I said that it might have been a little harmless fun to them but in the eyes of the law it was an offence.

We batted it to and fro for a while. I was rather enjoying making her squirm. I deliberately left one or two openings that she was too thick or too upset to perceive. The boy was more alert. 'You said "if". What is't that you're after?'

'Have you got anything for me?' I asked in return.

'Nae yet. Try me again the morn.'

'I'll do that,' I said. I turned back to the girl and told her that I might, just might, forget her crime if she answered a few questions, but any lies or evasions and she would find herself in court. After that, she was only too eager to please, but she was too unobservant or too self-centred to recall any frictions between neighbours other than the obvious ones already known to us. I concluded that she looked on all adults outside her own family as totally boring and not important enough to notice. But it was her own family that I was working towards. She must have been aware of the fires that had ended her father's earlier businesses and the variations in the family fortunes, but either she didn't see the implications or else she didn't care. She answered my questions to the best of her very limited ability. Yes, there had been some talk of yet another move. And yes, there had been a period of some months, ending around the time of Mr Fraser's death, when money had seemed to be short. But she was quite sure that her father only had the one rifle and she had never seen or heard of an adapter, nor seen anything resembling the sketch that I drew for her in my notebook.

This was all very unhelpful and I said so. I was almost sure that she was keeping nothing back but I kept the pressure on in the faint hope of some as yet unrecognised treasure. And, to my amazement, she suddenly produced the solution to quite a different case.

'You're going on and on about having sex with a minor,' she said suddenly. 'You know the row that's going on about somebody interfering with young girls?'

'What about it?' I said.

'If I tell you something really, really important about that, will you forget about the other thing?'

'Do you know who's doing it?' I asked her.

For a reason that was unclear at the time, my question threw her. She dithered for a few seconds and then rounded on Duggie. 'This isn't for your ears,' she said. 'You bugger off.'

I would have liked to have a witness, but I could see that she was not going to talk in front of him so I nodded. His self-satisfied expression made a sudden return and he slipped away through the dead ground.

'You could say that I know who's doing it,' she said, 'but that wouldn't be quite true.'

'Explain,' I said, 'or we'll head down to the nick.' I fished in my bag, looking for a pair of handcuffs to impress her. In addition to the dummy launcher and a dummy for it, another canvas dummy, some dog treats, a leather lead, a whistle, my notebook, my make-up case and some personal oddments, I had managed to collect no less that three pairs of cuffs. How in God's name did that lot get in there? No wonder my bag was heavy! Anyway, I produced one pair and she turned white and began to babble.

The burden of her tale was that nobody was doing it. The whole thing was a figment of schoolgirl imagination. The first girl had been to a pub with some boy and had had to stay away until she was sober enough to go home. She had made up the tale about a molester to distract from her own bad behaviour. Next day, she told the same story to her schoolmates along with a detailed account of her examination by the police surgeon. Her friends had been enthralled by the salacious tale and had appropriated it, each wanting to boast about having had a man 'looking up her snatch'.

At that point, Sandra suddenly broke off, produced a brilliant smile – which I had not thought her capable of – and said, 'Did you hear the story about the girl who'd had her purse snatched? She ran into the police station crying that her snatch was pursed.' I did not laugh, I promise you.

And that, Sandy, was the end of my day as far as the murder on the reservoir was concerned.

At first, Sandra was determined that her name was to be kept out of it, but renewed threat of prosecution soon changed her mind. She told her parents some tale and came in to Newton Lauder with me.

After consulting Ian, I took her along to what had once been our incident room. To my chagrin, Mr Blackhouse had come through to supervise, no doubt hoping for a quick arrest, preferably of some local bigwig, and a chance to preen on TV. His reaction when I walked in was mixed. He first tried to order me out of the room. Then he seemed pleased at the chance of a renewed victim for his irony, sarcasm and malice. Ian, however, had followed me up and he managed to persuade the DS to listen to me and then to Sandra. Then he was disbelieving.

Most of his team was out on enquiries, but DS Tomlinson and a woman constable were still present. I think that they had had their own suspicions, because the girls' descriptions of their molester had been generally identical but greatly differing in detail. I brought Sandra in and she spoke clearly and tipped the balance. I took her outside, gave her back her pants and told her to be much more careful about the ages of her paramours.

When I returned to the incident room, Mr Blackhouse had turned around from wanting to dismiss me as a time-waster and had accepted Sandra's version of events. None of the men fancied cross-examining young girls about their fantasy sex-lives and it was decided that I should interview them along with the woman DC. We set up in an interview room and the girls were fetched one at a time from school in the order in which they had made their complaints.

If they had stuck resolutely to their stories, I would have had egg on my face; but DC Otterburn and I played Good Cop, Bad Cop (I leave you to guess which was which) and luckily the first girl soon cracked. This produced a domino effect, but the taking of even very brief statements followed by explaining the truth to a succession of parents, in as unprovocative a tone as possible, took rather more than the rest of the working day. People are weird, Sandy – I know I'm not the first to notice that fact. But those parents seemed sorry to have the cause of their indignation stolen away from them. It was as if they would have preferred their daughters to be molested.

When I told Mr Blackhouse that the Case of the Phantom Molester was indeed solved, his first impulse was to rush to wherever the nearest media representatives might be and claim all the credit. But when he came to consider what questions he might be asked about what lay behind the inventions he suddenly realised what embarrassing pitfalls might lie ahead and he decided to let the furore die with no more than a statement that no prosecutions are expected.

I was late home once again. I had contrived to phone June and tell her to get the dogs out of the Range Rover. Even so, both of them were beginning to look at me as if to say 'Who is that funny woman?'

Never mind, lover. Every day brings your return a little closer. I am waxing in preparation. Be flattered that someone worships you enough to undergo such agony.

Lots of love,

Honeypot

8 July

Jeremy – no wonder Mr Symes was in a hurry to get out from under. He would have been well and truly landed in problems, quite a litter of them.

When were woken this morning by faint squeaks and squeals there were already three pups in with Suzy, all feeding avidly. She was managing perfectly well on her own so we left her to get on with it and by the time I left for work there were seven. When I came home there was an eighth. I got the vet in and he says that that's the lot and she and the pups are all doing well. Three dogs and five bitches, all black and all pure bred Lab as near as one can tell at such an age (and in accordance with the pedigree documents), sleeping in a snoring heap or waking simultaneously, squealing and scrambling all over each other to get at the milk bar.

And now I'll tell you something weird. Eight was more than Suzy would be able to feed, but Pippa got in with them, very gently, and within a few minutes she produced milk! I've known other bitches act as wet nurses but I didn't think that a spayed bitch could do that. The pups don't seem to mind whose teat they attach to, just so long as there's milk.

Hurry home. I am simply not equipped for a total of ten dogs. At present the pups and any bitch feeding them at that moment are penned into the space where my dishwasher will ultimately go, but what happens when they get bigger and their eyes open I do not know. Presumably you won't want to keep the whole lot so do you want me to keep my ears open for purchasers or advertise or what? If you clue me in as to how much you expect for them I'll see what I can do.

Love to Hazel. Oh, and no more dogs or I'll sell them to the Chinese takeaway.

Regards,

Honey

Sandy, my love – I know that I opened up the subject myself, but if there are any more jokes about women's handbags, the tender hospitality of my bed will be denied you. One of these days, I'll compare the contents of my bag with the contents of your pockets and briefcase. However, you have at least proved that you do read my rather long-winded emails. (Think of it as a test of fortitude.) If I go on and on a bit it's because you seem interested and ask the right questions. And I do appreciate the outlet. I have to keep a close guard on my sometimes wayward tongue in the work environment, now that I'm a full-blown DS and no longer a mere 'woodentop'.

My flat, which was beginning to seem quite homelike, is suddenly full of puppies which will all too soon be scuttling all over the carpet (which I must admit will be just as much like home as home used to be). They are quite gorgeous and a total pest. Would you like one for a wedding present? Thank God and Dad for lending me June who is coping brilliantly, with the dogs, the pups and all the visitors who arrive uninvited to coo over them. My landlords, Messrs Calder and James of the gunshop downstairs, have now lent me a huge whelping basket and sold me blankets to go with it. We now have a six-inch margin of walking space around it in the kitchen but we can manage.

However, you are an unsentimental and hard-headed Scot, despite your feeble attempts to convince me that you have a soft heart, and no doubt you will be more interested in the gruesome than in the sweet and cuddly. So back to our murder case.

This morning, after a short and gloomy meeting with Ian and the two DCs, I went up to the hill behind the houses to see whether Duggie, my desperate last resort, had sniffed out any useful scents to follow. The day was as gloomy as the discussion had been. It seems that the long spell of fine weather is about to break and you will return, eventually, to British summer weather – cold, windy and damp.

I would not have been surprised to find Duggie with Sandra or some other young siren, now that he has been introduced to the delights. (Whatever befalls, Sandy, we must keep them fresh and never take them for granted.) Now that I come to look at him, he has the signs of becoming a very macho young man, perhaps a stud in the making. I think that another sex maniac may have been launched on a grateful world. He was, however, alone.

I took a seat on my boulder and waited for enlightenment. At first, as evidence of his newfound preoccupation with the joys of carnality, he seemed more interested in my figure than in my conversation (a typical male, in fact) but in the end I brought him to the point. As I supposed, a small horde of children galloping around the houses, even if some of them were *persona non grata* in some of those houses, can hear, observe and remember a great deal more than their elders give them credit for.

Motive never makes a case but at least it gives you a starting point. One might suppose that I only wanted to know about disagreements between Fraser and the male residents, but I allowed the net to spread wider. You know as well as I do, Sandy, that violence can spring from the most remote and unexpected causes and that murder on behalf of a friend is far from unknown, so I listened patiently to a catalogue of quarrels such as only a cynic like me would expect in such an apparently placid backwater. The neighbours, it seemed, had been reluctant to air their dirty linen before the police. Now it was being hung out to dry – and these were only the disputes that the children had witnessed or heard being discussed. God knows what other rifts and dissensions remain undisclosed.

Mrs Fenwick and Mrs Andrews, for instance, although usually seeming to be good buddies, had only recently made up after a furious quarrel over some real or imagined insult concerning Mrs Fenwick's taste in colour schemes. Mrs Andrews, in fact, is generally quarrelsome and seems to have been behind a furious row between the Andrews family and the Dawsons over the relationship between Sandra Andrews and Julian Dawson. It seems that Mrs Andrews suspected Julian of corrupting Sandra, whereas the converse was probably closer to the truth if, indeed, any corruption was not a matter of mutuality. If ever there were two minds with barely a single thought between them, this was the occasion.

But, on a score of one to ten, the likelihood of quarrels between women neighbours being relevant to the death of Fraser seemed about one and a half. Quarrels between male neighbours, perhaps three. Mr Fenwick, for instance, had had a flaming row, which still smouldered, with Mr McPhee over the smoke from occasional bonfires. Mr Dawson had borrowed some garden tool from Mr Berenson and the dispute was over whether or not it had ever been returned in good order. The nearly new Audi of Mr Andrews had received a dent while parked behind the houses and, on suspect evidence, he had blamed Mr Berenson. If anyone had fallen out with Mr Glashan about his sexual orientation, nobody was admitting it; but there had been a running battle between Glashan and the Fenwicks over intrusions of the Fenwicks' dog through the mutual fence into Glashan's garden and rubbish bag.

Disputes between Fraser and the male neighbours obviously scored in the eights and nines. Fraser having been a quarrelsome old curmudgeon, there were plenty to choose from. Fraser was another who had raged at McPhee over bonfire smoke (which had blown over the water and choked him while he was fishing from his dinghy). He had told the Fenwicks to keep their noisy, unruly kids out of his garden or he'd call the police. Mr Dawson had threatened to report Fraser as a peeping Tom because Fraser had drifted past in his dinghy while Mrs Dawson was sunbathing in the garden and Fraser had retorted that he would row a mile in order not to be confronted with the spectacle of Mrs Dawson bursting out of an ill-fitting and unbecoming bikini. (I would have worded it more strongly myself.) Glashan, who was said to be fanatical about his trout fishing, had more than once raged at Fraser for fishing from his dinghy – poaching, in Glashan's view – along the bank fronting Glashan's garden. There was also said to have been a tension between Fraser and Mr Andrews that we could now suppose to have been the result of a little blackmail concerning Mr Andrews's past history and present intentions.

The children had been thorough. I cut Duggie off when his report began to descend into what the various neighbours had been saying behind each other's backs, gave him a tenner for himself and another that he promised faithfully to distribute among his informants and sent him on his way. While I jotted down the main headings of his report, my mind was rattling away like a sewing machine and out of all the faintly possible scenarios there was only one that fitted together logically and satisfied me on every point.

Our chances of getting another search warrant on the basis of very slim evidence were virtually nil, so I decided to pay one call on a woman down at the bottom of the hill. Can you guess which one, Sandy? Have you figured it out? Do great minds think alike?

As you probably guessed, the woman was Mrs McPhee at the smallholding, who cleans for Mr Glashan.

Mr McPhee was hard at it with a rotovator, but I caught Mrs McPhee as she was about to sit down for a nice cup of tea. She is a comfortably stout, maternal sort of woman with short, lank grey hair and a round, red face; everybody's idea of the perfect grandma or cook-housekeeper. She had no objection to chatting about Mr Glashan over a cup of the strongest, blackest, most revolting tea I have ever tasted. She is well aware of his homosexuality but, as she pointed out, this only meant that she does not have to worry about him coming on to her. He is, she said, the perfect gentleman. Usually he has his head down over his word processor with earphones on his head and Mozart 'or ane o' they chiels' playing softly and he wouldn't even hear the vacuum cleaner. He was just as fanatical about his fishing and when he wasn't at his desk he would probably be at the foot of the garden, casting a neat line over the water, very often producing a catch of well fleshed rainbow trout and often presenting her with a useful supper for her brood. About his shooting she knows very little because he only practices it abroad or along at the club.

She was able to tell me categorically that she has never seen any kind of firearm in the house. She goes in once a week and gives one room a thorough cleaning each time and a dust round the remainder, but when Glashan last went abroad to some competition he left the keys with her so that she could give the whole house a spring clean. She had done a thorough job, sending his curtains for cleaning, sweeping out the attic and even tidying every cupboard (except for his few files of papers and his sacrosanct stack of work in progress) and laundering whatever seemed to need it. The top drawer of his bedside cabinet had been locked, as usual (which raised all sorts of suspicions in her Rabelaisian mind) but otherwise she was in and out of everything. And, she added, the last two or three times that she had cleaned for him, that drawer had been unlocked and contained only a handkerchief and a bottle of aspirin.

She did not seem to be holding anything back, yet Duggie had been sure that Glashan used cannabis and if she was holding out on me out of loyalty to her employer about one thing she might be equally reserved about another. I probed gently, however, and she admitted that she had not paid much attention to various bottles and jars in his bathroom cabinet, so the likelihood is that he keeps his pot-pot there.

Far from my hopes being dashed, I was actually encouraged by her report. Can you guess why, Sandy?

If I close now, I'll have time for a little dalliance with the puppies before bedtime.

Love and all that goes with it,

Honeypot

9 July

Jeremy – all goes well. Suzy is a very good mother and the two dogs are keeping up the milk bar between them but of course, what with the milk I have to pour into them (along with the nursing dam diet) I am lucky to be left with enough for my breakfast cereal.

As soon as it became known that I had a litter of pups here, people wanted to visit and drool over them. As a result, I have had several offers for pups. Mr Calder has already picked out a bitch and my boss's wife, his daughter, is trying to persuade her husband. You'd better hurry up and let me know what you want to keep and how much you want for the others and I'll start to take bookings from owners I can trust. The pedigrees are good and prospective purchasers can see the dam for themselves.

Don't be silly, my reference to the vacant space for the dishwasher wasn't a hint and you don't have to buy me one. It's been a pleasure and you don't owe me a penny. I won't even charge you commission on any pups I sell for you.

I'm pleased for your sake that your research looks like bearing fruit. All the same, if this means that your return will be delayed my pleasure may begin to curl at the edges. An extended period with a pack of dogs starting at ten in number and not beginning to diminish for at least six weeks, all in a rather small flat, may begin to pall.

Longing to see you both again, and that's a hint.

Love to Hazel,

Honey

Sandy – perhaps I gave you too many hints. You were almost right on all points.

I'll run over them in sequence, just as I would have put them to Ian in our morning discussion if I had sorted them out in my mind by that time. As it was, they were still jumbled together and I could see that Ian was having to work hard to make sense of it all.

1. Glashan is a fanatical angler who had quarrelled with Fraser because the latter persisted in fishing the reservoir close to Glashan's house where he had laid ground bait of maggots. I'm not sure how the law stands on this but I think it might be regarded as poaching. (If you wade to the middle of a river and cast back towards your own bank, that is poaching.) It would certainly be cause for friction. Glashan places a high value on his fishing. It is his form of relaxation, his way of clearing his mind between bouts of creative writing.

2. Glashan is an occasional cannabis user. He had had a visitor who left early that morning. If there was an overnight session of drink and pot smoking, he could well have been stoned when he saw Fraser make a morning pass along the bank.

3. Glashan is a very competent pistol shot, an international competitor. He is not a man to be patient with legislation that even I can see to be ill judged and ineffective. He owned two competition pistols and it is recorded that he took them abroad before the ban. It would be consistent if he then smuggled one back, perhaps with a spare.

4. Mrs McPhee was given free run of Glashan's house and saw no sign of pistols but the top drawer of his bed-

134

side cabinet was usually locked except when he was abroad. It has remained unlocked since about the time of the murder. I have since had the opportunity to discover that the woodwork shows a trace of gun-oil.

5. Glashan is homosexual. He moved here because he had been targeted by homophobic toughs and his home invaded. If anyone were likely to keep an off-certificate pistol in his bedside drawer, it would be he. Right?

6. Henderson, the secretary and steward at the shooting club, is also homosexual. Glashan used to practice there and still goes there to shoot rifle. There is no suggestion so far of a sexual liaison between them, and that's unimportant. It does seem likely that Henderson would stretch several points, allow Glashan to get his very necessary practice with a pistol on the range (which is not overlooked from anywhere) and might store illicit firearms for an acquaintance of similar orientation. I had examined the club's guns and the usual storage, but that was as Firearms Officer and hardly constituted a search.

7. The clincher, for me, was the row between Glashan and the Fenwicks about the Fenwick's dog tearing open Glashan's binbag. All along, I had wondered how that one cartridge case could have got into the food chain. I just couldn't see any dog on the hunt for a tasty snack, picking up and swallowing a single brass case. But that a dog raiding a binbag and bolting down the edible contents might also swallow one, yes, that was feasible. And then the clue transferring to another, coprophagic dog. At a further guess, Glashan, still stoned, had dropped the cases tidily in his binbag. The spent cases spilled out when the dog ripped the bag. Glashan came to his senses, gathered them up and looked for the one binbag that was accessible to him but hidden from

neighbours' windows. He may not have intended to incriminate Andrews in particular, but just to get rid of the cartridge cases without having to go down his garden under the neighbours' windows and risk being seen throwing them into the water.

All speculative, I agree, but it is necessary to home in on a suspect in order to search for evidence.

I put this to Ian. He agreed but he was not a happy camper. His feeling was that, after two false alarms, the sheriff would not grant search warrants in respect of the club or Glashan's house on such a slender basis. On the other hand, he agreed with me that the police were entitled to search for clues and a gun club would be very unwise to object, bearing in mind that good relations with the police are essential to them.

There was, of course, one problem. If Glashan had shot Fraser, he would have been insane to keep the weapon around, where it could be linked to him and also to the bullets and cartridge cases. If the pistol happened to be an old friend with sentimental value, he could have buried it somewhere miles away for exhuming after the fuss had died down. More probably, I pointed out, he would have thrown it into the reservoir as soon as darkness returned. But he did not know that Fraser would drift around for a day and a night before anyone noticed that he was no longer fishing. Police activity might have begun within a few hours. If he had been prepared to wait for darkness, he would surely have thrown in the weapon and the cartridge cases together.

Ian said that that made sense just as I realised that it didn't. I explained that the little brass cases weighed very little and contained air. I had often disposed of my dummy launcher blanks by flicking them into the water and they never floated, but Glashan might not have been sure that they would always sink.

He thought it over, frowning. 'We've got to go through all the motions,' he said at last. 'I think I'll email in a request for one or more frogmen. And then we'll take our two beauties and go and give the gun club a good search.'

Not expecting him to move so quickly, I had come out in my

new silk and cashmere suit and I had no wish to go poking through dusty recesses in it. 'Remember that Henderson is of the same persuasion as Glashan,' I said. 'You don't want any warning phone-calls. Shall I come and keep watch on Henderson while you search.'

Ian shook his head. 'I can confiscate his mobile and disconnect the landline phone. But there's more than one way for news to get around in these backwoods. In the normal course, they'll send me a frogman in about three weeks' time but it's just as likely that the men are doing nothing and we'll have three of them diving off Glashan's house before lunch, which would really send up the warning signals. You'd better get out to the houses and see what other facts you can gather while keeping a sharp lookout. Any sign that Glashan intends to fly the coop and you'll have to think up some pretext to arrest him. Or, if he's too squeaky clean, call me straight away. We could get from the gun club to the junction before he could get there from his house.'

That suited me very well because, what with the puppies and the pressure of work, I had been rather neglecting Pippa. McKillop, my father's head keeper, is beginning to moan about getting his electronic collar and the dummy launcher back. I was thinking of buying my own, but meantime decided to give Pippa one last workout to remind her that even when she was out of reach or even out of sight, the long arm of Honeypot was never far behind. I darted home and changed into something a little less susceptible to damage by thorns, put Pippa into the Range Rover and headed out to the Moorfoot Road Houses. The day was still cool but sunshine had returned between massing clouds.

As I approached the houses, I was granted a brief glimpse along the waterfront and Fenwick's motorboat was not moored in its usual place. Fine. With Fraser's dinghy back in store as evidence, Glashan would need his car or would have to face a long walk. His garage was standing open and waiting inside was a very pretty little sports BMW. (You would have loved that car except that it was a truly horrible colour. I thought that Glashan had more taste!) I parked across the garage doorway, extracted Pippa, heaved out my shoulder bag and locked up the Range Rover. Mr

Glashan was not going anywhere until I wanted him to.

Pippa accepted the electronic collar happily as a signal of good things to come. There's a knack to fitting the collar – it has to be just tight enough to make contact but not tight enough to be uncomfortable. I hung the other component round my neck on its lanyard and we set off. Pippa was dancing with pleasure. I suppose that acting as wet-nurse to another bitch's pups might satisfy one instinct at the expense of others. Halfway up the hill I got out the dummy launcher and gave her several long retrieves.

Enough being enough, especially when training a dog, I soon headed towards where Duggie is usually to be found. There was no sign of him. I retreated to my boulder and sat down to think while running my fingers through Pippa's coat in search of ticks. Labradors, thank the Lord, do not pick up burrs like a spaniel. The action reminded me that she was still wearing the electronic collar. I prefer dogs not to wear collars in open country – I once saw a GSP bitch get a fallen branch through her collar and only be saved from strangulation by quick action on the part of her owner. But the sunshine was soporific and I postponed taking positive action.

Soon my thoughts gave way to passive observation. Looking down from the hill, I had almost a plan view of the scene, but there was little movement. McPhee was busy about the smallholding and two of his children were running amok among his raspberries. A figure that was easily recognised as Mrs Dawson emerged, took down something off a washing line and retreated indoors again. Otherwise the scene was remarkably placid.

What I didn't know but learned later was that Ian had found his wife in charge of the gun club. This was by arrangement with Ewan Henderson so that he could attend the funeral of some relative. Mrs Fellowes, as acting secretary and steward, had every right to give her husband full permission to carry out a search.

I roused and took more interest as Glashan walked down his garden with a trout rod in his hands. I was too far away to see the line, but from the timing of the rod I judged him to be a skilled caster. Sometimes a line of reflected light showed how the line had met the water.

Duggie arrived suddenly from behind me. 'Aye, Missis,' he said. 'You still want tae hear about folk bickering wi' him down there?' He nodded in the direction where Glashan was casting a neat line across the water. He waited with wide eyes, like a Labrador scenting food.

I let him see a fiver in my hand, but the story when it spilled out was worth more. On some unspecified date, which must have been around the beginning of June, one of the McPhee children went for a swim in the reservoir. He had swum level with Fenwick's house when Fraser, who had been fishing from the bank, got into his dinghy and let it drift on the breeze. The boy had been ticked off by Fraser in the past for swimming there – not for any particular offence but because anything that the local children did was, in Fraser's view, wrong. The boy tucked in among some tree roots under the bank, waiting for Fraser to drift away again.

Fraser's drift brought him to Glashan's frontage, where he began to cast his nymph (the boy was quite sure that it was a nymph rather than a fly) under the tree where I later saw the rabbit hanging. Glashan must have been taking a coffee break from his writing because he came down his garden in a hurry. He kept his temper at first, explaining (not, apparently, for the first time) that he ground-baited that bit of water and that whenever his writing hit a sticky patch he made his way down the garden and fished until the therapy of the actions freed his mind again. He made it clear that he resented Fraser spoiling the fishing by removing or disturbing the fish.

Fraser's reply, as quoted, was short and more than a little rude. An angry exchange followed. It finished with Glashan promising that, if the offence were repeated, he would put a hole in Fraser's boat. This was probably the kind of idle threat that men make under provocation, but when the provocation was repeated, it might have seemed to his fuddled mind that the time was ripe for action.

Duggie gave me the name of the boy – Bruce – and I remembered him as an intelligent and fairly articulate eight-year-old who would, I thought, make a good witness if carefully handled.

I gave Duggie his fiver and he made off, presumably in a hurry to spend it.

Glashan had stopped fishing. He was too far off for me to make out any details. (I had thought of bringing my binoculars, but the idea of making my shoulder bag even heavier was not to be contemplated.) However, his attitude, that of someone who was using a mobile phone, was almost unmistakable. Either the call had disturbed him or his mind had already been cleared by the therapy of angling, because he carried his rod up the garden and out of my sight.

Some minutes later, my mobile played its little tune (the duet from *The Pearl Fishers* in case you're curious). Ian was on the line. 'Henderson came away from the funeral in good time,' he said. 'He was seen sitting in his car, talking into his mobile. He must have seen our activity from the road as he approached. He may have been warning Glashan.'

'Glashan's car isn't going anywhere,' I told him. 'I've boxed it in. If he takes another car or the Dawson boy's motorbike, I'll call you back.'

The situation seemed to be under control but, even so, I felt that I should be closer to where the action might be. I called Pippa and we headed diagonally down the hill in the dead ground and approached the houses along the road. We were still some way off when Glashan began to play a fanfare on his car horn to summon the guilty driver back to the Range Rover.

With Pippa tightly at heel, I watched from behind a holly tree, a stone's throw away, waiting for Ian to arrive. The sun had vanished again and there was a definite chill in the air, or else my nerves were taking over – I had definite goose pimples. While I waited, I took the electronic collar off Pippa, ready to put her in the car if the need arose, but I was distracted before I got around to switching it off. Glashan tried the doors of the Range Rover without success and then tried to push the big vehicle. He retreated into the garage. When he returned with a large hammer, it was time to intervene. After all, he would only have had to break the driver's window, let off the handbrake and move the gear selector and the Range Rover would have rolled down the slight slope back towards the dam without need of his help. It might even have fetched up in the water.

'Can I help you?' I asked, stepping out of cover and approaching.

He knew who I was all right, but he decided to see whether courtesy would be enough. My being a policewoman accompanied by a large, black dog may have influenced him. Labradors are usually peaceable, but they can be trained to attack and they look purposeful. He laid the hammer aside on a shelf. 'Move your car please,' he said. 'You're blocking me in.'

'Yes, of course,' I said. 'I'm so sorry. I shan't be a minute.'

You know me, Sandy. I'm not usually one of those long-winded, garrulous women even if my emails do run rather to length. But I had a feeling that as long as somebody was speaking politely to him and he remained unable to get a word in, he would be more or less stymied. So I conjured up an image of my friend Poppy with the bit between her teeth and span out a combined apology and promise of urgent action until his eyes were beginning to bulge. While I spoke, as an additional delaying tactic, I unlocked the back of the car and put Pippa inside. This, as it turned out, was a mistake.

My monologue could have been spun out almost indefinitely. I was just getting into my stride and finding second breath. In fact, more and more ways of saying the same thing over again were occurring to me. But my mobile phone played its little tune. Deciding that it gave me an excuse to draw breath (I was beginning to see spots) I answered it. Ian's voice came with shocking clarity. 'We've found what we need,' it said. 'If he tries to leave, arrest him. The charge is murder.'

The phone died on me. I had one of those sinking feelings that one gets whenever matters are heading unstoppably in the direction of trouble. Glashan had heard every word and I did not think that he would stand idly by while I called back to request immediate backup.

He was coming round the Range Rover. That was when I began to regret shutting Pippa in the car. She could at least have given him a distracting lick.

'Give me your car key,' Glashan said, with emphasis on each separate word. He sounded very masterful but I was not in the mood to play the subservient female. I think I advised him not to hold his breath. I know that I told him that he was under arrest, though I suspect that he had already guessed it. My voice seemed to have gone up at least half an octave.

The key was in my shoulder bag. He was coming at me. I shrugged the bag off my shoulder, let it fall and, to spin out the delaying tactics, kicked it under the car without pausing to think of the damage to the beautiful suede. Even at that moment I felt relief at getting rid of the weight of it, but at the same time I was beginning to add that act to the growing list of rash acts that I might have cause to regret. Shutting Pippa in the car... Answering the phone... And now, with the key out of reach, Glashan's options would turn back in the direction of breaking my window glass; and, because the hammer was still only a few paces away, I stood a good chance of being knocked on the head. I could run away, but that was against my instincts and training. Besides, it might have resulted in the Range Rover going into the reservoir with Pippa inside. I turned to meet him. 'You heard the man,' I said. I repeated, 'You're under arrest,' and began to recite the statutory caution. Sometimes that has a sobering effect. When it doesn't, at least the fact that it was uttered may have a bearing in court.

His eyes were wild. Logic had gone out of the window. He jumped at me. My training suggested that I should turn and throw him over my hip, but practice in the gymnasium with a friendly instructor is not the same as being rushed by a homosexual murderer. Moreover, when I tried to grab him I found that I was hampered by the electronic dog collar still being in my hand. I managed to turn my back to him but I had lost my hold.

Glashan, on the other hand, caught me by the leather lanyard. The operating box was pulled up under my chin and I began to strangle. He was, I believe, solely obsessed with the need to get my car key off me, but in his state he was quite capable of killing me. I only had a few seconds to act. In the car, Pippa was going frantic.

It's weird how these things work out, Sandy. He, in his panic, could easily have killed me without intending to. I, for my part, could have pulled the balls clean off him on purpose. I grabbed with one hand to pull the cord away from my throat. The lanyard was too tight to grasp but I was able to grip the little box. I was close to the point of blacking out.

My grab at his vulnerable parts with my other hand was again frustrated because I still held the electronic collar. And this is where sheer chance saved us both from irremediable disaster. By chance, the two prongs of the collar – about two inches apart, blunt but designed to reach through fur to make contact with the skin beneath – must have been guided by a spirit hand. It almost gives one to believe in an afterlife and guardian angels. At the same moment, my grasp on the box of tricks as I tried to pull the lanyard off my throat must have pressed one or both buttons.

What he felt, I can only surmise. I noticed later that, during the struggle, the power had become turned up to maximum – a level that can fairly make a dog yelp at a hundred yards range. I felt the electric shock of it shooting between us and a convulsion ran through his whole body. He leaped away, jerking the lanyard as he released it and nearly dislocating my neck. Colour began to return to my world. He was tiptoeing round in small circles with his eyes shut, clutching his crotch and whinnying like a horse. I would never have believed that human tear-ducts could pass so much water. Mine were not much drier.

When my eyes stopped watering, I retrieved my bag from under the Range Rover and found a pair of handcuffs under all the other gear. He was being sick into the grass verge and in no condition to resist. He gave me no trouble once I had him cuffed.

Ian arrived a minute or two later. He asked how I had managed to overpower the prisoner. I was only able to croak modestly in reply.

The rest of the day was spent in locking up Glashan's property, the formalities of charging him – with assaulting a police officer as well as murder – and also with his complaint against me for unnecessary violence. We both received medical attention and the weal around my neck was carefully photographed. We are quite sure that his complaint against me will get nowhere because he had no symptoms detectable by the police surgeon, but I bet he'll still be feeling the effects in a fortnight's time.

I had some difficulty in swallowing my evening g-and-t but otherwise I seem to be relatively undamaged, you will be pleased to know, and at least using the keyboard is easier than talking. However, after all the excitement I do feel the need of a therapeutic half-hour with the puppies before taking to my lonely bed, so I will sign off now.

Your loving,

Honeypot

10 July

My darling Sandy – there's no need to fly into a tizzy. I am not harmed, nor is my beauty, as you so kindly put it, spoiled. I have a sore throat today and am rather husky, which gives me a sexy sort of voice – definitely a turn-on for my younger colleagues. Ian told me to take a couple of days off but the doctor pronounced me fit to work so I went in.

It has been a wild and woolly day!

It began calmly enough. Ian explained to me that they had found in the freezer at the gun club, beneath all the frozen pizzas and microwaveable chips, one good target pistol and one cheap and nasty semi-automatic pistol, probably Belgian, both of .22 calibre and each carefully greased, wrapped in polythene and stowed in a box that had once held pre-cooked meals, the whole then coated with ice. The hiding place was so convincing that they nearly missed it.

Glashan had by then, of course, started howling for his solicitor (Mr Enterkin yet again). While they conferred, the entire strength of CID in Newton Lauder, all four of us, searched Glashan's house without finding anything of much significance except for those traces of gun-oil in the top drawer of his bedside cabinet and a small quantity of cannabis in the bathroom. Those were the only items worthy of saving for Forensics.

The house was so neat and clean, almost sterile, that we had finished with it by lunchtime. It seemed a good time to celebrate a successful end to a difficult case, so I asked Ian whether he would mind if I treated the team to lunch in the hotel. I thought that he might have been embarrassed at my usurping what he might have regarded as his prerogative, but he said that he had never refused a good meal yet. So I bought a good meal, but with very limited alcohol, for the four of us. Then the two DCs returned to take a look around Glashan's garden, in the faint hope that he might have buried something and left traces of the deed, while Ian and I met Glashan and Enterkin in an interview room at the nick.

To my surprise, there was no air of hostility – more of relief

and expectation. Ian opened by stating that we had found the two
pistols and that Forensics would be asked to confirm that one of
them, almost certainly the Belgian semi-auto, had fired the fatal
bullets and imprinted the various cartridge cases. He added, 'You
must have been mad not to drop it into the reservoir.'

I expected to find that Glashan had been told to stay silent but
Enterkin stated that his client wished to make a full and frank
statement. What followed was not the ingenious evasion that I
had expected, attempting to incriminate somebody else or accus-
ing the police of planting the evidence. (Ian explained later that
Enterkin, though a shrewd and forceful lawyer, did not play that
sort of game.)

Glashan opened by apologising (and in front of the VCR cameras!) for losing his head and trying to choke me. His attack on
me, he said, had been in the heat of the moment and caused by
the shock of being intercepted while hoping to postpone arrest.
He trusted that I was suffering no serious after-effects. (I did not
like to enquire about his well-being – he might have told me in
excruciating detail. But he seemed to be walking normally.) He
added that he did not intend to pursue his complaint against me.
He paused to draw breath and then went on to say that the death
of Fraser had been entirely accidental.

That, as you know, is what they all say – if there is the least
chance of getting away with it – but in this context it seemed so
improbable that it caused a stunned silence. Ian broke it at last by
saying that he had some difficulty believing that a marksman as
highly skilled as Glashan could shoot a man accidentally so many
times in quick succession.

'I suggest,' Enterkin said, 'that you allow my client to tell his
story in proper sequence.'

Ian agreed and Glashan spoke up quite freely, seeming not the
least troubled by the atmosphere of incredulity. Perhaps the
writer of fiction becomes used to starting from a position where
he has to struggle for the reader's acceptance. He must have
known that we were not prepared to suspend disbelief in a hurry,
but he spoke with quiet confidence. I have a transcript in front of
me, but much of what he said at first was no more than confirma-

tion of what we had already guessed. His friend, who he still declined to name, had stayed and they had spent the night smoking cannabis and, latterly, drinking vodka. Any other activities were left unmentioned. By the time his friend left, Glashan admitted, he was stoned to the eyebrows.

On his way to bed, Glashan looked out of the window and saw Fraser fishing in what he regarded as his own private territory and he remembered his threat, which had been uttered in the heat of the moment, to put a hole in Fraser's dinghy. The moment now seemed to Glashan, in his condition, ripe for the execution of his threat. That, he thought, should bring Fraser to a sense of his vulnerability. Moreover, he could hear the helicopter approaching and he was confident that the noise of its passing would cover the muffled sound of a .22 shot fired from within his bedroom through a partly closed window.

As I supposed, he had taken his target pistols abroad when the ban was imposed but had smuggled one of them back again in order to practice surreptitiously at the gun club. But having twice been beaten up in his own home by homophobic thugs he had, on the principle of being hung for a sheep rather than a lamb, brought back also the cheap Belgian automatic, which he had bought on the spur of the moment. This was by no means new even then but it would be a much more sensible means of self defence. He kept it in his bedside cabinet, ready for the intruders who never came. When he went abroad, it was stored...elsewhere. (At that point, he declined to make any statement about the other hiding place, presumably out of loyalty to Henderson. This I could understand and almost admire.)

'I took aim at the dinghy,' Glashan said, 'being careful to avoid where I knew his feet and legs must be.' He paused and looked defiantly from one to the other of us. 'I pulled the trigger to fire a single shot and the damned pistol went fully automatic on me. It fired the whole magazine in a single burst and, of course, it rode up and to the right. And that,' he said, 'is why I kept the pistol. If the shooting was traced back to me, I wanted it as evidence to confirm that it was accidental.'

Ian (who married into a firearm-literate family but whose personal experience stops at the shotgun) was looking baffled. He evidently felt unready to tackle the technical aspect of Glashan's statement. He looked at me and I tried to convey in a single glance that I believed it to be possible. 'Assuming that Forensic examination of the pistol supports your story,' Ian said, 'why did you not come forward immediately? And why did you feel it necessary to assault my sergeant?'

Glashan glanced at Enterkin and received a nod. 'I hoped that it would blow over without the shots being traced to me. And one of the biggest competitions of the year takes place in Italy next week. I was determined to stay free for a little longer. After that, I would be prepared to take my medicine. When your sergeant detained me, I lost my head.' He paused and met my eyes. He is a very good looking man and if I didn't know his orientation – and if you weren't lurking in the background, Sandy – I could have been swayed. He looked back to Ian. 'I have already apologised and I'm quite prepared to go on apologising for as long as she'll listen to me. I meant the young lady no harm. I intended to return and face the music after one more championship attempt.'

'And how do you propose to satisfy a court that you did not intend to put the first bullet into Mr Fraser?'

Glashan half-smiled. 'It's common knowledge that a firearm kicks upward,' he said. 'Even somebody who has never fired a single shot must have seen the effect on the films. The only exception is when the actors are obviously firing blank cartridges because the director's working to a budget and doesn't think the viewer is intelligent enough to notice his carelessness. I've been on the set when one of my books was being filmed and I raised hell on the subject. The kick is always upward because the recoil of the firearm is above the grip of the user. So any court should accept that the first shot fired was the lowest one, the one that went through the hull of the dinghy. Mr Enterkin agrees.'

Enterkin had been allowing his client to speak freely. Now, suddenly abandoning his air of watching the children at play, he said, 'I take it, Inspector, that no bullets or bullet wounds were found in Mr Fraser below, say, the waist?'

'I'll make the post-mortem report available to the defence,' Ian said cautiously. 'We'll continue this interview when I have received technical advice and the report from Forensics on the pistol.'

'Your caution is understandable,' Enterkin said, 'but meantime my client would be sitting in prison on a murder charge while he would be willing to plead guilty to contravention of the Firearms Act and wasting police time.'

'And manslaughter? Reckless discharge of a firearm?' Ian asked keenly.

'That would be for discussion. I suggest, however, that he might well be bailed on the lesser charges. That would be up to the sheriff. It would give him time to finish the final draft of his current book. Matters would be hastened considerably if immediate help were to be sought from an independent expert. Your own father-in-law is an expert whose evidence has been accepted by courts of law on many occasions. We would be satisfied that his advice was not biased in your favour, and you would surely not suggest the converse. If he were not to be available, your own wife satisfies all of those criteria. Either of them might be asked for independent advice on the pistol now, this afternoon.'

Ian, I could see, disliked being hurried but he is a fair man and he could see the justice in Mr Enterkin's suggestion. He excused himself and left the room. I signed off and stopped the various tapes.

We talked about nothing. Enterkin was quite at ease and Glashan, apart from tightness about his lips, might well have been the same.

It was a full half-hour before Ian returned and resumed his seat. 'My wife will be here in a few minutes,' he said. He was carrying what looked like a pistol in a nylon bag and was accompanied by a thin balding man who I recognised as Mr Dartfield, the Procurator Fiscal. I had seen him prosecuting.

Ian started the tapes running again and went through the rigmarole of confirming the place, date and time and the people present. 'Mrs Fellowes is on the way,' he said. 'Meanwhile, I would like Mr Dartfield to know what went before and to agree to the proposed course of action.'

He wound back one of the two audiotapes and set it to play. We listened again to Glashan's admissions. When the tape came to an end, Ian set it to record again. Dartfield nodded. 'So far so good,' he said. 'Let's find out what your expert says.'

Mrs Fellowes was by then waiting on a chair outside the interview room. Ian brought her in, seated her and introduced her to the recording devices. 'The lady is my wife,' he said, 'but the accused and his solicitor agree to accept her as an impartial, expert witness.' He made eye contact with his wife. 'You understand and agree to give impartial advice which you will be prepared to repeat in court, under oath?'

'Certainly.' Mrs Fellowes, in a white overall and carrying a small case of tools, was a different person from the lady who had shared quite a lot of drinks with me, but she gave me a surreptitious glance.

'Very well. We do not yet have confirmation that this is the weapon although it is implicit in the circumstances,' Ian said carefully. 'Mr Glashan states that the pistol "went fully automatic" on him. I think those were your words?'

'Exactly,' said Glashan.

'We want Mrs Fellowes to tell us whether that is possible.'

'Such has been known to happen,' Mrs Fellowes said lightly. 'I can dismantle it?'

Ian caught the eye of the Procurator Fiscal. Evidently some signal passed. 'You may dismantle it,' Ian said. 'There are no fingerprints. I have a photographer waiting, to record every step of the process. It will also be recorded on the videotape. It would help if you gave us a running commentary.'

There was a delay while a photographer was brought in and set up two extra lights. Ian nodded to his wife.

Deborah Fellowes pulled on surgical gloves and removed the pistol from the bag. 'Made in some Brussels back street cottage, probably,' she said. 'And it does not appear to have been stripped and cleaned since it was made.'

Glashan shrugged. 'I never expected to fire it,' he said.

'Can I have a piece of typing paper, please?'

'You want to make notes?' Ian put a sheet of paper in front of her. 'We can furnish you with copies of the tapes.'

'A pistol like this,' Deborah said, 'has one first sear that holds back the action and only lets the pistol fire when the trigger's pulled. Blowback re-cocks the action, but the finger would still be on the trigger so that the pistol would fire again if it weren't for a second sear, the interrupter.' She was speaking more to the video camera than to us as an audience. 'If this pistol went automatic because the second sear sheered off, the bit should still be inside. Its presence, absence and condition might be evidence, so I want to catch it, not drop it on the floor.'

The pistol came apart in her deft fingers. She turned her hands so that the photographer and the video camera could see every movement. 'However,' she resumed, 'the sear, though worn, is unbroken. The second "bent" or notch in which the sear should engage is bunged up with the dirt of years mixed with soot and hardened oil.' She held it steady for the photographer. 'That would be quite enough to make any pistol go auto and I can say, from the polish on the parts in contact, that this pistol appears to have fired on automatic. Fairly recently, from the smell of burnt powder. And I'm quite prepared to state my opinion that, given a full magazine and a pull on the trigger, it would almost certainly do so again.'

Enterkin stirred. 'And in doing so, it would travel up and to the right?'

'Inevitably. All automatic weapons do so, unless they have some form of vent at the muzzle designed to counter that effect. Examples are the Thomson sub-machine gun and the AK-47.'

From the file on the table, Ian produced a photograph. 'Could that pistol have made this firing pin impression?' he asked. He placed his magnifier beside it.

Deborah studied the print and then the firing pin. 'The most I can say without comparing micrographs is that it might have done. It looks very similar.' She reassembled the pistol. 'Is there anything else I can do for you, or may I go home and see to my husband's dinner?'

Her husband had had rather a good lunch but he was clearly hungry again. 'I think that's all for the moment,' he said.

'Sergeant, would you please return Mr Glashan to the custody officer and then you can go. I think that Mr Enterkin, Mr Dartfield and I must have a short discussion.'

The custody officer was waiting. Glashan went with him without demur. He knew that he was in the clear for the most serious charge and now had to ride out the storm over all the lesser charges. I found myself walking out of the building with Deborah Fellowes. 'May I come and have another look at the pups?' she asked.

'What about Ian's dinner?'

'Won't take a minute,' she said. 'It's fish. Wallace James left me a brace of trout.'

I hope that she was right, because she drooled over the pups for half an hour.

More tomorrow.

Lots of love,

Honeypot

11 July

Jeremy – you have just made a young woman very happy. You can tell Hazel that my love for you is purely platonic but sincere. Yes, of course I'd adore to have Pippa. She and I have, as you suggest, developed a relationship and it was going to break my heart to part with her, but I never dreamed that that was why you decided to take Suzie on. Thank you, thank you, thank you. I have spoken to the Guide Dogs. They retained a right of veto, you will remember, but they see no problem.

I now have more than enough offers for the pups but if you've decided to keep one of them that means somebody else we'll have to disappoint. You'll be home before they're ready to leave their dam, so you'll be able to take your pick and then we'll choose owners for the others.

I'm only sorry that I shan't be able to see Sandy's face when I tell him. For my sake he will express delight, but I can always spot the slightly prune-like expression that he gets when he is only being nice and making a sacrifice for my sake. This time, however, he can look how he likes, I am adamant; but I'm sure that he will be almost as delighted as I am. He is a dog person too.

I gather that you have now gathered enough material for another book. I shall certainly read it. What's more, I shall go to the lengths of buying copies and handing them out as Christmas presents to any of my friends and relatives who I think might appreciate it. I can't say fairer than that.

And now I must go and walk MY dog.

Love to Hazel.

Honey

11 July

Sandy darling, it seems that we shall have an extra mouth to feed, but more of that later.

First an update. After I left the interview room and Glashan was returned to his cell, Ian and the two lawyers thrashed out a general agreement. Ian told me about it this morning.

Enterkin said that he was under instructions from his client, who insisted that he alone had hidden his pistols in the gun club freezer and that he would not plead guilty to anything if proceedings were to be taken against the club or Ewan Henderson. (While the rozzer in me deprecates such lack of co-operation, I give him full marks for loyalty. I should have such friends!) After some kicking around it was agreed that that version of events, though not even Enterkin seemed totally convinced, could just possibly have been true. Lacking any hard proof to the contrary, Glashan's condition was agreed. Deborah Fellowes's evidence was accepted and the murder charge was dropped.

At that point, I gather, negotiations nearly broke down because Enterkin objected strongly to a manslaughter charge on the grounds that Fraser had intended to cause no harm. Ian rather lost touch of the legal nit-picking, but after lengthy argument between Enterkin and the PF, mostly in archaic Latin that Ian couldn't have followed even if he had wanted to, it was agreed that Glashan would plead guilty to the firearms offences and to reckless discharge of a firearm leading to the death of Fraser.

(It was left to Ian to ask me whether I insisted on proceeding with the charge of assault. When, later, he put it to me, he pointed out that I had had my revenge and more. My possibly irrational liking for Glashan had returned and I said to drop it.)

Mr Enterkin said that Glashan was not particularly perturbed at the prospect of a period in prison, where he could expect to gather a great deal of background for his novels and be given some peace and quiet in which to write them. The publicity would be unlikely to hurt his sales.

It was therefore a surprise when, during that afternoon, Mr Enterkin suddenly approached the sheriff for an urgent hearing of a request that the nasty police be restrained from confiscating his virtuous client's passport and that bail be granted immediately to allow him to travel abroad to represent his country at a major sporting event. Substantial bail had already been deposited. His client had been arrested on suspicion of a very serious charge but that charge had been withdrawn and the charges pending were of a much less serious nature.

Whether the devious Mr Enterkin had chosen his moment with care I don't know, but Ian was having one of his rare afternoons off and was somewhere in the Lammermuirs, chasing rabbits with his father-in-law. I was suddenly required to appear before the sheriff and explain why, in the view of the police, this request should not be granted. With the Procurator Fiscal whispering in my ear, I pointed out that the request was sudden and that the competition was still several days away.

Mr Enterkin, the very picture of benevolence, explained that his client's arrest had been equally sudden, that his client was a respectable local man well known for his success in his chosen sport and that, with the ownership of pistols banned in Britain since the 1997 act, he would need every minute of the time available for practice in order to recover his form.

At this point, Sandy, I could perhaps have been more vehement but, as I said, I liked Glashan. He had always been polite and friendly to me (with one notable exception). He has a certain inexplicable charm and overall he is an attractive man. Such a waste, his gayness, or should that be gaiety? Anyway, I said that the charges remaining were still serious, which Mr Enterkin countered by pointing to Mr Glashan's status as a successful author and sportsman and a man of property. Glashan was called to appear in person and evidently made a good impression, because Mr Enterkin's plea was accepted.

The day's surprises were not yet over. Mr Blackhouse, alerted by Ian's emailed reports, suddenly arrived. Ian, I may say, with a generosity that would have been unthinkable in the Met, had given me full credit for my contribution to our successes.

I had already knocked off, changed into jeans and a hairy sweater and taken Pippa for a training session up at the reservoir, and that was where the DS sought me out. He was in an amazingly affable mood, expressed interest in her progress, greeted me as if I had been a long lost daughter.

'I always knew,' he said, 'that you were a clever girl.'

I could have said that he had kept his knowledge very much to himself. I could have said that I resented his patronising tone. I could have called him a liar. But such utterances are not considered good career moves, so I swallowed my bile. I couldn't bring myself to thank him, but I nodded and forced a smile.

He then invited me, with an air of conferring an invitation to a Holyrood House garden party, to join him almost immediately in confronting a media conference of which I had known nothing until that moment. I was looking the very antithesis of how I like to present myself to the world and the idea of going on television without a little preening time appalled me. (I can be a quick-change artist when the need arises, Sandy, as you very well know, but there are reasonable limits.) My protests were taken as mere becoming modesty. It seemed that, from being a *bete noir* and an irritating know-all, I had become his personal but platonic (I hope) favourite. He chuckled approvingly at my every remark and for two pins I think he would have patted me on the head as he did, rather nervously, with Pippa.

He had bravely hidden his disappointment when I explained to him that each case had turned out to be a storm, if not in a teacup, at least in a soup tureen. But that did not prevent him conveying to the reporters and TV cameras the impression that he and I, working as a team if not as a couple, had personally solved the riddles of Fraser's death and the molestation of schoolgirls. I had had about fifteen seconds to tidy myself. June had had warning and videotaped the news (on all channels), but if I uttered a word (which I honestly don't remember) it had been edited out. I looked like a fugitive from the fashion police, caught in an off moment. The DS seemed positively dapper by comparison, which may explain some of the bonhomie with which he bade me farewell when he tore himself away.

Ian missed all the fun. I only hope that he doesn't go into a huff when he catches up with events.

Love, love, love,

Honeypot

13 July

Sandy my love – sorry to have missed writing to you for a day, but I took the whole day off and went back to Dad's for two nights, leaving June in charge of the whole menagerie. Anyway, it gave me a chance to sort out my wardrobe, pick up what clothes I wanted to have with me and do some shopping. June seems to have coped.

It was only on my return here that I got your email and realised that I had left you to panic for a day. No, Sandy, I have not had a relapse from the damage to my throat. Nor am I pregnant. I'm much too careful for that. (Are you pleased or disappointed?) The extra mouth I referred to is Pippa. Hazel and Jeremy Carpenter, as I think I told you, also accepted another black Lab, the pregnant Suzy, now a proud mum and temporarily resident with me. As comparatively new dog-owners they had felt less than competent to cope with an impetuous and strong-willed Lab and have accepted the more biddable and fully trained Suzy, who they knew and had seen working. Their motivation all along has been so that they could bequeath Pippa to me.

I hope that you can accept us as a pair. Please don't make me choose between you. On the other hand, try very hard not make me jealous. I'm sure that you're going to love each other. Too many marriages have been broken up because of excessive devotion to a Labrador, though I have never yet heard of one being cited as a co-respondent. To celebrate her change of allegiance (I don't like to think of dogs as being owned) I have bought her a soft toy which she carries everywhere with great pride and devotion. The mini-supermarket next door had them as a loss leader.

When I turned up at the factory this morning, Ian was not too dissatisfied with the way that the case had gone, though when he heard the outcome of the afternoon's pleadings he was highly peeved and made remarks about the sheriff's probable sexual orientation that would have brought his career to a sudden end if they had been made outside the security of Ian's own room. (Please wipe this paragraph off your disk and expunge it from every crevice of the magic machine.)

I suspected that Mr Blackhouse was equally miffed, because he had spent the previous day trying to get me on the phone. My colleagues were left in no doubt, first that he would speak to nobody else and secondly that he considers days off to be the perk of the higher ranks. That, I thought, was the end of my short period of basking in the glow of his favour. Expecting a chewing-off, I put off calling him back for as long as I dared. Before I finally got round to phoning him, a long email came off the line. (Not for him the abbreviations and short cuts so commonly used. He is as longwinded in email as I am!)

The long and short of it is that the inspector in charge of the dog training and handling units has had to take early retirement for health reason. There is no obvious successor and none of the handlers has any experience of responsibility. Having noted what he considers to be both efficiency and facility with dogs on my part, Mr B has put my name forward to take over temporarily. This would be pending the permanent appointment of a suitable person to the vacancy, after which I would join his team.

I consulted Ian, who clutched his brow but said that I should go for it. But I don't know. What do you think, Sandy? I'm inclined to take the dog job on (I could commute from here) but as for transferring to Mr B's team I'm undecided. In my view, Edinburgh is essentially for quick visits to the better shops, not for living in. Too many addicts and too much traffic. It would put you and me closer together, geographically (I don't know that we could get a whole lot closer physically than we already have). And it would mean earlier promotion than I could possibly expect here, but I like Newton Lauder and I don't like Mr Blackhouse. Looking on the black side, I could commit myself to his team and then fall totally out of favour.

That risk would be immaterial if I were prepared to resign and become a good little housewife; but a life bound up with supermarkets and washing lines would never satisfy me now. I suppose that I could have got a proper job outside the police, but I have come to the conclusion that I am a career copper and not even motherhood, if such should be my fate, will turn me aside. I like the life. I like the sense of responsibility. I like everything about it except Mr Blackhouse.

If we both work on and if promotions come as they should, we could afford to keep June on without having to offend against your principles by allowing my well-heeled father to help us. ('Sponging' you would call it, you stiff-necked puritan.) I have had a tentative word with June and she would be quite agreeable. I think that she has enjoyed being out from under her mother's thumb.

I'm not asking you to tell me what to do. That isn't our sort of relationship. But I would appreciate your advice and comments. Soon, please. He is not the most patient of men and I have to give him an answer before he ruptures himself.

Not long now until your return. I look forward to your company. And you can help me swot for the inspector's exams. No doubt you can think of treats that I can give you in return. Hurry back to your loving,

Honeypot

My very favourite Daddy – yes Sandy is home and we hope to come for a visit soon, we're both due a little leave. I'll forewarn you now that Sandy intends to break it to you that we intend to marry in the spring. This is so that you can ready yourself to greet the tidings with the appropriate cries of amazement instead of the cursory nod appropriate to news that you probably guessed months ago. We have other news, but it can wait until we see you.

What a pity that Mum is not alive. She would have relished the occasion of her only daughter's marriage and would no doubt have taken over all the arrangements – which, frankly, I am too busy to think about. Do you think that Mrs Wallis would care to deputise for her?

When I saw you last month, you expressed interest in the Fraser case. I can now tell you (because it will be all over the media soon and, anyway, you have probably already heard it through that omnivorous grapevine of yours) that Glashan did not return and surrender to his bail. He is believed to be settling down in one of the pleasanter parts of North Africa, to continue his writing. No doubt he will be limiting his shooting competitive activities to countries that do not have extradition treaties with Britain. Any money that he sacrificed in bail or property he will doubtless recoup because his sales will go through the roof. The public will never believe his version of events and all the world loves a murderer who knocked off a blackmailer and got away with it. The fact that he did not know Fraser's true nature is irrelevant. To be frank, yes I do think that his version is the true one and Fraser's death really was an accident.

I wish him well. If he is heading, as I have heard whispered, to the lower slopes of the Atlas mountains, I would see if I couldn't wangle an invitation for Sandy and me to spend winter breaks with him – except that Ian Fellowes is still fizzing at being balked of the kudos that comes from a successful prosecution and would probably never forgive me for fraternising with the enemy.

Much more urgent, now is the time for you to start calling in favours and remembering guilty secrets. Sandy's boss is about to retire and I want that job for him. Who do you know who knows the Chief Constable or somebody on the Police Committee? If you have strings prepare to pull them now and oblige your ever loving,

Honoria

Book Two

THOROUGHLY NASTY NELLIE.

MORE COLLECTED EMAILS OF HONORIA LAIRD
(Née POTTERTON-PHIPPS).

Foreword

I am deeply grateful to Sgt Simon Young for introducing me to at least some of the mysteries of the Edinburgh Dog Unit, sufficient, perhaps, to avoid any total absurdities. With luck, this has also saved me from accidentally describing any real people. In case some such coincidence has occurred, let me point out that, with the exception of Pippa, all characters are fictitious.

(In editing these emails I have limited the inclusions to material relating to the particular story of Thoroughly Nasty Nellie plus any background material that may help to set the scene. Some passages have been omitted as being unsuitable for publication where they may be encountered by younger readers.)

G.H.

Poppy – such a pity that you couldn't stay up here for my wedding! But I understand. The needs of the twins must come first and we certainly wouldn't have wanted them spreading the jungle rot (or whatever it was) around among the guests. It was unfortunate that we had to bring the wedding forward – no, not for the reason you're imagining but because Sandy had to go abroad for an uncertain period.

Dad certainly pushed the boat out, but I suppose that was only to be expected of a very well heeled landowner and industrial bigwig with only one daughter among the sons. He allowed us the quiet service that we wanted, in the little local church with just family and very close friends, and I flatly refused to doll-up more than wearing a cream dress and carrying a small bouquet. In your absence, June stood in as my bridesmaid.

One of Sandy's colleagues stood up as his best man. He and June got on rather too well together. I had been trying to persuade June to move into Edinburgh with me as trainee housekeeper and bottlewasher. With Sandy and I both working, some domestic help is essential. When June realised that this would make her more accessible to Alec Innes (the best man) she suddenly turned eager to make the move, so at least Sandy and I can get on with our demanding jobs without the distraction of household chores.

Back to the wedding. At the house it was a different kettle of fish. Dad had invited everyone in Perthshire to the reception and most of them came. The wingding went on until nearly midday the next day and four people were arrested, so I suppose the party could be counted a success. Sandy and I were away by then, on our way to honeymoon on St Lucia. (If you ever go to St Lucia, don't fail to visit Magan's Bay. Superb! And that's not just a rose-tinted memory from a lovely, lovely honeymoon.)

I never explained about Edinburgh, did I? You visited me while I was still in Newton Lauder, a humble detective sergeant in the local fuzz. However, two cases and the participation of my dog brought me to the attention of a detective superintendent – a man I cannot thole at any price, but I don't suppose that I need see much of him. The sergeant in charge of the dog unit had to retire suddenly with hardpad or something and DS Blackhouse recommended that I take over pending a permanent appointment. It was hinted that promotion might well be in the wind if I transferred to Edinburgh. This seemed very suitable, Sandy already being a detective inspector in Auld Reekie.

We have bought a nice little house in Edinburgh, not too far from the Fettes Avenue HQ. We had to take out an astronomic joint mortgage but it's not as big as it might have been. (Sandy is still being a bit stiff-necked about accepting help from Dad, but I managed to pass a cheque through the vendor's solicitor which gained us what is, on paper, the bargain of a lifetime. Sandy may suspect but he can't be sure.)

Presumably the twins have finished spreading germs around so you would be welcome to visit again. Only this time, do remember that we are not far off the equivalent latitude to Cape Horn and wrap up warmly. I have plenty of room at the moment because, believe it or not, Sandy is back in LA. During his previous secondment there we discovered that a gentleman who we suspected of fire-raising over here was very much wanted in California in connection with a fire which had resulted in the loss of more than one life. We were not very long back from our honeymoon when Sandy was required in the States, to give evidence of arrest and then to wait around in order to introduce the villain's record from over here at a more appropriate stage. American legal shenanigans being what they are, the case keeps dragging on with more and more adjournments. My time, on the other hand, is taken up with running the dog unit and I can lead a nearly nine-to-five workday.

You say that, on the basis of your very short acquaintance with Pippa, you have decided to get a Labrador. All right, so they are very good with children and they take you out for walkies. And she's loveable. And all right, so by dint of very careful diet control Pippa farts very little and hardly ever scratches. But do think carefully. Either start with a puppy and face up to messes and chewing (do for God's sake keep it away from electric cables) or get a mature dog already trained the way you want it. And find out why it is looking for a new home. I took Pippa over at fifteen months because, as I discovered later, the Guide Dogs Association deemed her untrainable. But they had already managed to teach her all the wrong things, like walking in front – and chasing a ball. (Fetching a ball is all right for a gundog, chasing it is not.) I have almost cured the coprophagia and have learned to ignore the remainder of the habit. On the up side, she has a marvellous nose that can detect a shot pheasant at a hundred yards or a dropped crumb at twenty and I have been training her at tracking along with the full-time dogs. She has a memory that makes a goldfish look like Pelman personified, yet she has made her contribution to several criminal cases. I don't know what else I can tell you. Taken all round, a Lab is great company and marvellous for children but you have to take the rough with the smooth.

In answer to your question, yes, married life is suiting me very well. In fact, it's not very different to my salad days except that I am now a detective sergeant in Edinburgh instead of Newton Lauder, I'm more concerned with dogs and their handlers than with mundane enquiries; and my night-time frolics are now legitimate and much more fun.

Email me again soon with your news and tell me when you can come up again. Give me some advance warning so that I can book some leave.

All the best,

Honeypot

Sandy, my true but slightly retarded love. When several days and several of my increasingly agitated emails went by without reply, I was sure that you'd eloped with some anorexic starlet. Now that I've heard from you at last, I can't say the revelation that my husband, who promised to cherish me for as long as we both should happen to live, was ready to put his life on the line for no good reason is an awful lot better. You went over there as a witness, Sandy. A witness. It was rash to let yourself be tempted out on a shootout against bank robbers; but to emerge from that unscathed and then to get pushed down a flight of steps by an indignant prisoner and break several bones was… Well, you can put your own words to it. Your judgement will probably be more severe than mine, my dear idiot.

Anyway, I do understand that you couldn't fix up email facilities immediately on arrival, concussed, in hospital nor use your laptop with several fingers splinted. My thanks go to the hospital visitor who's doing your typing for you.

At least we've got Christmas over in this neck of the woods. During the interlude between being a child and having children of my own, Christmas doesn't seem quite so much fun. More of a commercialised rat race and a lot of work.

Deck the halls and spend your lolly, Fa la la la la, la-la, la-la.

And a lot of the associated rituals are gibberish. Have they ever seen snow in Bethlehem? You remember the words to King Wenceslas? (Not that the Good Wenceslas was actually a king. There was a King Wenceslas, but he came later.) What I want to know is, why would the poor man, who lived right against the forest fence, trudge a 'good league' (around three miles) to the castle and three miles back again, carrying his winter fuel, while the snow lay deep and crisp and even? No, my theory is that he was a spy and that Wenceslas went back with him to check on his cover story. You'll note that no more is heard of the poor man. I suspect that he ended up stuffed into St Agnes' Fountain. Poor man indeed!

Season for all sorts of folly, Fa la la la la, la-la, la-la.

You'll realise that I'm only waffling to give you something to read and to distract you from ogling the nurses or making love to your pillow.

Don we now our gay apparel, (and that doesn't mean quite what it once did), *Fa la la la la, la-la, la-la.*

I'm settling in to the new job. My superior is an inspector who has to oversee the mounted unit as well as the police dogs. He is more concerned with the horses and quite right too, because horses are necessary for ceremonial purposes and essential for crowd control and are even dafter than dogs, more nervous, more fragile and generally more disaster prone. So I have a pretty free hand. Incidentally, the nickname Honeypot seems to have followed me here even though I'm no longer Honoria Potterton-Phipps and am trying to get used to being addressed as Sergeant Laird. Was that your doing? Even the inspector calls me Honeypot. He says it seems very suitable somehow. I can't think why. Perhaps you can explain.

Sing this stupid Christmas carol, Fa la la la la, la-la, la-la.

In point of fact, Sandy, one hand may be free but the other is definitely full. We have a row of ten kennels with outside runs. The runs overlook the stable-yard, which is a sensible arrangement – the dogs have something to break the monotony and the horses get used to the smell and sound of dogs. The dogs go home with their handlers, so the kennels are usually empty except for any dogs whose handlers are away. Just now we have one German Shepherd (an explosives sniffer) and a Labrador (a drugs sniffer), both left by my predecessor; another German Shepherd (a general purpose dog – i.e. trained to search, track and detain), left for the moment by a handler who has gone on a course at Strathclyde to learn how to train handlers to train their dogs; and a pair of Springer Spaniels, in training as drugs sniffers, whose handler is on holiday. These all have to be exercised, fed, looked after and at least not allowed to forget their training to date. If I can't recruit any handler who has come in to get dog food, collect a van or lodge his time sheets, it's all down to me. I am supposed to be educating the handler who has gone on the course, bringing him up to scratch on matters of admin and management so that he can take over from me. I wonder who selected him – he's as thick as porridge.

After a damp and dismal Christmas, we now have the first snow. Only a light dusting so far, but it's very frosty. When the snow turns to sleet the roads get like ice-rinks. The vans are positively dangerous and I bless the Range Rover that dad reluctantly passed on to me. I hate leaving it in the street in case some maniac slides into it. We had one snowdrop in the back garden but either Pippa ate it or it pulled its head down again when it saw the weather.

That's about all the news I can think of for now. The plumber has been and has installed the new bidet and June is waiting for the decorator to come and tidy up.

Hurry up, mend and come home to your loving,

Honeypot

Sandy, you wretch, you never said that you were sharing a two-bed ward with an LAPD SWAT officer who was damaged in the same shootout. Anyway, I understood that you were to be released yesterday. Gratifying as it is to know that I have given amusement, my email was not intended for general distribution. Come to think of it, why didn't you leave hospital yesterday? Is there something you aren't telling me?

During all the fuss and flap over your injuries I forgot to say that, rather than become embroiled in Customs declarations and duty and all that jazz, I am keeping your Christmas presents here, awaiting your return. If I mention that I have been rather extravagant, that may give you a motive for hurrying back to my loving arms. For your part, you acted with unaccustomed intelligence in leaving my presents with June, who produced them suddenly on Christmas morning just when I was sure that you'd forgotten all about me. Well, well. Such an abundance of pretty silk and lacework. And so delicate that I'll be afraid to wear any of it, only to expose it to your rough handling. I like pretty things but I know which one of us gets excited by them. Really, I wonder for whose benefit it all is.

(Editor's note: The remaining eight lines of this paragraph have been omitted as being irrelevant to the story and possibly embarrassing to the reader.)

And the above, dear Sandy, should ensure that you don't go handing my email around this time, for the amusement of all and sundry.

That issue disposed of, I can now get around to my news. There's a hot time in the old town tonight, or rather out in the countryside.

Yesterday morning, I had more or less caught up with the admin. It was a busy time in the field, what with the terrorist scare and a tip-off about drugs coming into Leith on a cargo ship. Nearly all of the twenty handlers were busy, but two called in at the office to leave their expenses claims. I hinted strongly that they would get no expenses if I got no help with walkies etc., so

I was soon free. I have managed to pressure two of the handlers to take on my predecessor's two dogs as second dogs.

The vans were out, so I loaded a young spaniel, in course of being trained as a drugs-sniffer, into the Range Rover along with Pippa and sallied forth. My intention was to combine a little training with a visit to several of the teams, just to let them know that The Eye of Honeypot is always on them. However, I had only reached the Maybury roundabout when a message was relayed to me. My old boss, Detective Inspector Ian Fellowes (remember him?) wanted one or more tracker dogs near Newton Lauder, urgent.

A quick mental review assured me that the only suitable team that could be pulled out had to be Constable Ritchie with his two general purpose German Shepherds. He was at Turnhouse Airport and he had exclusive use of one of the vans. I decided that I would like to see him at work, because though he has rapport with his dogs he is sometimes lackadaisical in his work, so I set off while asking Control to relay an order to him.

The day was overcast and the first flakes of snow were drifting on the wind, which explained the urgency of Ian's request. Indeed, as I crossed the Lammermuirs the snow was beginning in earnest. I've never been so glad of the four-wheel-drive, but the snow let up as the road descended again into the Borders country.

Ian's message had been less than clear and almost certainly garbled in repetition. I called his mobile from mine. When he answered the call, I was suddenly aware how much I had missed his solid, comforting presence – especially since you went gallivanting off to sunny California, Sandy. I was certainly glad to get off the main road where the traffic was moving too fast for the conditions and a game of big boys' dodgems looked imminent. At Ian's direction, I found my way onto a minor road to the east of Newton Lauder. I soon began to recognise roads that I had travelled during my months as a detective sergeant in the area. There was a powdering of old snow and the tarmac showed black where warm tyres had cleared the snow.

The countryside was partly obscured by the dusting of snow,

but I recognised a typical low ground Borders scene of small to medium sized fields, with hedges and tree strips, all mingled with small woods, larger plantations and areas of setaside – charming, cosy countryside in summer but bleak and cheerless on a freezing January day under a black sky. Farms had originally been small, but changed farming practices had made small farms uneconomic and larger units had been created. Surplus farmhouses and farmworkers' cottages had become available for renovation and sale so that, as with many other rural areas, it was becoming a retirement and commuter paradise populated by families in search of peace and quiet or with rural aspirations. Some, no doubt would see the countryside through the eyes of Walt Disney, but that's another and sadder subject.

Ian's directions brought me to the mouth of a short drive leading to Stoneleigh House. This, clearly, was once a substantial farmhouse, but it was now stripped of its barns and most of the outbuildings. Slated and roughcast, it is well proportioned and has a friendly aspect with some of the wayward charm of a Labrador puppy. Wandering stems of clematis promise that it will be bright with flowers in spring or summer, depending on the variety of clematis.

Two police cars were parked outside the gate and Ian was waiting for me, stamping his feet for warmth. As soon as I pulled onto the verge, he climbed in beside me.

Ian was brought up in the countryside and has never lost the habit of exchanging courtesies before getting down to business. He greeted me almost effusively and asked how I was. He asked after you, having heard on the coppervine about your mishaps. 'I'm glad you came yourself,' he said. 'You brought Pippa?'

'Yes,' I told him. 'But I have a professional team on the way.'

'Pippa would have managed. I never knew a dog with such a nose.'

I let it go. Pippa does have a good nose. She also has every bad habit known to Labradors and would rather follow up a fox's droppings (did you ever smell anything so vile?) than a burglar's trail. Only good luck has so far kept her from disgracing me in front of my fellow officers. 'What's it about?' I asked.

'The cleaning lady expected the couple to be at home but she found the house open and empty. I've looked inside and there are no signs of deliberate departure and every indication that they expected to be around for a while. On the other hand, I didn't see any signs of violence. It may be nothing, a misunderstanding, but both the family's cars are in the garage and there are no tyre-marks suggesting that they were picked up by another vehicle. This snow's nearly forty-eight hours old. I caught the postman here this morning and he identified the only tyre-tracks as his own. For all we know, they walked out and collapsed or —'

At that moment my mobile played its little tune. Ritchie came on the line. He sounded frazzled. He is one of those rotund and unflappable men who seem able to surf over trouble, so I knew that it was serious. 'Sergeant? Problem. I'm halfway across the Lammermuirs. It's snowing a blizzard here and I've been run off the road and ditched by a mad bugger in an artic. I'm good and stuck.'

'Are you hurt?'

'I'm fine, Sarge.'

'And the dogs?'

'They're OK.'

'Radio in for help,' I told him, 'and make sure that your dogs are looked after. Did you get the number of the lorry?'

'I did that. I've radioed it to Traffic.'

'Then go home when you can.' And to Ian I said, 'It looks as though I'm all you're going to get. And we'd better get moving. It's snowing hard, between here and Edinburgh. A heavy snow-fall would make scenting very chancy.'

'Quite right,' he said. He drew a plastic bag from his pocket. 'One sock and a pair of tights from the linen basket.'

'You're quite sure that she hadn't been wearing wellies, with his socks on top of her tights? There'd be none of his scent.'

Ian waited while a call came in over the radio from Control, repeating McFadden's message. I acknowledged and signed off. 'Who knows?' Ian said. 'We can try again if you don't get a result.'

The wind was bitter. I was glad of my sheepskin coat and the matching boots and gloves. I let the spaniel out for a pee. He sniffed Ian suspiciously and seemed satisfied that he wasn't carrying any drugs. I put the springer back in the Range Rover and took Pippa out on a long lead. She sniffed the discarded footwear with apparent contempt. If she can't eat it or roll in it, Pippa doesn't want to know – until she gets the message that there will be an edible reward for a successful mission. I rather agreed with her about the tights. It seemed that Nellie was addicted to a rather strong perfume. Expensive but strong. I had smelled it before, on a top-of-the-range prostitute who I arrested for soliciting in one of the most upmarket roads in Edinburgh.

'We'll walk round the house,' Ian said. 'Don't worry about footprints. I've got McFadden touring round, photographing anything of possible interest, in case this turns out to be a crime scene.'

I nodded. McFadden is the more intelligent of his two detective constables and I knew him for a competent photographer. I could see his footprints ahead of us.

We set off round the back of the house, anti-clockwise. Pippa showed occasional signs of interest, which was only to be expected. I dragged her away from the dustbins. There was an untidy vegetable garden, mostly empty at this time of year, and a few bare fruit trees. Beyond a beech hedge were fields where the snow was still lying. At the front, an informal garden with rambling rockeries and beds of heather had been laid out and, after a fashion, maintained.

Near the front door, Pippa began to show interest. She nosed the footwear that was still in my gloved hand and then turned towards the door of the house, thinking that the tracks in that direction might well lead towards food. They were less likely to lead towards the absent owners, so I turned her and let her know that I was more interested in where the scent went to rather than whence it came.

She took the point eventually and led the way; nose down, across the untidy gravel and through the garden by way of what seemed to be a muddy grass path to a metal gate in a fence. This brought us into a windbreak strip of conifers and along a rough path to another gate.

We found ourselves back at the road about fifty yards along from the drive, but Pippa, who was now thoroughly into the game, led us across and onto another faint path through a stretch of mixed woodland. The path could never have been much used, except perhaps by wildlife. In many places it was barely visible and could only be guessed at by looking for the most level and open space, but Pippa seemed to be sticking to it and I followed along, uttering silent prayers that she was not on the trail of a rabbit, another dog or a pricked pheasant. The day was becoming overcast, but the deciduous trees were bare and the few conifers were tall and thin, so there was some daylight.

The path was narrow. Ian dropped behind and I spoke over my shoulder. 'Not that it matters,' I said, 'but who are we looking for?'

'I believe the house belongs to a Mr Duffus. George Duffus and his wife Helena.'

I stopped for a moment and Pippa nearly jerked me off my feet. We set off again. 'Not Thoroughly Nasty Nellie?' I said. 'If so, she isn't his wife unless there have been big changes in the last few months.'

'You know her?'

'I've met the lady,' I told him. 'And during my time in Newton Lauder, you had me acting as Firearms Officer whenever there wasn't any crime to detect. I was all over the place, checking firearms certificates and safekeeping and inspecting land for its suitability for stalking rifles. I used to get far more information over a cup of tea than any other way. Around here, Nasty Nellie was the prime topic of conversation. Her proper married name's Arnoldson and she has a husband living not far away.'

'She has, has she?' Ian said thoughtfully. The statistics tend to favour husbands and partners as suspects. Or wives of course. So be very gentle with me, Sandy, when you eventually come home.

'But don't bank too heavily on the husband,' I told Ian. 'She's reputed to have a hell of a temper and seems to have made enemies the way other women make beds. That's how she came to be called Thoroughly Nasty Nellie. After Thoroughly Modern

Millie, of course. I was told, for what it's worth, that she went for the man who first called her that with a milk bottle, so the name isn't used to her face any more. She has very white skin and flaming red hair. I never before believed the stories about red-haired people having hot tempers, but I do now.'

'And Mr Duffus?'

'I don't know much about him. Rather a nonentity, I gather, but he must have something if he tempted her away from her husband.'

'Money?'

'Very probably. I've only seen him in the distance. He was well dressed. Despite being into middle age at least, he looked to be quite a virile sort of man. That could be enough. She makes little secret of her sexuality.'

We were still following the kind of path made by sheep or occasional dog-walkers. There was no snow in the shelter of the trees. I thought that we were heading generally towards the north. There seemed to be no particular merit to this direction except that Pippa was towing me along it. I was still hoping that she hadn't picked up the smell of a dead rabbit or something even worse. But after what I guessed to be no more than a few hundred metres she turned off the path and began to sniff vaguely around.

We were in a small glade or clearing, a long stone's throw from the faint path. I began to have an uneasy feeling about it. A stand of evergreens had sheltered the place from the prevailing wind so that, like the path, it was clear of snow. The pines had given way to spruce with some dense underbrush and the area was shaded, but I could see untidiness to the ground which I realised looked as though somebody had been throwing the sandy soil around. As if he wanted to get rid of it. I felt a shiver run up my back.

Pippa left her first area of interest and moved to another spot, bare except for a small gorse bush. She began to dig. I pulled her away.

'Let her dig,' Ian said very quietly. He took hold of the gorse bush. Gorse is usually firmly rooted but it came up easily in his hand as if it had only just been transplanted. Pippa was digging as though her dinner was below, halfway to Australia.

Ian watched keenly. 'That's enough,' he said suddenly. I dragged Pippa away. She got the message and looked to me for her reward. I took out biscuits from my pocket.

Ian produced one of the nylon evidence bags without which no good detective ventures out and, wearing it like a glove, groped in the bottom of the excavation. When he straightened, I saw that he had uncovered what looked like a human hand, thickly crusted with soil. For some time I had been picking up a smell, an inappropriate smell, domestic, reminiscent of the garage and the kitchen and the smell was now much stronger. I realised that the smell was what Pippa had been digging for and the thought sickened me.

You know me by now, Sandy. I don't get the vapours at the sight of a dead body – I've seen too many of them. But I'll admit that the prospect of a corpse in that rather eerie wood, in that weather, under that black sky and with that smell of cooked meat would not have been my choice for a jolly morning. Also, when I came to think of it, lunchtime had arrived and almost gone. My midriff began to send me unhappy messages. I was shocked to find that my mouth was watering.

'I seem to have done my bit,' I said. 'If you don't need us any more —'

Ian looked surprised. 'Of course I need you,' he said, quite testily for him. 'You're a witness of what went before, you can be a witness of anything still to come and I'll be needing a statement from you. Stay clear of the site but don't leave the area.'

As instructions go, that left ample latitude. Without prejudice to Nellie or her partner, there was no sign yet of a second body and a virtual certainty that somebody had walked away from the burial site. Of course, they might have returned by the way they came; equally, they might not. I gave Pippa another sniff of the footwear in the bag and rattled the biscuits in my pocket. That was message enough. She cast about and then set off along a slant that brought us back to the line of the original path, still heading in what my sense of direction continued to assure me was more or less north.

Dogs can be remarkably articulate. They have voices but their body language speaks louder once you have learned to interpret it. Pippa was communicating all the time, but I would have given a lot to have had her tell me whether she was following the scent of Nellie, of her partner or of somebody completely different. Behind me, I could hear Ian using his radio, calling for backup, tarpaulins, the attendance of the police surgeon, a pathologist, SOCOs... His voice faded.

Pippa pressed on confidently. I guessed that a change of temperature was releasing scent from the ground. A quarter or maybe half a mile brought us to another narrow, tarmac road. To judge from the tracks clear of snow, this road was evidently more heavily used. I seemed to recall that this road joined up with the other about a mile to my right.

The trail had arrived at a dead end. I tried Pippa on the far side of the road and along the verges, but her interest had lapsed. I thought that whoever we had been following had probably left the area in a vehicle.

At that point, custom and routine decreed that we call for assistance in a fingertip search of the area. But I had noticed that the daylight was becoming colourless, which usually means that it is filtering through snow. As we started back, the snow arrived and the whole investigation was made a thousand times more difficult. The snow was not the fine powder that wets without laying down any depth but huge flakes drifting and whirling, settling everywhere, penetrating any crevice in the clothing, clinging to nose and ears, obstructing the very breathing and quickly building up on the ground. I had my sheepskin hat on or my hair would have been ruined. The path disappeared in seconds. I asked Pippa to lead me back, but she said that she was just as lost as I was. The contours of the ground had vanished. I thought that I could infer the position of the path from the gaps between the trees overhead but within a few paces it was obvious that any such attempt was doomed. Soon I was thoroughly disoriented. Several times I came to one edge or the other of the wood and turned back. I shouted, but you know how falling snow can muffle sound.

Belatedly, I thought of my mobile phone. I keyed Ian's number and to my huge relief he answered. He was, he told me, back at the house. He said that he had not worried because he knew that Pippa would look after me. (Sometimes that boy lives in a dream world.) At my suggestion, somebody went out to one of the cars and played a fanfare on the horn. (Unfortunately the Range Rover, which has the loudest horn on the market, was locked and I had the keys.) Soon, I heard a horn, not very far away, and we followed the sound. Pippa seemed relieved to be back in the Range Rover, dried with an already damp towel. Both dogs were getting anxious about their dinner and, to be honest, Sandy, so was I.

As you can imagine, the rest of the day was the sort of orderly chaos that usually follows the discovery of a body. I know that you like to have all the grisly details but I am writing this at nearly midnight after a day of exercise, fresh air and excitement and finishing with a large brandy. My last yawn made my ears pop. I'll bring you up to speed next time that I have a minute.

Until then, all my love.

Yours,

Honeypot

Well, I'm sorry if your ears are burning, Sandy. You were supposed to be getting out of hospital and anyway I didn't realise that emails sent to you in hospital went through the whole of the hospital mail system. But you're out of hospital now – true or false? I only hope that you didn't check yourself out early to escape any pointing fingers and hidden sniggers and that somebody – male or platonic – is looking after you in your lonely motel room.

And just in case you're in any doubt, I really did mean every word of what I wrote.

As you'll realise, at the point where I left you cliff-hanging, Ian Fellowes was in a quandary. We had an empty house, left unlocked and unexplained. We had a dead body some distance off and nothing but surmise and the opinion of a dottled Labrador to connect the two. The owner or owners of the house might walk home at any minute. Or one might have murdered the other and done a runner. Or perhaps one of them was buried beneath the other. Or perhaps all sorts of things. Ian solved the problem from the negative slant, deciding that what he could not do was to walk (or slither) away and leave the house empty. We had already gathered, for the sake of warmth and shelter, in the big living room with its pastel décor, watercolour prints and Swedish furniture. Therefore it seemed logical to give that room a careful search for anything suggesting wrongdoing and, when the room appeared as innocent and had been subjected to as much photography as a new baby, use it as a very temporary and unusually luxurious incident room. No computers but plenty of radios and telephones and people making notes.

DC Bright, who occasionally lives up to his name, had made a pot of tea and opened a packet of biscuits. We each put a few coins on the mantelpiece, in case the occupiers returned and made a fuss. While we enjoyed the poor substitute for lunch, I reported on the trail that Pippa had followed away from the grave scene (or possibly towards it). Ian had already made a brief report to Edinburgh. He had also managed to have a rough tent contrived from a tarpaulin before the snow had got too heavy. While he waited for the tarpaulin to be brought from Newton Lauder, he had uncovered enough of the body to be sure that it was a) human and b) dead. The latter went without saying but officers have sometimes been misled by animal remains.

The police surgeon had arrived in the Traffic Land Rover that brought the tarpaulin and had been taken to the death scene. (The snow had started in earnest by then and they had some difficulty finding it again until a waft of unholy scent led them to the spot). He confirmed both points but was unable to offer any opinion as to the cause of death. Ian had seen more of the cadaver than I had and he explained to me that a serious attempt had been made to destroy the body or at least to conceal its identity and the cause of death. It had been soaked in petrol and set alight and then, apparently when that blaze was on the point of dying down, charcoal had been packed round it in order to keep it smouldering. The body had then been covered over and, if not found before the rush of spring growth, might well have become lost forever. The charcoal, he said, had not completely burned, probably because it was surrounded by damp earth, and it had been in a form resembling barbecue briquettes.

We learned over the radio that the road at Soutra was still blocked and looked like staying that way. The chances of trained Scene Of Crime Officers (SOCOs) arriving that day seemed remote. When the Police Surgeon had been conveyed back towards Newton Lauder, our team now comprised Ian, me, Ian's two DCs and one uniformed constable who had come out with the Traffic Land Rover.

Ian had arrived at another decision. 'I think that I should have the house searched,' he said. 'If the occupiers have met trouble, I'll be doing the right thing. If they haven't, they may still be understanding. What do you know of them?'

'I wouldn't count on Thoroughly Nasty Nelly being understanding, Sir,' I said. (The 'Sir' was because junior officers were present and, although he had asked me to call him Ian, I only do so in private.) 'I've been told that Mr Duffus is the quiet, self-effacing sort, but Nelly enjoys making trouble. She would love an

excuse to kick up hell in the media. I think you should refer to
Edinburgh.'

He shook his head. 'If I do that, I won't get a decision until
after dark. Compromise. What I'm going to do is to start a search
and send a message to say that I'm doing it. By the time anybody
gets around to telling me to stop, I'll have done it.'

'And if there's a row you can say that you had tacit permission
because nobody told you not to. Very crafty,' I said.

'Probably not crafty enough, but it's what I'm going to do.'

In point of fact it was not exactly what he did, because just
then the pathologist turned up, ploughing through the snow in
his Mitsubishi Shogun. He left the car pointing towards the road
and met DC Bright on the doorstep. Bright brought him into the
room. He is a gingery, bustling little man named Waller. Ian and
I had met him before. He always seems to be acting in haste but
his autopsy reports are always thorough and almost always right.
He stands up well to cross-examination, which is the first
requirement in a good pathologist. He had provided himself with
Wellingtons and the fullest set of waterproofs that I ever saw.

The central heating was working and my sheepskin coat was
drying off beside a large radiator. Ian looked at me speculatively
but decided to be merciful. 'I'll take Dr Waller to see the body,'
he said, 'and McFadden can come with us and take photographs
of whatever we disturb.' (McFadden, who only had a mackintosh
and ankle boots for protection, sighed the sigh of the much put-
upon.) 'If we decide that it should be moved now, I'll call for
help, so keep your radios open. You can oversee the search,' he
told me.

I still had hopes of getting home before dark or before all the
roads were blocked, whichever came first. I thought that it would
still be possible, in the Range Rover, to make a long detour and
get home through Gorebridge. 'I'm only here as a dog handler,' I
pointed out.

'You're still the next most senior officer,' Ian retorted.

The three wrapped figures vanished into the whirling
snowflakes and we set about the search. I told the two PCs to do
a general search for signs of violence, hasty departure or anything

out of the ordinary while I looked more specifically for diaries, threatening letters, unpaid accounts and similar indicators.

There was no telephone answering machine, to my disappointment. I called last-number-redial from the phone in the hall and was connected to the local garage. I keyed 1471 and took a note of the last caller's number. Above the phone was a his-and-hers calendar showing idealised pictures of Highland scenery. The legible writing, mostly on the 'hers' side and in a round, clear hand, showed mundane appointments with tradesmen plus a few medical consultations. Mr Duffus, on the other hand, wrote in a scribble and used a personal shorthand combining initials and occasional symbols which conveyed absolutely nothing except the times of the appointments. That day and the day previous were unhelpfully blank except for a hairdresser appointment for the previous afternoon on the 'her' side. I phoned the hairdresser. The appointment had not been kept.

The PCs, I was pleased to note, were being thorough – lifting the lids of lavatory cisterns and taking out drawers for a careful look at the underside. I reminded them that everything must be put back exactly as we had found it or heads might very well roll. The only loose papers were in a bureau in a corner of the dining room, and they seemed to be made up of receipted bills and trivial business letters. Two chequebooks showed modest balances. There was a two-drawer filing cabinet, but any system was locked away in the mind of its originator and there was too much material for an immediate study. A quick sift though the files produced the usual spectrum of insurances, financial dealings and receipts. A glance at the bank statements showed nothing out of the ordinary. A file labelled 'Correspondence' seemed to contain only the most mundane of letters but would probably repay further study.

The bathroom was more interesting. There was a container for contact lenses, empty, and several prescriptions in the name of Mr Duffus, who appeared to suffer from mild arthritis and an ulcer. Two of those prescriptions were in the form of pills enclosed in pop-out plastic with the day of the week printed beside each. The day was Thursday, but neither Wednesday's nor

Thursday's medications had been taken and only one of Tuesday's.

The beds were neatly made but not turned down. Without knowing the habits of the couple, it was difficult to draw inferences, but the kitchen was clean and tidy and the dining room table was laid as if for a simple meal for two.

I was trying the pockets of the clothes in the wardrobes, in the vain hope of finding something more informative, when Bright's radio came to life. Ian Fellowes wanted to speak to me. He and the pathologist had decided that the value of an early post-mortem examination would outweigh any risk of damaging evidence which, in any case, might not surface again for days or weeks, depending on the thaw. In addition, he said, the crows seemed to have found the place and there were sounds as though a fox was lurking in the underbrush. Unless there was a volunteer to stand guard on the body overnight...

There wasn't. We agreed that, in the circumstances, a guard would be impractical and probably less effective than the tarpaulin with inches of snow on top of it. For the moment, taping off the emptied gravesite might only draw attention to it and would be left until the thaw seemed imminent. The mortuary van had been summoned and Dr Waller had brought a body bag with him. We were to collect the bag from the doctor's car, Ian said, bring a lamp and come.

The snowfall was becoming lighter and even stopping occasionally only to start again. The light was already beginning to go. All the landmarks had vanished or changed completely. Some of the trees looked familiar but we might not have found the place again if Ian had not come to meet us. I noticed that the ground was still warm enough to have half melted the fresh snowfall.

There followed an hour of the most disgusting labour. You can imagine it, Sandy, which saves me reliving it for your edification. The body was the most obscene thing that I ever saw and it had curled up as burned bodies do. We checked to be as sure as we could that there was not another body underneath or adjacent. When we had the body bagged and the tarpaulin pegged down to protect the site, we struggled back to the house. We had just reached it when a message arrived via Control. The mortuary van had slid off the road and was hopelessly stuck. There was no ambulance available to substitute. The snow had started again with a vengeance, the large, soft flakes that quickly put a deep blanket over everything.

Within seconds, we went from being a moderately well organised and disciplined party into a rabble of disputants. Ian phoned the motoring organisations but they were unanimous. The ploughs were out but snow was still falling heavily on the high ground and it seemed unlikely that even the main road would be cleared before the snowfall ceased. Dr Waller had brought the body bag, so it seemed logical that he should convey it back again, but he was adamant that that he only carried such containers in the empty state. My Range Rover was the only other four-wheel-drive vehicle with enough ground clearance to have a chance of reaching the mortuary in Newton Lauder, but I was not going to risk getting stuck in a snow-drift with a partly cooked and decomposing body in the car with me, along with a hungry and flatulent Labrador. I am not an unreasonable person, as you well know, Sandy, but I did draw the line at that. After intense bickering, it was decided that the body should remain in the house and under guard overnight. The others all had homes to go to, so I nobly agreed to do that duty and, even more nobly, lent Ian my car on his sacred promise to return it to me undamaged or to repair or replace it. By that stage, he would have promised anything.

The body bag was brought inside, the exterior wiped dry and the bag placed respectfully on the utility room worktop, with the window ajar and the radiator off. I turned the Range Rover for Ian and brought the dogs into the house. The party set off in the two four-by-fours and I was left in the house, alone with the body and two dogs.

At least I had heat and light. What I would do if the snow brought down the electricity cables I shuddered to think. I phoned the inspector in charge of animal units and he promised to have the dogs in kennels attended to and to lock up for me; and I let June know that she would be on her own. At least

Thoroughly Nasty Nellie's kitchen was well equipped and adequately stocked. The dogs were surprised and gratified to be fed tinned steak from soup-bowls while I steamed some fish for myself.

As you may imagine, I was restless. The owners of the house might, just possibly, return from a sudden visit to a dying relative to find their house occupied by a corpse and a woman detective sergeant. I tidied away the more obvious signs of our occupation. Somebody had dropped a half-moon of mud from under a heel and, to be safe, I gathered it into an evidence bag. Rather than be surprised by hysterical arrivals, I made sure that the doors were bolted as well as locked. Then I finished the interrupted search, without positive result. I had been aware all along of a faint sense of *déjà vu*. My younger self would have noticed nothing but since breaking away to make my own way in the world – more or less – I had become aware of fine shades of affluence. In this house I could see little sign of make-do-and-mend, of accepting best value for money instead of the absolute best. The wines in the rack might not be the ultimate but they were probably the best that the local wine-merchant could provide. It was impossible to judge the quality of the cuts of meat in the freezer but the cans in the cupboard showed an appreciation of quality. Furniture was good and the fabrics unworn.

There remained the question of where I was to sleep. I was tempted to borrow one of Nellie's nighties and her bed, but the prospect of a sudden thaw enabling her to return, though unlikely, was so dreadful that I contented myself with borrowing a quilt made with real duck-down. The day had slipped away and by the time that I had drafted my report and written and sent last night's email I was pooped. I slept on the couch and woke early with a crick in my neck. I seem to remember being roused by somebody trying to open the front door, or maybe I was dreaming. I've showered, borrowed breakfast from Thoroughly Nasty Nellie, made myself presentable and while awaiting Ian's return am taking the chance to update you.

I may as well admit, Sandy, that I am not your usual happy bunny. I have no wish to get involved in somebody else's murder and shall strain every sinew to escape back to my comfortable niche with the dog unit. But Ian, I fear, is determined or hang on to me, or more probably Pippa. He seems to credit the tyke with almost magical powers.

Is your leg really mending properly this time? When are you going to do your stuff in court and be free to return to your loving,

Honeypot?

7 January, evening

Darling Sandy – if you emailed me again, it hasn't caught up with me yet.

This morning came in bright and clear but frosty – a belated Christmas card scene. It must have snowed again during the night because the snow was deeper and yesterday's tracks had disappeared. I had my shower, resumed yesterday's clothes and then saw to the dogs, who had spent a comfortable night in the kitchen. I noticed that there was tinned cat food in the kitchen cupboard and a cat basket in the utility room so it can be assumed that a cat belongs with the house. Was it scared away by violence? Or do we have another mysterious disappearance on our hands? When we re-open the grave site, will another and tinier corpse be revealed?

The first arrival was the local farmer, a coarse but friendly man named Hapless whose house and farm buildings are only a field or two away from this house. He has lived alone since the death of both his parents within a week of one another, several years ago. He works the farm with the help of casual labour and the occasional contractor, but I gather that he was very much under the thumbs of very old-fashioned parents and he is still very slow to bring his farming practices up to date. He keeps a few pigs and cattle but most of the farm is mixed arable. I already knew him because I had visited him in connection with the deer rifle on his firearm certificate and he sold me half a milk-fed pig that June and I butchered between us for the freezer. (You've eaten some of it.) He's a very fit-looking man, as farmers often are what with good food and physical work, rather stocky with a dark and brooding air and a stubble which would look deliberate on a more urban man but on him was probably due to neglect. Ian had phoned him up to bring his tractor over and clear the driveway to Stoneleigh House. (This is Stoneleigh House, in case I haven't mentioned it.)

His instructions, as explained by Ian to me in an early phone-call, were to remove the upper layers of snow from the gravel in front of the house but to go no deeper for fear of destroying the evidence, if any, lying below. Ian had not told him anything about the absence of Nellie and her partner, so Mr Hapless was both curious and uncomprehending and I had to restrain him from scraping the snow right down to the gravel. (Or was he hoping to destroy evidence? I must suggest this to Ian.) The ground was now featureless and my recollection of the layout in front of the house, as seen before the bulk of the snowfall, was fading, so under my direction he probably wrecked several flowerbeds. God help me if vital clues are buried under the mountains of shifted snow. They won't thaw out until about April. I breakfasted on Nellie's bacon and eggs to the tune of the farmer's diesel.

News and rumour would soon be flying around, so the moment seemed ripe to begin enquiries. I took him inside (through the back door but avoiding the utility room), fed him tea in the kitchen and asked him the obvious questions. He had not seen either of the couple for several days – he was vague about how long. He knew Mr Duffus, had met him several times in the local pub. Duffus, he believed, was only in the mid-forties but taken an early medical retirement from a senior job in a major oil company. The two had exchanged pints and got on well.

Nellie was a different kettle of fish. He put her age at thirty-five. He could not find a good word to say for her except that she had an undeniable sexual magnetism. (He put it rather more forcefully than that but I would not sully your eyes or ears, Sandy, by repeating his exact words with agricultural similes.) I thought that he was rather enjoying telling me all this. He stated quite frankly that if she had been done away with it was no more than she deserved. Trouble had started soon after she and Duffus had moved into Stoneleigh House when, noticing that one of the farmer's beasts was limping, she had reported a case of foot-and-mouth to absolutely every authority that could possibly be interested. The vet had already been called to treat an injured hoof, but the farmer had still suffered endless official harassment. Nellie had further complained to him constantly about the smell of pigs, smoke from stubble-burning, noise of cattle, mud on the road and so on and so forth. Conversely, although Hapless, or so he said, had tried hard to be a good neighbour, his approaches to

her about the assaults of her cat on his poultry and about gates
left open during her searches for the cat had been met only by
denials and abuse. That, as I recalled it, was about par for the
course. He left, promising help and asking if I wanted another
half-pig because he will be killing one soon. We'll have to see if
we can arrive at an arrangement.

The dogs were in need of a good walk. Pippa would have been
all right but spaniels can turn themselves into snowballs, so I kept
them on the area cleared by Mr Hapless and hoped that their
deposits would not be obliterating any clues. One consolation
was that anything Pippa could have eaten or rolled in was still
covered by snow. It was bitterly cold and even the dogs were glad
to come indoors again.

Ian delayed his own arrival until he could be sure that Mr
Hapless had done his ploughing and had also dug out the two
cars at the gateway. To be fair, Ian was also starting enquiries by
way of the National Intelligence Model and obtaining instructions from Edinburgh. These latter consisted mostly of telling
him not to do what he had already done and to do what he
intended to do anyway.

Ian did at least manage to bring my car back without any damage, though heavily laden with constabulary flab. He was followed by a police Land Rover with more people and (Heaven be
praised!) the mortuary van (slightly dented) with Dr Waller. The
body was carried out on a stretcher and dispatched to Newton
Lauder in the care of the pathologist. Everybody else heaved a
sigh of relief.

We now had one Forensics man who had made it through
from Edinburgh, one SOCO, the same two DCs and four uniformed constables, these latter being all that the local super was
able or willing to lend. Edinburgh was not going to risk a mobile
incident room on the roads as they are, so Ian will have to make
do for the moment with the house and, later, with the one-time
gymnasium in Police HQ. He had also spoken, apparently, to all
of my several lords and masters in Edinburgh and has permission
to keep me for as long as is needed. Arrangements have been
made about my workload back at the dog unit. This, I know only

too well, means that everything will go ahead without anybody recording anything and I will have to clear up the mess whenever I get back. Thank you very much, Ian! I feel like an unexplained parcel in a Belfast pub.

The first task, obviously, had been to get the body on its way to a post-mortem. Once that was dispatched in the van, we had a conference in the temporary incident room. Taking more liberties with the property of the owners, I had lit a fire in the room and the two dogs were curled up in front of it.

Ian opened by saying that Messrs O'Brian and Gold (the SOCO and the Forensics technician) could make a study of as much of the site as had been sheltered by the tarpaulin. They could have DC McFadden to assist, witness and record. The rest of the area was now covered to a depth almost equalling the height of the average Wellington boot, so no further searching would be practicable. It was becoming an ever-safer assumption that something was amiss with the couple from Stoneleigh House and the probability of a link with the corpse was increasing. Just what had happened to the other occupant was anybody's guess, but the couple seemed to have been missing for several days so that the possibility of a survivor beneath the snow seemed impossible.

On that assumption, house-to-house enquiries could now begin. In this, he added with a mischievous sidelong glance at me, he had the support of the Edinburgh Detective Superintendent now nominally in charge of the case, DS Blackhouse.

(That, as you can imagine, Sandy, made my day. Although I had progressed from being Mr Blackhouse's whipping-girl to being teacher's pet, I still can not stand the man and had hoped to steer well clear of him. The only consolation was that he was monitoring us from Edinburgh for the moment and could be expected to exert control from the comfort of his office until the thaw or until there was thunder to be stolen, whichever came first.)

So far, Ian said, nothing had emerged from police records concerning the couple. He had followed up the phone-call to the garage but no taxi had been to the house for several weeks. Mr Duffus had been bitching about the bill for some work on one of the cars. The last incoming call had been from a Mr French in the village about an invitation to play bridge.

Ian then said that I seemed to have had most contact with the locality and could explain the geography and the personalities, starting with the missing pair.

Mr Duffus is or was a person who would not have stood out in a crowd and I told them so. My recollection of Nellie, and of what her acquaintances had said about her, was coming back, red hair, green eyes and all. I remembered her as superficially friendly to other women. With men she was flirtatious and exuded an aura of sexuality. Her figure was moderately good but she managed to make the most of it. She would wear a perfectly respectable dress that somehow managed to flatter her curves. She might have been in Marks and Sparks tights and a pantygirdle, for all I knew, but there was something about her to suggest that under that dress were lace pants and stocking-tops. (I don't know how she did it and I suppose it's too late now to find out.) I gave them a slightly Bowdlerised version of this general opinion, but I'm sure you'll know exactly what I mean. She was reputed to have the devil's own temper if crossed.

My contact with the area had been months earlier when Ian had had me acting as Firearms Officer, but when I thought about it I could recall a lot of detail. I started by summarising the location of the farm and what I had managed to extract from the farmer. I went on to explain that the road past Stoneleigh House ran for about a mile away from Newton Lauder and met another road at the tiny village where Nellie had lived before her affections and companionship were transferred to Mr Duffus. This was the road to which Pippa had led me from the grave site. The village of Kelvinside, I said, took its name from Kelvin Water and this was purely a local name and nothing to do with Glasgow. The village comprised only a few houses, a church which had been taken over as a furniture workshop and a remarkably good pub. At the mention of the excellent bar meals served by the pub there was a stirring of interest.

To be honest, Sandy, I had a much clearer recollection of the dogs pertaining to each house than of the people, but I had more sense than to say so. I just used the dogs as a sort of mnemonic and found that the method brought most of the people back to my mind.

I said, as nearly as I can remember my exact words, 'From this direction, you come first to a group of cottages on the left. The first seems to be occupied by an old woman. The other two have been knocked together and they – or it – is or are occupied by a young couple with a fat golden retriever. They look like first-time buyers in the process of doing the place up. After that comes the pub. Then there are two fairly substantial houses. The first of those is owned by a Mr Farquhar. He has a large German shepherd. He also has three shotguns and a rifle, so I've made his acquaintance. His certificates were in order, his security was well above the minimum and I found him a rather pleasant chatterbox. I met him again when I had lunch in the pub and he introduced me to his neighbour, one Kenneth French, the man who made the last phone-call to Stoneleigh House. I didn't meet Mrs Farquhar and I don't know whether there's a Mrs French. I assume not, because he chatted me up fairly aggressively and invited me on a date to a rock concert.'

'Did you go?' Bright asked.

'No.' I said firmly. 'I did not. The man fancies himself a damn sight more than I do. Nor do I enjoy rock music. Then there's the former church, where a down-to-earth character called Jasper Dunn runs a workshop. He lives in the former Manse behind the church with a very old corgi.'

'I've heard of him,' Ian said. 'Doesn't he make furniture or something?'

'Something is right. He makes reproduction furniture. If a stately home has a dozen matching Jacobean chairs and two of them get damaged by fire or woodworm, they come to Dunn for matching replacements. I'm told that only an expert could tell the difference. He also restores and polishes. Mr Calder – he was my landlord while I lived in Newton Lauder – used to take furniture to him for refinishing.

'There's one house beyond the church. That's where Nellie used to live; in fact I understand that her estranged husband is still there.'

'We'll have to see if he has a photograph of her. You haven't seen one in this house?' (I shook my head). 'I take it that this is Mr Duffus?' Ian got up and lifted a frame down from the mantel. It showed a portly but not undistinguished looking man chatting with another who I had no difficulty in recognising as a well known rock singer.

'The less dissipated one,' I confirmed. 'There's another cottage beyond Arnoldson's house. I think it's where the cleaning lady lives.'

There were no questions. Ian then spelled out the day's action plan. I was to have DC Bright for company and we were to search the two cars and then go to the village and begin house-to-house enquiries. Ian, with one of the uniformed constables, would make his own search of the house and then settle down to study the papers and make a few phone-calls in the hope of tracking down a next-of-kin for each of the missing pair.

He was interrupted by a call from a competent female voice, speaking on behalf of the pathologist, Dr Waller. The post-mortem would take some time but in the meantime he thought to let us know that the body had been definitely male. He was taking an impression of the teeth and the competent female was about to phone the local dentists in the hope of finding and consulting the dentist to Mr Duffus – she hoped that Ian was in agreement. He was.

The news was rather a surprise. When a couple vanish, it is often assumed that one has killed the other and the woman is usually cast as the victim. (I can't think why except that we are gentle and loving souls not given to violence, but don't count on it.)

Ian resumed. Bright and I would take the village. The remaining PCs were to visit the scattered cottages to ask a sequence of questions that Ian would spell out for them. I pointed out that I had never been properly off duty since yesterday morning, that I had not adequately slept or bathed or changed and that I would be leaving at dusk in order to arrive home in reasonable time. Ian reluctantly agreed but insisted that I return tomorrow 'for as long as it takes' and he promised that he – and his wife – would provide me with a bed. I could think of a thousand reasons why I would prefer to get back to my routine, but none that would have washed with Ian. I capitulated with as much grace as I could pretend.

The garage was approached from the house by way of a short passage. It was just the sort of useful space that we ought to have at our house if there was some way of getting a car off the road. The cars – a Volvo estate and a Ford compact – were both nearly new. They held very little of interest, just the usual debris that a driver tends to drop. The larger car smelled of rather good cigars. The smaller car reeked of the same expensive perfume as had been on the tights and which was also detectable in the Volvo. We left the cars and sealed the garage. Forensics could gather up the toffee papers and vacuum the mats.

I told DC Bright to sit in the Range Rover, ready for our trip to the village, and I re-entered the house to fetch the two dogs. We were leaving by the front door when Hugo, the spaniel, suddenly sat, facing the door of a small cloakroom, and refused to budge. Pippa looked at him curiously but, remembering that he was in training as a sniffer, I took notice. The cloakroom, I was sure, had been searched and its only interest for me had been that there seemed to have been enough coats, both warm and waterproof, to satisfy the needs of any couple, which again suggested that they had not walked out in any normal manner into the January weather. The spaniel followed me in and sat again, looking up toward a high shelf. Pippa imitated her, showing interest.

The shelf held only hats and gloves and I had seen Bright poking through them. There were several expensive scarves hanging with the coats but a rough, woollen scarf was rolled up at one end of the shelf. I took it down and unrolled in. Inside, neatly wrapped in foil, was a small block of cannabis resin. I let both dogs have a sniff and a reward.

As you can imagine, the processes of calling Ian, getting witnesses to the find and bagging it for Forensics took some more precious minutes. By the time that the dogs were back in the car and we had made our way cautiously over freshly ploughed roads to the village, noon had arrived. The village is a single row of houses on one side of the road, facing open country and some magnificent trees. I remembered it as a pretty spot in summer. Now, with the snow lying clean on roofs and gardens and trees, it was definitely picture-postcard material. Paths and pavements had been cleared, apparently by the residents themselves.

From my previous visit, I remembered that most of the mid-day drinkers and diners tended to arrive later. If we wanted a quick and private snack, now was the hour.

Sure enough, the cosy bar was empty and the landlady, Mrs Doughty, was pleased to make toasted sandwiches and mugs of tea. It was an excellent chance to conduct a first interview, so I invited her to sit with us for a minute. She is a roly-poly widow in her fifties with a jolly manner but a firm hand with unruly customers. DC Bright was happy to concentrate on his lunch and a pint of draught while I asked the questions.

Yes, she knew Mr Duffus and his partner (this with a disapproving sniff). She knew that they were missing because Mrs Macindoe, the cleaning lady at Stoneleigh House, helped her out with cleaning the inn and behind the bar at peak times. But word of the body buried in the woodland had not yet reached the village. I tried to probe very gently without giving anything away, but as far as I could determine nobody had mentioned seeing smoke or firelight in the woods, but the dense conifers and underbrush would have made that unlikely.

Yes, she knew the lady's husband. Mr Arnoldson came in for a half-pint and a sandwich at lunchtime on most days. The poor man had been made redundant from his previous job and seemed to be living on a pension and compensation, helping out in the furniture workshop for pocket money while he wondered what to do with his life. Mr Duffus looked in now and then but she hadn't seen him since Tuesday. Mrs Arnoldson had been banned from the inn for some months, but although the ban was now lifted she hardly ever came, perhaps because she knew that Mrs Doughty disapproved of her flighty habits. (One suspects a touch of jealousy here. I think that Mrs Doughty rather fancied being a sexpot if only she had the youth, the figure and the nerve.) But they had come in together about a week earlier. When I asked the reason for the earlier ban, her face darkened. It required some gentle pressure and not a little smarm before she would open up. There had been an altercation in the bar one evening. Mrs French (so there was a Mrs French!) had taken Mrs Arnoldson to task for spreading rumours and Mrs Arnoldson had seized a walking stick belonging to Mr Duffus and would have laid into Mrs French if she had not been restrained by three of the men who happened to be in the bar at the time.

DC Bright, either out of genuine clumsiness or putting on an act – I am never quite sure with him – asked what Mr Duffus had got that would tempt a woman to leave her husband. Mrs Doughty's answer was brief and to the point. 'Money,' she said. And if we'd like to know what *he* wanted of *her*, she would tell us. The answer was what men always want. There!

This would have been an interesting topic to pursue although I already knew what men always want. Women want it too, but not quite so overtly. (Hurry home, Sandy.) After a few more minutes it was clear that if she had answers to the other questions on Ian's list she was not going to produce them. There were signs that the lunchtime trade was about to begin. We settled up and left.

Friday afternoon is a bad time for door-to-door enquiries in the country. The need to shop for the weekend combines with the tradition of payday even after the menfolk have become self-employed or salaried. The furniture workshop in the old church was wrapped in the quiet lassitude that overtakes businesses during the lunch hour. Several cars were parked outside on tarmac that had been cleared of snow the hard way, by shovel, but only a dim-witted teenager was minding the shop. Mr Arnoldson had gone home for lunch, he said, and Mr Dunn was away with the van but would be back some time.

I could hear sounds suggesting that staff were lunching off sandwiches in a back room, but I knew of old that if people are disturbed at a meal they will give you the shortest possible answers in order to get back to the trough. I said that we would return.

Two doors to the right, we found Mrs Macindoe, the cleaning lady, at home. She is lean and stiff, starched even to the greying hair. Her cottage was small but very clean and neat and although the garden was in its winter sleep I could tell from the shrubs peeping above the snow that it was just as well kept. She welcomed us into a comfortably overfurnished room and forced more tea on us. Her husband, she said, worked in Newton Lauder and would not be home until six. She cleaned for Mr Duffus and his lady, twice a week, four hours a day. The rest of her working hours were spent at the inn.

It seemed that Mrs Macindoe went around in blinkers. The information that she could furnish was of the most basic nature. The vanished couple had seemed contented. They bickered occasionally, but who didn't? The madam was fussy about Mrs Macindoe's work but not too fussy in her own; it was left to the cleaner to pick up dirty clothes and do the laundry, wash up dishes that had often been left for a day or more, and to do the dusting and hoovering. I said that the place was clean and tidy when we found it, and Mrs Macindoe was sure that the couple must have been away since her previous visit on Tuesday morning. They did not do much entertaining but often went away for a week at a time, she had no idea where. When they did so, they would always leave a key with Mrs Macindoe, along with clear instructions as to when they would return and what preparations she was to make.

I took her through her information again and again but she knew, or claimed to know, nothing else about the couple's habits and activities, nor about what friends or acquaintances they might have locally. She never looked at any documents nor listened to any phone-calls. She seemed quite open and above-board but such a total lack of feminine curiosity was a bit much to swallow. In my experience, domestic staff know all that there is to know about their employers and sometimes more.

Back at the furniture workshop, it seemed that Mr Dunn had not yet returned and Mr Arnoldson had gone home again, feeling unwell. The Arnoldson house showed no sign of life and there was no answer to the doorbell. We sat in the Range Rover for a while, compiling a report on my laptop. When we gave up for the day, I drove Bright to the 'factory' in Newton Lauder and left him with the disk to print off and leave on Ian's desk.

So here I am, back home strictly for one night only, packed for a return visit to Newton Lauder and missing you, Sandy. The house seems empty without you and even June hardly begins to fill the void.

Lots of love and you-know-what,

Honeypot.

8 January

Sandy – I am writing this from the spare bedroom of DI Ian Fellowes, formerly my boss and once again temporarily granted that honour. His wife, Deborah, insisted that she was happy to have me. You'll remember that Deborah and I had more than a few drinks together while I was living over her father's gun shop in Newton Lauder. You may also recall that the Felloweses took on a black Lab puppy which was born in my care (and in my flat) at that time. That dog has grown into a very handsome Lab of the small and eager type. Known as Beel – short for Beelzebub, because he was so full of mischief as a puppy. You can still see the teeth-marks in some of the furniture-legs.

Ian was most insistent that I bring Pippa and Hugo, the spaniel, back with me. I think he hoped that Beel might learn the art of tracking or drug-sniffing by example, but since Ian has concentrated solely on teaching the dog retrieving, and not without some success, I have my doubts. Anyway, the three seemed to get along all right once Beel made it clear that this was his home and the others were only guests.

June helped me to get on the road before sparrow-fart on a freezing January morning, with the two dogs already walked and brushed and the car full of boots, waterproofs, dog beds, bags of kennel meal and, almost as an afterthought, changes of clothing. I did not dare to look in at the office – whatever is or is not being done there, knowing wouldn't change anything except my peace of mind. A low, bright sun made driving difficult but I made it to the HQ in Newton Lauder in time for Ian's morning briefing. This took place, as I had been warned, in the general purpose room that used to be a gymnasium and function room before the old building was overpowered by the new. Not only was the Victorian room familiar but I recognised the phones and the computer that had been brought in again to create a rather downmarket incident room. The excruciating chairs were also only too familiar.

The team was building up. Ian had managed to coax an experienced collator out of Edinburgh and several experienced PCs from here and there.

I know that you like details, Sandy. Sometimes you prove helpful, either by deduction or out of that phenomenal memory of
yours. Also, writing it all down helps to clarify it in my memory
Ian's briefing and action plan were fairly lengthy so I'll summarise his main points.

1. Dental evidence has now confirmed that the corpse
is that of George Duffus. The body had been substan-
tially damaged by fire and prolonged heat but the
pathologist had found a broken vertebra in the neck.
This could have been the cause of death – it would certainly have proved fatal. Tissue samples have been sent
for DNA testing, in the hope that the DNA and any
possible toxins haven't been cooked out of existence.
There was no soot in the lungs, so death had definitely
preceded the fire.

2. The SOCOs had discovered a hair and faint traces of
blood on the brick surround of the sitting room
hearth. (I flinched at that point, wondering what evidence might have been lost due to my recklessly light-
ing the fire, although I did examine the fireplace first.
Ian said not a word of reproof.) The hair matched one
from a man's hairbrush in the master bedroom.

3. I had forgotten to look in the dishwasher. It contained dishes, not yet washed, which judging from the
state of the adhering traces of food had been eaten off
at Tuesday's lunch or possibly evening meal. There was
no milk on the doorstep, but milk was never delivered
and Mrs Arnoldson was in the habit of buying milk in
Newton Lauder. Similarly, the couple did not get a
delivery of a daily paper. The last newspaper in the
house was Tuesday's.

4. It seems a reasonable working assumption, therefore, that Mr Duffus died around Tuesday afternoon or
evening or that night. This accords with the pathologist's tentative opinion although he did say that, after
the fire, the lapse of time and the changes of temperature at unknown intervals, he would not quarrel with
anyone who suggested that he was days out in either
direction. It also seems likely that either he was killed
by his lover who then fled; or that he was killed by
some other party and that her absence is explained by
her death, removal or fear, but in asking questions we
must be open to other possibilities. It is still possible,
for instance, that Thoroughly Nasty Nellie is away on
a visit or in hospital and does not yet know of her partner's murder. Whether Nellie could have carried his
body for that distance unaided requires investigation.

5. The body had been fired with petrol and then surrounded with charcoal. The petrol was high octane
pump petrol showing, on analysis, no trace of rubber
from a siphoning tube. Anyone might draw petrol from
a car by disconnecting a fuel line and many people carry
a can of spare petrol, so there's little help to be had
there. We should be on the lookout for petrol vehicles
that had lost fuel and for anyone in the habit of keeping barbecue briquettes.

6. The last phone-call made to Stoneleigh House was
traced to Kenneth French. He will be asked for details.

7. Examination of the Stoneleigh House refuse bin
turned up no information except that Nellie leaned
heavily on prefabricated meals from the supermarket.
The house itself was equally uninformative. Nobody
knew enough about Nellie's personal possessions to
tell which of them might be missing; but the absence of
her credit cards looks ominous.

8. As a matter of routine, I had included the half-moon
of mud with the few samples collected with the
Forensics team. This is reported to contain ordinary
clay mud, particles of china and a few grains of pine
sawdust.

With most of the evidence lost under the snow, possibly for ever,
many of the usual avenues for investigation were closed. The
action plan, therefore, said Ian, had to lean heavily on door-to-
door enquiries. He and I would concentrate on the village but
appointments had been made for us to see the local solicitor and
the manager of the only bank in Newton Lauder. This, it was
hoped, would also settle the vexed question of next-of-kin. Ian
apportioned out the houses and cottages round about and also
the more likely shops and businesses in Newton Lauder. A small
team would be left in Stoneleigh House, to field calls and to
check out the numbers in the book of addresses and phone numbers. And no statements whatever were to be given to any of the
media without Ian's personal authorisation.

No questions were asked, which suggested that the team
understood the action plan either fully or not at all. Time will tell.
The meeting was dismissed. Ian, who values his comforts, had
left his car for Deborah's use and walked in, intending to travel
with me in the Range Rover. (It would have served him right if
I'd arrived in June's old Mini.)

Saturday is not always a good day for catching people at home,
but in foul weather they tend to stay in and watch sport or a
video.

We went first to the former church, where we found the furniture workshop in full swing. A clerkess was working in a cubicle
just inside the main door and she directed us to Mr Dunn's office.
We passed a youth who was French polishing a bureau and,
deeper in the building, we could hear power tools at work. The
whole place smelled of polish and glue and sawdust. Mahogany
sawdust in particular has a singularly horrid smell. Mr Dunn took
us into his tiny office. He is a fair-haired and slightly drooping
man in his early thirties. His bad posture hides the fact that he is

quite tall.

He seemed to want to chat about anything but the local mystery and Ian allowed him to ramble for a minute or two. He had started his working life as an IT consultant, he told us. But he had always preferred to work where he could see some physical result at the end of the day and, having had a flair for woodwork, he had obtained a grant and set up the workshop. At that stage, he straightened up and would have given us an immediate tour, but Ian brought him back to the point. He had known about the disappearance but expressed horror at the news of George Duffus's death. Not, he explained, that he had known Mr Duffus well, only to repair a Victorian sewing-box for him. He had been acquainted with Mrs Arnoldson through refinishing an oak table for her – before the change in arrangements, he added quickly. He has one of those expressive mouths and it had a definite curl.

'You don't like the lady,' Ian suggested.

'Does it show? I find it hard to like any lady who leaves a trail of sex hormones on the air behind her.' He glanced at me and evidently decided to pursue that topic no further, so I shall never know whether he did or did not include me. 'I can't forgive her for the way she treated my friend Simon Arnoldson. Not that I'd wish her any harm and she did do him a big favour by getting out of his life. She'd had a lover for some time, or so they say, and I don't think that it was Duffus.' Ian asked him to explain and he said that sometimes, when Simon Arnoldson was away on business, a car would meet his wife outside the village. Mr Dunn had never seen the car and he did not know anyone who had seen it, because the driver had seemed careful to stay out of sight. From the sound, which he had heard more than once in the distance, it was definitely not the smooth and quiet Rover that George Duffus had been running at the time. 'But if you want an enemy's view of her, have a word with Kenneth French. Don't tell him that I gave you the hint.'

Bearing in mind the sawdust in the mud sample from Stoneleigh House, Ian probed a little, but the workshop never made furniture in pine and the last repairs or refinishing to pine furniture had been years ago. We would be welcome, said Mr

Dunn, to take samples from around the workshop for comparison.

Dunn had spent Tuesday afternoon, he said, at work in his office or in conference with Simon Arnoldson. He had spent the evening at home alone. He had little more to say and none of it to the point. We again declined his offer of a tour and borrowed his office to interview Mr Arnoldson.

Arnoldson is middle-aged, mild-mannered and balding. Despite a kindly expression and a ready and pleasant smile, I could understand how a woman might eventually find him unexciting.

He absolutely denied any feelings of enmity towards his estranged wife. 'We're still on good terms,' he said. 'There's no feeling of awkwardness at all.' (I noticed the present tense. Does he have reason to believe that she is still alive?) 'To be honest, although it would have been cruel to tell her so, I was relieved when she went. Financially, of course. And she's a champion non-stop talker.'

'What did she most often talk about?' Ian asked.

'Good God! I don't know. Nobody has enough time to listen to endless babble and her subject matter fell far short of interesting me. My wife has a spiteful tendency,' he said confidentially. 'She doesn't mean half of it, but her tongue runs away with her.'

'We're told that she could turn violent if upset,' I said.

Arnoldson nodded reluctantly. 'She can lash out. She's sorry afterwards.'

Or says she is, I thought. 'Do you miss her in other ways?' I asked.

'Not for the work she did around the house, that's for sure,' he said with a wry smile. He looked at me shyly, weighing me up. 'If you mean sexually, my libido doesn't run my life and I found her demands exhausting. Is that what you wanted to know?'

'More or less,' I said.

'I wouldn't have killed George Duffus to get her back. I might have done something rash to *not* get her back, but the question never arose.'

Nothing else of interest came out of our questions. He had last seen his wife about two weeks earlier, when Mr Duffus's car had let him down and Jasper Dunn had found the pair stranded beside the main road in the rain. Dunn had picked them up in his van and, being in a hurry, had brought them to the village for Mr Arnoldson to drive the rest of the way home in the firm's other vehicle, a people carrier.

He confirmed that he had spent the afternoon in the workshop, much of it with Jasper Dunn. He, too, had been alone all evening. (If they had given each other shockproof alibis, I would have been intensely suspicious.) On the way out, we consulted the firm's diary, which seemed to be in general agreement, at least about the afternoon in question. I had intended to take a sample of sawdust, but a glance around the building showed that there were a hundred holes and corners where traces of sawdust might have lingered for years. We would leave it to the Forensics technicians.

Ian paused beside the car. 'We'll give the dogs a walk along the street,' he said.

'Any particular reason?'

'Only desperation. We've so little to go on that we can't afford to miss a trick. Can you trust both dogs to sit outside a door?'

I said that I could, hoping that it was the truth. We walked back along the short street. I can read Pippa's body-language like a book by now and her reactions were only to the smell of food and other dogs. The spaniel just looked bored. At the furthest cottage, the old woman came to the door. She looks rather like Grandma in the old Giles cartoons and is just as cantankerous. We were not invited inside, which was rather a relief from the appearance of the place. She made it quite clear that she knew nothing about her neighbours and that, if she did, she would not have passed it on to the horrible police. I thought that it was inconceivable that an old woman could live in a village and not observe the comings and goings, but if she was determined to obstruct us it would be better to play a waiting game. We returned to the street. Rather than have a personal radio quacking confidential messages in the street Ian was relying on his mobile phone, which chose that moment to play its little tune.

He walked a few paces away from the houses for privacy before answering it. He returned, looking annoyed. 'A message from Control,' he said. 'A big wheel from the Fraud Squad is coming through shortly.'

'It can't be anything to do with this case,' I said.

'One would suppose not. Just the distraction that I needed at the beginning of a case with no leads! And Mr Blackhouse will be joining us for the meeting and a discussion of this case. You'd better keep my dates with the lawyer and the bank manager for me.'

I tried to hide my surprise. It takes a lot to fetch Mr Blackhouse out at a weekend, and especially so in horrible weather, but I suppose the chance to impress the big wheels was not to be missed. 'I can do that,' I said.

Ian looked at his watch. 'We have time for one more visit, if we make it a quickie.' But his phone chose that moment to demand attention. Ian took a few steps away from me again. I heard his voice go up. He returned in a hurry. 'It seems that we don't have time,' he said. 'Back to the car.'

He took one of the leads from me and we almost galloped back and slung two very surprised dogs into the back of the Range Rover. When we were moving he said, 'There's been a ransom demand. Get us back to Stoneleigh House.'

By then the roads had been sanded and salted, so we could make good time. We were back at the house before he had begun to amplify the facts. It seemed to be an occasion for haste and I think my driving may have taken his breath away.

DC Bright was holding the fort at Stoneleigh House along with a woman PC of forbidding aspect. They wore paper gloves and a small assortment of opened, incoming letters was neatly arranged on the table. Prominent was a missive on typing paper, printed in bold letters by a computer. 'WE HAVE YOUR WIFE,' it said. 'NO POLICE AND NO PUBLICITY OR SHE DIES. WAIT FOR INSTRUCTIONS.' The envelope, addressed also by computer, had been posted in Edinburgh, first class postage.

Ian stared out of the window. We were each busy with our own thoughts. 'The media know that there's been a body but they don't know whose,' Ian said, 'or if word's leaked out it hasn't had time to reach the public yet.'

'Two reporters have been here,' the woman PC said. 'We sent them off.'

Ian grunted. 'The first job is to make sure that word of Duffus's death doesn't get around. I'll phone Edinburgh and get them started placing an absolute embargo on everything connected with this case.' He caught my eye. 'You'd better get back to the village and warn Arnoldson and Dunn to keep their mouths shut.'

'You think it's genuine?' I asked him.

'We have to assume that it is. And if the kidnappers learn that her partner's dead, I won't give much for her chances.'

My immediate thought was that it was a kidnapping gone wrong. Mr Duffus had been killed in the process but they had gone ahead anyway, perhaps to suggest that the death had been none of their doing. In which case Ian would be right, Nellie's chances would be slim.

I asked Ian what else he wanted me to do.

'You look after the house-to-house,' he said. 'We'll have to broaden the enquiries. You know the sort of thing. Anything unusual happening, unfamiliar cars or strange phone-calls. And see the solicitor and the bank manager. I'll deal with Edinburgh and the visitors and join up with you if and when I can.'

I managed to contact two comparatively bright PCs who were on a tour of the least likely cottages, stretched their remit slightly and told them to tackle the village. I caught Jasper Dunn and Simon Arnoldson before they left the workshop to start the weekend. They quite understood that Nellie's life might depend on discretion and they seemed to be sincere in their promises of silence. They had talked only to their staff and they promised to impress on them the need for absolute discretion.

Then I drove into Newton Lauder with my mind buzzing. My first thought was that the phone-calls were unlikely to be helpful So many calls are made from untraceable mobiles these days. Also you get so many hang-up calls from call-centre canvassers who autodial a dozen or more calls at a time, give the sales pitch to the first person to answer and allow the rest to disconnect. If Simon Arnoldson was innocent but would prefer his wife dead, he might very well whisper the news of Duffus's death to a journalist. Was Nellie still alive or should we be looking for a second grave under the snow? Had I, in fact, walked over the top of it?

There was almost an hour to spare before I was due at the bank. I shook off the more morbid thoughts, which did not leave a great deal of constructive thinking to be getting on with, and got a bar lunch at the hotel.

The bank manager grumbled at being dragged out on a Saturday. I think he was on the point of complaining that we had loused up his weekend's golf before he remembered that golf would have been out of the question in that weather. In any case, I knew by his reputation that he welcomed any excuse to get out of the house at a weekend. With George Duffus certified as deceased, he made no objection to revealing the state of the dead man's two bank accounts but these were uninformative. They told a story of regular payments from a large, private pension fund and from well chosen PEPs and TESSAs; and there were equally regular withdrawals roughly commensurate with what I guessed to be the couple's standard of living. There were no payments to a building society, nor any that could be taken for rental, so I concluded that he had owned Stoneleigh House outright. I collected copies of his recent bank statements for more detailed study. The bank manager promised to keep George Duffus's death under his hat, but I was sure that as more and more people were admitted to the secret it would inevitably be public knowledge soon. I thanked him anyway and left him to return to his houseful of children – or not, if he preferred to use us as an excuse for playing hooky.

The solicitor, Mr Enterkin, was an acquaintance and almost an old friend, (literally old, and fat with it, but always on the ball). He was waiting for me in his old-fashioned office overlooking the Square. He at least did have one or two surprises to offer.

To start with, Mr Duffus had a wife still living – in Inverness, with the proprietor of a large garage and workshop. Duffus's extant will was in favour of the wife but he had been on the point of changing it in favour of Thoroughly Nasty Nellie. Mr Enterkin also acted for Nellie and first steps had been taken towards a divorce which Mr Arnoldson was contesting, on the grounds that if there was any divorcing to be done he was going to be the one to do it. This, Mr Enterkin explained, was because Mr Arnoldson was determined that no ex-wife was going to claim a share of the business that he had spent years building up. Nellie's next of kin was her sister in Venice, Italy, living with a hotelier. (It occurred to me in passing that it is the younger generation that marries, though perhaps not always as early as they should; their elders are more likely to cohabit indefinitely. This is not illogical. As the probability of children recedes, there is less need for a formal contract; and, later in life, questions of property loom larger.)

I was free at last. Ian was still closeted with his visitors. Daylight was fading and I wanted to give the dogs a walk and then settle in and unpack my clothes before the folds become permanent. That accomplished, I had several drinks and some nibbles with Deborah, Ian's wife, then settled down in their sitting room and studied Duffus's bank statements in more detail, without turning up any signs of corruption, blackmail or anything else of interest.

I am eager to hear how Ian had got on, but he has only just arrived home in dire need of food, a hot bath and rest, so I must restrain my impatience.

Pippa sends you lots of sloppy kisses. These may not be the benison you might suppose, in view of what she picked up and ate when I walked her. I send mine, which are more hygienic.

Love,

Honeypot

Sunday today, but days off tend to be rare during a murder enquiry. At least I'll be due for some rest days when you finally make it back home. Shall we go away for a few days? Somewhere warm?

Which said, Ian started off the morning conference by referring to the non-murder case that had brought the visit from the Fraud Squad man – a Chief Superintendent. There seems to have been a succession of credit card frauds of mysterious origin. The first that is ever known is when a customer finds a very expensive item of jewellery or similar charged to his account. The item has been ordered by phone, giving all the correct credit card details, and is delivered (with others) to a rented address which by then has been abandoned, each time, long before any enquiry begins. The phone-call is never traceable but the despatch addresses – Edinburgh, Glasgow, occasionally Newcastle and larger towns within that triangle – prove to be accommodation addresses or temporary lets taken in false names and now abandoned. They seem to centre on this very general area. We are to watch for anything suspicious, though just what we could be expected to see remains as mysterious as how the fraudster obtained all the credit card information in the first place, and how the goods are disposed of. Any ideas?

DS Blackhouse had stayed at the hotel overnight, by the way, and sat in on the meeting – as an observer he said, every time that he butted into the discussion. He greeted me like a long-lost daughter although we had seen each other only ten days ago on the occasion when a child went missing near East Calder. (The child turned up in the house of her half-witted grandmother after we had combed miles of countryside and a golf course, and the River Almond had been dragged.) He asked after Pippa and made a point of visiting her in the car after the conference broke up. He even seemed to enjoy having his face licked, which will undoubtedly bring him out in spots, I hope.

Back to the murder and possible kidnapping. Ian had been busy. Forensics, it seems, had also been working late but to little effect. There were no fingerprints on the letter and although there were prints on the envelope they can be assumed to be those of post office staff. (But this will have to be laboriously checked.) Nor was there any DNA on the back of the stamp or the flap of the envelope, which suggests a certain level of sophistication on the part of any kidnappers. Even the postcode was correct. Other traces in the house and cars were of doubtful value. Three sets of fingerprints presumably belong to the occupants of Stoneleigh House and to Mrs Macindoe, the cleaner, who was most indignant at having her prints taken. She was assured several times that they would be destroyed at the end of this case, but I don't think she was convinced.

The media had published the finding of the body before the embargo was in place, but without an identity. Any intelligent kidnapper, however, would probably make the connection, which may explain why no ransom demand has arrived. On the other hand, any ransom demand might now be directed to Mr Duffus's widow in Inverness or to Nellie's sister in Venice – either of whom, on yet another hand, might have a financial motive for disposing of either of the couple. (Which of the two would have the larger motive for murder, or to not ransom Nellie if a demand arrives, might depend on whether Nellie's death, if it has occurred at all, occurred before or after that of Mr Duffus and whether it was known that he had procrastinated over changing his will. Could she be being kept alive in order to avoid any suggestion that she pre-deceased her lover?) The sister has been kept informed. She insists that no ransom demand has been received but will inform us immediately if one arrives. The widow had so far proved unavailable.

The post-mortem examination came up with some minor medical findings such as arthritis and an enlarged prostate, but no signs of violence other than the broken vertebra, nor any signs of drowning or poison. Of course, burning might have destroyed any number of superficial clues.

The identities of the persons concerned in the case have been circulated to other forces and to the Police National Computer, but so far without turning up anything criminal. Enquiries so far have produced little else. A great deal of background information has been gathered from various, possibly reliable, sources.

There have been no reports so far of suspicious or unfamiliar persons or cars. If a body or a kidnap victim was carried out of the district, it would have had to be taken through Newton Lauder. Intensive enquiries have found no witnesses to anything that might point in that direction, but who would remember a nondescript car with the boot closed? There have been no signs of a female having met an untimely end at the right time other than an old lady in Bootle who drowned in her bath. Neighbours, the more likely sources in Newton Lauder and contacts from earlier lives have been questioned and little of interest has emerged except for accounts of Nellie's talent for exacting revenge and making enemies.

I'll attach a note of what's known about the characters so far, just as I took it down at the morning meeting, to this email.

All in all, it looks hopeless with no starting point to get hold of, if I may mix my metaphors. But, though most cases have an immediate and obvious suspect, others always look hopeless until you get that sudden break. Sometimes, of course, the break never comes and the case may be shelved, forever or until advances in forensic science open up a new avenue for investigation. One thing, there is no shortage of people who would cheerfully have seen Nellie burned at the stake. She seems even to have managed to 'put it about a bit' (her husband's words, not mine) without making any real friends. Contrariwise, her temper undoubtedly has a hair trigger. The least disagreement seems to have blown up into a state of war. Much of her spite seems to have been dissipated in mere words, back-stabbing and rumour-mongering, but there are cases of downright malicious acts or even violence. Of some, including a recent outbreak of cat-poisoning, she was only suspected but of others she openly boasted.

As an instance, Kenneth French (who lives just the other side of the furniture workshop from Nellie's estranged husband and her former home) has a small yacht (about four tons) on a trailer in his back garden. Years ago, Nellie had told tales (true or false, we don't know) to Mrs French who then moved out for several months. As a result he fell out with Nellie, to put it mildly. It developed into a slanging-match of epic proportions and in public. French told Nellie that she was all mouth and no knickers. I believe he put it rather more strongly than that and it rankled.

French asked Mr Arnoldson, who has a photocopier, to copy some plans out of a yachting magazine for him. (Very naughty, depriving the designer of his royalty on the design.) Nellie found out and abstracted the photocopies. She had once worked in a design office and was quite able to use drafting instruments. Using white ink, she removed certain lines and dimensions and replaced them before photocopying again. From what French told the interviewing officers, at some length, she slimmed down the bow, fattened the stern and moved the mast and the keel slightly forward. French spent two years building the boat, buying the best of materials through the furniture workshop. He finished the work laboriously, to a very high standard. I have had a look at the furniture, all mahogany, beautifully varnished, and you can't see the joints or get a penknife into the crack around a door or drawer.

When the boat was finally launched, Nellie made a point of being present at the launch at Berwick-on-Tweed. Legend has it that she laughed so hard that she wet her pants. The boat floated with its stern cocked away up in the air and, though ballast eventually brought it back almost to the designed waterline, it sailed like 'steering a cow by the tail', as French put it. He has spent his leisure in the subsequent eighteen months rebuilding the hull with great labour and expense. One has to feel that Nellie's revenge, though excessive, revealed considerable ingenuity, not to say artistry. The interviewing officers admitted that they had been hard put to it not to laugh in French's indignant face and there was some amusement when the story was repeated to the meeting. An immediate reaction was that French was due for serious scrutiny although many others had almost equal motives. One viable theory, of course, is that something nasty was planned for Nellie and Mr Duffus got caught up in it, with fatal consequences.

At this point, DS Blackhouse spoke up. Money, he said, was a much stronger motive than revenge (which tells us something about him!). Nellie's sister should certainly be questioned, and without waiting for her to return to Britain. Did anybody present speak any Italian? He knew from my CV that my Swiss finishing school had left me with a smattering of Italian and I could tell that he was watching me out of the corner of his eye, so I had to put my hand up.

'Ah!' he said. 'So DS Laird must fly out to Venice and make enquiries.' I think he thought he was doing me a favour, but flying around in mid-winter is not my favourite pastime. He then piled Ossa on Pelion by telling me to get HQ in Edinburgh to book my flights. I already knew that sergeants fly tourist class but I had it in mind to pay the difference myself for an upgrade. Well, at least he didn't call me Honeypot. The rain in Italy should be warm.

I am sending this from home. My remaining time in Newton Lauder was limited, but I gave a hand with the collation for the rest of the morning and came home after lunch to see to luggage and tickets and to make arrangements with June for both dogs. I also checked that somebody was doing my work for me – which they are, in a haphazard sort of way. I fly out at some ungodly hour tomorrow morning. But not in your direction, lover. The other way.

Be good. I am being a pillar of virtue. If my bum happens to get pinched in Venice I think I may be able to resist temptation, but there is a limit to how long virtue can be stretched.

Fly home soon to your loving,

Honeypot

9 January – attachment to email.

(The following information has been derived from various sources. These include the individuals themselves but checked as far as possible with original records. All addresses, unless otherwise stated, may be taken as being in or near the village of Kelvinside, Newton Lauder.)

The late George Duffus of Stoneleigh House. Age 46. Born Newton Lauder. Educated Watson's, Edinburgh and Herriot Watt University. Worked for several Internet companies rising to General Manager. Set up own company in Edinburgh designing web sites. Married Pauline (née Eliott) but separated after five years, no children. Invested heavily in private pension policy. Legacy from mother assisted him to afford early retirement and return to Newton Lauder three years ago, soon after which Helena Arnoldson left husband to live with him. Lived a generally quiet life. Enjoyed good food but ate and drank moderately. No known history of mental illness. No previous history of unexplained absences. No criminal record. Next of kin, wife.

Pauline Duffus (née Eliott). 118 Ness View Drive, Inverness. Estranged wife of George Duffus (above). Age 31. Born Leith, Educated Leith Academy. Studied accountancy and worked under the staff auditor of a major oil company until her marriage to George Duffus. Marriage failed. Now living in Inverness with a Donald Macdonald, garage proprietor. No criminal record. Not presently available for interview.

Helena Arnoldson (née Finlay). Missing person. Of Stoneleigh House. Age 33. Born Morningside, Edinburgh. Educated Watson's and Technical College. Frequent job changes, finishing with Hamlyn Design. Married Simon Arnoldson. No children. Marriage unsuccessful. Left husband to move in with George Duffus (above). No known history of mental illness. No previous history of unexplained absences. No criminal record, but several officers remember being called to violent disputes which had calmed down before their arrival. Officers were also called to complaints of cat poisoning. Cats had certainly died of poison but there was no evidence pointing to Mrs Arnoldson and the poison might have been put down for rats. Next of kin and heir, sister, Rebecca, née Finlay but now the Signora Viticelli, Bellavenista Hotel, Venice, Italy.

Simon Arnoldson. Age 49. Broombrae, Kelvinside, Newton Lauder. Estranged husband of the above. Insists that they remain on good terms and that he was friendly with George Duffus, doing his tax returns and partnering him at bridge. Born Dalkeith. Educated Fettes College and Herriot Watt University. Accountancy degree. Took early retirement, largely on health grounds. Still in business in a small way, doing accounts and tax for small local businesses and helping out at the nearby furniture workshop. No criminal record. Had not seen George Duffus or Mrs Arnoldson for over a week.

Jasper Dunn. Age 36. The old Manse, Kelvinside, Newton Lauder. Born Falkirk. Educated Falkirk High and Glasgow University. Degree in Computer Sciences. Most recent employment was with Internet Access. Left to set up Arnoldson Woodworking in the Old Kirk, Kelvinside, Newton Lauder. Unmarried. No criminal record. Business appears modest but interviewer noticed signs of affluence in personal life. Had not seen Mr Duffus or Mrs Arnoldson for about ten days.

Isobel Macindoe. Aged about 50, not prepared to be specific. Bridgeway Cottage, Kelvinside, Newton Lauder. Married. (Husband works in Newton Lauder, spends his leisure fishing or beating for local shoots and so has less contact with Kelvinside residents.) Mrs Macindoe was cleaner to Mr Duffus and partner. Cleaned house as usual, Friday 2nd January. The couple were both present and seemed to be on good terms. No special occurrences. Returned as usual on Tuesday 6th January; house unlocked but unoccupied. This seemed very unusual so notified police. Speaks of Mr Duffus with affection. When she heard that he was dead and that Mrs Arnoldson had disappeared, her first comment was that it was 'just the sort of thing she'd do'. Asked to elaborate, could only make vague references to ructions. It seems that Mrs Arnoldson had given her the sharp edge of her tongue and Mrs Macindoe had retorted with some home truths and threatened to throw up the job. She was the only cleaner prepared to travel as far as Stoneleigh House, so matter was resolved by a grudging apology and a gift from Mr Duffus. She 'helps out' at the inn and sometimes in the Dunn and Arnoldson houses and, according to her, her liking for Mr Duffus and dislike of Mrs Arnoldson is universally reflected.

Maggie Thomson. Aged 86 and apparently proud of it. Hawthorn Cottage, Kelvinside. No information to offer. Major quarrel with Mrs Arnoldson in street stemmed from suggestion by Mrs A that Maggie T was smelly, to which MT replied indignantly, drawing attention to Mrs Arnoldson's perfume. Thereafter the two never passed without an exchange of insults. Mrs A spread a rumour that Mrs T had once had a child due to an incestuous relationship but there seems to be no evidence to support this.

Charles and Janet Able. 28 and 23 respectively. Bridgend Cottage, which is the other half of Maggie Thomson's pair of cottages. Married less than a year. She is pregnant. First-time buyers working hard to renovate the cottage with a view either to trading up or to incorporating Maggie Thomson's cottage when it becomes available. He is an apprentice solicitor with Mr Enterkin. She works as receptionist in Newton Lauder Hotel. Friendly with the Frenches (below). They do not have a good word to say for Mrs Arnoldson but their views appear to be secondhand from the Frenches. Only criminal record is that Charles Able was recently prosecuted for non-payment of a speeding fine.

Kenneth French. Age 41. Kelvinbank, Kelvinside, Newton Lauder. Engineering degree from Glasgow. Married with teenage daughter. Expensive (and beautifully finished) yacht sabotaged by Mrs Arnoldson tampering with plans. Quality timber purchased from furniture workshop. He is connected with oil industry, often offshore. No criminal record.

Priscilla Doughty. Licensee of the inn. Widow, aged 33 by her own account, 46 in fact. Very strict enforcer of the licensing laws, not so fastidious about the morals of occasional residents. Very anxious not to become known as a tattletale but, on the promise that sources would be protected, she opened up. She has overheard most of the local residents discussing Mrs Arnoldson. Kenneth French, in particular, has been outspoken in his anger. In addition to the boat incident, it seems that Mrs Arnoldson accused Mr French and Mr Farquhar of a homosexual relationship on the grounds that they often visit the pub together. General belief is that Mrs Arnoldson, who adores her belligerent cat, resented the fights her cat usually started and set about poisoning neighbours' cats.

Ian and Betty Farquhar. Not immediately available for interview, believed to be on holiday in Switzerland. Aged 46 and 38 respectively. Hollytree, Kelvinside, Newton Lauder. Mr Farquhar travels for an agricultural chemicals firm; Mrs Farquhar is part-time bookkeeper at the Newton Lauder Hotel. They resent Mrs Arnoldson (see above). Neither has any criminal record.

Thomas Hapless. Farmer, Loanend Farm Nr Kelvinside. Age 48. Unmarried. Reputation as a womaniser. Admits to disagreements with Mrs Arnoldson, mostly over cats. No criminal record.

10 January, from Venice

Detective Inspector Ian Fellowes. Re: Credit Card Fraud.

I have received some advice by email, which I now copy to you, concerning the case of credit card fraud now under investigation. The email reads as follows.

It is assumed that the victims have been questioned to determine whether each used the credit card in the same shop or restaurant, opening up the possibility of cloning. Assuming also that efforts have been made to track the culprit through his telephone or accommodation addresses and that these were unsuccessful, the most likely modus operandi would be as follows.

In this instance the cards have not been cloned. It would therefore have been necessary to obtain full credit card details of the victim. The fact that goods have been ordered by phone suggests that the credit card information was obtained by intercepting similar telephone calls. The number of instances suggests that this could not possibly have happened by chance. One possibility would be continuous wire-tapping at a major telephone exchange. Telephone exchange staff should be investigated and the equipment examined.

The victims should also be asked whether they each placed orders and gave credit card details by mobile phone or cordless extension. If so, this opens up the possibility of sophisticated listening equipment. In view of the distribution of victims, the culprit would probably have a small computer and a radio receiver in a van or a car boot, perhaps even a suitcase. The computer could be programmed to monitor randomly selected traffic on normal communication wavelengths, to recognise and store any conversations containing strings of numerals, erasing all other calls.

I hope that the above may prove helpful.

Det Sgt Laird.

10 January, from Venice

Sandy, my angel. Many thanks for your email about the credit card frauds. I've passed your suggestions on to Ian, for onward transmission. The Fraud Squad officers will no doubt have had the same thoughts, but just as surely they will have failed to pass them on to the troops. Your suggestions will at least tell our motley crew what they should be looking out for.

Edinburgh, quite predictably, had booked me a seat in Economy. (Sergeants do not rate Business Class. Do inspectors? It's time that I took the inspector's exams. Perhaps you can help me to swot for them when you return, whenever that may be.) I quite understand that your dour, Calvinist conscience hates me to use any of Dad's money for your pleasure, but you have never objected to me spending it on myself. (The logic seems a little obscure, when my pleasure is to spend it on you, but never mind. We'll come back to that topic another time.) Having the foresight to be begotten by a landowner and captain of industry and then suffering the cramped accommodation, excruciating seats and plastic food in Economy does nobody any favours. I transferred myself to First Class, paying the difference, and travelled via Amsterdam in comparative comfort compared to the squalor of Economy – and no risk of DVT. The very charming German in the next seat chatted me up but I remained faithful to you although I am beginning to forget what you look like.

Our lords and masters, being also masters of the false economy, had jibbed at the expense of the Bellavenista Hotel which, being just behind St Mark's Square, is very expensive. I had more than half a mind to transfer to the Excelsior, even more expensive and much more luxurious. However, when I came to think about it I realised that certain enquiries would be made easier if I were on the spot so I transferred to the Bellavenista, again paying the difference out of my own, or Dad's, pocket. (Nothing is cheap in Venice. Each of the porters suggested that I put my handbag with the rest on the luggage on his trolley. Apparently I was not expected to know that they make their charge per item. I would not have put Pippa to bed in the grotty hole that I had first been booked into. And if the police enquiries benefit from my self-indulgence, so be it. I am a public-spirited citizen. I avoid tax but do not evade it and I never spit in the street.)

The Bellavenista turned out to be a classical marble building, probably built as a minor palazzo but successfully modernised internally. Naturally the rooms are huge. The cuisine turns out to be above average even for Italy. Venice is at its wintry best, with sunshine that in Britain would be considered summery though the locals consider it quite arctic. A brisk breeze is removing the canal smells and chucking the gondolas around.

The local *carbinieri* had been informed of my impending visit. Resorting to the Italian that I had learned in Finishing School, I made a courtesy phone-call from my room to let them know that I had arrived and where I was staying.

My reservations had been made on the assumption that I would need a clear day in Venice, so there was no great hurry. The day was already well advanced. I had dinner (a remarkably good dinner) and then asked to see Rebecca Finlay. I was met with incomprehension. Eventually I remembered that that she had married her Gianni and that I should have asked for Signora Viticelli. But it seemed that the Signora and her husband were out for the evening.

At that point, I switched into chatterbox mode. (You may say that this is my natural persona, but only if you wish to lose all marital privileges.) The receptionist is a black-haired lady with a matching moustache and a mellifluous voice. She is little more than my age but shows every sign of being fat before she's forty. She was having a quiet time and pleased to enjoy a little gossip. She has been at the hotel for three years. It is a good job and the hours suit her because she in engaged to the hall porter who works a similar week. The signor is a good employer, firm with slackness but appreciative of work well done. She had little to say about the signora, but from her tone and expression I gathered that the signora might take after her sister. It was, she said, a respectable hotel. As if joking, I asked whether they ever had *Mafiosi* staying there. She shrugged. Who could tell? They were outwardly respectable these days. At least there had never been trouble. If the police visited, it was only to check on visitors' passports.

I dragged the conversation round to the couple's absence that evening. Hotel keeping, I said, was a terrible tie. Ah, but the staff were good. Only a week ago, the signor and signora had taken a few days holiday – they had gone to his sister near Trento who had a lodge in the hills and enjoyed the skiing there. The hotel had continued to run with perfection – the signor had complimented all the staff on his return. I pretended an interest in skiing (although, as you know, I value my legs too highly to risk them on the piste) and noted down the address and phone number of the ski lodge.

The other topic almost raised itself. I was curious as to whether my friend Mavis Something-or-other had paid a visit recently as suggested by the same friend who had recommended the Bellavenista to me. My brief description of her may have sounded much like Nasty Nellie. I was assured that nobody of that description, other than the signora herself, had stayed here within the last fortnight. She even showed me the register – not, presumably, that the proprietor's sister-in-law would necessarily register.

I was tempted to visit Harry's Bar where the celebrities go, but by local time it was almost my bedtime and there are few things quite as tiring as sitting still. I decided to have a refresher in the bar and then turn in, but I had hardly settled down with a Martini cocktail before a man arrived from the *carbinieri* on a courtesy visit. He had probably prepared himself to speak halting English to a stout British copper reeking of beer and chips, so I may have come as a surprise to him. He did not seem disappointed. Far from it. He was wearing a wedding ring, but that did not deter him from coming on to me as only an Italian can. At least his attitude predisposed him to make a lot of rash promises to get the Trento alibi thoroughly checked. He would also find out whether any of the local *Mafiosi* had been approached, though general opinion at home had been that the presence of a Mafia hitman in the vicinity of Newton Lauder would have been as conspicuous as a two-headed yak.

I had to be very firm with him in order to get to my room unaccompanied, but I assure you that I succeeded in the end and shall have few complaints if you are remaining as staunchly virtuous. I am writing this from a large and comfortable room smelling slightly of the Grand Canal (the room, I mean, not me). I have all day tomorrow to 'pursue my enquiries' and I go home again on Wednesday.

You haven't been very forthcoming about how your leg is mending. You may be trying to spare me the need to worry, but I assure you that such reticence only causes me to envisage all sorts of the direst calamities. Next time you email, please report. If you can borrow a digitiser, append X-rays. Better still, fax them.

Love,

Honeypot

14 January, from Venice

Sandy – your email came as a relief. So your fingers have healed and your leg is well on the way to mending. You've given your evidence and are only being kept hanging on in case you're needed for further cross-examination. Wouldn't it be better and cheaper if they flew you home to where you can live for the cost of your feed and be cared for without the expense of American nurses? If you don't agree, say so and I'll know that you're enjoying being cosseted by glamorous nurses with big tits. I've seen them on the box.

It was a safe bet that Rebecca Viticelli and her husband would not be too early to rise after their night at the opera (doesn't that sound like an old Marx Brothers film?). I treated myself to the sort of leisurely breakfast that is seldom possible for me, even with June to share the burden, while I have a husband to feed, dogs to walk and a job to go to. Even so, Signora Viticelli was not immediately available so I returned to my room and conversed with the chambermaid while she cleaned and tidied.

She confirmed that nobody answering to Nellie's name and description had visited the signora. She has a crafty look about her and struck me as the sort of woman who might have contacts with the lowlife of Venice (if lowlife can exist in Venice without drowning). To pass a little time and to furnish some extra material to pad out my report, I probed a little. My Italian must be a little bit too elementary for subtle hinting, because she caught on only too well. Madam was in need of a man to visit Britain and perform a removal? But that would be no problem. For a fee to be negotiated, her Luciano would be happy to oblige.

As the maid was writing down her Luciano's address and telephone number, my acquaintance of yesterday evening telephoned. Even over the phone, I could feel his hot breath in my ear. He wanted to come round and tell me his news in person but I managed to persuade him to cough it up over the phone. It amounted to no more than that the signora's alibi proved impregnable. She was indeed skiing in the lower Alps when Duffus died and Nellie vanished. He promised to phone me if anyone of

Nellie's description arrived at the hotel, or even to fly over in person to give me the news. I said that I was sure my husband would be pleased to meet him and show him over the Fettes Avenue HQ. I didn't mention that said husband was stuck in LA with no immediate prospect of escape. By then the maid had finished up and left. To introduce a more innocuous subject, I read him the name of the maid's lover. He said that that particular Luciano was small fry and a con artist of low magnitude. He would certainly take a fee for a contract killing but would then disappear until the money was spent.

When I came downstairs again, Signora Viticelli was free and waiting for me. We sat down in a private parlour. At first glance, this seemed to be as ornate as the Doge's Palace though a second glance revealed that the faded décor was not by Tintoretto but some much lesser artist. The drawing was poor although the colours were good. Signora Viticelli rather resembled the photographs I had seen of her sister, which explained some of the puzzled glances I had received when describing Nellie. The air of sexuality was there which, combined with the blondness, would be bound to drive any Italian male clean out of his skull. I tried hard not to let it prejudice me against her. The maid had hinted that the signor was fiercely protective.

She seemed concerned at her sister's absence but not excessively so. She was quite frank and open and I could detect no signs of dissembling. (I can usually spot a liar at fifty paces, so don't bother trying, Sandy.) She had, of course, been notified of Nellie's disappearance and the death of George Duffus. She was quite willing to fly over if there was anything she could do to help but at the moment she could not imagine herself being anything but a distraction.

When I told her that a ransom demand had been received, addressed to the deceased Mr Duffus, she was perturbed and surprised. Either it was a fraudulent attempt to cash in, she said, or the kidnappers were surprisingly ignorant – either of Duffus's death or about the existence of a sister as next of kin. She would, of course, notify us immediately if she received any such demand. I enquired, as tactfully as I could, whether she would be able and willing to produce a ransom. She said yes, but without any great enthusiasm and I guessed that there were unspoken provisos as to the amount and the safeguards.

She and Nellie had grown up together in Edinburgh but they had never been close – indeed, she admitted, any attempt at closeness had always ended in a hissing, spitting, hair-pulling fight or, later, the kind of quarrel in which the contestants vie to see who can utter the least forgivable insult.

She must have found me a good listener because she became quite frank. Her body language showed the relaxation of somebody who was relieved to spill the beans at last. 'Partly, I blame myself,' she said. Her Edinburgh accent remained stronger than what I could recall of her sister's. 'I could have done more to help her. I can't pretend that we were poor or grew up in a slum, but there were some tough kids around and they tended to pick on anybody better dressed then themselves. Fair hair also helped to single you out. I soon found that I could survive by a series of tricks. I had a temper but I learned to control it. I became the class humorist. I cultivated friends. And I learned to set my enemies against each other. Divide and rule, that sort of thing. Get them to kick each other up the bum instead of me. With friends like me, who needs enemas?' She produced a sudden grin and I looked at her sharply. This mildly blue humour showed a new side to the Finlay family.

'Helena was younger than me. I suppose it was my job to give her a lead, but by the time I realised that she was confronting the same problems but from the wrong angle, it was too late. Her answer to bullying was to lose her rag completely, grab the nearest weapon and start laying about her. She got into trouble sometimes; but they stopped messing with her, so I suppose you could say that it worked, after a fashion, even if it didn't make her any friends. Perhaps I should have seen that it was becoming a habit set in concrete. At home, she could fly off the handle if I thwarted her in any way, though she reined herself in with our parents. I don't think that they ever realised what she was becoming. I certainly didn't, not until the day that her boyfriend decided that he liked me better. She went for me with a walking stick, making sure that our parents were out at the time. I could only be thankful that there wasn't anything sharp handy at the time. I was a student and it was easy to move out into student accommodation.'

Things had improved, said the signora, when, after several years of no contact, she had settled in Italy while Nellie remained in the Borders. Contact was established, of necessity, when it came to dealing with the estate of their parents. At a distance of more than 400 miles, they could be friends. They had never met again and neither was given to writing letters, but they had spoken regularly on the phone, enjoying the exchange of acerbic comments on world affairs or gossip about acquaintances which, she admitted, was often malicious, at least on Nellie's part. Nellie would even boast about her tantrums and the effect that they had had on her adversaries. The signora took a tolerant view of her sister's jaundiced attitude without quite sharing it, or so she claimed.

Malicious gossip on Nellie's part might easily contain the seeds of whatever calamity had overtaken her, but, as it turned out, her sister was as doubtful about the accuracy of Nellie's scurrilous anecdotes as I was and so had not bothered to memorise any of it. Moreover, not being familiar with the people involved she had little recollection as to who was the subject of any particular barb. It was not difficult to connect the suggestion that somebody was defrauding the VAT inspectors with Jasper Dunn. An allegation that one of the locals was recording child pornography off the Internet was probably the purest fiction and in any case had no identity attached. The last phone-call, however, was tantalisingly just clear of the bullseye. The conversation was fresh in the signora's mind and Nellie had, for once, seemed sincere. She had come across some information about a neighbour – possibly more than one, she couldn't remember Nellie's exact words – and she was going to 'light a firecracker' under them.

There was one other area in which either Nellie or her sister might be reticent, so I approached it on tiptoe. Signora Viticelli was perfectly frank. Yes, she was aware that her sister had had lovers before and during her time with George Duffus. Nellie had been quite frank about her activities and the attributes of her paramours. She had led her sister to believe that the men concerned had been prepared to overlook any defects in Nellie's manners or reputation on account of her talents and adventurousness in the bedroom, and the signora, pursing her lips, said that she could well believe it. Unfortunately, Nellie had been more reticent about naming her lovers. There had been a current man in her life, and the signora was sure that Nellie, while remaining discreet about his identity, had let slip that he was a neighbour, insofar as a household in open country can be said to have neighbours, but that the relationship had been carefully kept from George Duffus. Nellie had referred to him casually as 'a tiger.' Mr Duffus had not been under any delusions about her past, but according to Nellie he had had no doubts about her present fidelity. She may, of course, have been deluding herself.

That was absolutely all that she could recall for the moment. Nor could she suggest anyone who might have a grudge against George Duffus. I steered the discussion gently in the direction of who might benefit from his death. She took the point immediately and was visibly shocked. She pointed a shaking finger at me. 'So that's why you're here,' she said. I saw for a moment a trace of Nellie's famous temper.

She was quite correct, but I had already established her innocence subject to further checks so I was able to deny it. She regained her calm but had to be prompted about the probable date of the death before she thought to produce her alibi.

Staff were arriving at the door and demanding decisions about hotel business. The signora promised to think hard and to phone or email any snippets that returned to her memory; and she would be available for more discussion later in the day if I could think of any more useful questions.

Clearly I was being dismissed, but I already had all that I had come for. I phoned the airport and tried to bring forward my flight home, but a medical conference was just breaking up and there was no chance of any seat other than in economy class. Another night in Venice would be no great hardship though I can't say the same about the early start tomorrow morning.

I had an early lunch and took a stroll across St Mark's Square, resisting any temptation to stop for a coffee – not even Dad's wealth can stand up to St Mark's Square prices. In accordance with tradition, I rubbed the stomach of the lion for luck. Unfortunately, I'm a month too early for the *Carnivale* or I might have hired a costume and gone on the razzle. I thought of going again to see the glassworks, but I would only have ended up buying something that would be impossible to transport home unbroken. In the end I went to the Gothic fantasy of the Doge's Palace to admire the Tintorettos. Do you fancy frescoes on the walls of our dining room? I know a teacher at the College of Art who enjoys doing slightly erotic murals...

Enough for now. I'm being virtuous. Be the same.

Lots of love,

Honeypot

12 January

I flew back today. All day. The first plane was delayed by the captain needing a pee or something, so I missed my connection. I was not happy. I had to hang around Schiphol Airport for donkey's ages. Some penny-pinching bureaucrat had booked me with two different airlines and when I upgraded my seats I couldn't change that. As a result, neither airline wanted to know about my problems and in the end I had to come back from Amsterdam Economy Class among screaming babies and argumentative drunks. Another consequence that I put down to falling between airlines was that my bag got lost and hasn't turned up yet.

I'm home now, altogether pooped out but at least I've had a decent meal at last. More tomorrow if I feel strong enough.

Love,

Honeypot

13 January

Sandy, my sweetheart. My return to the frozen north coincided with the beginning of a thaw, so the double investigation may be able to take several steps ahead. There remains about ankle-depth of slushy snow but the thermometer's well above freezing and there are signs of rain, so I think most of the snow should clear today.

As a further bonus, Ian Fellowes phoned me this morning, just as I was preparing to leave for Newton Lauder. Anita Duffus, who has now reverted to her maiden name of Foster, is back in Inverness and ready to be interviewed. She is employed as office manager at a wholesaler of car parts (which I assume to be how she met her garage proprietor partner). She will stay at home to await a visit. I was nearest so I was elected to go and hear what she has to say and then check it. Meanwhile, there have been no new leads and no further ransom demands.

As you may imagine, I had had a bellyful of flying for the moment and I was caught out once before when some other plane broke down. On that occasion, the Inverness plane was switched to replace the other and they substituted an aircraft only one step up from an open-cockpit biplane. The trains have been disrupted by flooding on the line so, leaving Pippa with June again, I set off by car. (Hugo's usual handler has returned and claimed him. I shall miss the little spaniel. So much better behaved than Pippa!)

I don't care what they say about the A9, it's a good road if you keep an eye on what the other idiot's doing. I did the 125 miles in two hours and a quarter through thin drizzle, listening to Dave Brubeck on my new set of CDs – the first chance I've had to listen all the way through. The local fuzz (sorry, Northern Constabulary) had been notified that I would be poking around on their patch, but I decided to make Ms Foster my first port of call and let her get back to work. She and her partner have a luxurious flat almost next door to his garage and showroom so that parking, unusually for Inverness, was no problem. The buildings are new and smart but not quite in keeping with the stolid image of the Highland City.

Inverness traffic is terrible but not quite as bad as in Edinburgh.

Ms Foster is tall, thin and dark and looks too straight-laced to have a lover, but there was a trace of a twinkle in her eye and a Mona Lisa sort of smile. A woman with hidden passions like an underwater volcano, which is how I like to see myself, so we had something in common. She gave me coffee in a contemporary sitting room that managed to be both comfortable and even tasteful although the pictures seemed to have been chosen more for their sentimental content. She sat bolt upright but her apparent physical stiffness may have been the aftermath of surgery or possibly tight corsetry and not due to guilty nerves.

She apologised for not being available earlier but she had been in hospital, she said, having her gall bladder removed. The message about her estranged husband had only reached her yesterday and of course it had come as a shock – he was an old stick-in-the-mud but she had been very fond of him, much as she might have been fond of a favourite poodle; just not fond enough to vegetate at the back of beyond with him. Lowering her voice as though the furniture might be eavesdropping, she hinted that he had not been more than adequate in the marital bed, which remark made me revise my first opinion of her, which had been that the shoe might be on the other foot. It also explained why Nellie might have found it necessary to take a lover or two.

About Nellie she had little to say and none of it good. They had only been neighbours for a few months but I sensed that that had been long enough for the usual antagonism to erupt. Without quite saying so aloud, she managed to convey that Nellie, as soon as she had realised that George Duffus was a better financial proposition than her own husband, had begun putting in the poison under the guise of friendly gossip. When Mr Duffus began a flirtatious friendship with Nellie, Ms Foster (or Mrs Duffus as she was at the time) was willing to let the marriage fail. She had, she admitted, already met her present partner when George Duffus was changing his car and Mr Macdonald had the only model in stock of the colour that they wanted. They must have clicked, because Macdonald had paid court to her by phone, letter and in person.

Her recollection of Nellie was complete but not very helpful. When I asked her who had had good reason to dislike Nellie, she placed herself quite frankly near the head of the list – for a multiplicity of reasons but the root cause had been cats. 'I had a lovely cat,' she said, 'a neutered female tabby. She used to stand up on her hind legs to be stroked. She disappeared mysteriously at a time when cats were being poisoned. I knew who to blame.'

'The cat-poisoning rumours were true, then?' I asked.

'I'm sure of it. She boasted about it to one of her very few and temporary friends – she never kept a woman friend for long, and not many men. This was when Nellie was still in the village, of course.'

'Who was the friend?' I asked.

'That was Mrs Garrett, who had Bridgend Cottage before she moved away to live with her sister in Blairgowrie and the Ables bought it.'

I had a suspicion that Nellie had enjoyed alienating other women so much that she might easily have made a false boast. But Nellie's own cat – a large, neutered ginger tom – was in quite a different category, according to Ms Foster. 'When Mr Dunn nearly backed his van over the brute, Nellie gave him an earful of abuse. You really wouldn't credit the language! And she told him to look where he was reversing although how he could look under the back wheels once he was in the driver's seat of a van I do not know. But she was never reasonable with other folk although she expected others to be reasonable with her. That's the way she was. Self-centred.'

Lunchtime was approaching and Ms Foster had said that her partner was expected home, so I managed to spin out our talk until he arrived – a rather craggy-faced man with a mane of black hair. He would have been perfect type-casting as the handsome villain except for an undershot jaw and upper canines that came below the otherwise perfect alignment of his teeth. He turned out to be a soft-spoken Highlander with a slight lisp, Donald Macdonald by name. He had been told about the death of George

Duffus and in the course of a slightly tense exchange between the three of us I sensed that he was not totally delighted that Ms Foster was now free to marry.

He had been away on business when Ms Foster had her operation, including the period during which George Duffus died. He was visiting the main importers in Glasgow at that time, to be briefed about a new model. It did not take long for them to realise that my questions were directed towards whether or not he could account for himself at the time of the death. I could see for myself that, if he was as reluctant as he seemed to offer marriage, he had little or no motive; and I'm sure that they could see that I saw it. All kinds of emotions were bouncing around unspoken. After that, relationships cooled.

I was not invited to stay to lunch. I had quite a respectable snack in a nearby hotel and then went to visit Northern Constabulary. The desk sergeant was going to refer me to the duty inspector, but it can be a mistake to aim too high. You can't bully a superior officer into being frank or helpful. I explained what I was looking for and why and his rather bland face came to life.

'You want DS Munro,' he said. 'She lives somewhere nearby.'

A woman DS with local knowledge was exactly what I wanted. DS Munro, when she arrived, was dumpy and rather plain in a warm but unflattering woollen dress, but she was ready to smile. She took me into an interview room and listened to my outline of the case.

'I know the couple you mean,' she said at the end. 'I see them most days. I don't know either of them to talk to. There's nothing known against her but we've been keeping an eye on him. We suspect him of clocking cars and doing other naughtiness with trade-ins and write-offs. The Trading Standards Office is watching him and I think he knows it. I think I'd have heard if there had been any sign that either of them had any contact with more serious crime, but I'll ask around.' She promised to pay a personal call at the hospital and check the dates of Ms Foster's operation. As you know full well, Sandy, a phone-call only connects you with a voice that can't be bothered or may even have pocketed a fat bribe.

For the same reason, I decided to check Mr Macdonald's alibi in person. Glasgow was not so far from my route home. I thanked DS Munro and shot off back down the A9, switched to the motorway and just managed to catch the main agents before they closed. He was certainly with them on the relevant two days and on the evening in between he went out for a meal and theatre with two of their staff. He had not had the forethought to take one of them to bed with him so he could, I suppose, have sneaked out of his hotel during the night and driven to Newton Lauder to do the deed but it is almost impossible to envisage why he should have done so nor how. If he married Ms Foster he might, I suppose, fall heir to George Duffus's money in time; but Duffus's pension will have died with him, so to my mind the money motive could only apply to somebody with financial troubles, of which Macdonald shows no signs.

So here I am, back at home rather late and tired and with an early start to join Ian at Newton Lauder tomorrow. Pippa is sitting with her head on my feet, farting gently from time to time.

When exactly can I expect you home?

Love,

Honeypot

14 January, from Newton Lauder

Sandy - here I am, back in Ian's spare bedroom, this time with two Labradors groaning and farting on my feet.

Driving through this early morning, as a damp and windy day dawned, I could see that the thaw was complete except for traces of snow on north slopes and wherever the shade had lain. I could make a good guess at what was ahead and I did not look forward to it.

DS Blackhouse was present at Ian's morning meeting and he was in a mood which, even for him, was unusually sombre. To be fair, nobody was particularly cheerful. The lower ranks had been warned that the time had come for a damned uncomfortable search of the countryside. Ian, Mr B and I were even more aware that the case was in a mess. Endless house-to-house enquiries had turned up nothing to be recognised immediately as significant. In most cases of foul play, the nearest and dearest are the obvious suspects, but in this case the nearest and dearest were either dead or had the sort of alibis that criminals can only dream of. A list of those with cause to dislike Nellie included almost everybody who had ever met her, while Mr Duffus seemed to have been mildly liked and respected. They must have made an unlikely couple and if they had killed each other nobody would have been at all surprised. This could still have turned out to be the case but it seemed highly unlikely.

After I reported, very briefly, the results of my travels or the lack of them, Ian announced that the SOCOs could now get busy around the site of the burial. (And the best of British luck to them, I thought. The site had been trampled over in rotten weather and had then no doubt been picked over by carrion-eaters hunting for the origins of the cooked-meat smell.) At the same time, the general search of the area would be carried out, paying particular attention to any ground that might have been disturbed. Anything that seemed to be unusual or out of place was to be noted, photographed, collected and its precise location recorded.

At that point, Mr Blackhouse took the floor. He began to rant.

It was not the sort of rant that a senior officer should perform in front of junior ranks and there was a great deal of embarrassed shuffling and coughing. The general search, he said, should have happened days earlier and Ian's head would be firmly on the block if another body turned up, unburied. There would be an immediate and obvious implication that earlier action might have saved a life.

Ian tried to point out that by the time that we knew that any-body was even missing, two days had passed and the possibility of finding the victim of an attack still alive under the deep snow and in a black frost had become so remote as to be non-existent. He added that such a search might have destroyed more evidence than was to be found. He was indisputably correct but Mr Blackhouse, once having pronounced, was not going to lose face by changing his mind. In point of fact, he would have earned more respect if he had had the sense and grace to back down, but he has never stood out as either sensible or graceful – or should I say gracious? He would have none of Ian's soft answers but, his main thrust having been parried, he became more vague and so more ominous until he ran out of steam. He really is a prime example of a man promoted to the level of his own incompetence. (Sandy – do not print this out and do delete it totally from your laptop's memory. My career and probably my life will be at risk if this ever surfaces.)

I was becoming convinced that the truth, if it lay anywhere, was more likely to be found in the house-to-house enquiries than anywhere else. The right questions just had not been asked of the right person. Or, more worryingly, perhaps they had been asked but not answered truthfully. Even worse, perhaps the magic words had been uttered but not recognised. I wanted to read the reports made so far and then go over the ground again myself but, when I said so, Ian and Mr B were for once of like minds. Pippa must certainly go out on the search and because she had never worked for anyone but me I had better tag along.

Not being a complete idiot, I had provided myself with good Wellies, my thornproof trousers and the tweed coat with the hood and the Goretex lining. I was carrying my thumbstick with the built-in whistle. I also had a flask of coffee and a smaller one of brandy. Squelching around the countryside in search of the debris of past horrors would not have been my chosen occupation to pass a cheerful morning. Even so, such are the vagaries of the human psyche that if I had been in pursuit of pheasants, as a Gun or a picker-up or even a humble beater, I would have set off with enthusiasm. As it was, I stumbled and plodded and cursed Pippa, who was thoroughly enjoying herself. (Her habit of hauling on the lead is infuriating at the best of times, but when the feet of the person on the other end of the lead are stuck deep in mud it can only lead to a messy and undignified tumble, to the great amusement of those round about. About once in three, my thumbstick saved me.)

I tried to think of happier times, which was not difficult. What put the lid on it, as far as I was concerned, was that Ian had ordered that Pippa, and therefore yours truly, was to be called whenever any interesting object or patch of ground was discovered. That meant that we walked about ten times as far as anybody else. And, believe me, it was hard going. The ground had begun to drain but it was still very muddy and almost every pace meant dragging many kilos of boot out of a glutinous mire. I consider myself to be passing fit. My regular visits to the health club make sure of that, but by the time that the out-of-condition officers around me were sweating big drops my thighs seemed to be on fire, and no sign of a husband to do his marital duty and massage them better. I was soon giving serious consideration to pleading migraine, pregnancy or a period and escaping.

We were to begin with a sweep of the nearby fields, hedges and rough ground, ending, when the SOCOs had finished at and around the site of the grave, with a fingertip search through that wood. A local sergeant who knew the ground was directing operations. Every man or woman who could possibly be spared had been pressed into service. There were also civilian volunteers. Even after the exclusion of the young, the old and the obviously unfit, we had a long line for him to control and for me to traverse whenever somebody found a lost glove, a discarded handkerchief or some part fallen from a tractor. Once I had to hurry the whole length of the line because some ass had come across the place where a farmer had marked his sheep with red dye and had spilled a puddle of it. I had given Pippa a refreshing whiff of Nellie's perfume before we set off but she showed less interest in any of these finds than in the occasional cattle-dung or rabbit carcass. I was just in time to stop her rolling in a long dead salmon that must have come up the Kelvin Water to spawn and die and had then been carried into a field by a scavenging bird or animal.

The temperature was just above freezing, which always means that the moist air can suck the warmth out of you quicker than the dry air of a frosty day would do; and a brisk breeze was adding the wind chill factor. Stumbling around generated some warmth but at midday a van brought sandwiches and more coffee and there was a scrambling competition for what shelter could be found. We were all muddy but I was the muddiest of all. The SOCOs joined us for the meal. These – three men and a young woman – clearly considered themselves to be a race apart. They unbent enough to let us know that they had nearly finished with a site that had been almost destroyed by the incompetence of less specialised officers trampling over the ground and removing the body. If anything of what little they had found had any relevance, time alone would tell.

After a further short break for relief – women one side of the hedge, men the other and a lot of banter between – we set off again. We were threading a last strip of woodland, really a continuation of the wood where George Duffus had been found, and were almost back at the road when the man on my left raised a shout. At the same moment, Pippa hurled herself to the limit of the extending lead and almost jerked me off my feet again.

Half hidden in a depression in the ground was what at first looked like a dumped bundle of damp clothes. At second glance, it was a woman's body. She was lying on her back and she looked very like Signora Viticelli. Unless there were another sister somewhere, this was Nellie and we had arrived close to the point where Pippa had lost the scent after we found the body of George Duffus. Even in death there was a vicious twist to her open mouth or, I wondered, was that just a cruel trick of rictus? She wore no coat and court shoes, so she had certainly not walked there. Her woollen dress was undisturbed except for a tear and a splash of blood but there was remarkably little blood around the gash in her throat.

I was carrying a personal radio. I got onto Ian straight away. Then I cleared everybody back from the area and had the line halted. Ian arrived, out of breath from hurrying while talking over the radio. I had heard him sending for the police surgeon. For once, there were SOCOs nearby and available. During the inevitable delay, I let Pippa put her nose down and lead me straight, as I half expected, the few dozen paces to the road, close to the point where the scent had petered out once before.

It seemed to me that my part in the exercise was finished. Nobody was going to want a large Labrador snuffling around and showing interest without being able to explain what was causing it. Mr Blackhouse made a beeline for Ian, who managed to draw him slightly aside. I tagged along, dragging Pippa with me and hoping to get a word in. I wanted to free myself to read over the statements again and then start another round of house-to-house enquiries. In their agitation, neither seemed to notice me.

Mr Blackhouse led off. It was just as he feared. The poor woman had been lying there and a search would have found her. Ian said that, while it was for the pathologist to say how long she had been dead, the body looked remarkably fresh. Exactly, said Mr B. In such cold weather, the body would hardly have begun to deteriorate. Almost hiding his triumph, Ian pointed out that Mr B seemed now to be suggesting that the body had been dead for some time. Mr B said that he wasn't saying that at all, he was saying that the poor woman had been lying injured under the snow and had only just died. Ian, without quite saying aloud that the DS was an idiot, pointed out that there was remarkably little blood for any such explanation.

Before they came to blows and Ian ruined his career for all time, I decided to intervene. 'Excuse me,' I said, 'but I think I should point out that there's a scent trail now between here and the road that was definitely not there a week ago.'

I could sense Ian's relief. 'So the body was brought here

recently?'

'If you believe the dog,' I said.

One of Mr B's foibles is to believe, or to pretend to believe, that Pippa is more intelligent and reliable than any of the officers assisting him (whereas I know that she is only more intelligent and reliable than some of them). The arrival of the police surgeon, who had been attending at the scene of a car accident only a few miles off, gave him an excuse to drop the subject.

Nellie – I was quite sure that the body was hers – was photographed, examined and pronounced dead, presumably killed by the slash across the throat although the police surgeon also noted the lack of blood. The SOCOs began work, but leaving the body undisturbed for the pathologist, who was said to be on his way.

Mr Blackhouse was in his element, hurrying around and countermanding everybody else's orders, so I was able to get Ian alone. He was in a nervous state and wanted to thank me for jumping in, but I was more concerned to explain what I wanted to do. He agreed immediately. He had more than enough men to complete the search of a single wood. He would be tied up, dancing attendance on the DS, but I could have Bright and McFadden if I wanted them. I said that McFadden would do for what was left of the day but that I would like both of them tomorrow.

I brought McFadden back to Newton Lauder with me and we settled in the Incident Room. The Collator, a thin and wrinkled sergeant approaching retirement, had been thorough. He had already done most of the work, so with McFadden's help I condensed everything of probable significance onto a single, separate disk and printed it out. Door-to-door enquiries work well when every question can be spelled out but, as you know well, Sandy, your average constable, told to go and ask about this or that, is rarely steeped in the subject enough to chase down the implications of what he gathers up. There are still loose ends to the Duffus case and of course the discovery of Nellie's body produces a whole lot more. This time around, Forensic Science should be able to turn up a lot of extra data; but questions asked before the news gets around or while it is still shockingly fresh may produce something new.

We knocked off at last, hopeful that we could make some progress tomorrow.

You really think that your evidence is finished? Will he be convicted? Either way, hurry home. Yes, I do know that American defence counsel can dream up all sorts of late technicalities relating to the legality of the arrest, but surely that stage must have gone by. Start kicking up hell. Tell them that somebody here still loves you, for the moment.

Yours,

Honeypot

15 January

Sandy darling! So now you're only waiting for your flight details to be confirmed. Yes, I know that there's been a terrorist scare – probably another false alarm, I hope! – and also that plane services are disrupted; but I see that there's a deep, deep depression heading your way, bringing the threat of blizzards, so if you can get a flight to anywhere in Britain I'll tell Ian to manage without me and come to fetch you. And yes, I know that you're perfectly capable of catching a train but I can't wait that long and couldn't risk a train strike. If you can only get a flight by travelling First, do it. I'll pay for the upgrade. Sit on the captain's knee if you have to, or get into a box and send yourself air freight.

In spite of my missing you desperately, life has become quite interesting. Unpleasant but interesting.

The morning briefing was cut short. One fragment of interest was that the first DNA report is now in and the blood on the hearth at Stoneleigh House did come from George Duffus. Another was that the second body was confirmed – dental evidence again – as having once been Thoroughly Nasty Nellie, although following the principle of *nil nisi bonum* that sobriquet is rapidly dropping out of use. Detective Superintendent Blackhouse was beating his fat chest again and telling Ian all the things that, in hindsight, he should have done. Ian was trying to stand up to him without making matters worse, which I know from experience is an impossible task. Argument was going to go on for ever, but they came down from their high horses long enough to agree that we three of the lower orders should resume house-to-house enquiries in the village. I drove out to Kelvinside this morning with DCs Bright and McFadden in the back of the Range Rover and Pippa (who had had a second breakfast of something I couldn't even bear to look at) breathing foul vapours down the backs of their necks.

There is a small parlour at the back of the inn that Mrs Doughty had allowed the team to use as a *pied-a-terre* and I bespoke the use of it again. I left my two bright sparks with two mobile phones, to do some telephoning for me while I buttonholed Mrs Doughty.

Innkeepers know only too well that it pays to stay on the good side of the police. Prompt attendance if trouble breaks out and a blind eye turned to minor infringements of the licensing laws are the benefits, while a jaundiced eye and an unfavourable report when the license comes due for renewal may await the licensee who has proved disobliging. Of course, I would never have said any such thing aloud; but I did mention that we would certainly make a note of any help that she could give. She took the point. There was no more mention of the value placed on discretion and how a reputation for tittle-tattle can damage a licensee's trade. She was suddenly eager to be of assistance, but this eagerness was offset by the fact that, to her, one day tended to be very like another.

It was necessary to give her a fix on the days of the previous week. She had closed the inn on Ne'erday, January 1st. Nobody, she said, fancied much to eat or drink so soon after Hogmanay. The denizens of Kelvinside do not favour a lot of after-midnight visiting, so there had been a great deal of handshaking, kissing and New Year's greetings in the bar on the 2nd, limited next day to the few who had not seen each other since the New Year came in. Things were back to normal on the 4th except that some firms had sensibly decided that there would be little work done that week and had remained closed with the result that the inn was comparatively busy for a Tuesday. It was the day, she recalled, of the light snowfall, two days before the blizzard.

It was also the day on which George Duffus had almost certainly died.

Carrying bodies around in open countryside is more safely done in the hours of darkness. The culprits might have waited until the middle of the night or the early morning, but any traffic movement and any firelight among the trees at that sort of time would have been more noticeable and more probably remembered. Comings and goings during the hours of evening opening might prove important. Mrs Doughty, now that she had brought the evening to mind, was not only helpful but, when uncertain, was wise enough to say so. Mrs Macindoe, who often helped behind the bar in the evenings, had come in to assist with the cleaning and she was invoked to jog Mrs Doughty's memory whenever it failed.

The farmer, James Hapless, had come in for a dram and a game of darts with Charles Able but left after losing the first game. The pregnant Mrs Able had watched for a minute, but had felt squeamish and had taken only a small tonic water before going home. Kenneth French had come in to buy his son a shandy in late celebration of the New Year, but the son had left early. Mr French had lingered until closing time and had got mildly plastered while bitching about Nellie and his yacht to Mr Able. He had then made a pass at a woman visitor, wife of a tradesman from Newton Lauder, and had got into a quarrel with her husband that Mrs Doughty had defused with a mixture of threats and promises. Simon Arnoldson and Jasper Dunn had come in together but Mr Arnoldson had received a call on his mobile phone and the two had left again. The other customers had been farm folk from the outlying cottages or travellers from Newton Lauder seeking to dine out cheaply on Mrs Doughty's bar snacks and avoid anybody who they'd quarrelled with or made a pass at on Hogmanay.

Now that Mrs Doughty was in a more talkative mode, I broached another subject. How, I asked, did she cope if she suspected that somebody was smoking a prohibited substance in the bar? After a moment of hesitation, she said that she would order them out and warn them that they might be putting her license at risk and that if it happened again they would be banned from the inn and the police would be informed. So far, there had been no recurrences. When I asked for names, she froze. She couldn't possibly remember, she said, but behind her back Mrs Macindoe looked up from her dusting and winked at me.

There was a conspicuous NO DOGS sign outside the door with a smaller note to say that guide dogs were excepted. Pippa had shown interest in the small block of cannabis that Hugo had detected at Stoneleigh House. I thought that a quick visit might prove interesting before Mrs Doughty had time to object. I might also be able to catch Mrs Macindoe alone for a discussion of cannabis users.

I went out to the car to fetch her, but was distracted by something more immediate. Outside Hollytree, the Farquhar's house, was not a holly tree but a slightly rusty silver Saab. A stout man in a Barbour jacket was taking cases out of the back while a thin woman stood by, telling him (to judge from his disgusted expression) to do all the things that he was going to do anyway. Apart from the difference in their figures – although thin, she was large-busted – there was a resemblance between them, each being round-faced and red haired. Even their hair was similar, because his, though thinning, was long for a man's while hers was short for a woman's. If the Farquhars had anything to say, now was the time to hear it before their insights were contaminated by those of their neighbours.

I caught them at the gate and introduced myself briefly. In any couple, the woman is usually the more communicative but of this pair the wife looked the more tight-lipped (and tight everything else) while the husband had a more approachable air. She was carrying her handbag and one small plastic carrier while he was humping two large suitcases and at the same time managing to carry the sort of smaller bag that one uses for shoes and things. 'Let me help you with that,' I said, and I relieved him of the smaller bag. The small front garden was deep in snow, but I remembered it from a previous visit to Kelvinside as being unimaginatively covered with granite chips. My help at least got me over the doorstep.

Standing in the doorway of a nice enough but uninspired sitting room, I explained that there had been dark doings during their absence and I hoped that they might be able to reflect a little light into the darkness.

Mrs Farquhar looked as though she would not warn me if I happened to be on fire, but her husband murmured something about not being sure how they could be of help but they would certainly try. She was bursting with curiosity but it would have been against her principles to show it, so she said something about putting the kettle on and disappeared, leaving doors open. We took seats in chairs that felt damp after their owners' absence.

A light was blinking on an answering machine but I decided that it could wait.

Mr F was suitably appalled when I explained that both Mr Duffus and Mrs Arnoldson had been killed, presumably murdered. That brought Mrs Farquhar back into the room, without bringing any tea or coffee, on the pretext of dusting and tidying.

I shrugged off their questions for the moment. 'I believe you've been in Switzerland,' I said. 'Skiing?' There had been no skis on the car but these things can be hired.

'We don't go in for that sort of thing,' the wife said over her shoulder. 'We were visiting my sister. We flew out the day before Christmas Eve, leaving the car at Glasgow Airport.' That agreed with the information we already had. From Mr Farquhar's expression, I gathered that the sister was no favourite of his and that he had been dragged to Switzerland, leaving skid-marks.

I heard the kettle come to the boil and switch off but it was ignored. 'And no news of these unhappy events reached you?' I asked. 'By phone perhaps?'

'We're not on those sort of terms with people around here,' Mrs Farquhar said with a sniff. Where her husband's accent was the kind that passes anywhere, hers was a poor imitation of what she thought an aristocrat might sound like.

'Tell me what you thought of Mr Duffus and Mrs Arnoldson.' I suggested.

Mr Farquhar opened his mouth but his wife got in first. 'It was a crying scandal,' she snapped. 'And among respectable people! When you've promised to stay together, for better or worse, that's what you should do.'

Her husband looked as though he would have liked to give her an argument about that, but thought better of it.

'I wondered what you thought of them personally, not whether you approved of their liaison,' I said.

'I rather liked George Duffus,' Mr Farquhar said. 'He was a well-meaning sort and quite approachable. He promised to take me indoor bowling in Newton Lauder and introduce me to the club.'

'Another excuse to go boozing, I suppose,' said his wife, facing us at last.

'And Mrs Arnoldson?' I asked.

'I only met her once or twice,' Mr Farquhar said. 'Dear me – I shouldn't speak ill of the dead but I thought that there was something sly about her.'

'You only say that because she was a woman,' said his wife. I couldn't decide whether she was merely being contradictory on principle.

'What did you think of her?' I asked her.

The lady put her nose in the air. 'Until she left her husband for a man with more money, I thought she was a respectable body.' Mr Farquhar looked at her with his eyebrows up but she ignored him and turned back to her dusting again.

I asked her husband, 'What were relations like between the couple and the other residents of the village?'

'They didn't seem to visit here as a couple,' Mr Farquhar said mildly. 'Mrs Arnoldson had put a lot of backs up before she even left here. I think her husband was one of the few friends she had in the village. I think he liked her better when she was several miles away. Nobody had a good word to say about her. Except my wife, of course, and she always sees the best in people.' I had the impression that he possessed the only sense of humour in the family and that his tongue was firmly in his cheek but Mrs Farquhar, who had been swelling with indignation, deflated and nodded complacently. He went on thoughtfully, 'I wouldn't go so far as to say that any of them would have. . . been violent towards her, but I don't expect to see many sad faces at her funeral.'

Mrs Farquhar humphed.

'We didn't see a lot of George Duffus,' her husband resumed, 'but he sometimes looked in at the inn on his way back from a meeting or a visit. I think he was well liked. I certainly liked him.'

I was more than ever convinced that this case was not really about George Duffus. 'Who in particular had Mrs Arnoldson quarrelled with?' I asked.

'The Frenches in particular. And Jasper Dunn. And myself,' he added, colouring. 'She made some appalling aspersions which I will not repeat.'

We had already learned about those aspersions from other witnesses, so I had no need to press him further. If I asked whether the aspersions had any truth in them I knew what answer I would get, but general opinion locally was that there was not. Mrs Farquhar appeared to agree. I was going to probe into the cause of any ill-feeling between the late Nellie and Mr Dunn when Mrs Farquhar, probably just trying to be obstructive, noticed that the answering machine beside her husband was signalling that it was holding messages. She leaned across him and pressed Play.

The machine informed her that she had six messages. The first two were hang-ups. The third was a dressmaker in Newton Lauder, to say that some alterations to a dress were completed. The fourth, we were told, had been made at 3 p.m. on January the 4th. A pleasant, deep voice with a trace of a Glasgow accent came on the line. 'George Duffus here, Ian. I can't remember when you said you'd be going away, but if you haven't gone yet would Saturday suit you to go bowling? Give me a call some time. If you've already gone to Switzerland, I hope you're enjoying yourselves. Call me when you get back. My regards to your good lady.'

The remaining two messages were again hang-ups.

I stopped Mr Farquhar before he could delete the messages and asked him to play them again at higher volume. As I thought, behind George Duffus's voice, others could be heard. One, a woman's, seemed to be raised in anger. Then, just before the message ended, a man's voice was also raised and I could clearly hear George Duffus say 'Now, don't let's —' before his receiver was fully down.

I asked whether this was the sort of machine that lost its messages if it was unplugged, but Mr Farquar said no, that it was an old model with a tape. At my request, he took out the cassette and handed it to me. His wife began to protest, again on principle.

'I have a spare,' Mr Farquhar said.

'And you'll get this once back eventually,' I promised, hoping that it was true. If not, I'll buy him one myself.

I excused myself and got out of there. From the car, I phoned Ian and told him that I thought the technicians could probably extract the message. He seemed distracted and I guessed that DS Blackhouse was still harassing him, but my message brightened his day. 'Take it straight in to Edinburgh,' he said. 'Go yourself. If our chaps can't work the magic, ask them who could and go there. Provided that it's in the Central Belt, of course,' he added cautiously, visualising more trips to Venice or Inverness. He sounded excited. I nearly told him to be prepared for a disappointment.

DC Bright was already knocking on the window of the Range Rover. I started the engine so that I could open the window. 'We got it,' he said. 'Old Maggie Thomson's next of kin. It's her son in Gorebridge. He's a foreman painter. We have him on his mobile. He says that if we let him speak to his Mum he'll sort her out.'

I thought quickly. I was rather glad of the excuse not to have a session with the old woman. She might have been perfectly charming and fragrant, but she looked as though she had a navel full of dandruff and old toffee papers. 'I have to go into Edinburgh,' I said. 'You two go and talk to Maggie. Let McFadden do the talking, he has the softer touch. You know what I want, but if she has anything else to tell us, get it. OK?'

I left them to it and left a trail of rubber in to Edinburgh. At the Forensic Science Lab they tutted over the tape and suggested that I try one of the independent TV studios – right at the other end of the city, of course. A technician there met me and said that he thought they might be able to do something with the tape. First he would have to perform some incomprehensible technical magic which I understood to mean that he would make a copy without the background voices and use that to eliminate the main conversation. I asked when and he looked surprised. He said now. I had forgotten that in the media world it tends to be now or forget it.

So I came out to sit in the car and I'm writing this while I wait for him to wave his magic wand over the tape. Maybe, just maybe, this is the first stroke of real luck that we've had and I have a suspicion that I may be very busy for what remains of the day. I'll get this away to you as soon as I can. I also want to trim this down into a proper report for the records. I'll write again this evening if I have time.

Love etc., etc., etc., etc., etc.,

Honeypot

15 January, evening

Sandy, I'm just snatching a moment to finish off today's tidings before flopping into my lonely bed. I'm back at home for the moment, which means an early start again tomorrow.

The technician returned the tape and two copies to me, saying modestly that he was afraid that it was the best that he could do, but to my mind he's done brilliantly. The cassette from the Farquhar's answering machine was a commonplace audio one. My sound system in the Range Rover only takes CDs, so I dashed home and had a listen. The phone-call can still be heard faintly but now the background argument comes through loud and fairly clear over the top. Maddeningly subject to Sod's Law, it is tantalisingly too short and only stops being drowned out by George Duffus's voice when tempers start to fly. The woman's voice cries out, 'Yes you will or I'll —' at which point the man's voice cuts in over the top – 'Try anything like that and so help me God —'

You can put your own imaginary top and tail on the exchange and make it mean almost anything, but the only credible explanation is that threats were being exchanged. Which ties in with Mr Duffus's words as he put the phone down. 'Now, don't let's —' Don't let's what? Forget our manners? Get excited? Lose our tempers? Have any violence? It might be no more than a quarrel over a hand of cards. On the other hand, that exchange might very well be the precursor to murder. If only people would be longer winded and articulate with greater clarity, a policeperson's job would indeed be an 'appy one. Sod's Law prevailing again, none of the men in the case has a different pitch of voice from the others and I wouldn't care to make a selection based on a recorded phone-call and a doctored tape.

I phoned Ian, who seemed to have escaped from the baleful presence of Detective Superintendent Blackhouse for once, and played him the full tape and then the doctored one. He agreed that there would be little or nothing of the day left if I hurried through to Newton Lauder and he could see the wisdom of what I proposed, which I'll come to in a minute. He also relayed a message from DC McFadden, that Maggie Thomson's son had told her not to be a silly old biddy and to help the nice policemen. She was so tickled to have heard from him over what she regarded as a miracle of modern technology that she turned into quite a friendly old soul, producing tea, scones and raspberry jam. She even announced her intention of allowing her son to have a phone installed in her cottage, a gift that she has hitherto refused. Ah, the wonders of modern science! Her cottage is the nearest to where the road splits and, as I hoped, she has little to keep her occupied except to maintain a disapproving eye on her neighbours. Our boys had ended up with their occurrence books almost filled with a detailed account of who went where and in particular the vehicle movements over much of the relevant periods.

There was no time to hear the details if I hoped to get back to Forensics before everybody disappeared for the weekend. I asked Ian to phone ahead and insist that somebody wait for me. I told June to walk Pippa again and to expect me back for a meal and then trailed back there through the rush hour traffic. (And if you're hoping that traffic conditions have got any better during your absences, you're living in a dream world. Council policy remains to make life as difficult, expensive and inconvenient as possible for the motorist and never mind the effect it has on business or law and order. I couldn't possibly have done it all by bus.) I saw the same chap as about two hours earlier and asked him the one vital question. Could he get a useable voiceprint off the tape? He tried it and said that he could make a print of sorts. If I brought him tapes of the voices of suspects, it would be adequate for us to determine which of the neighbours was speaking but (and now the bad news!) that the quality was poor and he would not be able to swear to an identification in court.

So now all that we have to do is to get tape recordings of the voices of everybody known to have had any contact with Nasty Nellie or her partner and shuttle them back to the helpful technician. Guess whose job that will be. We make progress in another direction. When the technician came out to me with the tapes, he put his head in at the Range Rover's window and sniffed. I thought that he was looking at me in a peculiar manner so I hurried to explain that I had a flatulent dog, which tended to perfume the car.

'I recognised the smell,' he said. 'I used to have a mastiff with the same problem. I got fed up with being told to try things like charcoal biscuits. So I got my pharmacist to write down the active components of one of the antifart medicines made for humans and I checked them with the vet. He said that it wouldn't do a dog any harm. He also said that he didn't think that it would do any good, but in fact half a tablet after the main meal worked wonders.' I found a chemist's shop open late on the way home and bought a packet. So far so good.

Still no word of your flight home? When I didn't find an email waiting for me I hoped that it was because you were over the Atlantic, or at least high above the USA. But apparently not.

Despite your total lack of consideration, I still love you.

Honeypot

Sandy – still no email from you. I keep watching and listening to
the news but there's been no mention of another 9/11. I am reasonably but not totally confident that if you had been run over,
shot or succumbed to an embolism, somebody would get around
to telling me. Part of my mind pictures you missing a connection
due to heightened security and being stuck in some airport, or on
some runway, with no facilities. Another part visualises you getting off with some light-skirted trolley-dolly and enjoying yourself too much to bother, in which case I could feel free to bestow
my favours elsewhere. Just bear in mind how much more talented
and willing I am. *(Three lines omitted in order to spare the reader's
blushes.)*

If it's any encouragement to you to hurry home, we now have
one of those perfect days that sometimes occur in winter and
make you think, quite wrongly, that spring is just around the corner. Still cool after an overnight frost but now calm, bright and
sparkling. A perfect day for getting out into the countryside with
a dog. So of course I spent most of Sunday indoors with Ian, DS
Blackhouse and the collator, leaving Pippa in Deborah's care. Just
my luck, but it was the sensible course of action.

The first decision was to send Bright and McFadden forth.
Sunday in midwinter can be a good occasion to catch people at
home. They were to find each of the men living in Kelvinside and
ask them where they were at the date and time of the phone-call
and then to account for any movement of their vehicles as
recalled by Maggie Thomson. That should take long enough for
their voices to be recorded on the tape recorder hidden under DS
Bright's rather baggy macintosh. He will sweat a bit if he can't
take his coat off, but he does that anyway. When they've seen all
of them, or as many as they're going to get today, they were to
send the tape in to Forensics by Traffic car and get back here. Mr
Blackhouse would then get on the phone and demand that somebody was available to deal with it.

We three, with the collator, then settled down to a rehash of
the facts both known and inferred. If I make my summary sound

as though we had a neat and orderly discussion, I'm in danger of misleading you. We rambled. Mr Blackhouse kept diverting the discussion with arguments about what Ian should have done. He kept reverting to questions of motive although we know that motive is sometimes a snare and delusion. For the killing of somebody with habits as malicious as Nellie's, everybody had a motive. Stripping away all the rambling and diversions, this is roughly the line that we followed.

Nellie was a sexually attractive but mean-spirited woman who had left her husband for a retiring but wealthier man. She had already antagonised almost all her acquaintances except, surprisingly, her estranged husband. It seemed generally agreed that the two remained on civil terms.

At 2.58 p.m. on 4th January (according to the recorded voice on the tape) there had been visitors, raised voices and an apparent exchange of threats. Unfortunately, this seems to have been the one time that Maggie Thomson takes an afternoon nap, so that we have no indication what vehicles may have been on the move at the time. In any case, Stoneleigh House is within walkable distance of Kelvinside village and we have no witness as to who was afoot either.

Later, George Duffus died. No cause of death has been found other than a broken vertebra in his neck. It must be assumed that he died as the result of an act of violence or there would be no reason for what followed. Later still, presumably that evening or during the night, the body was moved to a grave in the nearby woodland and an attempt made to destroy and hide the body, first by fire and then by burial.

Questions – Why dispose of the body? Were there some incriminating signs destroyed by the fire? Was Nellie strong enough to move it alone and if so where had she been in the interim? Or was there another murderer and was Nellie kept under duress? If so, where?

During the evening of the 4th, according to Maggie Thomson, two cars and a van left the village on the road passing Stoneleigh House. One of the cars did not belong in the village but she has seen it before and she supposes it to belong to a courting couple heading for a small quarry which provides a secluded parking place. She thought that the van belonged to the furniture workshop but could not be certain. She heard another vehicle during the night after she had retired.

Questions – Were vehicles necessary at all? Certainly they would not be practical for conveying a body from Stoneleigh House into the wood. Why did the trail, presumably of Nellie, that Pippa followed from the grave site lead to the other fork of the road? The burial party may have preferred to be picked up there rather than be seen near Stoneleigh House again. If the burial party were on foot he, she or they might well have preferred not to be seen on the Stoneleigh House road.

Later, Nellie was killed. It must now be assumed that the ransom message was a diversion. The pathologist states that the signs of post-mortem lividity are confused but it would seem that she was moved at least once after death. Well, we could guess that. But we do not know whether she was kept in the warm or the cold and therefore his estimate of the time of death is subject to a very wide bracket – he thinks between noon on the 13th and 6 a.m. on the 14th, the day that she was found. Forensics found orange and blue nylon carpet fibres on her dress, suggesting that she may have lain indoors; an earlier rather than a later time is therefore likely. Her last meal – chicken – would have given us a more certain idea of the time of death if we had the faintest idea when she ate it. I suggested that analysis of the chicken for additives might at least give an idea of where the chicken had come from.

The wound suggests extreme violence. There must have been a great deal of blood but our officers have seen little sign of it. The pathologist is sure that the wound to the throat was made before death and would have bled copiously. He suggests that the blood was washed away carefully, even tenderly, after death. There were signs of blood on her underwear (very fancy stuff as I expected) and he thinks that a fresh dress was put on her after death – to keep blood off who or what? There were certainly indications that the body had been dressed by somebody else after death – the smoothing-down actions of a person dressing can never quite be duplicated by another person handling a limp body.

At this point I kept my head below the parapet because arguments were beginning to fly. Ian, with perfect logic, pointed out that if we could search the cars and houses in the village and (if that proved unproductive) the outlying cottages and farm buildings, we could find a carpet with fibres to match those on Nellie's dress and quite probably the signs of blood as well. DS Blackhouse said that he could well imagine asking a sheriff for search warrants on such a massive scale and the kind of reply he would almost certainly get. I must admit that I agreed with him. Sheriffs usually want evidence pointing to a particular house before they will authorise a breach of the general public's privacy. On the other hand, innocent people, when approached with a polite request for a look around in order to eliminate them, will usually give you the guided tour along with the provenance of any object of the least possible interest. The few that refuse can then be focussed on.

Seniority prevailed. Mr Blackhouse decreed that the Frenches were to be subjected to testing scrutiny – this apparently on the basis of intuition inspired by motivation. I would have had to admit that, of all the motives revealed to us so far, the tampering with the yacht plans, while being the most brilliantly conceived, was also the least forgivable. Close behind followed the matter of cat-poisoning, but it had never been proven against Nellie and we could not identify anyone who was still mourning the loss of a beloved moggie. The other slights had been mere words but Kenneth French's yacht definitely fell within the same category as sticks and stones. If somebody had committed me to two years of spare-time work and a lot of money rectifying such faults in what had begun as the ultimate labour of love, I might very well have inclined towards murder. But that does not mean that I would have given way to the temptation.

I opened my mouth to suggest that other motives might be found in the use of drugs, but each of my seniors was following his own line and was disinclined to be diverted. Ian, standing firm for once, was adamant. We could expect a useful lead from the voice prints, but evidence would be needed to back it up. Under the guise of continued house-to-house enquiries, visits would be made tomorrow to each house, in descending order of probability. Access would be sought by requesting a formal statement, followed by a request to use the bathroom, in the hope of obtaining sight of an orange and blue nylon carpet. In parallel, a look would be taken inside each car. The latter, he said, would be my job.

I was shaken out of my role as an innocent bystander. 'Why me?' I asked.

Ian failed to meet my eye. 'You're a woman,' he said. 'People will expect you to be curious. You can say that you're thinking of buying the same sort of car.'

'I wouldn't be seen dead —' I began.

Ian ignored my false start. 'Also,' he said, 'Pippa might detect the scent of Nellie.'

I could have said that I didn't need Pippa to detect Nellie's scent. But I admitted to myself that even attar of garlic might well have faded by now.

We seemed to have missed lunch. The few hours remaining of Saturday would have to do instead of a weekend. I decided against going home. I felt like having a long walk with Pippa and then several strong drinks with Deborah, for lack of a husband to unwind with. June is becoming an excellent housekeeper but she is no fun as a boozing companion.

Kelvinside is as good a place to walk a dog as any and I had never had a chance to follow up the wink that Mrs Macindoe had given me. I drove a little out of Newton Lauder and walked Pippa the rest of the way there. Mrs Macindoe was at home and had no objection to the dog being brought inside. Her husband gave Pippa a pat and then tactfully went out into the garden.

We settled in rather hard chairs covered in imitation leather. Mrs Macindoe's house smelled of soap and air freshener. I was becoming overcome by hunger, so I accepted a large slice of a very fattening cake and a cup of tea. 'You gave me a wink,' I said, 'when the subject of pot-smoking came up.'

She nodded. 'Aye. But you won't let on that I clyped?'

I assured her that any guilt in that respect would stand or fall by what we could find.

'Well, then. There may be others, mind you, but one I'm sure of is Mr French. Mrs Doughty warned him. Very serious she was. Said she could lose her license.'

'And you've never smelled the same smell again?' I asked.

'Never.'

I was just finishing writing the above when your email of yesterday arrived. I wouldn't have seen it at all if I hadn't forgotten to disconnect from the phone-line. (I am still angry with Ian and perhaps running up his phone-bill was a Freudian way of exacting revenge.) So somebody banged into you and damaged your leg again! Kill the idiot from me. Thank God your insurance covers it!

But they can still fly you even if you're back in a cast. If your leg won't bend, ask for an aisle seat, or one beside the emergency exit where they always give you more leg-room. I'm sure that we can adjust the seats in the Range Rover to accommodate your leg; if not, I can hire a helicopter to bring you from whatever airport you land in. Never mind details – problems are for solving or, to put it the other way, there are no such things as problems, only solutions. Just come home. Come. Come. Come. Funny how those words ring a bell.

Love,

Honeypot

17 January, from Newton Lauder

Sandy – come home, almost all is forgiven.

As ordained, while Messrs Blackhouse and Fellowes started asking the Frenches some unkind questions, I did a rapid survey of cars. Kenneth French had been working on his boat behind the house, but they had caught Mrs French on the point of leaving for church so, when they all trooped inside, the garage was open. The boot was unlocked and their Audi has blue carpets throughout.

Simon Arnoldson's Mini was standing outside his house. It had rubber on the floors. Jasper Dunn at the old Manse was away in the firm's van but his BMW estate was standing out. It has black carpets and a nasty dent in a rear wing. Neither Mrs Macindoe, Mrs Doughty nor Maggie Thomson owns a car (confirmed by the DVLA, Swansea). Mr Macindoe has a motorbike and sidecar with ribbed rubber on the sidecar floor.

Charles Able is a likeable, open-faced young man with the face of a Greek god. Unfortunately he doesn't have the height to go with it. He was polishing his DAF and cleaning it out with a portable vacuum cleaner. The boot was standing open. Black carpeting but buff in the boot. He explained that a can of oil had leaked on the original carpet in the boot and he had scrounged an offcut to replace it when new carpets were put down in the inn. He still had the original carpet, roughly cleaned and rolled up to form a kneeling pad. I was satisfied that the replacement was weeks if not months or even years old.

A message came in over my mobile phone. Detective Inspector Fellowes did not have his mobile or his radio switched on. Would I pass a message to the effect that the voiceprint from the telephone tape did not match any of the locals as recorded? Somebody at Forensics, it seemed, had worked instead of going to the kirk. Well, I thought, that was a hole in the head, except that Kenneth French and Jasper Dunn had proved unavailable when the two DCs were getting voices on tape. I knocked on the door of *chez* French and Ian came to the door looking frazzled.

'You look fed up,' I said.

He glanced over his shoulder to be sure that Mr B was not eavesdropping. 'Up is exactly what I am fed,' he said softly. 'The DS is determined to extract admissions while it becomes more and more clear that the Frenches have none to make.'

I lowered my voice to match. 'French is a married man,' I said, 'but he came on to me.'

'I'd be surprised if any man didn't,' Ian said.

That startled me. It was the nearest he's ever come to a compliment on my appearance. 'He would certainly have made a pass at anyone as overtly sexy as Nasty Nell,' I said. 'He has the virile look and men who look like that can never resist using it, nor boasting about it if the subject comes up. Try that on him while his wife's out of the room.'

'You're vicious,' Ian said, but he looked a little happier. I gave him the message from Forensics and told him that the cars were coming up clean. He looked unhappy again. 'We may have to spread the net a bit wider,' he said, 'although we haven't had any promising leads to any of the outlying properties or to any in the town. Finish off and then join us. I'll leave the door off the latch.' He turned back into the house, a dispirited man.

There was no sign of life at the Farquhar's house although a large dog barked when I rang the bell. The furniture workshop van was not back yet. I decided that while I waited for the two vehicles to return I might as well watch DS Blackhouse at work.

Nobody paid much attention to me as I slipped in and took an inconspicuous seat at a small corner table. From the atmosphere of mingled patience and exasperation, I gathered that the evidence was being gone over for the second time or more. Ian Fellowes was listening in silence but I noticed that a small tape recorder, placed quite openly on his knee, was running. 'But you did have a cat?' Mr Blackhouse was saying.

'Yes,' said Mrs French. 'We had a cat. A beautiful Persian. She was run over by the baker's van. I told you.'

'So you did.' Mr Blackhouse managed to suggest that he had serious doubts about the cause of death.

'And that was before the Arnoldsons came to live here,' said Mr French. 'Any of the neighbours would tell you, those that have been here long enough. Or ask the baker's vanman. I can give you his name.'

'That may be necessary. Mrs Arnoldson told tales about your relationship with your neighbour Mr Farquhar?'

Mr French's naturally mottled face turned a deeper colour. 'I do not like your choice of words, Superintendent,' he said firmly. 'Telling tales suggests that there is some truth in the stories. There was and is not and I can assure you that none of the neighbours gave them any credence. You can ask them for yourselves. And if she had ever made any such positive statements, we would have gone after her for slander, but she only uttered hints and stayed just this side of what would have been actionable.'

'I see.' The superintendent put heavy emphasis on the words, but without explaining what exactly he saw. 'But you resented them?' He was looking at Mrs French.

'Of course we did,' she said hotly. 'Who wouldn't? But I knew that they were just part of her usual pattern of beastly lies, made up to hurt.'

Ian Fellowes opened his mouth for the first time since I joined them. 'What was your personal relationship with Mrs Arnoldson?' he asked suddenly. 'Did she have reason to believe that the story about yourself and Mr Farquhar could not possibly be true?' He glanced at me. It was almost a wink.

Kenneth French looked baffled. His wife said, 'My husband is not gay. And he did not have any kind of an affair with Mrs Arnoldson. You can take that as gospel.'

The DS returned his glower to her husband. 'And you resented the trick she played, tampering with the plans of your boat?'

'When I first realised the problem and where it came from, yes.'

'You were furious?'

'I was angry, but I got over it.'

Mr Blackhouse looked disbelieving. 'We know, of course, that you smoked cannabis. Did you ever smoke it with Mr Farquhar?'

'No. I deny that I ever indulged.' For the first time, he was less than convincing.

'Nor you, Mrs French?'

The lady had been listening to the exchanges with an anxious air, like one who is watching over adventurous children. It not did seem to be the attitude of a woman whose husband is vulnerable. When suggestions were made about sexual misbehaviour she had seemed complacent, but I could not make out whether she tolerated it or was totally confident. But at the detective superintendent's suggestion she tensed. 'Absolute nonsense!'

'You won't mind if we bring in a sniffer dog?'

'Not if it's house-trained.'

Mr Blackhouse moved on into what I gathered was new territory. 'Mr French, did you go to Stoneleigh House on January the fourth in mid-afternoon?'

Mr French looked at him in blank incomprehension. 'I haven't been to Stoneleigh House since Christmas day. George Duffus asked us up for a drink along with one or two neighbours. That was the last time that we saw either of them. What are you suggesting?'

Wisely, the DS shied away from the subject of voiceprints. 'There was a quarrel at Stoneleigh House that afternoon,' he said. 'You were not there. Nor Mr Farquhar? Or perhaps both of you?'

Kenneth French got to his feet. 'Superintendent,' he said, 'I don't know what you're getting at and I don't want to know, but I am not answering any more questions except in the presence of my solicitor. Please leave.'

Mr Blackhouse showed no sign of intending to leave but I had just seen a van go past the window. It looked remarkably like the van belonging to the furniture workshop. I slipped out of the room.

The van turned out to belong to a visitor. It deposited several children and an old lady at the inn.

This may not have sounded like a busy morning but it had all taken time. I had no wish to return to the French's house to witness Mr Blackhouse banging his head against what I was more and more certain was a brick wall. I decided on an early lunch before the inn became busy and before Ian and Mr B arrived to patronise it.

Mrs Doughty, assisted by Mrs Macindoe, provided me with a

defrosted and microwaved lasagna, some biscuits and cheese and a glass of almost respectable wine out of a box. I followed it up with a cup of coffee. I don't know what they did to the coffee, but it was awful. Charles Able and his wife were lunching, as was another couple who I didn't know, but I left them in peace and ate in a corner of the big bar, which was peaceful and quiet until the arrival of the party with the children. I was still slightly stunned by Ian's remark. I mean, I know I am blessed with my mother's looks, and she was much admired, but I never think of myself as looking sexy no matter how passionate my secret nature. I do get my share of passes but don't all women? You'll have to explain me to myself some time.

Opposite the string of houses there are fields and some broken ground. I managed to give Pippa a short walk while still keeping an eye on the comings and goings. The large four-by-four that arrived had to be the missing Farquhar's, besides being a very suitable vehicle for a traveller in agricultural chemicals. I returned Pippa to the Range Rover, to her annoyance. She thought we were going for a proper walk.

The Farquhars proved friendly and amenable. They made no objection when I examined the vehicle (buff shagpile throughout, non-standard but not new.) Mrs Farquhar was, or is, a cheerful woman, turning distinctly tubby as she nears the change but cheerful with it. Her chestnut hair was carefully curled and any grey tinted out. Each was tidily dressed and I guessed that they had been attending the kirk in Newton Lauder. They had left a cold lunch prepared for themselves, they said. I would be welcome to join them. I had already eaten, I told them, but yes please, I would kill for a cup of coffee, almost.

Their house seemed to be furnished with a mixter-maxter of colours and styles. The overall effect was totally uncoordinated but pleasantly homely. A shaggy, dull red and grey carpet seemed to have been laid throughout. While Mrs Farquhar made coffee, her husband seemed ready to take me through every word of the statements they had already made. He was as portly as his wife, and as jovial, but he was on the way to being as bald as an egg. I dragged the talk round to the question that I had been waiting to ask. 'There have been allegations of cat-poisoning,' I said. 'Enquiries have been made in Newton Lauder but nobody from here seems to have bought rat poison...or anything similar. Alphachloralose, for instance. It occurs to me that you're in agricultural chemicals. . .'

He was nodding like one of those dogs that you used to see in back windows of a certain sort of car. 'We had an outbreak of rats, some years ago,' he said. 'Mark you, there are rats everywhere, but at that time the weather seemed to suit them and we had a population explosion. I opened a sample bag of rat poison and anyone who wanted to put poison down only had to come to me and I'd let them have a small supply along with a lecture about how to use it safely and in a way that wouldn't endanger pets or other wildlife. But that was before the Arnoldsons came to live here.'

So much for that idea. Anybody in Kelvinside could have had rat poison available and the skill to use it. I would have made my escape, but at that moment Mrs Farquhar called out that both lunch and coffee were ready. We went through to the cramped dining room and while they lunched I had to tackle a cup of coffee that was even worse than Mrs Doughty's. How do they do it? In this day of good instant, it takes a special genius to make really bad coffee.

When I made my escape at last, the firm's van was back outside the Manse. There was carpet on the van's floor but the day had turned dull and the smoked glass made it impossible to be sure of the colours in the back. Jasper Dunn came to the door in answer to my ring. He is a tall and rather sallow man with a grooved face and weary eyes. I said that if he was at lunch I could come back later.

He seemed not the least perturbed at being revisited. He even smiled. 'No problem,' he said. 'I had lunch in Kelso. Come on in.'

I explained that I had no need to come in and disturb him. 'I just want to look inside your van,' I told him. 'If you let me have the keys I'll return them in a minute.'

The smile vanished. His face was expressive but I was undecided which expression dominated. There was surprise and concern and calculation but I thought that annoyance, verging on anger, came first. 'It's not convenient,' he said.

'Why not?'

He looked at his watch. I think that he was going to say something about lunch but remembered that he had told me about Kelso. 'I don't like people going through my things,' he said. 'I have trade secrets.'

I told him that I was not interested in his patent polishes. He asked me what I was interested in. It seemed an unnecessary question, so I put on my most enigmatic smile and waited him out.

'I want my solicitor present,' he said at last. 'Come back on Monday.'

'All right,' I said. I took out my mobile phone and called Control in Newton Lauder. 'Get on to Traffic for me,' I said. 'I'm at Kelvinside. There's a van here that I want clamped and guarded, prior to its removal to the police garage.' I put away the phone and got out my book. Making a written record often gives a suspect a reminder of his vulnerability.

Concern was now definitely heading the list. 'You can't do that,' he said. 'You've no grounds. I know my rights.'

When somebody says that he knows his rights, you can be fairly sure that he doesn't. In this instance I had no wish to debate the legalities with the urbane Mr Enterkin, who seems to be everybody's solicitor for miles around. I was relieved to see that DS Blackhouse and Ian Fellowes were leaving Kelvinbank without taking either of the Frenches away with them. I caught Ian's eye and gave him a half-wave, half-beckon.

My two seniors hurried to join us. Ian had already interviewed Jasper Dunn. I introduced Mr Blackhouse, making his rank sound as impressive as I could. 'Mr Dunn doesn't want to let me see inside his van,' I said. 'I think we should remove it.'

Mr Blackhouse may have his faults but when it comes to dominating a witness he is in his element. He drew himself up from his usually slumped posture until he topped even the tall Jasper Dunn. 'And what is so sensitive about your van?' he demanded.

Mr Dunn mumbled something about trade secrets. The DS

snorted. 'No need to wait for a recovery vehicle,' he said. 'Break the glass.'

Jasper Dunn gave in and produced the van's keys. Ian opened the sliding door and then the back door. The van had a carpet of an unusual grey colour. On close examination it proved to be made up of tightly woven orange and blue fibres. Behind the seats was a large, metal toolbox.

'Well, well, well,' said Mr Blackhouse. 'Where did this carpet come from?'

'What?' I could have sworn that Dunn's puzzlement was genuine.

'Did you carry the dead woman in this van?'

Dunn's voice went up into a squeak. 'Certainly not!'

'Where was she, from when she disappeared until she died?'

Dunn said that he hadn't the faintest idea.

'And the carpet? Where did you get it from?'

'Is that all that you're on about?' Dunn blew out a long breath. 'About six months ago a carpet fitter stopped at the inn for lunch. There was a skip outside the inn because Priscilla Doughty was having some alterations done to the toilets. The carpet fitter dumped some offcuts in the skip and I saw that there were two pieces of this colour which together would cover the van's floor. You can see that it's joined. I thought that it would make it both warmer and quieter, and so it did. There now!'

'And where did the carpet fitter come from? What firm?'

'I've no idea.'

Mr Blackhouse came to a decision. 'We'll have to take the van away for forensic examination,' he said. 'See to it, sergeant. As for you, Mr Dunn, you can come inside and explain yourself.'

Jasper Dunn's body language was pouring out unconscious signals. He had ranged from near panic through urgent puzzlement to rapid thought. 'I can manage without the van for a day or two,' he said, 'but can I take my toolbox out?'

My two superiors exchanged a glance. Ian gave a small headshake. That was enough to decide Mr B. 'Bring the box in with you,' he said.

Jasper Dunn, protesting that he had no idea what was going

on, climbed into the back of the van and, after a little fumbling, emerged with his large, metal toolbox. I was sure that he was feeling more at ease. The three men went into the house.

I called Control and modified my earlier instructions. I locked the van. That seemed to exhaust my responsibilities for the moment provided that I remained within sight to hand over the keys. I got Pippa out. But something was nagging at me. Why had Dunn had to fumble before he could lift a toolbox out of a van? I unlocked the van's rear door again. I could see the rectangular depression in the carpet where the box had sat. And that was not all.

Pippa, like Mr Blackhouse, has her faults but if told to sit and stay she will do just that. I could have climbed into the back of the van but there was less risk to some rather good nylon in entering the front. I unlocked the driver's door and knelt on the seat. Two bolts were sticking up through the floor. They were rigidly fixed and I thought that they engaged with holes in the bottom of the toolbox to prevent it sliding about. And there was something small and silver close by. It resembled the sort of terminal that plugs into a television set. I lifted it and found that I was pulling what appeared to be coaxial cable out from under the carpet. It seemed to lead forward in the direction of where the radio would have been if the van were fitted with a radio.

With the van re-locked, I picked up Pippa's lead and headed towards the front door of the Manse. The door was open and the inner door was unlocked. I could hear voices, petulant voices, from the room on my right. Pippa jerked me towards a door on my left. Surely she hadn't developed a new talent? The room turned out to be a small bedroom. Had Pippa remembered Nellie's scent – which, to be sure, was hard to forget? The toolbox was sitting just inside the door. It was fitted with a small padlock but there was a padlock key on the ring with the van's key.

Inside the toolbox I found no tools. Instead, there was electronic gear. It appeared to comprise a radio and a tape-recorder. The radio was not your standard off-the-shelf item but something more sophisticated in a purpose-made case. Pippa, meanwhile, was whining at the door of an inbuilt wardrobe. I looked inside.

Seconds later I was at the door of a shabby sitting room. The three men looked at me enquiringly. 'Gentlemen,' I said. I was enjoying myself, rather. 'It seems that we have the credit card fraudster with us. And there is enough cannabis stored next door to keep the whole of Edinburgh stoned for a year.'

As you can imagine, the rest of the day was taken up with arrests and searches. So far no more of the same carpet, blood-stained or otherwise, has turned up; but Forensics will be busy about the place for the next day or two.

I must finish up and spend a little time turning the salient parts of this waffle into a coherent report. Then, for tomorrow or whenever I get a clear moment, it occurs to me that there's one voice and carpet that we've forgotten and I'd better take a look there, just to round off.

Keep in touch and get a flight as soon as you can.

All my love,

Honeypot

Sandy – I'm taking it that no word from you means that you're on the way back. I'm trying very hard not to think what else it might mean. Do please try to let me know.

As you would suppose, the first outcome of our discoveries was a search of Jasper Dunn's house, the former Manse. We whistled up the scattered remnants of our team and all turned to. The result left little doubt for us, or room for manoeuvre on his part. It seemed clear that he was either propping up his business with his illegal activities or using the business as a cover, possibly both. (Legal and illegal enterprises often develop a symbiotic relationship, don't they?) There was the stock of cannabis, which he tried to insist was for his personal use although if one man had got through that quantity in a decade he would have been absolutely kippered and far too stoned to run a business, let alone two businesses and one of them high-tech. It was evident that his frequent trips around this part of Scotland were devoted to dealing in wacky baccy and gathering credit card details for his other side-interest.

The radio has gone to an expert, to download and investigate the microchippery controlling the recording function; but we found enough tapes of phone-calls, every one of them relating to a purchase by phone and credit card, to convict him of systematic fraud. These were tapes of people phoning orders, complete with card numbers, names, addresses, postcodes and all the details that vendors insist on. This must have been the crucial part of the operation and it was soon clear that only a small proportion of the calls were likely to be productive. If I could tell, on a quick listen, that a certain combination of address and accent might suggest a set limit adequate for a dozen scout hats and woggles but not for an emerald tiara, a supplier could draw the same conclusion. But of course, given details of one credit card from a good address matched with an educated voice, the account might be used a dozen times before anybody twigged.

There was also a stack of catalogues from the best shops with marks against some of the goods priced at just the right sort of level. There were two turquoise necklaces and some expensive watches, already parcelled and addressed to his brother-in-law in London; who is no doubt already trying to answer some unanswerable questions; and a notebook half filled with an easily decoded personal shorthand listing dates and addresses. In the trash were several credit card receipts that had been enclosed with the goods. The fraud officers are already rushing around like ants from a trodden-on nest, trying to connect up calls made from Dunn's mobile phone, orders, temporary addresses and so on. There will be a field day in court when the case comes on.

As I suspected, Mr Enterkin is Dunn's solicitor. He arrived at the nick breathing fire and announcing that his client would undoubtedly sue for false arrest, but when he saw the weight of the evidence there was not much left for him to do except to start gathering up evidence of previous good character. With Mr Enterkin present, Jasper Dunn was questioned. Under advice, he stayed quiet on the subject of fraud and drugs, but when the matter of murder was broached he was indignant in his denials. So far, Forensic Science has failed to find any other evidence than the carpet fibres to connect him with Nellie. We live in hope, but the carpet in the van, though uncommon, can hardly be unique and, if his explanation is true, the presence of offcuts in the skip suggests that somebody in the area was having a larger area of it laid. DC Bright has been sent off with a sample from the carpet on a tour of the carpet shops and warehouses. If he finds it, we might consider ordering some for our bedrooms – the mix of bright, contrasting colours gives a rich but subdued, almost luminous, effect that would go well with most of our furnishings.

As the officer who made the discoveries, I was involved in the questioning. I was also deputed to monitor the considerable telephone traffic generated. And as if that were not enough, the reporters, who had given up hope of a dramatic solution to the deaths and instead were probably filing the details in readiness for future articles or documentaries about unsolved murders, suddenly woke up to the fact that a major fraud had been uncovered. Mr Blackhouse, perhaps because he only had a vague understanding as to how the frauds had been committed, was for once not thrusting himself into the limelight. Ian is too much of a gent to hog the credit and I am still the DS's blue-eyed girl, so they agreed to appoint me as media liaison. Of course, a woman officer with (dare I say it?) a touch of glamour was meat to them. I was carefully briefed as to what I could or could not say – as if I didn't know the rules – and I appeared on the telly last night and in all the papers today.

Luckily I remembered my lines and parried the more provocative questions. I was wearing my Armani suit and had had my hair styled not too long ago, so I don't think that I disgraced you. Any jealousy among my colleagues has been obviously just that. But one of the reporters wants to do a feature about me and the Edinburgh Dog Unit, and if that comes off it may put pussy among the pigeons.

It's been a hell of a day and I'm too pooped to drive home. Anyway, I have a visit to make tomorrow, if you remember. Can you guess where?

Love,

Honeypot

19 January

Sandy – still no word. I see from the TV that blizzards are sweeping across America, so I refuse to panic yet. Communications are badly disrupted and you're too sensible to get stuck in a snowdrift (though not too sensible to get pushed down a flight of steps by an angry prisoner).

George Duffus's body is being released and the funeral is tomorrow. (He is being buried. If there had been any question of cremation I expect they would have held onto him; after a burial, if any further questions arise, up he comes. I don't suppose the mortuary staff like having him around in his state.) I expect that there will be the usual police presence, ostensibly out of respect but in fact to watch and listen. It's not unknown for the mourners to whisper to each other the killer's name.

In the middle of Ian's morning briefing, a bombshell! Nellie's credit card was used to draw money in Kelso on the 13th, the day before her body was found. Ian and Mr B had their hands full with Jasper Dunn. (The DS is still trying to connect him with at least one murder, so far without success.) They are also being plagued by reporters and I think that the DS, who is accustomed to grasping any media coverage that's going, felt his nose out of joint, what with all the publicity I had been getting. So, to get me out of the way, I was deputed to go to Kelso and ask questions.

I left Pippa with Deborah, drove to Kelso, clocked in with the local station and then visited the supermarket where Nellie's card had been used. I could assume that Nellie had avoided the hole-in-the-wall in case a stop had been put on her bank account. The supermarket (a very small one, nothing super about it) gave substantial cashback against some modest purchases. The girl responsible had no recollection of who had presented the card – she was concentrating on her job, being a good employee and a worthless witness. Nellie's photograph didn't ring any bells with her, but they still had the signed copy of the credit card slip and the signature looked very like hers. It may have to go to an expert if any doubt arises, but as things turned out I don't think that that will happen.

Over a cup of coffee in a nearby hotel, I scratched my head while I thought all around it. Of course, whoever killed Nellie might have taken the opportunity to draw cash on her card. But the date seemed to suggest a coincidence. She had been missing for a fortnight by now. About ten days into that fortnight, money was drawn on her credit card. Then she had come or been brought back to Newton Lauder and dumped close to both of her former homes. At what point along the way she had been killed was still an open question. Where had she resided in the meantime? The sudden need for money at the end of her stay strongly suggested that she had been staying in some hotel or guest house, using another name in case the call was out for her and therefore unable to use her chequebook. Getting cash at the end of the visit would be to settle her account. A hotel might have taken her credit card but if any questions had been asked she could hardly have made a run for it with her luggage under her arm. A guesthouse would probably not have taken a credit card at all. So a guesthouse or a B and B was the best bet. However, I would have to go through all the motions.

The chill wind had got up again and I was not exactly eager to plod around Kelso on foot, but it had to be done. I made notes from the yellow pages and began. One of the hotels provided me with a Tourist Information list of guesthouses and a tourist street map.

She had, of course, stayed in the last place that I tried. Silly thing to say, of course it would be the last place. I wasn't going to go on slogging around on foot after I had cracked it. But I really had covered almost every hotel and guest house (and although Kelso, thank the Lord, is relatively small, you'd be surprised how many there are), before the landlady of a small B and B, a very small lady with a Northumbrian accent, took one look at the photograph and said 'That's Mrs Farquhar'.

'You're sure?' Anybody less like Mrs Farquhar than Nellie was difficult to imagine. But it would be in keeping with Nellie's malicious sense of humour to invite trouble for one of her former neighbours.

'Of course I'm sure. She was here for more than a week.'

The house was a typical double-fronted family home. I could imagine the family shrinking until, with the deaths of the parents, the remaining daughter was left with little income and a house too large for her needs. Filling the empty bedrooms with guests in season would be the logical step.

She led me inside, into an old-fashioned parlour with framed photographs everywhere but not a speck of dust. There was an appetising smell in the air. Nellie, who had not been one to miss her comforts, would not have remained for so long if the cooking had been second rate. 'She seemed quite respectable,' said the landlady, whose name was Ella Forbes. She declined to tell me whether it was Miss or Mrs and insisted on Ms, which seemed remarkably modern in a lady who seemed as old-fashioned as her parlour. 'But there was something sly about her and – would you believe it? – she tried to sneak away without settling up. But I kept her luggage and got her car keys off her,' Ms Forbes said with satisfaction, 'so she went away and came back with the money. Next thing you know, the Public Health was here to inspect my kitchen and I'm sure that was her doing. But there's nothing wrong with my kitchen, no way! I sent them away with a flea in their ear. And now the police are here asking questions? What's she been saying about me?'

'Nothing whatsoever,' I told her.

'Well then. What's she done?'

I said that that was what I was trying to find out. 'How did she spend her time?' I asked.

Ms Forbes thought back. 'She was a quiet guest, there were no complaints about that. No noisy music and no men in her room. She spent the evenings in her room and went out during the day, usually in her car, and where she went the Lord alone knows. Out of Kelso, I think.'

I thought so too. She would have no wish to be spotted by the local Bobby. And she had a car with her. But both cars were left at Stoneleigh House. Somebody was going to have to try all the car hire firms. 'Where did she leave the car overnight?' I asked.

'There's a back lane. It's very rough and muddy, but she didn't seem to mind.'

She probably minded, but she would not want to risk leaving even a hired car where the number might be noted. I asked to see the room.

The room that 'Mrs Farquhar' had occupied had been re-let to a commercial traveller and cleaned every day. After a little persuasion she let me examine the room, which was now disengaged but there was no trace of Nellie, no conveniently overlooked receipts or hurriedly pencilled notes, not even a sniff of her perfume. We sat down again in her small and stuffy sitting room.

'When were your bins emptied?' I asked.

'This morning.'

Wouldn't you know it? 'How did she seem?' I asked. 'Happy or sad? Frightened or excited? Hyped up? Depressed?'

She thought about it for a while. I thought that she might have forgotten Nellie or had misunderstood the question, but I wronged the little person. She was all there. 'Determined,' she said at last. 'Impatient. That's the best I can put it. I'm half guessing, you understand?'

I said that I did.

'Thinking back, the best I can make of it is that she was going to do something and she could hardly wait to get on with it. She was worse after her visitor.'

That woke me up. 'She had a visitor?'

'Not to call him a visitor. But she was picked up near the door by a man in one of those big, boxy-looking vehicles.'

'A Land Rover?'

'Something like that. I think it was dark green, but it was a long time since it had seen a car wash.'

That didn't sound like any of the cars at Kelvinside, more like one of the outlying farms or cottages, but cars can be hired or borrowed. 'You saw the man?' I asked her.

'Sort of.'

This, I could tell, was going to be like pulling teeth. 'Was he large or small?'

'Hard to say. I only saw his head and shoulders.'

'You're sure that it was a man?'

That made her ponder again. 'I think so,' she said at last. 'I suppose it could have been a large woman with short hair but I think it was a man. He had a hat on,' she added.

'Could you describe his face?'

She had a short answer to that one. 'No.'

'Would you know him again?'

'I might.'

It was my turn for a little thought. To show her photographs of the men in the case would be to invite destructive cross-examination later by a defence counsel. Any kind of Identikit or Photofit would invite guesswork. 'If I fetched you tomorrow —' I began.

'Hey! I can't just walk out. I have a business.'

The house seemed very quiet. 'How many guests have you at the moment?'

'Well, none. It's not the season.'

'What do you do when you go out?'

'I leave the key with Mrs Johnstone, two doors away. And she leaves hers with me. We take bookings for each other at busy times.'

I had already encountered Mrs Johnstone, a hard-faced old battleaxe in a floral pinny. 'But this isn't a busy time. There's a funeral in Newton Lauder tomorrow,' I said firmly. 'I want you to come and see if you can pick the man out.'

She lit up. There's no other way to put it. 'Hey, is she the woman that was found murdered?'

I had to nod.

'The poor soul,' she said happily. 'But it's not her funeral, so quick? Is it her fancy man?'

That was not quite how I would have put it, but I nodded again.

There was no more talk about not getting away. 'What time?' she asked.

By then, I was at the furthest corner of the town from where I had left the Range Rover and my poor, tired feet were sending me messages of hurt and despair. All the same, I trod lightly all the way through Kelso.

Back in Newton Lauder, things had moved forward but into

another dead end, or so I believe. See what you think. Mr Blackhouse and Sandy had interrogated Jasper Dunn again in the presence of Mr Enterkin. I begged a copy, on disk, of the transcript and I'll send a section of it as an attachment to this email.

Contact me soon.

Your loving Honeypot.

Attachment to email of 20 January:

Excerpt from interview at Divisional HQ, Newton Lauder. Present: J. Dunn, prisoner. R. Enterkin, Solicitor. Det Supt Blackhouse, Lothian and Borders Police. Det Insp Fellowes, ditto. Transcribed by DC Bullock.

Fellowes: We'll change the subject now. I want to ask you where you were on the afternoon of January the fourth.

Dunn: I don't remember.

Fellowes: I think that you do.

Enterkin: Come now, Inspector. You can hardly expect my client to recall the details of an afternoon nearly three weeks ago – an afternoon that had no particular significance for him at the time.

Fellowes: Then I'll refresh his memory. Mr Dunn, do you remember visiting Stoneleigh House that afternoon?

Dunn: No.

Fellowes: Mr Dunn, during your non-visit, while you were speaking with Mrs Arnoldson, Mr Duffus made a phone-call. Do you remember that?

Dunn: No.

Fellowes: That's strange. You see, Mr Dunn, that phone-call was to Mr Farquhar, who was abroad on holiday at the time. That call remained on the Farquhars' answering machine until we recovered it recently. Your voice can be heard in the background, engaged in a quarrel with Mrs Arnoldson.

Dunn: I —

Enterkin: One moment. Has my client's voice been identified with any certainty?'

Fellowes: A voiceprint was isolated from the other voices in the room. It has been compared with the voiceprint of your client, taken from the tape made, with your consent, during a previous interview.

(Sandy – This was very naughty of Ian. Forensics was sure that the voice was the same but would not have been prepared to swear to it. However, the bluff worked.)

Dunn (after a pause): I was there.

Enterkin: You don't have to say anything. I advise you to remain silent, at least until we have been able to confer privately and the voiceprint has been confirmed.

Dunn: No, I'd rather speak out now. I don't want them thinking that I killed somebody. And if they're concentrating on me, whoever did either or both killings is getting away with it and they're not looking for the real culprit so I go on getting the blame.

Fellowes: That's very sensible. Tell us about it.

Dunn: It goes back to the time, before Christmas, when I picked George and Nellie up in my van.

Blackhouse: They'd had a breakdown?

Dunn: You know about that? Yes, George's car had developed some electrical fault. If I could have just driven past and left them at the roadside, I'd have done so. But I knew that they'd recognised me. George had already tried to fix the fault. He was a better electrician than I'll ever be and anyway it was a gremlin deep in the electronics. So I said that I'd run them home. What else could I do?

Fellowes: Not a lot.

Dunn: That's right. George was troubled by his back so Nellie said that she'd go in the back. Women sit more easily in a bad position than men do. I said OK. I had some parcels in the back – I've already admitted to the credit card thing – but I always carried them with the address side down, just in case. Nellie noticed the coaxial cable going into my toolbox and she lifted the lid. 'What's this?' she asked. And George looked back and down into the box and he was curious.

I tried to pass it off as an ordinary but top-of-the-range radio, but Nellie asked me to play some music and I said that it wasn't working just then and she said that I'd have to get George to look at it. I was glad to get back to Kelvinside and send them home with Simon Arnoldson in the people carrier. Later, I noticed that one or two of the parcels had been moved.

Blackhouse: She'd noticed that the addresses weren't yours?

Dunn: And that they were different from each other. Yes. She must have talked it over with George and between them they put two and two together and made three and a half. I thought that they'd forgotten about it. Then, on the morning of the fourth, Nellie called me up and said that I'd better pay them a visit. She didn't make any threats but she made it sound ominous.

Fellowes: So you went?

Dunn: Of course. The vehicles were in use so I walked to Stoneleigh House that afternoon. Nellie took me into their sitting room. She threatened to tell the police about the radio and the parcels unless I told her the whole thing. That left me no alternative.

Blackhouse: Alternative to what?

Dunn: To telling her. I had to tell her all about it. I've already admitted it to you so there's no point going over it again. I told her how the credit card thing worked. I thought she was telling me that it would have to stop. But instead, she said that she wanted half of everything I could get from then on. That's when George walked in and made his phone-call. We argued on, almost in whispers, until we got a bit heated and raised our voices.

Fellowes: Let's be clear about this. Did Mr Duffus know about Mrs Arnoldson's attempt at blackmail?

Dunn: Apparently not. He seemed to be shocked when he realised what she was saying.

Fellowes: What happened then?

Dunn: I went home.

Fellowes: Oh, come now. There was certainly more to it than that. What was Duffus's reaction when he realised what was going on?

Dunn: Like I said, he was shocked. He said that there was going to be no blackmail.

Fellowes: And then?

Dunn: Then I went home.

Fellowes: We can't accept that. Mr Duffus was a respectable man, outwardly at least. No man would learn about a series of crimes and find out that their partner was trying a bit of blackmail, and leave it at that. He had three options. To quash the blackmail attempt and go to the police. But that would have laid Mrs Arnoldson open to a charge of attempted blackmail. He could make a conscious decision to let sleeping dogs lie. Or he could go along with the blackmail.

Dunn: I —

Enterkin: I don't think that you should say any more at this time.

Blackhouse: I suggest to you that Mr Duffus decided to go along with the blackmail and that you killed him because of it.

Enterkin: You do not have to answer that.

Dunn: But I want to answer it. That isn't what happened. George Duffus told Nellie flatly that there were to be no more threats. The last thing that I wanted was to get into an argument about the future so I got out of there and went home. I got hold of Simon Arnoldson. He didn't know anything about the credit card fraud.

Fellowes: I find that hard to believe.

Dunn: I dare say, but it happens to be the truth. I told him that I was in trouble. I coughed up the whole story and we arranged that if I went inside he'd run the business for me. He'll bear me out.

Fellowes: Is it your suggestion that after you'd left, the argument flared to the point at which Mrs Arnoldson killed her partner?

Enterkin: My client has absolutely no more to say on that or any other subject, but if you want my opinion your suggestion seems logical.

Interview concluded at 16.28 GMT.

Sandy – that explanation seems to fit the facts. I can't explain the gap of a week or Nellie's death any other way. So we still want Nellie's killer.

H.L.

Sandy – I phoned your service provider and spent twenty minutes going through the rigmarole of 'If you want to wish us a happy Christmas press nineteen'. Then, after being put on hold a dozen times to the tune of music I didn't recognise and hated, I was connected to a harassed voice that eventually admitted that they had a technical problem. Well, I could have told them that. In the end, he said that he didn't understand the details but they'd had one of their several computers crash and about a million incoming emails were backed up. I would probably get a whole rush of them, one of these weeks. But he thought that you were probably getting my emails so I'll go on writing and try to stop worrying. Instead of trying to save two pence a year, why don't you get a reliable Internet service from one of the big boys? Or phone me.

Ian wanted me to be at his morning meeting (which turned out to be a bit of a non-event, with Mr Blackhouse monopolising the discussion and mostly criticising Ian). So I arranged for a panda car from Kelso to collect Ms Forbes and deliver her to me at the church in Newton Lauder in time for the 11 a.m. service. I did at least manage to get their attention long enough to make a report. It was decided to leave the funeral to me with our two local DCs while the chiefs conducted one last interview with Jasper Dunn prior to his release on bail.

The Old Kirk in Newton Lauder is set in a large plot, complete with cypress trees, on the corner of two side streets. To judge from the gravestones the churchyard must be nearly full, but they had found room for George Duffus. I could see the open grave waiting with the earth piled neatly to one side.

The panda car from Kelso was there ahead of me and the driver agreed to wait. I took Ms Forbes into the Range Rover. Cars were parking along the streets but the only car answering the description of 'boxy-looking' and of a colour that she might have remembered as being dark green, belonged to a very old man with an equally aged wife. The two of them ambled very slowly up to the porch, causing a tailback of other mourners. Ms Forbes said that she was sure that that was not the car in which she had seen Nellie driven off.

There was a much larger turnout than I expected. I discovered that the late George Duffus had been a valued member of several clubs and President of the Scottish Society to Provide for the Homeless. He was also remembered by former employees and customers, who attended in strength. Ms Forbes wanted to sit through the service anyway, but with such a full church it would have been impossible for her to pick out a face half seen through glass days earlier. I had to revise my plan. Bright and McFadden were already in the church, with instructions to mingle after the service and to pick up any gossip that was being bandied about. I led Ms Forbes back to the Range Rover. She is so small and the car so high that I expected to have to lift her up like a child, but she hopped up nimbly. I moved the car into a position from which we could have a good view of the emerging mourners. The police car from Kelso drew up behind us.

After what seemed an age the coffin, laden with flowers, was carried reverently out into the graveyard, followed by the congregation in slow procession, George Duffus's sister leading. There was a cold wind again to ruffle their uncovered heads and I hoped that they were all well wrapped up. One funeral too often makes another. A man with a video camera was recording proceedings; I took him to be a reporter. Not everybody from Kelvinside was present but I drew her attention to Simon Arnoldson, Ian Farquhar, Charles Able and Kenneth French. To avoid any risk of later being accused of coaching the witness, I also pointed out several other men who had no connection with the case.

When they were all clustered round the graveside to watch the interment, I said, 'Well?'

She sighed. 'I'm sorry,' she said. 'So sorry. I just can't be sure at all. Of course, when I saw him in the car he had a hat on and these are all bareheaded. It could be the last man you showed me. I couldn't swear that it wasn't.'

The last man I had shown her had been a stocky, well-built man with a rubicund face who I had sometimes seen standing around importantly in the Newton Lauder Hotel. I rather thought that he was the manager.

'Oh well,' I said. 'It was worth a try. Thank you anyway. Before I send you home, we'll have one more shot at it.'

I got on the phone. The connection was bad but useable. Ian was still in his office and Dunn had not yet been turned loose. We made our arrangements for an hour later. I thought of filling the time by taking Ms Forbes for a coffee in the hotel but as I reached for the ignition key there was a rap on the glass of my window. I turned my head and nearly jumped clean through the sunshine roof – which wasn't open at the time – because there, outside the window, was Thoroughly Nasty Nellie looking in at me and mouthing.

As you know, Sandy, I'm not a superstitious person. I have more sense than to walk under ladders when there may be some-body with a paint-pot on top of it, but Friday the thirteenth is, to me, the same as any other day. As to whether there is a life after death, I am prepared to wait and find out. Or not, of course. But I do have the universal atavistic instinct to fear the undead. I had never encountered an example before and don't wish to again.

Before I could succumb completely to the threatened heart attack, I realised that the spectre was saying, 'I thought it was you,' and at the same moment Ms Forbes said, 'Mrs Farquhar! Is it? Is it?' and I recognised Nellie's sister, Signora Viticelli. Sending up a little prayer of thanks that I had – just – managed to retain control of my bowels, I completed the turning of the igni-tion key and lowered the window. 'I saw you look into the church before the service,' she said. 'I was going to ask for you at the police station but then I spotted you again out here.'

My heart was slowing down, almost back to normal, and a lit-tle saliva returned to my mouth. While I prepared to get out to talk with her, Ms Forbes, who seemed to take a delight in funer-als, saved me the trouble. 'I'll let you talk in private,' she said. She slipped out of the car and hurried over the road to join the throng surrounding the open grave.

The signora took the vacated seat beside me. She was very neat in an appropriately grey coat and skirt of Italian cut that, between you and me, I envied. 'I flew over yesterday,' she said. 'Bloody awful trip and my luggage got lost in Amsterdam and hasn't turned up yet.'

'Mine only turned up yesterday,' I mentioned.

'Hellish, isn't it? I have some of Helena's business to attend to. George Duffus was a sort of brother-in-law to me, so I thought I should pay my respects.'

'Very proper,' I commented.

She shrugged. 'I'd have been at a loose end otherwise, because the solicitor who she named as her executor is at the funeral anyway. He says that they'll release Helena's body very soon, so I'm staying over to see her decently buried and to tidy up her affairs.'

'Is there a lot to tidy up?'

'Not a lot,' she said. She gave me a sideways look that made me think of Nellie again. 'This is your area of interest, isn't it? She changed her will in my favour but George Duffus never finished changing his will.' She turned towards me. 'My sister may have had some malice in her. I don't think she was after Mr Duffus's money, perhaps just a more comfortable style of living. She didn't go hard on her real husband, Mr Arnoldson – in fact, he tells me that she didn't even clean out the joint account when she walked out, as most women would have done. He's a pleasant enough man, by the way, but I could imagine her getting bored with him. She put her all personal savings into premium bonds and even any prizes went back in. She also had a life insurance with Mr Arnoldson as beneficiary and she never changed that, but it isn't for a lot and he's decided to pass it over to me as her heir. If I gain enough for another skiing holiday, I'll be satisfied.'

What she was saying was in line with what we had gleaned from Mr Enterkin. 'You weren't going to seek me out just to tell me that?' I suggested.

She smiled for the first time. 'You're right, I wasn't. After you left, I carried on thinking about the conversations I'd had with Helena on the phone. We weren't very close but she was my sister and I'd like to see you catch the swine that killed her. And that might well be a lover, don't you think?'

'The statistics support that view,' I said.

'There you are. Bits and pieces came back to me. No names,'

she said quickly. 'Helena played fair that way. She never gave away any names but while she was in Kelvinside I know that she had affairs with two of the neighbours.'

'And after she moved to Stoneleigh House?'

'She told me at first that she was being a good little girl. The novelty of a new partner, I suppose. But even when we were teenagers we knew that we each had an appetite for men and Helena was the more adventurous. I'm more the stay-at-home type, probably because I'm afraid of being found out.' She laughed self-consciously. 'So I married an Italian instead. Helena told me that she was embarking on a new relationship, and not with either of her previous local lovers. That's all she said about it, except that I remember one little thing that might help you. Referring to her new boyfriend. . . lover. . . paramour, whatever you want to call him —'

'The one she referred to as a tiger?' I suggested. I had been thinking about you a lot and the word had stuck in my mind.

'That's right. But she did say something else. I was thinking back over our last conversation and it came back to me that she referred to him laughingly as "a bit of rough". But that could mean almost anything, couldn't it? Not necessarily that he had dirty fingernails and hair growing out of his ears?'

'I've known it used to mean that the gentleman was not very gentle on the bed,' I told her. 'But we'll bear it in mind.'

'That's all I ask.' The interment seemed to be over. People were trickling towards their cars. 'I'll have to be going,' she said. 'I'm going to Stoneleigh House with George's sister. We have to sort out what's mine from what was his. I'll be at the Newton Lauder Hotel if you want me again.'

I thanked her for her help and she hurried away. Ms Forbes took her place, but before driving off, I got out and hurried to catch the man with the video camera before he disappeared into a battered Audi. As I thought, he was a reporter. I took his name and phone number and he promised to let me have his videotape after it had served his editor's purpose. You never know when that sort of record may turn out to be invaluable.

I drove to the nick with the Kelso panda car following and I settled Ms Forbes on a moulded plastic chair just inside the main doors. With her very light weight, I thought, she might even be comfortable in it. I got out of sight beyond a glass corridor door and, some time later, watched as Jasper Dunn was brought to the desk and told to go. Mr Enterkin left with him. They both put on hats.

I emerged from hiding. 'Well?' I said. 'Well?'

'I'm not sure,' she said. 'But it could have been the fat one.'

Mr Enterkin, I was sure, would be less than delighted. I looked forward to telling him, verbatim, on the next occasion when he made cracks about policing methods.

She was thrilled to be given lunch in the canteen. It took me most of the afternoon to get her statement down in coherent form and signed.

Please let me know you're all right.

Love,

Honeypot.

24 January.

To: Detective Inspector Laird.

From: Southern General Hospital, Edinburgh

Sandy – I quite understood that you were away on a case, but I missed your usual visit today. That's the curse of a police area covering almost everything between the Firth of Forth and the English Border – you can't always get home at night. When I was with the Met, I was never more than a taxi-ride from home.

So we're back to communicating by emails. June brought in my laptop and my mobile phone with a new battery, so I'm back in touch with the world. She also slipped me a secret bag containing snacks and a hip flask of gin and tonic. That girl is becoming a treasure. The hospital food is adequate, but it's not the same as home cooking. I'm feeling a lot better today, but maybe that's the effect of the g and t. I'll probably be home before you are and then watch out! I've been going short of my ration of love!

I don't think that I ever told you the first part of what happened that day. It fills in a gap in the story.

At about the time that your plane landed at Turnhouse Airport, I drove away from Ian's house. The battery of my mobile phone had gone kerblooey and the local shop couldn't match it, so I left the phone at home. I knew that it would be easier to get a new battery in Edinburgh and I wasn't planning to be anywhere that didn't have a phone.

As I'd hinted to you, it had been occurring to me that there was one person who had never been interviewed because she was usually away, either at school or on some girlish ploy. And in my experience children and teenagers can make your best witnesses. They are out and about at quite different times from everybody else and they notice and remember far more than we think. When you are young, a day is a significant proportion of your life; but as one gets older it becomes progressively less significant and therefore less worth remembering. So I turned off my shortest route and went on as far as Kelvinside.

A minibus acts as the school bus along that route and I was quite prepared to follow it back to the High School, but I was lucky. Priscilla ('Cilla') French was waiting at the roadside. She's a pretty child of fifteen, soon to be a beauty, with black curls, pert features, large eyes, a mouth made for kissing and a skin to die for. I did a U-turn and offered her a lift to school. She hopped in beside me so confidently that I felt obliged to warn her not always to be so trusting with strangers. She laughed and said that she knew exactly who I was and if you couldn't trust a police-woman who could you trust? Which confirmed my beliefs in her intelligence and her powers of observation.

I parked outside the school and led her through most of the points in evidence so far without adding a thing. Then I worked round to the real objective of my questions. Who was Nellie's secret lover?

In better weather she was out and about a lot, collecting wild-flowers, looking for mushrooms in season and walking the fam-ily spaniel-poodle cross. I suspected that she was also having secret trysts with boys, but it was soon evident that she was very shy about all matters sexual. I had to dress Nellie's escapades in a cloak of romance for fear of scaring her into silence. But in the end I brought her to the point.

She had twice seen Nellie in a car heading away from Stoneleigh House on days when she knew that George Duffus was away. She was more knowledgeable about cars than most teenage girls, which suggested that her virginal innocence did not extend to a total absence of boys from her life. She was sure that the car had been a dark green Daihatsu Fourtrak and could swear to it. That, of course, checks with Ms Forbes's vaguer evidence. As to the driver she was less certain but she rather thought that it was you-know-who.

Now that I was sure of my witness, I wanted to get away; but I had beaten the school bus to it. Pupils were only trickling in. She was too early for school and she had a question of her own. 'What is all this about boys and love and sex and things? When I ask my Mum she says that she'll tell me all about it some time but I bet she doesn't.'

'Why me?' I said, or something equally stupid.

'Somebody said that you got married not long ago, so you must know all about it.' (As if anybody knows all about it!) 'And,' she said, the little madam, 'they don't call you Honeypot for nothing.'

Well, Sandy, that took the wind out of my sails. I hadn't realised that my regrettable nickname was in use outside the Force. You'll probably tell me again that it suits me but you never say why; and I keep telling people that I'm not Honoria Potterton-Phipps any more, so the joke ought to be over.

Anyway, she had answered my questions so I owed her an answer or two. And it isn't the first time that some teenager has asked me that sort of question. Does that say something about me? Probably it does. I do feel that the subject is so important that such questions should never go unanswered. After all, it's what life is all about. Mrs French will probably have a stroke if she finds out that I've enlightened her ewe-lamb but that can't be helped. As it happened, I had been giving that question some thought, in your regrettable absence. I explained that that sort of love came in three packages.

First there is affection. This is having somebody you can laugh with. Somebody who knows what you enjoy and takes trouble over it. Somebody who will hold you when you cry. Who isn't shocked by your bodily functions. Whose smile makes you light up inside like an electric bulb. Somebody who needs you in return. Somebody just like you, Sandy, although I didn't tell her that. I do have some discretion left.

Then there is glamour, or romance, or call it whatever you want but never laugh at it. Glamour is soft lights and sweet music. It is a favourite wine. It may be no more than a sidelong glance or a blush. It is a cuddle in a deep armchair. It is being clean or shaved and wearing very little of the right perfume or aftershave. It is stolen glimpses. It is silk underwear, stocking tops and the touch of a friendly hand. It is all those little things that make the occasion different and special.

Then there is sex, but sex is only the touching together of the parts of the body with the most concentrations of nerve endings.

It can be divine and make for lifelong bonding, but without the other two it is no more than the scratching of an itch – one of the things like food and money that only become important when you don't have them.

I fed her the above in a slightly Bowdlerised version, laying more emphasis on the first two than on the third. I tried not to shock her but she seemed a little pink when she got out of the car. I think and hope that I gave her a standard that may make her less inclined to throw her knickers over the windmill and her virginity after them, but who can be sure?

Anyway, I'll be out of hospital soon and you'll be home and we'll send June to the pictures and find out if I've got it all right.

Love, and I mean love in all three packages.

Yours,

Honeypot

24 January

To: Detective Inspector Fellowes.

From: Southern General Hospital, Edinburgh

Ian – thank you for the flowers that Deborah brought in yesterday. She said that they were really from you. She also brought me
all my bits and pieces that were left at your house, for which I'm
almost as grateful. These included my laptop and June has
brought me a new battery for my mobile phone so that I can now
report. I know you must be rushed off your feet, so I don't
expect a visit.

You've had word from Sandy but I promised to tell all in more
detail and here it comes. I'll turn it into a formal report later. I
suggest that you take a printout and mark up anything you particularly want included or left out.

As you know, Cilla French provided information that caused
my vague feeling of suspicion to become the sort of certainty that
makes you wonder if you haven't gone off the rails. How could I
be seeing something that had bypassed everybody else? Did they
all know something that nobody had bothered to tell me? With
my mobile phone out of action and no radio to hand, I nearly
detoured to the nearest public phone or came into the office, but
I knew that you were closeted with the Detective Super and I did-
n't think that you would appreciate being interrupted. Bright and
McFadden were out doing your errands. I had no desire to
explain myself to some outsider, nor to find that I was making an
idiot of myself by barking up a completely wrong tree. I could
make a discreet enquiry and retire. That's what I thought. I dare
say that most of the world's major errors, including the Iraq war,
have seemed just as logical at the time.

My way to the farm took me back through Kelvinside and a
long way round by road. The farm is over the hump of the hill
from the village and from Stoneleigh House although it's an easy
walk from either. It's in a different postcode and the junction of
two OS maps comes between. Perhaps that's why we neglected it

after a single visit by two of the Edinburgh officers.

As I drove, I was pondering how to get the information I wanted without alerting him. I had only been to the farm once before, when you were using me as firearms officer, but my first impression came back to me. This was that the farm had been in the family for generations and that, although the farm machinery had been brought up to date, give or take twenty years, the farming was still old fashioned in philosophy. No great harm in that – modern farming, with hedges removed, chemicals everywhere and animal feeds containing offal of the same species – has done more damage to the environment than the motor car. In the end, I just drove up to the door and stopped in a yard that was rather cramped for space between a tractor and trailer, the farmer's car and a badly parked disc harrow. The tractor had a small ring of diesel oil under the fuel pump and I could see several marks on the tarmac where fuel oil had been dripped at other times, which explained the 'parafinny' smell that Mrs Macindoe had noticed on Nellie's shoes.

A few chickens were pecking at scattered grain between the vehicles. At the corner of the barn, some pale grey grit had been deposited for them. Several facts began to come back to me and to link themselves together in one of those moments of revelation like the road to Damascus. Birds need grit in their crops, to grind their food. I had spent hours with Dad's keepers, putting out grit for grouse. And in my youth we had been visiting one of Dad's tenants, an old-fashioned farmer. The farmer's wife had just dropped a plate and he was busily smashing the remains to powder to add to the hens' grit. He swore that it made the best grit in the world. The grains of china in the half-moon of mud on Nellie's carpet were explained. If the hens were given wood chips to scratch and nest in, that would have been the source of the sawdust.

It looked like being all too easy. Without even getting out of the car I could see that his car was an olive green Fourtrak. As you may remember, it was a beautiful day. The front door stood open and the carpet in the hall was a rich grey, which I could guess was made from a tight mixture of two contrasting colours. It looked very much like the carpet in Jasper Dunn's van.

It was a moment of mixed triumph and apprehension, like jumping across a chasm and being almost sure of reaching the other side. I had broken all the rules of procedure and common sense in visiting a man who had already looked guilty, at the very least, of complicity in a murder; and coming alone without telling anyone where I had gone.

Perhaps it was not too late to rectify my mistake. From the approach road I had seen another tractor working in a distant field, ploughing the last of the stubble, and I hoped that the farmer was driving it. But it was not my lucky day, by a mile. I was about to back round and drive away when the burly figure of Thomas Hapless appeared in the doorway and walked towards me. 'Aye lassie,' he said. 'What can I do for you? You're looking to buy another half-pig?' His manner was politely enquiring but I could see how well he fitted Nellie's description of 'a bit of rough'.

In a lightning-burst of thought so urgent that it that nearly gave me a stroke, I realised that I could only get out of there by making at the least a six-point turn and the first leg would be enough to warn him to stop me. To lock my doors would be the first give-away and he looked quite capable of tearing a car door off its hinges. Failing that he might even flee or commit suicide, leaving me with egg all over my face and elsewhere. Whatever happened, I would be wrong and, worse, seen to be wrong. I also thought of buying a half-pig if he had one to sell, but he would probably remember that for my previous purchase I had come well provided with plastic bags to protect the car. Rightly or wrongly I decided to bluff it out.

'Just a few points concerning your earlier statement,' I said, dismounting.

'You'd best come inside.'

I hefted my shoulder bag and followed him into the house. The flecks in the carpet were, as I supposed, orange and green and the same carpet continued throughout. The remainder of the décor and furnishings was old, worn and shabby and I could only conclude that the previous carpets had suffered too much from dirty and probably tackety boots. He led me into a shabby sitting room. It was much as you'd expect in a farmhouse where the farmer had lived alone since, as I recalled it, the death of his mother several years earlier. My pale linen suit was almost new and quite spotless, so I accepted an upright chair that looked cleaner than its more comfortable neighbours did.

Mr Hapless dropped heavily into an upholstered easy chair that had certainly belonged to his parents and probably his grandparents before him. 'What points?'

My shoulder bag was beside my chair. I dipped into it and came up with my book and a pen while trying hard to recall the details of his previous statement. I riffled through the book as if looking for my notes. 'When did you last see Mrs Arnoldson?'

He looked at me in surprise. 'Whenever I said in my other statement. I can't remember now. I told the other 'tecs about it around ten days ago and it must have been about ten days or a fortnight before that. What does it say there?'

'That's near enough,' I said. 'You haven't made a statement since we found her body.'

'That hasn't changed the day whenever I last saw her.'

'Of course not. Was Mr Duffus with her?'

'Here! You trying to trick me? I told those others. I met her in the doorway of Kechnie's supermarket.' I was sure that he was fastening on some earlier encounter in order to keep the account straight and consistent.

'I'm sorry,' I said. 'We have to double-check. And your earlier statement was given to two officers from Edinburgh who were called back there for another enquiry. Their report isn't complete.'

After a pause, he nodded; but I could see that he was not wholly satisfied. 'She was coming out as I was going in,' he said. 'We stopped and passed the time of day.'

'When you came to clear the snow at Stoneleigh House,' I said, 'you gave me the impression that you were at daggers drawn.'

He shrugged. 'We'd had an argy-bargy on the phone a few days earlier, about her cat and my hens. Coming up here,' he said indignantly, 'chasing them around and putting them off laying. Only ever caught one of them, though, and that was only a little 'un. Fat bastard was too slow to catch a proper hen. Anyway, that came after I'd met her at the supermarket.'

'So sometimes you were quite good friends?' I was labouring under the difficulty of having only the vaguest recollection of his previous statement while groping for sensible sounding questions and waiting for an excuse to leave.

He looked at me hard and I realised that the question might seem to be barbed. 'There's no point having enemies,' he said at last. 'We were polite.'

'How was she getting on with Mr Duffus? What was your impression?'

He shrugged. 'They weren't the types to be lovey-dovey. Not in public. Too old and too toffee-nosed for that sort of thing. I'd say they were contented.' He grunted. 'That's all anyone can expect and more than most get.'

'Your bottom two fields overlook Stoneleigh House,' I said. 'From there, did you ever see any visitors' cars?'

While he gave it some thought, I began to relax. I had let him see a reason for my visit and at the same time had given him a chance to dangle a red herring. 'Sometimes,' he said at last. 'An olive-green four-by-four, much like mine. But I'd put it down as a Discovery or a Shogun.'

I probed a little further but, wisely, he was vague about dates. I sensed that he was rather pleased with his talent for improvisation. That made two of us.

As soon as I reasonably could, I snapped my book shut and dropped it into my bag. 'Thank you,' I said. 'You've been very helpful. We'll be in touch if we need any more.'

He came with me to the front door, towards the sunshine. Relief and complacency were written on his face. My emotions were the same but I was trying not to be so transparent. A large, ginger cat was approaching the house, passing among the chickens. They paid it no attention. It came back to me that Nellie's cat had been described as a large, ginger tom and that the cat had not been seen again since Stoneleigh House was first found empty. And that, between relief at making my exit and rapture at the prospect of laying my gifts before you, was the moment when I blew it. I rather like cats and they always like me. I bent down and stroked the ginger beast. 'You don't chase the hens any more, do you?' I said.

It took each of us a second or two for the penny to drop. Perhaps stupidly, I tried to bluff it out. 'Well,' I said, 'it seemed logical. Nellie's cat hasn't been seen around since she vanished and these are the nearest buildings. It could easily have come up here, and if it turned its attention to the rodents you might have welcomed it. But perhaps it's a different cat?' My voice had a quaver in it.

He made no answer aloud but I could sense disbelief falling like a curtain between us. He was half an instant quicker than I was. Just as I braced myself for a quick sprint to the car, a hand gripped my arm and I was caught off balance. I was jerked into the house and hauled back into the dingy sitting room.

'They know where I am,' I said quickly.

If I thought that the lie would save me, I was wrong. My shoulder bag had fallen to the floor, open, and as ill luck would have it, among the tissues and make-up and my occurrence book, a pair of handcuffs (without which no responsible woman officer leaves home) popped out. Without losing his grip on my arm, he stooped for them.

You know most of the rest, Ian. I'm ashamed to say that I was overpowered. What you don't have are the details of what he told me. They won't be admissible in court – for one thing, I was in no position to give him the statutory warning – but you'll need the facts in order to put the case together. What he told me then will tell you where to point the Forensics team and they should be able to produce all the evidence you need.

But at this point I'll have to break off. I'm sorry, Ian. I'm tired. And I didn't realise just how exhausting I would find it, typing half propped up. The nurses are just coming round again. I'll have to suffer their attentions with as much grace as I can manage and I'll finish off tomorrow.

Love to Deborah.

Yrs etc.,

Det Sgt Laird

25 January

From: Southern General Hospital, Edinburgh

Ian – nobody tells me anything, but Sandy came to visit this morning and they told him that I can go home tomorrow. So it will be goodbye at last to hospital food and to hard beds with just the wrong sort of pillow.

I promised to finish bringing you up to speed. I ended yesterday at the point at which the farmer, Thomas Hapless, and I had rumbled each other and he had hauled me back ungently into his sitting room. He had his eyes on my handcuffs and his intent was obvious.

It seemed to be a case of now or never. I raised my right arm to break his hold by twisting against the thumb. It half worked but he still managed to keep a grip on my sleeve, which hindered me from making use of almost any of the unarmed combat moves that I had been taught at Hendon. With full use only of one arm, I was limited to a one-handed blow to his midriff. My fingers are rather long and thin, so a straight-fingered jab to the solar plexus would have gained me nothing but broken fingernails. Instead, I swung a punch, using all my strength. That did not work either. I had intended to follow it up with an uppercut and a sprint for the car, but I might just as well have punched an inflated tyre. My fist bounced off his stomach muscles. Not being a gentleman nor imbued with respect for the Law, he retorted with a fist to my jaw.

Although I didn't know it until later, he had cracked my jawbone. I went down, of course, on my back with my head almost against one of the radiators. It hurt like hell and my head was ringing. He then followed me down, kneeling astride me. He could reach the handcuffs and he knew how to apply them. Before my head and my eyes began to clear, he had snapped one cuff onto my wrist, passed the link behind the pipe that came up through the floor to the radiator and cuffed my other wrist.

He got to his feet. I took a kick at him. It was all that I could do. It was a feeble kick, but that did not deter him from replying with a much harder kick to my ribs. I tried to roll away from it but I couldn't. I was still conscious, which was regrettable.

'They know where you are, do they?' he said thoughtfully. 'We'll see about that.' He took a mobile phone out if his pocket. (Does everybody have those damn things now?) 'What's the number of the nick?'

He drew his foot back. He would only have had to open the directory or call Directory Enquiries, so I told him. That was when I discovered that talking hurt rather worse than hell. All the same, I drew breath, which hurt almost as much. My intention was to scream as soon as he was connected, but he saw me fill my lungs or sensed my intention. He left the room.

My eyes had almost stopped watering. The radiator pipe was not very thick and it looked as if it might be of copper. The connections would have to be a weak point. I tried a pull, but that made my ribs scream – we found out later that he had cracked two of them – and I only pulled myself closer to the radiator, action and reaction being much as Newton said they are. I managed to roll onto my side – the side with the undamaged ribs – and got my feet against the radiator. Ignoring the agony from my poor, abused rib cage, I hauled at that pipe but it was as solid as a concrete gatepost. I gave up at last and rolled back to where I had started. We were back to square one, except that there was a furnace glowing among my ribs. My skirt was now up around my waist and there was nothing that I could do about it.

All the time, I could hear his voice in the distance. 'Detective Sergeant Laird, please... Out, is she?... Do you know where I could find her? It's personal but urgent... Yes?'

He came back and looked down at me, smirking. 'They say you went off on some ploy of your own. They've been trying to contact you.'

'I left a note,' I said. 'They just haven't found it yet.' Speaking was now even more agonising than drawing breath, but I managed it between clenched teeth.

'We'll see.'

He delved into my shoulder bag again. Then he left the room and I heard his footsteps outside the window. I considered trying to roll onto my face for the sake of modesty but my ribs were too painful. My car's engine started. I could hear Pippa barking furiously. Many times I had blessed the dog-guard that confines her to the extreme rear of the car, but now I wished it away. Not that the soft old thing would have given him more than a nasty lick, but he didn't know that. On the other hand, I suppose she might have been killed. He manoeuvred to and fro and both noises faded away, which gave me the comfort of knowing that Pippa was alive. I guessed that he was hiding the car away from the sight and sound of visitors.

Eventually his footsteps returned but I could follow his progress through the house and back again. He returned with a shotgun over his arm and a strip of duct tape dangling from one hand. He laid the gun gently on a side-table and stooped over me in order, much less gently, to tape my mouth. The pressure on my cheek hurt so much that I would have screamed if I could. I rather think that I passed out for a few seconds.

He took the chair nearest to my feet and sat, studying me. He was enjoying my plight and my humiliation. 'I'm not going to run away,' he said suddenly. 'Leave a damn good farm? Not likely. If the worst comes to the worst, I'd sooner put in a manager while I do my time and have the farm waiting for me when I come out. So we'll wait. If they come looking for you, maybe I can bluff them. If not, you're a hostage.' He grinned cruelly. 'If they don't come at all, I'll dig a deep hole with the JCB and put you where they'll never find you. But I'll have a little fun with you first.'

Panic is for when all hope is gone and I was not quite ready for that. Help would come some time. Whether help would arrive before his patience ran out, only time would tell. Meanwhile – put it down to feminine curiosity if you like – I wanted to ask questions, but with my hands drawn hard against the radiator I would have had no hope of reaching the tape on my mouth even if he had not been sitting over me, gloating.

But that did not matter. He was in the mood, which so often comes over a criminal once his misdeeds become known, to talk. We're coming now to the bit that you really want to have on record. These, as I remember them, were his very words. Significantly, perhaps, he wanted first to talk about Nellie.

'She could drive a man mad, that one,' he said. 'She had allure, that's the word, more allure than all the rest of the womenfolk put together. And when she'd got you, she was a greedy tigress but clever with it. She wanted all there was and more, but she could make a man fit to give it. I've known some women in my time and I'll know you too before we're done, but nobody could ever hound a man on like that. She turned me into a raging bull.

'But along with that much passion, she had a temper like a terrier with toothache. She could fly off the handle at the least upset, turn into a screaming vixen, get violent and throw things. She even picked up an axe once but I got it off her and no harm was done. While she was with me, I thought I could handle her. She was worth the trouble of watching my tongue and keeping her away from anything sharp or heavy.

'We only met for a time or two now and again at first, while she was with her husband and again after she was with Duffus, whenever she was left alone for the day. She'd phone me and I'd pick her up – outside the village always. I was the only one who really turned her on, she said, but while my mum lived she couldn't move in here and when Ma died it was too late. The only difference was that she could come back here with me. Just as well, maybe. We were happy enough to go on as we were. But if she'd come to me here first, maybe George Duffus would still be alive and we wouldn't be in this fankle.

'Then, one day, she phoned me out of the blue. The Tuesday it was, about a fortnight back. She didn't say much on the phone. I thought she wanted picking up for another good bulling, so I had a quick wash and shave. I drove round to Stoneleigh House because she didn't like mud tracked into her house. And, when I got there, what did I find? Not just Nellie tricked out in her silks and scent. George Duffus had said no to her at last over something trivial and she'd turned on him with her fingernails. He'd stepped back, so she said, and tripped and hit his head on the hearth.

'I told her and told her that it was an accident and the law would deal kindly with her, but there was no denying that she'd made a mess of his face. She was sure nobody'd believe her. In the end, she convinced me. Can you understand that?' He was looking into my eyes. I thought he was talking to himself but it seemed safest to nod.

He resumed. 'There was no way I could turn it into a simple accident, like a trip on the hearthrug and a fall against the kerb, not with his face ripped the way it was. He had to vanish or else be found in a way that the marks couldn't be seen. I made her wash her hands and scrub under her fingernails. I looked outside and there was not a soul to be seen. I thought of burying him the way I'll bury you, but she wanted him away from the house altogether and I wouldn't have him on my farm – I don't know why, folks' minds work funny sometimes. We carried the body between us into the wood. I had him by the clothes and I had a spade in my spare hand.

'I carry enough dead meat around in the course of my work that I wasn't too bothered, but she was getting hysterical so I sent her back to go in my car to fetch a bag of charcoal briquettes left over from the time I tried to make a barbecue to please my Mum. I carry a can of petrol in the back of the car. She was to drive the long way round and meet me at the far end of the wood. The last thing I wanted was for my car to be seen around Stoneleigh House again that day. While she was away, I dug the hole. After she came back, I sent her to sit in the car again while I did the necessary. It was half-light, so I guessed neither the smoke nor the flames would be seen at any distance. Nobody goes into that wood much, not until summer and they gather bluebells or fir cones and the ground would have grown over by then. I popped a young gorse bush on top of him.

'I told Nellie she should go back to the house, let some time pass and then let her man be treated as a missing person.' The farmer sighed. 'A body with a temper like that has no business being so damn frighted. But she couldn't face it, she was sure she'd give herself away, so I kept her damn cat for her – she thought the earth of that beast though she thought nothing of poisoning other peoples' cats. I hired a car for her in Coldstream and led her to a boarding house in Kelso. I thought it was far enough off. We had it peaceful for a while and I was able to sneak away and visit her once, but then she saw somebody in Kelso she thought she knew and got in a tizzy. She was sure they was after her for murder and in the end she set her mind on coming home with me. In a way, it made sense. I live alone and she could have kept out of sight forever.

He fell silent for a full minute, living in the past. He seemed to be relaxing, a little at a time. 'So we had a week,' he said suddenly. 'It was a damn fine week in most ways and I could have lived that way long enough with a secret woman. She was no damn good about the house but she made up for it in other ways.'

He sighed. 'It was too good to last. That temper of hers was lying in wait. There's a patch of rough ground behind the barn and I was cutting the weeds with a sickle ready to dig it over for veggies. She came up behind me. It's no fun living in the country and never going out, she said. I told her I couldn't drive her around while she was a missing person with a murder charge waiting. So, she said, let's have a holiday abroad. Get away to the sun for a while. I said I couldn't afford it and anyway I didn't want to. She went on and on and I went on and on saying no. I was expecting her to say that she could pay for the both of us, and that would have been all right by me except that I didn't see how we could get her out of the country if they really were watching for her. I asked her if she wanted to show her passport at an airport and she said we could buy a stolen one and change the photo. There was just no reasoning with her.

'She was getting angry and because I knew her temper I was keeping an eye out behind. Even so, it took me by surprise when she screamed at me and came at me with a pitchfork. I thought she'd learned her lesson. Bloody dangerous, a pitchfork can be. And I had a sickle in my hand.'

That was all he said before he was interrupted but it was enough. There was only one way for the scene to have played out.

The interruption came in the most blessed form possible. I heard a vehicle in the yard. A door slammed. Hapless jumped to his feet. I think we both expected a voice to call out, the voice of some visitor who could be fobbed off. Instead, quick footsteps approached and the shadow of an arrival darkened the hall beyond the room door.

The farmer turned quickly and made for his shotgun, but that brought him within reach of my feet and I pushed one between his ankles. He fell heavily, but in the act of getting up he aimed a deliberate kick at my ribs. I passed out from the pain of it, but as it turned out I had done enough.

I had been hoping for a gallant knight to gallop to my rescue but I never expected him to gallop a matter of some 10,000 kilometres. As I learned later, Sandy, who had been brought up among farmers, had picked up on the mentions of powdered china and sawdust and the smell of diesel. Perhaps there was also an element of telepathy or male intuition or something – I honestly believe that two people who get really close develop a telepathic link. But call it hunch if you like. He became uneasy when I mentioned my intention of taking a close look at Mr Hapless. Despite the blizzards and the terrorist panic, he managed to bribe his way onto an oil company charter flight to Turnhouse. He tried to call me after he landed but my mobile phone was not answering. He called the nick at Newton Lauder, only to be told that I had gone off on a ploy of my own and they had been trying to reach me – much the same message that they had given to the farmer. On no more than his hunch, Sandy had taken a taxi home, grabbed his own car and burned rubber all the way to the rescue, God bless him. I'll have to find some way to reward him.

I'll wait to hear from you before submitting a formal report. It seems that I shall be stuck at home for a while with not much else to do.

One other happy ending, by the way. Pippa's smells became so bad that I consulted the pharmacist about preparations intended for people with flatulence problems. The vet assured me that they contained nothing harmful to a dog, and June assures me that half a tablet of Nofart, or whatever it's called, given after her dinner, has worked wonders. A fortune awaits the company that makes a preparation especially for Labradors. I know that you had the same problem with Beel so I pass the tip along, hoping that it will help you to overlook my rash behaviour when you make your own reports.

Yours etc.,

Det Sgt Honoria Laird

24 January

To: DI Fellowes

From: DI Laird

I understand that a complaint has been made against me, alleging unnecessary violence during the arrest of Thomas Hapless.

This I absolutely and categorically deny. It must be remembered that during that arrest DS Laird was incapacitated and that Mr Hapless was resisting arrest with murderous fury. In addition, I had recent, incompletely healed fractures, incurred in the line of duty. In the circumstances, it was not a confrontation during which I could afford to take any risks by being excessively gentle. I had to subdue him quickly without giving him an opportunity to aggravate my injuries. I did not have CS spray available at that time.

I shall be happy to elaborate on these points before the Police Complaints Committee and DS Laird will support me.

Yrs etc.,

DI Laird